An Eternal Truth

Book One

Defiance

By
PATRICK SPENCER
And
Mason McNay

Forward

By Patrick Spencer

The Spartans were maybe history's most alien culture. Even in their own time they were one hundred eighty degrees different from their fellow Greeks (referred to in the text as the Hellenes, the authentic ethnic name of the Greeks). They had a dual monarchy (you will be introduced early on to the two kings, Kleomenes and Demaratos), were extreme isolationists, wore their hair long, and held themselves not primarily as individuals but as equal parts of one greater, perfectly harmonious and unbreakable whole. No other Hellenic peoples comported themselves even remotely the same in these or innumerable other respects. Their entire society truly was utopian and dissimilar to the outside world.

Today the Spartans are perceived as even more unrelatable because of the vast societal and cultural gap that separates us from them. But they were still men. They still breathed, ate, slept, fought, and loved the same as you and I, and it is the unequivocal goal of the ensuing six books to bring them to life in all of their reality and humanity.

It is my belief that they set an unparalleled example for all of mankind by rising to a plane of existence otherwise unknown. They embraced the raw brutality of life and in turn, as the diamond is formed from its environment's relentless pressure, attained the truest beauty that exists in this unbelievable, mysterious thing we call life. They set the unflinching precedent that nothing good in life comes without effort, that what you put in is what you get out, and that the proportion of your efforts is a direct corollary to your yield. They to this day stand above all other men, because they went the furthest down the less travelled, treacherous road of greatness. They pushed themselves to the very brink, the most frightening place that man can go. No one understood them in their own day, and they are even more horridly misunderstood today. But *An Eteral Truth* brings to life the real men and women we know as the Spartans.

The premise of this series focuses very simply on who the Spartans truly were, on animating them as they truly would have been 2,500 years ago. You, the reader, are meant to experience their actions, emotions, conversations, their entire world just the way they did. That experience, that brightest of illuminations begins with this first installment, which itself begins where the life of every Spartan and in turn the very foundation of the Spartan state, known to the Spartans, themselves, as Lakedaimon (also called by its geographical equivalent, Lakonia), began: with the introduction to the crucible known as the agoge.

It was this unrivaled, utterly unique educational system (of a military focus) that made the Spartans who they were. Without it, I never would have written a word of these five hundred pages, because there never would have existed these alien people called the Spartans. Everything that they were, everything that we still know, love, and remember about them and all of the reasons that we do hark back to them is because of this singularly vital pillar of their society. The agoge (literally "the upbringing") created unbreakable men, upon whom the Spartan state was built. Each and every individual Spartiate, or full Spartan, comprised the whole of Lakedaimon, which, itself, stood unbreakable, because of its invincible people. Without the agoge, there were no "Spartans." We would just be talking about another, relative city-state of ancient Greece that played its part in the larger Hellenic story but did not truly, when juxtaposed with its contemporaries, stand out for any particular reason.

That crucible, the very way of the Spartans and their world is shown through the eyes of one boy, in every way the same as any other Spartan youth but in so many ways starkly different. He is the representation, the manifestation of everything they were, and through his story, which begins as any Spartan's at seven years old, is the Spartan world painted with unmistakable vividness. Surrounded by his mentor, Krateros, his friends, Tellis, Alpheos, and Maron, as well as his several foes (foremost among them the inimical Thrasilaos), he attempts to navigate the impossible task that was surviving a Spartan's youth, of becoming a god among men.

Perpetually shadowing Dienekes' journey is the Persian Empire, which looms just across the Aegean Sea, threatening to devour the whole of Greece. It is somewhere between the impending Persian invasion and the story of Dienekes' youth that the plot hinges, and these two primary elements, neither more important than the other, work in harmony to tell this first episode in the Spartans' story.

SKYTHIA
BLACK SEA
THRACE
HELLAS
SKYTHIA
CASPIAN SEA
SKYTHIA
SAKAI
BAKTRIA
KAPPADOKIA
LYDIA
IONIA
AEGEAN SEA
KROTON
SYRAKUSE
PILLARS OF HERAKLES
MEDITERRANEAN SEA
SYRIA
ASSYRIA
MEDIA
PERSIA
SUSA
KISSIA
INDUS RIVER
INDIA
LYBIA
EGYPT
ARABIA
PERSIAN GULF
RED SEA
ARABIAN SEA

KORKYRA

THESSALY

▲ Mount
Olympus
Tempe ▲

ASOPOS

Thermopylai ✕

▲ Mount
Parnassos

■ DELPHI
• PHOKIS

• ORE

✕
Plataia

ELIS

ARKADIA

ZAKYNTHOS

KORINTH •
PHLEIOUS •
ISTH
• NEMEA
• MYKENAI

ARGOS •
MANTINAIA •
Sepeia ✕
• OLYMPIA
Thyrea ✕
TEGEA •

Alpheios

PARNON

MESSENIA

SPARTA ◉

LAKEDAIMON

TAÜGETOS

Eurotas

Marathon

ATHENS

MEDITERRANEAN SEA

Part One

Agoge

∧

One

Feel no fear before the multitudes of men
Do not run in panic
But let each man bear his shield straight, towards the front ranks,
Regarding his own life as hateful and holding the dark spirits of death as dear as the radiance
of the sun.

Krateros recited the words to Rhoda on a wooden bench outside her home. She knew the poems already. All Lakonians knew the laws of Lykourgos, writ in verse by the bard Tyrtiaios. She had been preparing herself for this day for seven years. Still she was not ready.

Krateros saw how her eyes glazed over, staring unfocused at an apparition miles away. He saw how her fingertips vexed a phantom itch on her wrist. He laid his hand over hers before she scratched herself to bleeding.

She squeezed his hand in hers until she felt a lump of cold in his fist and scowled.

"I hate that thing." She pushed his hand away.

"I like it neither." The big man sighed and chafed the iron ring with his thumb. "I wish I'd never told you what it meant."

"And I wish you weren't here to take my child." She did not hide the accusation. To her surprise, his shoulders slumped.

"Nothing we can do for the pain but bear it."

His remorse angered her. It was her day to grieve, not his.

"Oh?" She needled at him. "Does your jewelery hurt you so? You'd think a polemarch could manage to have a ring resized."

"The ring does not hurt my hand, Sister."

She snorted.

"Are you ready?" He changed the subject.

"It is my duty." There was flint in her voice. There were men already inside her home, ready to enforce the law should she resist.

"The others will be by to see you soon."

"The others?"

"The other mothers. For you to lean on each other. After your duty is done."

She tried to speak, but shuddered.

"I think I'd rather be alone." She finally managed.

"All the same." He brushed a lock of hair behind her ear. "They will be by. It's how these things are done. Everything we do in Sparta, we do together."

"Well maybe it's time we did things differently." She spat. They both flinched at her words. "I'm sorry. I don't. I can't... You don't under-." She crumbled. Tears coursed down her cheeks into the rictus of her scowl. She covered her face and they dripped through her fingers.

"It's alright." Krateros, stunned, rubbed his broad hand over her rocking shoulders. "It is never easy." He waited, awkward and confused, for her to calm. His eyes wandered to the mountains in the distant north, purple in the morning light. The titan of Sparta. "See there?" He pointed. "When you next see the boy, he will be as tall and strong as the summit of great Taygetos. A giant." He meant it as consolation but she only cried harder. He struggled to remember the day he had been taken, so long ago. His mother had cheered for him until he dropped out of sight. He realized now how hard that must have been for her. How she must have wept when he faded from view. "Cry then. We will wait. It will not do for him to see your tears."

"No, no." She shook herself and stood. "Best to do it now." She dried her eyes on the shoulder of her dress and steeled. "Wait any longer and I might not let you take him." Her lip still trembled but there was a savage glint growing in her eye. "Strike me."

"What?"

"You heard me. Strike me."

"Rhoda, I could never."

"Are you a man or not?"

Krateros tapped her on the cheek with his fingers.

"That's it? Is that all your strength, Polemarch of Lakedaimon? I said hit me."

"I don't underst-"

"Just do it!"

He hesitated, but did as she commanded. He hit his friend in the face. Regret pulsed through him the instant her face spun away, but she turned back smiling darkly.

"Good." She said. "Now I'm angry at you, Krateros, son of Alkibiades. And I will cling to that. Go and fetch my boy."

Krateros was a general of Sparta. He feared nothing. Nothing, save for Spartan women.

Λ

"I've heard…" He met her smoldering gaze with difficulty. "I've heard it is easier if you do not look him in the eye." She snorted and waved him off, then followed at a distance as he circled to the back of her house.

"Dienekes!" The aging warrior called. A boy ran to him through fields of barley, cheeks flushed, blonde curls bouncing. He was fast, despite his limbs gangling from a recent growth spurt.

"Ready to race at Olympia, are we?" Krateros faked a smile and slapped the boy on the shoulder.

"Just like you did!" The boy flexed his muscles triumphantly.

"Ah, but I didn't win." Krateros kneeled to the child's level. "I could have done our country greater glory had I not lost to that bastard from Pellene." He made a face, eliciting a giggle from the boy. "We will see that one day you surpass old Krateros. Succeed where he failed."

Krateros stood. Rhoda nearly broke down again, seeing the old weathered oak tower over the fresh sapling; the present and future of a nation, basking in each other's in pride, until a shadow cast over the scarred face of the warrior.

"Dienekes, I want you to look at your mother." They both turned to the woman, proud and beautiful but weary. Her eyes turned to the clouds. "I want you to remember everything she has taught you of our ways. The Austerity. Humility. Obedience. It is your foundation she has given you, on which the rest of your life will be built."

Dienekes gave a nod. He had indeed learned these rudiments of his people. He could recite the words of Tyrtaios backwards and forwards, even if their meanings still escaped his understanding.

"Come," the soldier said again. "It's time". He led them back to the house where a rap on the door summoned the Spartiates waiting inside. Apart from his size, they were indistinguishable from Krateros in their crimson cloaks, bronze armor and moustacheless beards.

"You know why these men are here."

Dienekes instinctively shrank towards his mother, to wrap himself in her skirts and their smell of hyacinths and barley flour. But she turned from him. He reached for her hand, but she pulled away. There were four of them. Two to see the boy safely to the capital, two to control his mother should she try to stop them. They carried no weapons, but custom had learned to wear armor when collecting students of the agoge. It was not rare for frantic mothers to reach for knives.

"I know you're frightened. I know." Krateros was not unsympathetic. "This is but your first test. The first of thousands. None of which you will pass unless you master your fear. Remember, you are Sparta. And Sparta has but one master. Fear is not its name."

Λ

Dienekes was still paralyzed. He'd known for as long as he could remember about the *agoge*, the military education of the Spartans. He'd known his day would come, but in his heart the day always lingered somewhere a distant future. To be ripped from his mother, from his home… He always thought he would be ready. he was not.

"Dienekes listen." Krateros took the boy's soft, tiny hands in his own calloused leather paws, a final act of mercy. "Your fear seizes you, like the bonds of a slave. But you are no slave. You are privileged to be Lakedaimonian, the freest of all men, but that freedom is not without cost. You will pay for it today, as we all do. This is the price of our lands and the due for our strength. Be brave. You will make your mother proud. You will make me proud."

Dienekes was numb to his mentor's comforts. Water dammed up red in his eyes, and he held his breath to keep from bawling. He looked again to his mother who chewed her lip and would not return his gaze. Her nails had found the itch in her wrist and clawed it as she spoke.

"Master your fear, my son. Or it will master you. You are to be a Peer of Sparta, but it is a right you have to earn. So I say again." Her breath hitched. "Master your fear, or you will not make it out alive."

"It is time," Krateros said, delicate but resolute. Dienekes would receive no more ceremony. Two of the strange soldiers advanced, each wrapping a fist around one of the boy's arms. He did not struggle until he was already in their grip. They marched him without care up the road to Taygetos, and it was not until his home was a speck on the horizon behind that he truly began to cry. Tears blurred his vision, grief numbed his hands and feet. His only measure of time was the moment he could no longer smell the hyacinths that lined the Amyklaian road to his former home.

Λ

Two

They tossed Dienekes into the barracks and slammed the door on his childhood. He teetered in numbness where he had barely landed on his feet and rubbed his arms where he could still feel the soldiers' fingers clench. There were no bruises. They hadn't harmed him, but he felt no less violated.

His eyes adjusted to the dark, to little use. The stone room was bare but for a row of boys murmuring softly on a bench against the wall. Most of them stared at him. For no more reason than that he looked away, feeling exposed. He occupied himself by digging his toes into the hard dirt floor.

"Hey, whatcha staring at?" Said someone over his shoulder. It nudged him in the back when he didn't answer. "What, something down there? Don't hide it from me, now. No secrets among us Spartans, yeah?"

Dienekes, unwilling or unable, still did not respond. The boy circled to meet his eyes but Dienekes angled away. The stranger was bigger and stronger, it only took a hand on a shoulder to turn him back.

"Cmon mate, are you shy or just stupid? Neither will do for you here."

Was it both? Dienekes broke into weeping. The sounds he choked out trying to quiet his cries were more pathetic than had he bawled outright.

Master your fear, his mother had said. Master your fear, which he was not doing.

"Ah, shit, shit, no." The boy hissed, and pulled Dienekes to a corner. "You're kidding me, mate. Cut it out now, come on." They leaned against the stone wall. "You know what'll happen if they catch you like this?"

Some of the other boys started to snigger until the new stranger glared them down.

"Enough alright?" The boy ruffled a fist into Dienekes's flax tunic, pulling it up to dry the tears from his face. "They'll be making fun of you now, no helping that, but that's nothing to what'll happen if you're caught carrying on like a little girl."

It wasn't exactly comforting, but the boy was on his side. Maybe even a friend. He didn't feel so alone anymore. His chest stopped heaving. He got a hold of himself.

"You alright then?"

"Yeah." Said Dienekes. His first word spoken since being ripped from his mother.

Just like you Krateros.

He nearly wobbled back into tears again at the thought, but steeled.

Just like you Krateros. He made a fist.

"Good." The boy punched him softly in the chest. "I should hope so. For both our sakes." He pointed at himself and said, "Tellis."

"Dienekes," he reciprocated, drying his eyes further as he took Tellis's proffered arm, hands locked over wrists.

"I didn't mean to send you into fits, mate." Tellis apologized. "Only poking fun. I mean… look where we are. Didn't think I'd make it any worse."

Dienekes nearly spoke but only nodded.

The door flew open again and two more youths were thrown inside. Tellis pushed Dien's head down, and faked like they were play wrestling so the soldiers wouldn't see his grief-swollen face. When the door shut and they stood back up, his eyes were still red but he wore a weak smile.

"Tellis." He introduced himself to the two newcomers, and they took his arm in turn.

"Alpheos."

"Maron."

"Hope you don't take it personal, I won't be able to keep you straight."

"It's alright," they grinned. "No one can." They were identical twins. "Hold on, mate. You been crying?" One of them pulled Dien's chin up.

"I punched him," Tellis shrugged

"Then his eyes'd be black, not red." Maron kept tugging on the struggling Dienekes for a better look.

"And I threw sand in his face."

"Really?" said Alpheos, "I don't see any."

"And then I poked him in the eyes. Alright? Both. And spat in them." He interjected himself between Dien and the twins, arms crossed. "And you'll leave it, or I'll do the same to you."

Maron looked like he was about to accept the challenge, but Alpheos gave a smile and a wink.

"Course, mate, we're with you." He bumped a fist off Dien's shoulder. "Don't let him get away with that any more, eh?" After a silence he changed the subject. "So what a day then. We're finally here."

Three of them shared nervous glances, sweat on foreheads, chewed lips. But not Tellis. He beamed.

"Do you feel no fear?" Alpheos asked him.

"Not at all." Tellis seemed surprised at the question.

"Why not? Don't you know why we're here?"

Λ

"Of course. But we are Sparta, aren't we? We were born for this. Why should I fear that for which I was made." His smile bordered on madness. Frightening, but infectious.

The door flew open again, and Tellis pawed Di's head back down. A man stormed in. He was young, in his early twenties, but his moustacheless beard just shaved at the New Year indicated his full Spartiate status. Slender and short compared to Krateros, but he still towered over the boys. He carried a huge white shield in his left arm. Four smaller shields were painted on its dome. Where the peel of his cloak exposed his left arm and leg, tawny ropes of muscles squirmed under leathery skin. He prowled around them like a predator. A shiver ran down the spines of his initiates when he ran his tongue hungrily over his teeth. They had been filed into points.

He was *eirene*. Their instructor. It was his responsibility to make their lives hell. The boys needed no introduction. They lined up for him at an awkward and shambling attention.

The eirene silently appraised them, pacing from boy to boy.

"Spartans do not bow." He said to Dienekes, eyes still downcast. The boy flinched, but did not look up. "You hear me boy?" The man barked. "Pick your fucking head up." Dien complied, and his teacher's eyes widened in disgust. He would have looked back down, but the man snatched him by the chin and drew him up. "Tears." He growled.

"Sir, if I may-" Tellis chanced.

"No you may not!" He fell on Tellis like a stormcloud. "Who do you think you are? Where do you think this is?" The boy withered. "Look at me! Who told you to look away?"

"No one, sir."

"Who told you to speak?" Spit splashed off the boy's face. Tellis would not be giving any correct answers today. The eirene turned back to Dien, whose face he still clutched in one hand. "An insolent shit and a weeper. What a way to start. Form up on me." He thundered and marched out the door. Twelve boys followed him out like ducklings, trembing despite the sun and trying not to think about the whip wrapped around their instructor's fist. He led them down to the dusty training fields and uncoiled it, cracking a stripe in the sand.

"On the line!" He roared. The boys bounced off each other, racing to obey. "Today begins your misery. You will learn to love suffering. Embrace torment. They will be your only friends. Not I. I am your enemy, and I will do my best to break each and every one of you." He stared into every pair of eyes on the line, swearing his oath to each of them individually. He peered at Dienekes a moment longer. It took all Dien's will not to bow his head again. "You will learn to expect no quarter and give none. Mercy is not a word in the Spartan language. But toil is. Agony is. And you shall

∧

come to think of them as though they were your mother, for you will be born again through them. If you hesitate, if you falter, if even one of you withhold in the slightest, there will be hell to pay for all of you." He recoiled the whip slowly as he spoke. The boys watched it, hypnotized as it wrapped around a forearm as thick as their thighs. "You are here to learn to live and die for Lakedaimon and become the invincible sentries she requires. This is your duty as obliged by our state, by our gods, and by our blood. You will succeed, or you will die." He paused a moment to let it sink in, but only a moment.

"Sparta's word is law, and I am her voice. You will obey. There is no alternative." He turned and pointed at the horizon. Half a mile off, barely a speck from where they stood, was a boulder glinting metallic in the sun. "On my command, you will run, you will touch the stone, and come back. And again. Until I tell you to stop."

"Sir we haven't got any shoes-" said one of the boys, yet unnamed. The whip cracked across his chest, the boys beside him were misted with pink splatter. He cried out, but bit his tongue when the eirene's arm raised again. The man's lip curled up into the faintest glimmer of a smile.

"Now run."

∧

Three

The boys fled. With the smell of atomized blood in the air and a predator behind them, they scattered like deer. They were all Spartan boys. They could all run, and fast. But as panic subsided and they fell into their stride, something became clear.

Training for Olympia, are we? The old warrior's voice echoed inside Dien as he found his feet. He felt the man's palm wrapped again around the beginnings of muscle in his arm.

Just like you, Krateros.

All Spartan boys were swift. But Dienekes could fly.

He had outpaced the larger boys in moments, left Tellis huffing and puffing in a distant second. He descended deeper into calm each time his bare feet beat the earth. This he could do.

The dash to the stone was over in a flash, half a mile done. Bronze spearheads jutted from fissures in its surface. Dien pictured himself driving one into the stone as he clapped his palm on the sunbaked rock and wheeled.

Loose clusters of other young Spartiates loitered around the stone, polishing armors, oiling their hair. They fell silent to watch the new recruits parade by. Dien hazarded them a breathless smile as he started his second lap. He was first. He looked to them for encouragement. A cheer, a fist in the air, a nod of approval... They gave him only cold stares.

He and Tellis touched fists as they passed each other, but none of the other boys looked at him, resenting him for being better. He dared not slow to spare their feelings. Their displeasure would be more forgiving than the whip he was fast returning to. The boy furthest in back moaned as he dogged on, the bleeding on his chest already slowing, caked and scabbed with sand.

Dien's stride shortened only once as he bore down on the starting line. The eirene rolled the handle of his whip in his fingers and the length of it writhed in the dirt. Reminding the boys-

Until I tell you to stop.

He rounded his teacher and started his second lap. The loitering warriors paid him no mind when he touched the stone the second time. Or the third time. Or the fourth. Or the tenth. He lost count of how many more times he ran the loop.

Sweat stung his eyes as he started to lap the other boys. They cursed under their breath and beat their legs harder to catch him but could not sustain. The bleeding boy had pulled himself out of last place. The pain of his punishment motivated him more than the threat to those who hadn't tasted it yet. Dien heard the crack of leather as he touched the stone for what could have been the thousandth time. A boy had fallen screaming but quickly found his feet again. Tellis vomited on himself, desperate not to slow. For fear or for exhaustion, Dienekes was unaware of the liquid shit purging down his thighs.

He rounded the eirene again and received the command he'd given up hope to hear.

"Halt!"

Dien collapsed. They all collapsed.

"Halt does not mean finish early!" The eirene cracked his whip into the air and the rest of the boys jogged, stumbled, or crawled to the line. "On your feet! Suck wind if you have to, but you'll do it on your feet like men!"

The boys quaked and retched, but stood, their tunics stained with sweat, some with worse. The twins leaned on each other, dry heaving. Some were too slow to erect themselves, and their teacher casually flogged them. Not with the crack, but the body of the leather bent double in his grip. What passed for gentleness in Sparta.

"Who among the enemy will give you reprieve?" He barked and strode down the line, knocking boys down just to make them stand again. "When you press them shield to shield, who will spare you a moment to catch your breath? To gather your thoughts?" He flattened Tellis with a kick to the chest. "You think it's hard to stand now? Wait till you're straddled with seventy pounds of bronze." He gestured to his bronze armor. "Wait until you've not eaten or slept for days and men don't stop trying to kill you. Wait until all the world is red and you can't tell whose blood is whose."

"Look beyond the plains." He pointed his whip at the mountains. "Taygetos stands the soldier. Never faltering, never failing. Never does she kneel. You will be the same! As you have run today, so shall you run whenever and from however far Lakedaimon may call. You will not stop, even if it means your last breath. And if it means your last breath now then so be it, and you will die in the shadow of the mountain to prove that you will never surrender, you will never abandon the call of home. Your victory is acceptable. Your death is acceptable. Your surrender is not acceptable!!" He cracked another stripe into the sand.

"Everyone but Weeper and Insolence on the line." The boys wobbled to comply, only one still had enough fluids left in him to hurl. "Now run!" He waited till the other boys were obscured in a cloud of their own dust before snarling at Tellis and Dien.

"You'll be the first ones back, or I will strip the flesh from your spines. Go."

Λ

Four

Dienekes plunged into ice. He woke, sucking water into his lungs. Mortal panic animated his tortured limbs. He thrashed and thrashed, not swimming, but fighting the water as the current dragged him downstream.

Not today. He gritted his teeth against the spectre of death encroaching from the corners of his eyes. Fear withered beneath the heat of his anger.

Not today.

A flailing hand stroked the surface. He kicked off the bottom and shot up towards air. Towards breath. He howled above the waterline, a wailing tenor fury followed by his swinging fists. Frenzied, unaimed blows at an enemy he couldn't see but was certain was there. He pummeled empty air. Eleven boys laughed at him from a safe distance. The water was only knee high.

"The weeper lives!" They cried, splashing him and slapping his aching back which, he realized as he fell back into the water, was blissfully unflayed.

Strip the flesh from your spines, the threat echoed in Dien's head. He remembered catching up. Passing every other boy as they rasped curses at him. And then when he could see the eirene growing larger on the line... he remembered nothing else. He must have collapsed.

"What happened?" He asked.

"You bit the dust." They confirmed.

"Then how? The eirene said... If I didn't make it back first..."

"You did make it back first." They laughed again at his confusion. "You should have seen how you fell, too. All at once. Slam. Down in the dirt. Like snuffing out a candle. Thought you were dead. Then he carried you."

"Carried me?" Dien sat up. "Who?"

They pointed at Tellis, who wallowed on his back in the shallows. He gave a weak wave and a groan then resumed caking himself in mud to cool the burn in his muscles.

"Carried me?" Dien repeated again, dumbfounded. "The whole way back?"

"Nope!" The boys laughed too hard for what they had just gone through. Their rigors had clearly touched them in the head. "Not even close. Made it maybe ten yards before he dropped you on your skull." Said the boy who'd taken the whip on the chest. He smiled bitterly as he picked grit from his wound.

"Definitely thought you were dead that time." Said Alpheos. He and Maron were helping another boy clean the lash on his back.

"He dragged you by the feet another ten before he collapsed too." Said the whipped boy, and anticipating Dien's next question, answered. "We did. We carried you back. All of us. Lucky thing we dumped you over the line first. Teacher didn't tell us till after what he'd threatened you with. He thought the whole thing was a hoot. Almost even smiled." He spat a jet of river water.

The river Evrotas in the fall was chill, but Dien in the heat of his pain and exhaustion did not care. He let his head sink below the water, the silence of the current calming the chaos of his thoughts.

"I don't know how I'll ever repay you." He rose, humbled.

"For starters, you owe me a new tunic." Said a boy on the bank.

"A tunic?"

"Yeah," said the boy. "You shat all over mine." And he pelted Dien in the face with his soiled shirt. The boys laughed till they choked. Dien gagged at first but realized how little it mattered with how filthy they all still were head to toe. The clear stream waters slurried brown with the muck and grime sloughing off their bodies. He waded upstream of the growing cloud and scrubbed himself as the others did, making a note not to submerge his head anymore.

A whip cracked. A dozen naked boys sprained themselves standing to attention.

"What a disappointment." Said their master. "Having a splash and tickle in the spring, I thought it was the muses inviting me to come bury my cock. A sad sight. But by all means, keep playing like little girls and I just might have it in me to treat you as such." The boys squirmed. He basked in their embarrassment. "No laughter? No songs? Yet another disappointment. I think that's what I'll call you now." He licked his pointed teeth.

The sun was getting low.

"It is almost time for Disappointment to sleep. If you want beds, you can make them yourselves. Your mothers taught you to giggle and frolic like nymphs, I assume they taught you to weave a mat." He pointed with his whip to the reeds growing along the bank. "Except for you two. Weeper. Insolence. You will dig graves for yourselves. You died today. You sleep in the dirt like dead men."

Unceremoniously, he left.

The boys finished scrubbing and wove their mats. Dien and Tellis assisted despite not having their own, wanting to help as they had been helped. They worked in silence. In part for fear of their teacher but mostly lacking the energy to speak. Eyes and heads were drooping while they still crouched naked in the stream.

They wobbled from the river to their barracks, and when the command came to

Λ

sleep, the boys hit the floor with a thud.

Λ

497 BCE

Five

It wasn't quite a kick, but it was still a foot in his ribs.

"Wake, boy." He must have only been asleep a few minutes. "You have a guest."

Some kind of trick. Dien thought. Some kind of test. He knuckled sleep from his eyes in the dark, windowless barracks and complied, zigzagging towards the door he could not see, on feet he could not feel. Impatient, the eirene took his shoulder and steered him through the blackness to a voice Dien recognized before his bleary eyes could bring the face to focus.

"Disturb your meeting with sleep, did I?" Said Krateros. The boy nearly ran to embrace the old warrior, but remembered his teacher looming and dared not. "Come, let us not take long." And then it was just the two of them. Dien felt as if years had passed since he had seen his friend only yesterday.

"Thrasilaos told me of your first day's training." Krateros smirked. His eyebrow inclined.

"Who?" Dienekes yawned.

"Your instructor. His name is Thrasilaos."

Dien nodded, and wondered at how knowing his name somehow made him a fraction less terrifying. A very small fraction. He staggered, sleep nearly dragging him back to the earth.

"Sit." Krateros settled the boy on a grassy hill before his legs betrayed him and joined him with his own legs crossed. "Walking is the last thing you'll want to be doing now." The dewed leaves felt like a feather bed beneath Dien's screaming bones. His mentor's face softened, wistful, watching the child grimace and wince. He remembered the days of his own torture with a twisted fondness. How weak he had been. How strong he had become. "We all know the feeling, little brother." Said Krateros.

All.

He meant the corps of Peers, the graduates of the agoge. The survivors. Through the fog of sleep, Dien pieced the information together from snippets of old half-heard conversations that had before only happened above his head. Things that held no significance to his little life until now.

"We all did just as you have done." Krateros continued. "But tell me. In your own words. How did it feel."

"It hurt." Dien sniffed. Krateros roared laughter and woke the quartermaster's hounds.

"Profound!" Krateros giggled like a child, hand over mouth. And glanced over his shoulders like he'd be caught sneaking. He whispered now, so he wouldn't upset the dogs. So not to wake the resting children, Dien realized. There was no one sleeping in earshot but trainees and their masters.

Sparta whipped her boys. Ran their feet bloody. Shaved their heads and starved them and shoved them out in the cold. But she would be careful not to disturb their rest when they had earned it. Dien was learning a strange compassion.

"Tell me more, child. What did you do when it hurt."

"I kept running?" Dien shrugged.

"Why did you keep running?" Krateros led the thought.

"I... didn't want to give up."

"Why not... did you feel obligated? Did you want to impress the other boys? Did you want to win? Or was it fear of your master's whip."

Yes, yes, yes, and yes, Dien thought. But still no. Something else. More than running for something, he felt he had been running against. He had run fastest when Thrasilaos had threatened him, but not for risk of punishment. After twenty laps he no longer spared a worry for the whip or the man who held it, nor had he been concerned with competition. He had no awareness for anything but the burning in his thighs.

I didn't want to give in to... to pain?."

"A smart boy." The big oak nodded and proudly ruffled the young sapling's hair. "I always told your mother so. You know the word for that? What you felt?"

Dien shook his head.

"The word is defiance."

"Defiance," Dien repeated in a whisper. He liked the taste of it. "Was it the same for you?"

"It was. It was the same for all of us."

"All?"

"Every single one. I know all the boys in your line all seem like strangers, so different, but they are all Sparta and they all felt what you felt. It's our tradition. Laid out in our laws and steeped in our blood. It was Defiance that first staked us a home in this land, and Defiance that has kept it. Defiance that tramples our enemies like wheat when they fall against us in the crush of battle." He curled a fist. "So we cultivate it. Breed it. Why the infirm young are left for the wolves. Why not all initiates survive

Λ

the agoge. They may die, but their sacrifice strengthens those who survive. You cannot break a chain if no one link will fail."

"Defiance." Dienekes nodded, rolling the word around in his mouth.

"But that is only one half of the whole coin."

"Oh."

"Dienekes, do you know what intuition is?"

He shook his head again. As desperate as he was to learn from Krateros, the singing crickets were tugging him back into slumber. Krateros sensed the child's fatigue. He glanced over each shoulder again, and assured no one would see, slipped a linen-wrapped parcel to Di from within his tunic.

"Here." He said. "Eat."

Dienekes did not even look at the heaping portion of smoked meat in his hand before thrusting it down his gullet. His nose pointed him to the bounty and he dove in. Krateros laughed and continued his lesson.

"I will teach you, and you will need to remember. For defiance is only the backbone of the fight, the backbone of the phalanx, backbone of the nation. Intuition-" He jabbed Dienekes in the forehead with a finger and the boy's eyes fluttered open, meat slipped from his mouth. "Intuition is the mind. The other half.

It is thought before thinking, it is seeing before looking, it is feeling a presence before it appears. It is a voice you listen to, but you don't listen with these." He tweaked Dien's ear to keep him from falling asleep in his dinner. "You listen with this," and poked him in the heart.

"How?" the boy garbled around a mouthful of flesh.

"A big question, Di. And my honest answer is that I cannot give you an honest answer. It is something we all have to find for ourselves. But I trust that you will learn. Now that you know its name you can be searching for it. Look ahead not into space, but into time. See before you the world's possibilities unfolding and the voice will speak to you clearer and clearer each day."

"Like magic?" Dien asked, incredulous.

"Ha, not like magic, no." Krateros rubbed his eyes, for the first time appearing tired himself. "But not logic either. It does not stand on sense, or reason. It is stronger than reason, and can take you where rationality cannot go. A kind of instinct. Some attribute it to the divine, a spectral quality given to us by the gods, and I am inclined to believe such notion." He shrugged, hung his hands. "But I am a simple man with no concept of the great mysteries of the universe. I see no reason why all men cannot harness such gifts. But what I do know, is that out of all men, it is Spartans who harness it best. Spartans like us." Dienekes reminded himself that he was no true Spartan yet, but his mentor's acceptance, his faith, it warmed him.

"Dienekes, do you understand?" The question hung unanswered while Dien sank

Λ

in and out of sleep again, The empty kerchief falling from his hands.

"No, Krateros." The boy replied honestly. "But I will learn. I promise."

The old oak swelled with pride again as the seedling grew inches before his eyes.

"Good. Just open this ear for now." He nudged Di in the chest again. "It will come to you."

And Krateros was on his feet, hand on his xiphos. A twig snapped in the dark, and the old warrior had reacted before it even made a sound.

Intuition. Dienekes marveled.

In the dark, Dienekes first thought it was a helot. He had seen them on the fringes of his mother's *klerois*, but knew little about them except that he was supposed to hate the nervous little men dressed in rags and doghide caps.

"Shukxa, my boy!" Krateros greeted the stranger warmly. Had Di been anymore awake, he might have taken more interest. Whether in his dress, in his speech, his name, even in his complexion, the young man was clearly not of Sparta.

"King Kleomenes requests your presence, Lord Polemarch." He bowed, addressing Krateros, who addressed Dien.

"And one must oblige the king. Back to sleep with you, so your legs may carry you again in the morning."

Even at this hour, Thrasilaos stood at attention by the door of the barracks. Krateros pulled his ward aside before they were in earshot.

"Repeat to me what you've learned tonight, little brother."

"Defiance."

"And?"

"Intuition." Dien might have smiled if he hadn't felt his eirene's eyes boring into him.

Krateros nodded and ushered Dien inside. The sapling bent to sleep in the dirt, and the oak tree left to meet with his king.

Λ

Six

Krateros stepped into the king's home. His four fellow polemarchs, Sparta's warlords, were already gathered.

"Seems I'm late to the party." He said, taking off his helmet. It was irregular for Spartiates to dress in full wargear when at home and at peace, but Krateros wore the full panoply daily. He told any who asked that part of his duty was to stand as a symbol of their military might. But in truth, experience had taught him cruelly how it was better to have and not need than need and not have.

"You are forgiven for your tardiness," said the king. "However, I will never find it in me to forgive you being born prettier than me." It was a joke, but he only barely smiled, and not at Krateros. The sad smirk was for the dark young man peeking his head around the door. Shukxa smiled shyly back and disappeared. Kleomenes shifted back to business, itching at the iron ring on his finger. He wore many rings, but only the one simple black one seemed to vex him. Krateros took his place around the war table, absently thumbing his own ring.

"Demaratos is not here?" Krateros noted the absence of half the diarchy, Sparta's second king.

"Perhaps his messenger got lost." Kleomenes shrugged in exaggerated innocence.

"Perhaps his messenger was commanded to get himself lost?" Krateros knew his king.

"I will neither confirm nor deny." Kleo winked. "My generals." He addressed his warchiefs. "Aristagoras is dead."

The five men groaned. They knew what it meant.

"Without his leadership, Persia will soon retake Ionia. The Hellespont is once more in the fist of King Dareios. Klazomenai, Kyme, and Lydia are back under siege, if they have not fallen already. Once they have, the Persians will again control the coast."

"How long for them to cross the Aegean?" Asked Krateros.

"Cross?" Another general, Noemen, turned to him. "The might of Xerxes is in his infantry. Would he not first march north? Through Skythia and Thrace?" He pointed on the map to the lands that separated Europa and Asia, on either side of the

Dardanelle Straits.

"Two years ago, Athens sent a fleet of ships to assist Aristagoras in his rebellion." Krateros responded. "Dareios thinks himself a god? Then he will revenge the personal insult first. Undo those who aided his enemy before making new foes. And now that he controls a coastline he can take his time assembling a beach invasion."

"Sounds like a problem for Athens, then." Noemen growled. The alliance between Athens and Sparta was shaky at best.

"Had I perceived the threat to only endanger the immediate objects of Persia's wrath, I would not have assembled you tonight." Began Kleomenes again. "Whether a friend of Athens sends aid, or whether Persia already has her sights on Hellas, we can trust that further invasion is inevitable. Dareios fancies himself a conqueror like his grandfather Cyrus before him. Whether it begins in Athens or Skythia or Thrace, it will spread. Dareios will come for us all."

"What stance would you have us assume?" Asked Opites, another Polemarch.

"A quiet one." Kleomenes shrugged and wrung his hands, testing in his palms the weight of two poor choices. "I would not draw the aggression of an already angry beast absent proof that it will strike. But short of proof, I trust that it will. And we will be ready to send him sprawling back to Asia when he does. Call up your banners. Drill. Accomodate the newly graduated Spartiates. We'll not be caught bent over."

"But, Kleo," Noemen interjected, "I thought you liked it from behind?"

"Oh? Are you offering?" There was laughter. Nothing, not even the conquest of the known world, was so serious that a Spartan couldn't laugh.

"How many can they call up?" Krateros asked.

"I do not know." The king responded. There was silence.

"How could we not know?" Asked Opites. "Our spies and allies must have sent word. Someone has seen."

"Many have seen."

Realization dawned on some of the Polemarchy.

"Do you know this nation, Opites?" Kleomenes pointed at the map, a finely engraved bronze rendering, and Opites nearly rolled his eyes.

"Of course, it's Ionia. Where Aristagoras held until his death."

"Good, and this is the forefront of the Persian invasion. Do you know this nation?" The king moved his finger east.

"Yes, sir. It's Lydia."

"Good. And these?"

"Cappadocia. Armenia. Phoenicia."

"Excellent. And this area?"

"Syria. And what was once Mesopotamia, but I do not know-"

"Yes, precisely, Mesopotamia. And this one?"

Λ

"I do not know, sir."

"Then I will tell you. It is Media. This one is Baktria. This one India."

"Alright but how-"

"And there's also Damaskos. Memphis and Egypt and Phoenecia, and Gods know what other nations north."

"Forgive me, but I don't understand what Persians in Ionia have to do with the rest of these territories."

"Xerxes controls them all." Kleomenes admitted. "And everything between." He rested a finger on Sparta, a tiny city on a tiny speck of an island in the Aegean Sea that they shared with Tegea, Messenia, Korinth, Arkadia and more. He touched his other hand to the far side of Persian control, deep in the Orient. The entire modern world spanned between his arms. At one end sat his tiny kingdom, and all the rest was enemy.

"You ask how many they can call up." The king said gravely. "We do not know, because it may be infinite."

"But Athens..." Spat Onesimos, another polemarch. "If we can know such things in Sparta, then surely Athens with its weak-backed scholars knows this and more. But still they provoke an attack from..." He gestured to the table. "From this? From a continent? How could helping the Ionians be worth such a risk?"

"Some alliances are not wise." Kleomenes continued, patient. "Nor even always strategic. Athens and Ionia share a lineage, I assume it for kinship that they sent their aid. I spent some time there, helping restore their oligarchy. I can tell you that these democrats who have come to rule the city are arrogant, out of touch with the world. They think they are beyond consequence behind their ivory columns, and from behind them extend their notions of right and wrong regardless of how impractical those notions may be."

"Democrats," scoffed Onesimos. "Let them spend one day in Lakonia, enduring as we do so they can see what it's like to earn suffrage instead of mewling for it. And how they waste it with their endless bickering. They'd sooner fight each other than Persians, and thanks to their folly we now will."

"Spoken truly, my friend." The king conceded. "But there are more in the world like the Athenians than there are of us. It is Lakedaimon that stands apart. Let us not," and he begrudged a proud smile "allow our indignation at the inferiority of others to distract us."

"I have called in some of our envoys from around the Aegean. You will know their news as soon as I do, and we will understand how to best proceed. We will pray to the Gods for the success of Ionia, but I fear their minds have already been made. Thank you for your ears. I will send for you again when there is more to be done. And my suspicion is that when the time comes, we will have to take arms against men of

Λ

Hellas before we see the spears of Asia."

The polemarchs departed, save one.

"Tell me." Said the king. "Of your protege."

"My protege?" Krateros played dumb. It was not couth for a Spartan to pick favorites, but Kleomenes saw through the polemarch's feeble ruse.

"Yes, him. The son of our old friend. Tell me of the boy. Dienekes."

Λ

Seven

Training continued. No day yet had been as hard as the first, and Dienekes was grateful. But there is always consequence. The boys ran less and fought more. Which meant Dien began falling behind. Falling behind meant tasting the whip. They learned wrestling, then boxing, and then a sport called pankration made from the nastiest bits of both. The larger boys threw him around like a doll, beat him until his teeth rattled loose in their sockets. Light on his feet, he could usually avoid their blows for a time before Thrasilaos saw his coward's dance and made him fight them two on one.

The days blurred together. They rose with the sun and took their tortures, not resting until they were told to, long after dark. Most nights they were already asleep on their feet before collapsing on their mats.

Thrasilaos starved them. They were given bowls of foul tasting black broth morning and night. It nourished their growth but never filled their stomachs, especially in the first few weeks when they gagged most of it back up.

They could smell meat cooking in the officer's quarters, saw helots porting baskets of olives and bread and cheese. Their mouths would have watered if not already dried out from struggling under the sun. They contemplated stealing, but did not have the strength, and worse, feared the whip that awaited were they caught. Once a day, sometimes twice, they were allowed a fistful of fruit. They wasted none, licking the juices from their fingers and chewing on stems, seeds, rinds. It was only ever enough to remind them they were still hungry. Only enough that they would not die. Some boys woke in the morning to find bruised and bloody bites down their wrists and hands, having gnawed on themselves while they dreamt of food.

Each day after training they were sent to the Evrotas to bathe. Each day in the river, Dienekes wallowed below the icy waters and listened to the echo of his stomach's growl.

"We need to eat." He floated to the surface and barely whispered. The other boys laughed or ignored him. They had grown accustomed to his complaints.

"And how do you suppose we do that?" Said Aristaios, casually scrubbing his whip scars. Pain seemed to affect him less than the others.

"We can steal it. From the servants" Dien mumbled, thinking of the helots with their thin wrists and hunched backs. But he knew it was a fruitless idea. He did not need to look behind him to feel the eirene's eyes boring into them from some far off vantage.

"We draw straws," said Tellis. "Short straw gets to be roast pig."

"Being roast pig doesn't sound much worse than another day with Thrasilaos." Maron speculated. "Maybe I'll volunteer."

"Curled up next to a nice warm fire with an apple in your mouth? You'll have to fight me for it!" Alpheos pushed him, Maron pushed back. They tumbled into the water, fighting feebly with new techniques they had learned that day.

"Wait, do we eat the winner or the loser?" Tellis called after the twins flopping downstream.

"I'm serious." Dien appealed to his squad, to Disappointment. "My insides are tearing me apart!"

"Tell me exactly," Olympikos doctored the flayed soles of his feet, "why your hunger is so much worse than ours that we have to keep hearing about it."

"That's not it, I know we're all hungry, it's just that-"

"It's just that you're the only one bitching."

"I'm not bitching! We're starving!"

"Way I see it, you're starving less. We're all given the same amount of food, but you're half our size. Means you're eating twice as much as us."

Dienekes balked. "I didn't choose to-"

"Maybe you're right. Maybe I do need more food. Maybe I steal it from you." The boy rose, pink stains swirling in the water around his ragged feet.

"...You wouldn't dare." Dienekes shrank, painfully reminded of how much smaller he was. An hour earlier, Olympikos had been shoving his face in sand.

"I think I should. There's nothing you could do to stop me."

Anger surged. A river stone leapt into Dien's fingers and flung itself at the larger boy. It bounced off his head with a harmless thunk, and before he had gotten over his own shock, Dien was under the current with hands around his throat. He could hear the muffled shouts of the other boys from somewhere far away. Saw his own breath purge upwards in a stream of bubbles as blackness crept in from the corners of his eyes.

He never imagined it would be Thrasilaos to save him. His limp body was hurled onto the bank alongside his squadmate, both of them forced to their feet while Dien still coughed up water.

"I see we've not had enough for one day." Their teacher thundered. "Should have said so. If it's more fighting you want, it's more fighting you'll get."

Anything short of total obedience had long since been beaten out of the boys.

Λ

Though they trembled from panic and exhaustion, they raised their fists and squared at each other. Olympikos grinned at his odds.

"No." Thrasilaos corrected them. "Today, Disappointment fights me." He unstrapped his cloak and let it fall to the ground. "Show me what you have learned."

They gulped, terrified at the prospect, but would stand in a bonfire if their teacher ordered, knowing that the consequence of hesitation would prove worse. The boys charged together.

So much faster and stronger was Thrasilaos that he didn't bother with technique. He tore Dien off the ground by his ankles and swung him like a club into Olympikos. They fell in a knot. The bigger boy was first to collect himself but didn't miss the opportunity to ferret a few blows into Dien as they untangled. He rushed in by himself and caught an open-hand swat that spun his jaw. His body torqued to the ground unconscious. Dien was left alone. Thrasilaos circled.

"What's the matter, Weeper? Afraid, Weeper? Don't want to throw any more stones, Weeper?"

The eirene badgered him with harmless but infuriating blows to the face. His reach doubled Dien's own, and he lorded it. Spatterings of blood flecked the boy's lips and nose, harried by a thousand tiny slaps. This was no pain compared to the trials he'd grown accustomed to, but the humiliation was unbearable.

Weeper Weeper Weeper. the Eirene parroted.

Hot tears burned in his eyes, and his shame deepened. He clamped them shut and bowed his head so no one would see. Thrasilaos battered him side to side until Di yoked his neck and pushed forward like a dumb animal, swinging blind and wild.

Weeper Weeper Weeper.

Somewhere between the hunger, the shame, and the violence, Dienekes felt a quickening. A brushfire was catching in his strength, and it grew. The seed sprouting up through the rock that Krateros had called defiance. He let it take over. Screaming and spinning his arms, Thrasilaos no longer battered him, only sidestepped and danced out of range. The quicker the Spartiate evaded, the harder Dien pressed. The sprout of defiance shot upward in him and blossomed into intuition. You have him on the run. It said.

You have him on the run?

Intuition screamed alarm. Thrasilaos would never run from him. Something was wrong.

Stop. Think. It's a trap. Said the ears in his heart, but Dienekes did not listen. It felt too good to rage.

The eirene stepped toward instead of back, his hands by his sides. Dien did not feel his right fist crunch into his teacher's bronze breastplate, did not hear the crack like split stone, not until after his left followed and rang the cuirass at a bad angle. It snapped along the wrist. Through misted eyes he looked at his split knuckles. Inside the twisted sheath of skin, his bones shifted and grated on each other like shards of pottery. The foot of his master stamped into his guts, and Dien saw stars all the way to the ground.

"This," Thrasilaos roared to the rest of Disappointment, who had climbed out of the river and stood naked and terrified on the bank, "is what failure looks like." He tufted his fingers into Dien's blonde ringlets and dragged him aloft. The boy could not resist with his hands mangled and squirmed as his teacher made an example of him. "This is what happens when you forget self-control, when you forget discipline. Thoughtless of restraint, mad for the kill, for some pitiful little personal strife you broke the line and impaled yourself on the enemy." Thrasilaos dangled Dien's ear by his mouth and whispered, "But what's worse than that, Weeper?"

Dienekes did not know the answer and would not have had the breath to speak it if he did. The pain dissociated him from his body, and in a strange way he was glad that Thrasilaos had kicked his wind out. If there had been any air in his lungs he knew he would have been sobbing openly. The teacher released his hair, and he crumpled to the ground.

"Worse than that... He struck one of his own. He turned the rank on itself. You are brothers! And you fight amongst yourselves?" He gestured to the body of Olympikos, who he had taken to calling Pigfat, still limp in the dirt. "You would throw rocks at he who will one day hold a shield for you? You would drown he who kills the man that would kill you?" He was not addressing the two who had come to blows, but all of Disappointment. He held them all responsible. "If you hold your own life, your own comfort," he spat the word down at Dien with unsheathed hate and put another foot in his ribs, "above the lives of the men next to you, then it is at YOU where the line will break. And it will be YOU to blame when all your brothers have died."

Dienekes mewled at his feet. Olympikos stirred, but only barely. The other ten boys stared, sheepish and petrified.

"No mats. There are traitors in your midst, and they have broken the line. There were no survivors. You all dig graves to sleep in tonight."

They all slept poorly, but none so bad as Weeper and Pigfat. Rest is unforthcoming with freshly bloodied backs.

Λ

Eight

Dienekes was not permitted to see the healers till morning.

"He will recover. But he must be removed from his current training." The *archiatros* said to Thrasilaos. He was an old white-bearded man with twisted, useless legs and a scar knotting his left eye closed. He gave no words or tinctures to comfort the boy, but his hands worked with a gentle compassion, even when setting the boy's bones. He did not ask how Dienekes had come by his injuries. Why should he care.

"Removed?" Thrasilaos snorted. "Hear that Weeper? Not even a year in and already you're to fall on your sword."

The healer laughed a wet breathy rasp.

"You misunderstand. I said the hands will heal." His laugh deteriorated into a damp, rattling cough. Dienekes thought he must be over 90 years old. "The fractures are severe. He'll need three, maybe four months. He won't be able to fight or hold a weapon, lest we ruin him for good. But the agoge -the upbringing- is thirteen years long. There is still time for him to serve his country."

"What am I supposed to do with a boy who can't hold a weapon?"

"His legs still work." The surgeon washed his hands and returned the black iron ring to the finger he had removed it from before treating Dienekes. " And speaking of work, mine here is done. Hand me my own legs, boy." He waved to where his crutches leaned against the wall, and Dien snapped to obey. His hands found the crutches, but broken and bandaged, could not hold them. They fell to the dirt floor, and the old man croaked phlegmy laughter at him. "They fall for that every time. Don't worry, you'll adjust." He picked up the crutches himself and hobbled to the door while Dien tried desperately not to live up to his new name.

Weeper

"What good is a Spartan who can only run away? The little shit's too inclined for it already." The eirene glowered at the healer.

"It's your job to purpose your little toys. I just put them back together when you play too rough."

It was not the first time concessions had to be made around an injured boy. Not for the sake of the child, but for the state. If every boy temporarily injured in the agoge were cast out, there would be none left to man the phalanx. So Dienekes was made to run. And run. And run.

While his squadmates learned their weapons, he sprinted tedious laps around them and Thrasilaos casually flicked at him with the whip. He ran urgent messages for his ereine to distant trees and boulders.

"I am a worthless blubbering infant." He was made to tell the stone.

"I'm a whimpering cock sheath." He told the oak.

Thrasilaos had him run in small circles around other officers without explanation until they grew annoyed and struck him down. He was made to run while singing embarrassing songs to make it impossible to catch his breath. At least once a day he would faint from exertion, wake to a kicking, then run yet more lest he take further kicking.

There were unintended consequences, good and bad. Already gifted with speed, his alacrity flowered significantly under his teacher's disdain. Constantly dashing about by himself made him more visible than he had been training with Disappointment. It was not a common thing for a boy of only eight to cover ground like an Olympian, and there were whispers. He heard them call him elafakia. Baby deer. He risked taking a small pride in this.

It was better than Weeper.

He liked the running, though he wouldn't admit it, but he lamented being separated from his squad. As far as the eriene was concerned, he had two squads now. One of eleven boys, and another squad of only one, called Disgrace. Dien was collecting many names, it seemed. He had not exactly been close with the other boys but being shoulder to shoulder with anyone was better than suffering alone. The cut of loneliness was worse than the whip, and every day he had to watch his new brothers advance their fighting skills without him. Already diminutive in size and strength, he feared that he was losing more ground than he would be able to recover once healed.

"You feel ashamed to not train beside your brothers. " Krateros said. He had sent for the boy after training.

"Yes." Dienekes felt ashamed of everything. I am a worthless blubbering infant. I am a whimpering cock sleeve.

"Why?" When Dien did not answer, he repeated the question.

"Because they are better than me."

"Better than you…" Krateros scoffed. "There are men under my command who are stronger than me. Faster than me. Better with spear and shield. They still obey me. We all find our strengths. Sooner or later, Lakonia makes equals of us all."

"How can I be equal? I'm a cripple."

Krateros laughed. Dien knew the laugh was at his expense, but he still warmed at

Λ

the sound. It reminded of happier times that he could still feel somewhere inside, even if he could no longer picture them in his mind.

"You were stupid, and you broke your hands. It is not the last thing you will do, nor do I think it will be the most stupid. You will heal soon. You will fight again."

"But not like them." Dien remembered how Tellis and Olympikos grappled, tumbling like gymnasts in the sandy palaistra, already becoming masters of violence.

"Keep whining, boy, and I'll beat you." Still smiling, he whipped the boy with a long stem of grass. "This is how the Upbringing works. It breaks you down and forces you to overcome. So your brothers are bigger, stronger, better fighters. Well one day soon, they will do something stupid, and the Upbringing will break them down and hold them back. That is where our strength comes from. You think you are falling behind, but it is them who trail after you. For your trial has become greater, and overcoming will yield greater reward. Be ashamed if you must, little deer, but overcome."

It was cold comfort.

"You are a soldier, Di. Soldiers do not compare their orders to those of their comrades. They simply obey. One day you will be every bit the wrestler and boxer they are, but for now your duty is to run, and you will do it. Smaller boys than you have gone through worse and come out stronger for it. Be patient."

Patient. As the whip cracks across my shoulders, as my brothers grow stronger and I grow weaker and my insides eat themselves from hunger.

Dien nearly lived up to his name again. But Krateros said something that gave him pause.

"You know, the King has been asking about you."

"What? Kleomenes? Asking about me?" Technically, there were two kings, but it was Kleomenes who had the greater love and trust of his people. Krateros nodded and smirked. "What did he ask? What did you tell him?"

"That is for the king to know, my boy. But do your duty, and remember what I have told you. The world is watching."

He sent the boy back to his barracks. Dien was careful not to wake the others as he stumbled to his plot. No mat again. The others had woven theirs while he spoke with Krateros. His eyelids sank like anchors, but sleep did not come. His mind reeled.

The king? Ask about me?

He was too deep in thought to hear the scuffle of bare feet circling him until a punch in the shoulder snapped him alert.

Four of his squad mates loomed over him. He panicked, lurched upright, tried to spring away. When they grabbed him, he kicked and bit, but they were too strong and would have easily pinned him flat even with the use of his hands.

"Dammit, Weeper, stop being a shit!"

Λ

It was Tellis. Dien calmed reluctantly, and they let him go.

"You little cunt!" Tellis rubbed the rosy welted teeth marks swelling on his neck. "Don't catch me doing you any more favors!"

"What?" Dien did not understand.

"They fed us again while you were talking with the polemarch. Here. Hold out your hands."

Dien complied, hesitant, and felt them fill with a sticky wet mass. He poked a wrapped finger through it, baffled. "Tellis, is this your…? You didn't…"

"No, not me. Well. Yes, me. But all of us."

All of us. Eleven little pieces of fig.

"All of you? Even…?"

"Yes, even Pigfat," said Tellis. Olympikos grunted assent beside him. His jaw was still sore from when Thrasilaos dislocated it.

"I don't understand."

"Just shut up and eat it, alright?"

"I will! I'm sorry! I just… I thought that since…"

"That since you don't train with us that we don't like you?" Maron cut him off. "Well guess what."

"We DON'T like you." Alpheos finished for him. "We think you're a whiny little turd." Dien could feel the twin's smile instigating his own through the darkness.

"But you're OUR whiny little turd." Said Tellis. "It's like Thrasilaos said when he was beating you to death. We're in this together. Brothers. And thanks for that, by the way. It was quite the show. And he's been going easier on us since you've been taking the worst of it."

Dien didn't see how that could be true.

"I don't know what to say."

"Say 'thank you', asshole."

"Thank you!"

"Sshhh! Not so loud! You're absolutely hopeless, Weeper."

"Eat." Olympikos grunted, and smacked Dien lightly in the mouth. Weeper did as he was told, and the other boys, satisfied, went back to their mats.

"Tellis?" Dien asked after he finished licking his fingers.

"Gods, what now."

"Does he really treat me worse?"

"Of course he does. It's cause you keep crying."

"I do not!" Dien's voice cracked, and tears crept into his eyes. The other boys laughed at him, sensing his discomposure, but it made him feel better somehow. Not alone anymore. To Olympikos he added, "I'm sorry I got you whipped."

"Would have happened eventually," Pigfat grumbled through his stiff jaw. "You

Λ

got the worst of it anyhow. Still can't believe you scored licks on Thrasilaos." The rest of the boys murmured agreement. It didn't seem to matter to them that the blows had no effect.

"I know he calls you Disgrace," Tellis murmured. "But you'll always be a Disappointment to us." Tellis laughed at his own joke and the others through clods of dirt at him.

Dienekes broke the silence after almost a minute.

"Did you mean it though?"

"For fuck's sake, Weeper, some of us are tired!"

"But did you mean it?"

"Mean what?"

"The part about… about being brothers."

"Yes, Weeper. Brothers."

Λ

Nine

Nine thousand men, every one a veteran of combat in war or otherwise, loitered in the acropolis as the shadows waned their shortest. Other Hellenes plunked their asses on luxuriant limestone rotundas with carved stairways and columned gates, to argue and shake their fists in the shade. Spartans were satisfied to squat in the grassy hollow of a hill and patiently wait to hear their kings speak. King Demaratos sulked on one side of a flat and barren stage in typical Lakonian fashion, absent attendants and unadorned but for his arms and armor in solidarity with his subjects.

Kleomenes was assumed present, but was obscured behind a theatrical maze of Tyrian purple curtains that hung from the spears of a dozen royal knights on white horses. Those who cared to look saw busy feet dancing back and forth in the crack below the cloth walls, and heard muffled bickering. Floutists, drummers, harpists droned from inside the veil. Fragrant smoke billowed from between the creases. The longer Kleomenes suspended his dramatics, the more Demaratos steamed. By the time his rival monarch's musicians kicked their melodies into a fanfare, lamb would have broiled on his helmet.

A helot, wearing rams horns and having great difficulty keeping a straight face, stepped from the wings and proclaimed.

"Hail! The first of his name, and first among the Peers! Ear to the gods and descendant of Herakles! The greatest soldier Lakedaimon has ever known!" Some of the audience took insult to this blatant self-aggrandizement. They did not tolerate open hubris and knew the consequences of such folly.

"I present, for your terror and awe! King Kleomenes!"

The curtains flourished open. Floutists keened. A giant, twice the height of a man emerged from the tumult of fabric.

Indignation gave way to surprise, to confusion, to mirth.

Kleomenes teetered into view wearing a tunic ten times too large, to conceal the two squires holding him aloft by the legs. His wicker shield could have been a small fishing boat. His lance, an untrimmed sapling, sprouted a bouquet of spearheads from its leaves. The Spartans laughed at their king. He brandished his unmanageably large weapons until his tree-spear hitched one of his squires in the groin. The three of them toppled and rolled out of the costume.

A final cheer rolled around the amphitheater as Kleomenes popped to his feet with a shameless grin and waved away the entourage with his mess.

"I suppose today, I have learned-" he shouted over the dying voices of his peers. "What befalls a man-" and now he stared directly, emphatically, at Demaratos "-when he takes himself too seriously."

There was yet more laughter, and Demaratos boiled in his armor.

A Eurypontid captain sat in the front row, and had brought his young son to see how Sparta conducted her affairs. Kleomenes removed his ridiculous costume helmet and gave it to the boy.

"Is it not time we address our business?" Demaratos grumbled.

"Yes! Thank you, absolutely." Kleomenes upstaged him and shed his theatrics like a vapor. "Peers of Sparta! I will waste no more of your time. Most of you know why we have come. For those who have not heard, or heard only rumors, Ionia has fallen. Aristagoras is slain. Our neighbor Athens sent troops to aid the fight, and Dareios of Persia is not one to forget such enmity. It is clear that Dareios has no intention to limit his westward conquest, and it is my belief, that rather than continue marching on new enemies, he will sail across the Aegean to conquer the ones he already has. Here. In the heart of Hellas. On our very doorstep."

Demaratos interrupted, knuckling his brow.

"Athens is not, and has never been our friend. Who they fall to is none of our concern."

Kleomenes wheeled on him.

"-Said the sheep to the goat when they saw the lion eat the ram." Then to his subjects, "Rest assured the lion ate them both next." The crowd murmured assent.

"So you would have us send soldiers to Athens?" Demaratos was losing his composure. "To waste Spartan lives to defend shriveled bureaucrats while our own home lies undefended?"

"No. I would have us march north. To Argos!"

"What does Argos have to do with-"

"Patience, Demaratos, and I will educate you." But he only faced the crowd, striding further into their masses, meeting every pair of eyes that tracked him like a hawk.

"Argos, our bitterest enemy," the audience growled with him, "has few friends left among the Hellenes, if any. They remember their hatred of us, and how we crushed them at Thyrea. When Persia comes, Argos will surely side with the invader against Athens, and then again against us as they move to take all the great cities."

"You speak for the gods now, do you? You see the future? You make

Λ

unsubstantiated prediction and-"

"Unsubstantiated prediction? Demaratos, can you honestly claim that Persia, an entire continent behind them, will sail to Athens, teach the liver-spotted aristocrats their lesson, and sail away home?"

"I claim that such events cannot be known!"

"You may not know, but I do. And I am not content to sit and wait to be proven right at the cost of our entire nation. Hear me, brothers!" Kleomenes raised his hands. "We are the greatest fighting men the world has ever seen! If Persia comes for us, we will throw her mutilated corpse into the sea. If Argos comes for us, we will crush her on the rocks of Parnon." He stifled the growing cheers. "If Argos and Persia come for us together, with their forces combined." He lowered his hands, but not his eyes. "We will not win."

Silence rang.

"If Hellas is to win in the coming war, and I promise you, war is coming, it will take all the Hellenic cities united to cast off the conqueror."

"Sparta fights for Sparta, and Sparta alone." Demaratos spat through clenched teeth. "We are neither caretaker nor bodyguard to nations that cannot defend themselves. I will not hold with the proposal that we fight for strangers who would not fight for us."

"I do not propose that we fight for strangers. I do not even propose that we fight alongside strangers. Brothers. I propose that we lead them. I propose that we take our rightful place on the throne of men and show our cousins how we deal with infidels from the front! I say we drive our spear into the heart of the enemy for all of Hellas and Persia to see so that when the foe is scattered and torn and banished back to the holes in the ground from which they crawled, their mothers and sisters and daughters can ask the cowards who has slain them. And the whole world will shout back-SPARTA!"

Demaratos tried to refute his rival in vain, drowned out by clamoring soldiers rising to their feet with their fists in the air.

Kleomenes urged the ephors call for a vote. The voices rang 'yea' so loud in favor of war that they need not call for 'nay'. They dismissed the assembly to prepare for campaign. Lakonia did not idle after decisions were made.

Demaratos thundered down on his rival, smoke nearly pouring out of his ears. Kleomenes beckoned his minstrel troop to re-envelop them both in the curtains. As much as Kleo enjoyed shaming his fellow monarch, it did not do for the children to see their parents fighting.

"Is this is a game to you?" Demaratos roared.

"Everything is a game, cousin. It is only the stakes that vary." Kleomones poured two cups of wine and offered one, only to have it slapped out of his hand. "Wasteful."

Λ

He sighed, and shrugged. He finished his own cup in one pull and poured another. "You!" He snatched the collar of the squires who had carried him. "You were supposed to drop me! I should have racked your jewels harder, you imp, you nearly cost me my charade. It would have been all for nothing if they had not seen me fall."

"What is this nonsense?" Demaratos gestured at the curtains, the sconces of foreign incense, the flute girls making eyes at Kleomenes. "This... This frivolity." He spat the word as if there were no greater insult.

"This?" Kleo pretended to be hurt. "This was all for you. Did you not like it?"

"I most certainly did not."

"Well, thank you. That was the point."

"All this just to irritate me?"

"No, not irritate." Kleo scratched his chin. "Distract. Disarm. Discredit. You're rather a poor persuader when you're flustered, aren't you? I'd say it worked like a charm. It was simply a bonus that our subjects found it comical. I do so love to see my children happy."

"You debase yourself as a traveling minstrel, to make me angry? This is worth subjecting yourself to the laughter, to the ridicule of the Peers?"

"They voted on my behalf, cousin." Kleo finished another cup. "They may be laughing, but I assure you, it is not at me."

"They will sicken of your extravagance, Kleomenes. They will become disenchanted with your ridiculous expenses and your noisome masquerading. You are like a child with your whims and follies, and Lakedaimon will cast you out for it. You have become too grand for yourself."

"Extravagant... noisome... perhaps. But grand? I think not. It is the pompous man, the arrogant, that they despise. I am but silly. I humble myself before them, and they love me for it. You, on the other hand... I don't know what they make of you... So unoriginal. So timid."

Timid.... Kleomenes had gone too far.

"You're insane." The grinding of his teeth rattled nearly as loud as his voice.

"The philosophers have been known to say," Kleo did not miss a beat "that madness walks hand in hand with genius."

"I will not be party to this disgrace anymore. You'll soon find that Sparta will not be either."

Demaratos stormed from the violet canopy, leaving Kleomenes with his victory, and his wine.

Λ

Ten

Of the five regiments Kleomenes could have called to battle, he brought four. He left behind little more than a single *mora* of a thousand men, with a single polemarch, to fester with jealousy under the pretense of guarding their home. A sea of scarlet marched up the road north. The march to Argos could have been made in two days if needed, but Kleo took a leisurely four before his men lined the banks of the Erasinos, the river defining the edge of enemy territory. He wanted his men well rested. He wanted to give his enemies time to wallow in fear.

Crossing the border of another nation is a dramatic event. To do so without the favor of the gods bodes poorly for an invasion. Any other nation would have consulted with augurs and oracles for their insight in the flight of birds and the wafting of smoke. Among the Spartans, the king was the oracle. Kleomenes conferred with the gods himself, brow furrowed, his arm elbow deep in the chest of a screaming goat.

He frowned, and stoically wrenched its liver into daylight. The animal's kicks slowed and eventually stopped as the life drained from the rent in its body. Kleomenes inspected the organ close enough to smear blood across the tip of his nose. He sniffed, prodded, tore off a small piece and tasted the specimen until he was satisfied in his verdict.

"We do not cross today." He proclaimed. His army hardly waited for the end of his decree before rising ready for the next command.

"A riverbank is hardly the place to field a phalanx." Krateros said, talking himself through Kleo's reasoning. "Where should we camp, then?" He suspected he knew, but wanted to hear it from the mouth of the king.

"To Thyrea." It meant retreating a considerable distance of the miles already travelled. "I want to see it. Where we marched over their bodies." Said Kleomenes with blood still on his face. They all wanted to see it.

Camp was a solemn affair.

Krateros ran his fingers through the tall grass of the Thyrean plain, fertilized by blood and offal from decades before. He could hear the ancient iron pounding bronze like a dull gong, feel the insufferable itch in his sword hand urging him to finish the fight that had ended before he had been born. He felt the pangs of loss echo through time and wrench at his guts, the bones of the fallen calling out from where they were buried beneath his feet. They had not been defeated that day, but neither could they call it a victory.

"I was there, you know," said the king.

"You were?" Krateros had never heard him speak of it.

"No. I lie." Kleo sighed with a wry smile. "I still had yet to crawl out of my mother. But do you know the feeling? How sometimes we let ourselves believe things would have been different had we been there. Better. That we are somehow special enough that our presence could have driven the past down a different course."

Krateros hesitated before speaking.

"This is hubris."

"Yes, my friend. Only hubris. Only folly." He crouched, pulled a handful of dirt from the ground and ran it through his fingers. Held the earth to his face and breathed deep. "Or is it?"

"I am but a soldier, Kleo." Sometimes, only sometimes, did the king's strange ways grate on his old friend. "I do not understand your philosopher's riddles."

"It is hubris that angers the gods, beckons them to strike us down. But without it? Without that dangerous wanton pride, what would we be? Ants that work and never strive. To live and die in mud and obscurity, resigned to the fate of the forgotten. It is the folly of believing we are somehow greater than we are that drives us to do the great things we never would have otherwise chanced." He reached in the collar of his cuirass and produced a leather pouch on a cord and filled it with the Thyrean soil. Kissed it, slid it back under his armor.

"Are you saying it is good to anger the gods?" Krateros snorted.

"Nay." Kleo chuckled. "Angering the gods only ends one way for us mortals. But I say that to win their love we must sometimes risk their wrath. A precarious balancing act."

"Sounds like nonsense. Athenian drama."

"Perhaps. Perhaps. But look at Achilles. Thetis warned that he would die at Troy, and he went anyway. Die he did, but did he not get what he wanted as well?"

"Immortality." Krateros conceded. It was a strange concept for a graduate of the agoge, their successes were something achieved together, as a united force. Victories were rarely feats of the individual, but they did happen. Krateros had nearly done it, been crowned in a wreath of olives. But he had only been second fastest and returned home unadorned and unknown until finding renown in the phalanx, joined with the strength of others. Sometimes the loss still burned in him. As burned his nation's memory of the battle at Thyrea.

Λ

"Immortality." Kleo repeated. "The gods killed Achilles for his hubris, but bestowed him with the greatest gift a man can receive. They punished him and rewarded him with the same act in the same moment. So perhaps to the Gods, so much wiser and more complex than ourselves, to be loved and to be hated are the same."

"The gods are many. And seldom are they of one mind. Athena loved Achilles. Apollo hated him. One lifted him up and the other struck him down."

"A wise distinction, Krateros. But would he have been struck down had he not been exalted? Had he not been the greatest of men, a rival to the divine, he would have drawn neither their affection nor their ire. Achilles, Herakles, Bellerophon, Jason, countless more… The greatest of men they were, and they all met terrible ends. For us mere mortals, it would seem few things are more fatal than greatness."

"I am but a soldier."

Such musings frequently reminded the polemarch that his liege, like all first sons of kings, were exempt from the agoge. His mind and body had not been conditioned like those who followed him. They were carved from stone. But their king was flesh and blood. And something else entirely.

The king and polemarchs had brought squires. Promising youths with drums and pipes granted temporary exception from training so they might glimpse leadership in action. They would soon be proud men of Spartiate status, but were still boys a little longer. And boys want stories. The story of Thyrea.

Kleomenes, with mist in his eyes and gravel in his voice, beckoned them to sit with him in the darkness and fire. Then he told them.

Λ

Eleven

It is an old dilemma, provoked since nations first drew borders, to continue through time for as long as borders remain. Lakonia claimed Thyrea belonged to Lakonia. Argos claimed Thyrea belonged to Argos. Both would kill for their claim. Both would bleed.

War brings out the boast in a man. To hear the soldier speak, all his enemies are frail and inhuman, all his causes are just, all his acts endorsed by the will of the gods. All battles righteous and won before they began. For without such certainty, what man willingly marches to his death?

A wager was struck. Three hundred of mine against three hundred of yours. King Anaxandridas brokered the deal with whatever man spoke for the squabbling Argolid democracy, and they left the field with their armies. They would not watch, lest they be tempted to intervene. The three hundred best of each nation remained with orders to let none of the foe survive. Victory would be total or not at all.

The Gods take challenge when men think in such absolutes. Sometimes they favor neither side. Sometimes they favor both. Sometimes their blessing is the same as their curse.

Sparta fought with strength and discipline, Argos with cunning and guile. The battle was brief, but the choking dust they kicked into the air hung for days. Two men of Argos, blinded in its fog, could find no more enemies to kill. Weary and haggard, they limped home to declare themselves victorious. They were too eager.

A single Spartan remained alive, gravely wounded but unwavering in his task. He stalked the empty battlefield a day and a night for anything still breathing, friend or foe.

The following day they found him, Othryades, alone on the field. He too declared victory, as his enemy had fled. He had not seen the pair escape, but he knew. He had counted the dead.

Anaxandridas declared him a hero, but Othryades was deaf to the praise. His brothers were gone. In his heart he had failed them and could not bear the guilt. He reported the battle to the king, sparing no detail, then he fell upon his sword.

Sparta claimed Sparta had won Thyrea, as it was they who held the field. Argos claimed Argos won Thyrea, as it was their soldiers who survived. The deal broken, the wager abandoned, both nations returned by the thousands.

The three hundred best of each nation had drawn a stalemate, but Argos learned a powerful lesson then. The greatest among them may have stood equal to a Spartan, but the last of the Lakedaimonians stands equal to the first. There would be no dispute a second time, no stalemate. The foes of Sparta were trampled like wheat.

Λ

Twelve

T he next morning, using iron ingots as currency, Kleomenes chartered sailors to ferry his six-thousand men across the bay instead of the Erasinos so they would be less likely to expose themselves to ambush. He announced to they who asked that his omens boded well, but no one saw him kill the goat.

The Aegean bay was wide, and to shuttle four mora across was no small task. It took till nightfall for their entirety to assemble. A braver leader would have attacked while the Spartiates made landfall, but the Argives instead entrenched themselves at a place called Sepeia. Adjacent to an ancient and sacred wood so the gods would walk amongst them and lend their strength.

For all their austerity, the Spartans were more superstitious than most. They feared no man, but they feared the gods. To fight in the enemy's holy places prickled their doubts. They would be sure this time to watch their king garner his omens. With all eyes on the goat in its throes, none saw how the king failed to observe his own sacrament. He watched not the animal, but from under his furrowed brow studied the enemy only a few hundred yards away where they made sacrifice of their own.

He shook his head wordlessly. Poor omens. They ate the meat and would not mobilize that morning.

The entrails at noon read the same. Either ill or inconclusive, Kleo would not say, but he gave no order to attack. Neither did the Argives taking augury from flights of doves. He ordered his men to rest and eat. As did Argos. At midafternoon he called for another sacrifice which also failed to yield a blessing, and their enemy did the same. He paced the field of battle alone and silently watched the enemy camp until dusk. He called for another goat, but before slitting its throat, he roared the call to arms. His troops were surprised, but leapt to the ready. They were in formation in mere moments and patiently waited for the struggling Argives to fall in line. Some wondered why they waited for their foe to organize, tripping over each other and bleating on trumpets, why they did not sweep the blight away in their panic. But all wondered why the king, before the enemy had even fully composed themselves, dismissed his phalanx and sent them back to their campfires. The Argives hesitated, gripped by suspicion, and trembled in their lines until they saw every Spartan eating and drinking in their camp before doing the same themselves.

Less than an hour later, only moments after Kleo saw his enemy settle in did he order his soldiers to once again form up. They were bitter about abandoning their still hot meals, but a Lakonian does not hesitate when battle calls. Again they stood and waited while their enemy foundered in disarray. And again, when the enemy had dragged themselves into formation, did Kleo give the order to rest for the night. The men were baffled, but obeyed. Spartans on the battlefield think with one mind. They do not question their orders.

Krateros and the other polemarchs were waiting by his tent when he returned. They spoke not, but the concern in their faces was plain.

"Peace, brothers." Kleomenes brushed a hand over each of their shoulders as he passed. "All will soon become clear." He strolled into his tent without stopping before ducking his head back out the canvas flaps. "Bring me my Thrasilaos."

Krateros bit back the questions waiting on his tongue and fulfilled the command. He contained his questions and the urge to eavesdrop on the king's whispers to the eirene. The young soldier trotted from the tent minutes later, barefoot, wearing only a tunic and a small knife. Krateros need not ask where he was going.

"It is a brave man who runs naked among enemies." Krateros called out, and the young Peer turned back.

"I shall hope they say such things about me one day."

"You know they do already, you little shit. And more." The two embraced, smacking each other's shoulders and backs. "But be more than brave tonight, yes? Be smart. Be prudent."

"There is little glory in being smart. And none in prudence." The boy's eyes were wild, his smile manic.

"There will be glory enough later. You have a duty."

"I do as my king commands. And happily." He had the taste and the reputation for night work. The riskier the better. He licked his sharpened teeth.

"Your duty is not only to your king." Krateros barked. "You still have a duty to Hegisistratos." Thrasilaos sobered when he heard the name and the old soldier drove the point with a finger in the younger's face. "You will be smart, and you will be prudent. Take no unnecessary risks. So you may live to fulfil all of your duties."

"No glory tonight then." Thrasilaos bowed his head. "For the son of Hegisistratos."

"May he one day grow to look after your son, as you have watched over him."

"Let's hope by then he has learned not to weep."

They shared a laugh.

"I hope" Krateros raised his voice to the darkness of Thrasilaos's shoulder. "That the spirits in the dark will watch over our scout this night?"

Λ

"Do not leave it to hope." The shadows answered. Shukxa stepped from them with a bow. "A polemarch must be certain."

Krateros smiled, grateful for friends in the dark. "Certain or not," He embraced the young brown man. "An old man will always worry for his boys."

"Worry away." Shukxa punched Thrasilaos, who punched him back. "But trust that I'm watching out for my little brother."

Softer men might have reminisced, but Lakonia bred men of action. They touched heads and Thrasilaos ran off into the night with his companion.

The veteran stood silent attention by his king's tent until just before midnight when Thrasilaos returned, his word kept. Still wearing the stolen armor of a murdered Argive, the scout made his report to Kleomenes in private before the king invited his generals inside.

Λ

Thirteen

T hank you for your patience, brothers. It has been an interesting day," said the king. "It was not my intention to keep you uninformed, but our spy-" he gestured to Thrasilaos, who paused from climbing back into his own armor to salute "-has only just confirmed my suspicions. Tell them what you've told me."

"The Argives are shitting themselves." Thrasilaos grinned. "Their oracles foresaw their doom before we even crossed the bay."

"Then I'm impressed they did not break and run. Perhaps there is honor among them yet." Xanthippos murmured. A crooked scar fused half his mouth together and muffled his words.

"Perhaps not." Thrasilaos's eyes glittered, made hungry by the stench of Argive fear still thick in his nostrils. "The soldiers do not know. Their leaders keep it secret from them. They hound their soothsayers as we speak to find better omens in smoke and bones but…" He shrugged, palms up, licking his lips. "Tyche sees only death."

"You learned this how? Strolled up and asked?" Asked Onesimos.

"Thrasilaos has my trust. He won a crown of olives for boxing at Olympia, and in addition to the agoge, he received more strange trainings from my Skythian friends. His time in the Krypteia and as a scout for me since have demonstrated that his skills as a treacherous little bastard are even greater than his fighting."

"Then why have we not attacked? Kleomenes, have you not seen the same omen in your readings?" Xanthippos, while a valiant leader, was youngest and hastiest of the polemarchs. He still shared Thrasilaos's fever for challenge. For blood.

"Only the night before last did I tell the boys of Thyrea. Have you forgotten already?"

Xanthippos looked puzzled. Krateros, in his infinite patience, enlightened him.

"Tyche may call for the destruction of our enemies, but that does not mean she doesn't call for our destruction as well."

"You may be the wisest man in Sparta, old friend." Kleomenes raised his mostly empty cup of wine to the general. A squire wordlessly refilled it. "Tell them the rest, Thrasilaos."

"They have no plan. They're too busy scurrying between sacrifice and soothsayer to strategize. They wait, ripening on the other end of the field for us to walk over and pick them like fruit." The Argive armor in the corner indicated that one at least had already been plucked. The polemarchs noticed silently that there was no blood on Thrasilaos's knife or hands, but flecks of it had dried into the beard around his sharpened teeth.

Strange training indeed.

"At first it was mere suspicion. But the simpering Argives replicated every order I gave yesterday, regardless of the reason I gave it. My apologies for keeping you in the dark, I had to be certain first lest I look the fool."

Krateros laughed mightily. "I am learning," he said, "that wisdom and folly often appear the same." The other polemarchs laughed with him.

"So that's why you had us run around like idiots." Xanthippos shook his head, jaw dangling as slack as his ruined mouth would allow. "Using us to measure the enemy, you clever bastard. We were worried you'd finally gone mad."

"Not yet, little brother. Not yet." Kleomenes winked and drained his cup. Krateros was grateful to see it set aside and not refilled again. "So here is my plan. You will tell your subordinates, and they will tell their subordinates till every man knows. Our success demands that every Peer be complicit. At dawn our pipers will call for breakfast. Our men will line up to take their meals, and we can suspect the enemy will call for the same. But unlike us, they do not sleep in their armor. So we will have our bronze and iron and they will not. I will give no order to attack. Instead, the signal will be when the pipers stop playing. No formation, no hymns, no phalanx. Tomorrow we fight as individuals. No battle. Only murder. Krateros and Thrasilaos each will lead a small squad to lie in wait on their flanks in hopes that none escape too easily. There will be a reward for him that brings me the most heads."

Onesimos hesitated before speaking. "It feels dishonorable. To rely on deception."

"Maybe it is, brother," Kleo admitted. "But you are merely following orders. So it is I and not you who will face judgement for such trickery. Besides, this way fewer of our own will die. And the more men survive today, the more we will have to fight the Persians."

"But we are not yet even certain that Persia is coming. We may come to regret dishonoring ourselves on suspicion. A worthy suspicion, but a suspicion nonetheless."

"With utmost respect, sir..." said Thrasilaos. "You're wrong." He basked in the moment. "I heard more than oracles in the Argive camp. I heard their diplomats converse in no uncertain terms. There were foreign soldiers in their midst. Asiatic mercenaries. They have already sold themselves to the invader. Surrendered to the Persian Empire, and the price Dareios promised in exchange for their loyalty is Sparta."

The polemarchs had trusted their king's theories, they would not have marched

Λ

with him otherwise, but they were still affected to hear his predictions laid out in fact. In his strangeness he had a way of knowing the truth long before truth should have been knowable. They watched him as he fondled the pouch of dirt collected the night before.

"I promise, on the soil of Thyrea, and on the bones of those who fell there. Tomorrow." He glowered. "Argos dies."

Λ

Fourteen

Dawn came and went. Kleomenes raged through the empty enemy camp. He tore down tents, hurled shields, smashed pots of water, drank the pots of wine and hurled curses at the Argive cowards cowering in the trees.

The battle had been won and not a single Spartan life lost, but his mission had failed. No one expected for the Argives to not even attempt to fight. When the northerners saw the host of Lakedaimon silently streaking towards them through the mist, they broke and ran, many of them naked from their beds. Kleo had hoped to wade through their bodies by the thousands, but took instead a scant few hundred, only the stupidly brave or those slowest to flee. The remaining survivors, the entire Argive expeditionary force, now hunkered emasculated in their sacred wood.

"I can't tell, Kleo." Noemon laughed. Unlike his king he was satisfied with their victory. "Did your plan fail? Or did it work too well?"

"I thought I was fighting men." The king fumed. "I would have planned differently if I knew we waged war against insects! Rodents! Vermin! Why did you not follow them into the trees? I did not give the order to stop!"

The polemarchs glanced at each other. They were no more willing to storm hallowed ground than a temple or a shrine. They may have hated the Argives but they worshipped the same gods. Noemon said so and was shouted down.

"Do you see any Gods?" Kleomenes spat, arms stretched to the surrounding grounds. "I am king! I speak for the gods here! And I will continue to do so until they decide to come down and correct me themselves!"

"We would have lost the advantage. Better to remain united." Onesimos found the only answer that did not stem from reverence. "They know the terrain. Our men would lose each other in the trees for the cowards to pick us off and slip away between us. Like catching mice through a fishnet." He saw his logic take hold and risked a small flattery. "We must save our ranks for Dareios, must we not?"

"Catching mice in a fishnet..." Kleomenes mumbled as he calmed. "...Remain united." His unfocused eyes danced back and forth as he thought, rapidly calculating what the others could not see.

"Alright." He snapped back to lucidity. "Noemon will take a single lochos back to guard our camp, and the remaining troops will circle the forest. It's wide but not so wide that six thousand men can't surround. The front lines will scour the ground to the edge of the wood and stack whatever you can into a barricade. Branches, rocks, their wagons and carts and tents, all the trash the cowards left behind. It doesn't have to be impassable, just an obstruction." After a short pause, "Send runners to their city. They will have sent their own already and will hear of their defeat just before our runner arrives to offer to ransom their soldiers back."

"Ransom? For nearly six thousand men? What city has that much wealth?" Asked Opites.

"None. But we must at least be seen to offer."

"I do not understand."

"And that is why I am king. No more questions. Go, now. Build my wall. And send a messenger to summon the Argive general to parley, if the rat is not too craven to crawl out from his hole." And as an afterthought he added, "Their campfires. Put them all out. Save all their firewood, separate from the wall." The Lakonians obeyed, not knowing why.

"I'm sure Noemon will be bitter about you banishing him to the baggage train."

"Noemen is always bitter." Kleo sipped his wine.

"Do you think yourself so popular that you can afford to aggravate the ire of your generals?"

"*My* generals?" The king blew a raspberry. "Noemon is a creature of Demaratos, and both of them are impotent. I fear no plot hatched in their court, and no man who keeps their council."

"Demaratos keeps my council as well. Do you not fear me?"

"I would." Kleo laughed. "You are certainly a terror. But you have a fatal flaw that would never allow you to turn from me. Or by your advice, allow them to turn from me."

"And what's that?" Krateros humored him.

"You're too damn trustworthy."

It took some time, but the enemy commander did present himself. The sun hung at its peak and Kleomenes had calmed his temper, awaiting his enemy with open arms and a crocodile smile.

The commander trudged down an aisle of silent Spartan sentries. He had emptied his hands and his scabbard, removed his helm. He held his head high in defiance of his defeat. He might be beaten, but he was still Hellene, and a leader of Hellenes. Dignity was as much to him as bread and water.

"So it ends?" Klemones asked when they clasped hands. A question, an earnest question.

Λ

"I can only hope." The Argive general answered. And then he flinched. It was the flinch that saved Kleomenes's life. The king may not have suffered the Upbringing, but he was no less tempered to assault. His training acted on its own, no thought, only reflex. The dagger that had been concealed fell to the dirt from the general's hand as Kleomenes twisted his wrist to the point of breaking. He drove the commander to his knees with one hand and with the other, stroked the face of his enemy as if he were an old friend.

"For without hope, the heart would break, no?" Kleomenes released the general and plucked the fallen dagger from the dirt. A curved Persian weapon, concealed beneath his cuirass. "A fine blade." He remarked. "A shame it did not serve you better. But all the better for me, for now we may talk." His eyes remained fixed on the weapon, studying its alien craftsmanship while his men dragged the general into the command tent that had only this morning been his.

"What is your name?" Kleomenes asked as his personal guard slumped his enemy onto the stool before him.

"My name is Argos." The man sighed, both truth and a lie. He did not look at Kleomenes, but instead his eyes scanned over his maps and his compasses, his wartime accoutrements and heraldry that had failed him, that he had failed. As one of his feet stood on the earth and the other in Elysium, so did his vision fail to see either fully. He was a dead man. A broken man.

"I am sympathetic to your loss." Kleomenes still inspected the dagger.

"Are you?" The Argive responded rhetorically.

"After a fashion." Kleo's attentions remained on the dagger, but he rose and with his offhand poured two cups of wine, uncut by water. He handed one to the general who took it but did not drink. "I have tasted loss many times. But so far only in my dreams. I fear loss in the waking world…" He drained his cup. "May prove more than I could bear."

"This is why you conduct yourself with such dishonor." The Argive looked at the king in the eye for the first time. "Such deceit."

"My friend, you have only just attempted to assassinate me like a common brigand and I give you wine for it. Do not claim a moral high ground with me."

The general did not respond but to let the cup spill out of his hand onto the floor. Kleomenes shook his head at the dark puddle.

"You're here to discuss the terms of your surrender."

"I'm here, aren't I? What more do you want?"

"The surrender of your people then."

"They will not."

"Won't they?"

"You have shamed us, King of Sparta. You have shamed me. But that is all." His

Λ

eyes lolled in his sockets as he droned like a man possessed. His body sat here in this room, but inside he was already gone. "There are hardly fewer of us than there were this morning. If you storm the forest, my men in their holes will find you before you find them and take from you more than you brought to bargain with. And that is if you are brazen enough to anger the gods with your trespass."

"I wonder if they might prefer the trespass of an unbowed man, rather than the piety of soldiers who fled naked from their beds and now cower in the bushes."

"They are only embarrassed. Not beaten. Not dead. I had my scouts in your camp as I'm sure you had yours in mine, and we know you are not supplied for a siege of any length. Reinforcements are already on their way from the capitol, and even if they weren't, you are in a strange land surrounded on all sides by those who would have you dead. You are not prepared for what you have brought on yourself."

"Your men squat in their own piss. Who is left to fight? Women and children?"

"A leader of men should know full well how even women and children with rocks and sticks can drive great beasts from their homes when they have to."

"It will take more than your women and children, however many, to drive me and my great beasts away." Kleomenes was growing bored.

"You misunderstand. Our remaining men do not come to meet you here. They have set sail. They are to attack Sparta."

Kleomenes glowered. His polemarchs who had stood silently shared fevered glances. Krateros and Onesimos stormed from the tent to mobilize a response.

"It is too late!" The Argive called after them. "Your messages will not arrive in time! You see, Great King? You cannot hope to lay siege to the forest, you cannot hope for my people's surrender, and your home will be sacked unless you turn tail to defend it. You are beaten. In your little backwater valley you forget how the rest of the cities live, oh wise king " He spat venom. "Your army may outnumber mine now by some small margin, but your army accounts for every last one of your men. Without my army, there remain thirty thousand at least in the great city of Argos, countless thousands more in the surrounding lands, and all of them hate you. Had you killed us all this morning, you would still be hopelessly outnumbered."

"If I am so undone," Kleomenes raised the Persian dagger between them. "Why try to kill me?"

"Ah. Alas. That was for me."

"You hate me so much you would forfeit your life to take mine?"

"My life is already over. Do you think the other soldiers will be blamed for how you chased away their manhood? No, they have already forgiven themselves, forgiven each other. It is I who will stand accused. Their leader, who disgraced his home and his people. They will kill me, imprison me, or cast me out. I can never show my face again in my city."

Λ

"So you wanted revenge."

"I wanted to preserve my legacy. That my dying deed be a blow struck for my home, to redeem myself in some small way…"

"For your failure…" Kleomenes finished for him.

"For my failure." The general hung his head.

"I must say I'm a little flattered, that my death means so much to you. So I extend you this small courtesy. It is not too late. You can still surrender. All your men can return home alive and embrace their wives and children this very day."

"Have you heard nothing I said?" The Argive began to laugh. Sick, hoarse laughter, mad with loss. "It is too late. For me, and for you it is over. We have both of us lost here today, but Argos will carry on. Argos will always carry on." His laughter broke and he narrowed his eyes at Kleo. "Even after Lakonia broke its promise at Thyrea. Argos carried on."

A runner burst into the tent, breathless and flushed. He started to speak, but hesitated when he saw the general in his Argive livery.

"You may speak freely." Kleomenes waved the messenger in. "This man, apparently, is already dead."

"My king," the runner still eyed the Argive warily. "The city has-

"Stop, stop, stop." The king interrupted. "Little brother, what is your name?""My name? Pantites, sir. Son of Xandridas."

"Good. Pantites, son of Xandridas. What do our northern cousins have to say."

"The city has offered no terms for surrender, and has denied our request for ransom."

The general's sudden laughter nearly knocked him off his stool.

"A ransom?" He sputtered. "You thought the greatest city in Hellas would buy back a disgraced general and his men who fought as hard as wet cloth?" He howled. "We always knew Lakonians for stonebrained troglodytes, but I never thought you'd be so greedy too."

Kleomenes ignored the commander in his throes.

"No matter." He said, and thanked the messenger. "This is the response we expected. All we needed was to be seen extending the offer."

"Offer? What offer? To sell back men you haven't even captured yet?" The general wiped tears from his eyes.

"So you will not surrender?" Kleo changed the subject, and his foe hardened.

"No, I will not surrender."

"And your men will not surrender?" Kleo rolled the handle of the knife through his fingers.

"No. My men will not surrender."

"Never?" The king leaned forward and his prisoner leaned in too, their faces nearly

Λ

touching.

"Never."

The knife plunged low in the belly of the Argive. With a sound like the tearing of wet fabric, Kleomenes split his captive up the middle from navel to neck, plunged his hands inside the gaping rent and gripped. The dying man slumped to the ground and his face splashed into the puddle of wine he had poured out barely a minute before. His insides unspooled from within his body as he fell, his guts still clenched in the grip of the king.

Kleo inspected the organs, a liver in one hand, a rope of intestines in the other.

"Good news, brothers." He turned with his blood-flecked smile and showed the entrails to his polemarchs. "The omens bode for victory."

Λ

Fifteen

There was no more blood on his hands when Kleomenes emerged from the tent. He had wiped them clean on the canvas inside.

"How's my wall coming?" He asked no one in particular, his entourage flanked him as he marched with purpose to the scrimmage line.

"The men make... efforts." An officer struggled to reply. Lakonians were not known builders. Eager they were to follow orders, but this was not a maneuver they had drilled. "Supplies are scant."

"But 'scant' implies that supplies do in fact remain." Kleomenes chided him, if patiently. "Stack boulders. When there are no more boulders, stack sticks and stones. When there are no more sticks and stones, you will stack pebbles and twigs. When there are no more pebbles and twigs, stack grass if you have to. The Argives will not attack without leadership, so I want every single Peer building, poorly as that may be." He stopped, backtracked to a passing squire with a wineskin, took it and drank deeply. "And you," he added to his messenger while he wiped his chin. "Fetch me my Thrasilaos."

The polemarchs flanked him as he strode all the way into the shadow of the sacred trees. Sparta did not use slings or bows in battle, but all the other Hellenic nations did. Krateros and Onesimos tried to close their king in their shields, but brazen, he shrugged them away.

"Good news, my honorable foes!" He bellowed into the forest. "Your general has surrendered! Our fight is done! My messengers have returned from your capital, and your countrymen have accepted my offer for your ransom!"

The Spartans astride their leader did not blink, but each of them internally flinched. Lies did not become them. The forest remained quiet, not a man in sight.

"Hear me, brave men of Argos!" Arms outstretched, he wandered further into the dark of the trees. His men moved to follow but he hissed them back like dogs. "The strife of today can be over! We need not remain enemies! Throw down your weapons and I promise I will see you safely into the arms of your wives and daughters this very night!"

No man or beast replied. Kleomenes hailed them one last time before turning back.

"You have until sundown! Any man who presents himself before dusk is free to sleep tonight in his own home, in his own bed. Think on it. And think on the faces of your families."

The entourage returned to the Argive camp where Thrasilaos and Pantites presented themselves.

"Tell me, Pantites, son of Xandridas." He lowered his voice so that only those closest to him might hear. "At the city of Argos, did you see a harbor?"

"Yes, I did. Not from the city, but I saw it from the road." It must have been a wonderful view for Argives in their home country, but a grave tactical error.

"And tell me, what did you see in this harbor?"

Pantites hesitated, wracking his memory. He had not been dispatched as a spy, but a Spartan messenger is conditioned to take in any useful information, not just what he is told.

"I saw ships, sir. Many ships. A fleet. Loaded to the necks with men and supplies."

"And these ships. Were they moored or setting sail?"

"Moored, sir. But they were ready. Surely they were only waiting on the tide. Where might they be going? Do they flee?"

Kleomenes spat.

"Thrasilaos," he said instead of answering. "Which way does the wind blow?"

"Is this a riddle, my King?" The young captain grinned, familiar with his leader's strange ways.

"No riddles. Tell me which way the wind blows."

"It prevails to the east."

"Then you will take all the firewood I ordered saved from the Argive camps, ours too, we no longer need it, and you will stack it to the west. As high as a man, as wide as it goes until there is no more wood."

"We are smoking them out then?"

"I shall hope it doesn't come to that. The waiting wears on me, and I'm homesick already." The king joked loudly but lowered his voice once more, whispering only to the two young Spartiates. "Pantites goes with you. Aside from him, no one knows but your own small squad. Stack the wood inside my wall. Build it against the trees themselves. Then you soak everything in oil. Everything. As much as you can find."

The two saluted and rushed to obey.

The sun was hanging low, and Kleo was disappointed to find that only fifty men had trudged from hiding to accept his terms of surrender. Each of them was pinned on his sides by a pair of Spartiates. They did not need to hold the Argives to keep them still, their submission unconditional.

"Where are the rest of your brothers?" He asked of the man who stood most

Λ

proud among them, some low level officer who had removed his marks of rank in shame.

"They do not come."

"I see that, soldier. I ask where they are. Why do they not join you?"

"Still in the forest. They do not believe you."

"I'm wounded." Kleomenes put a hand to his chest. "They doubt my word?"

"I doubt your word as well." The man seethed, being mocked face to face by his sworn enemy. "I do not think our general surrendered. I do not think that Argos will pay for us, nor do I think they even have the funds. I do not in my heart believe that you will let us go."

"Then why do you take my offer?" The king's brow furrowed in a genuine display of sympathy.

"I have four daughters. And a newborn son." The man's eyes misted. "I thought of their faces. The gods have already decided my fate, but it was for me to decide that if I am to see my children again, it would be as a man standing. Not skulking like a coward in the weeds."

Kleomenes, gently, gravely, laid a hand on the man's shoulder.

"Thank you, soldier of Argos," he said. "You have taught me a very valuable lesson today. It will not be soon forgotten. But before I bid you farewell, are you absolutely certain there is no way we can convince your comrades to leave the forest?"

"There is none. Their minds are made."

"Very well." The king nodded to his men. "Kill them."

The Argive did not even have time to be surprised before a Spartan shortsword punched through his spine and out his belly. His forty-nine brothers fell in pieces around him.

Kleomenes left them without ceremony, whistling to himself as he marched west.

"What is this treachery?" Krateros caught up to him and spoke softly. They were old friends and could speak with candor, but to be overheard questioning his king could be seen as sedition.

"I only do what is required." The king inclined his head humbly.

"To kill an enemy in battle is one thing, but this is murder. This is deceit! How many lies have you told in only this one day? What will our people speak of you when you are gone?"

"I do not care what they speak of me, old friend. So long as our people remain to speak."

"Sparta is not threatened here. We may walk on a battlefield, but we are safe in victory. We need not debase ourselves with dishonor. With falsehoods and tricks.""You heard the general yourself. He was right. We're not outfitted for a siege. Thirty thousand peasants is enough to swamp us, and if their fleet left with the tide they may be on our shores by morning.""A thousand men? At the most? They are no threat. Our reserves will trample them to dust."

"Only if they offer pitched battle. Which they won't. They'll kill our livestock, burn our crops, salt our lands, and cut down our helots then run back to their ships and sail home. They won't fight us, or the city. They'll just ruin us. Ravage the kleroi. He was right, we've been outmaneuvered. We can leave to defend our home and find it already sacked and the vandals gone, or we can stay and be harassed to death by women and children with rocks and sticks. Or," he wheeled on Krateros, fire in his eyes, "I can lie to them, in order to keep my word."

"Your word?"

"I made a promise last night. That Argos dies today. Not Tomorrow, not in a year, not in my lifetime. Argos dies today, by my own hand if need be." Crickets chirped in the silence hanging between them.

"What now then?" Krateros felt the urge to say more, but could not find the words.

"It is a nice night. Warm, with a strong easterly wind. We are but two friends taking the air. All I want right now is to stand next to a nice warm fire and watch the sun set over the sea."

As the light on the horizon bled red and purple and gold, Kleomenes, still whistling, made himself a torch, lit it, and ambled liesurely toward the edge of the forest.

"You will face the Ephors for this…" Krateros took care to sound more advisor than critic. Kleomenes did not care either way. "…for this madness."

"Madness." Kleo sighed. "Why is it always madness I'm accused of? How is it that I must so often defend my actions from my own people when I give them victory after victory?"

"They are not fond of having their victories sullied by lies." Krateros shared in their sentiment.

"Then this I promise to them, and to you. No more lies today. Only promises kept."

"At what cost, Kleo?" The wind still prevailed east, but Krateros could smell the oil thick on the sticks that Thrasilaos and his men had stacked. He was a simple man, and set in his ways, but he was not stupid. "These woods have been dear to the gods since before the fall of Troy. Since before Herakles birthed our nation. You do not risk their wrath in this, but beg for it. This is too far. This is not greatness, brother. There will be a price to pay."

"Indeed there will be." Kleomenes' face flickered in the light of his torch. "Which is why I act alone. It will be my hand that undoes our enemy, and on my head the price will fall. A price I am prepared to pay for my people."

Λ

Krateros nearly moved to stop him, to wrench the torch from the hands of his friend, his king. To commit treason for the sake of his virtue. But he did not. He was but a soldier.

Kleomenes touched the torch to the pyre. The dry wind licked at the blossoming red tongues and scattered them in a frenzied storm through the gnarled canopy of old oaks. Here and there, silhouettes of broken men would stumble coughing from the treeline and attending Spartans casually cut them down. Whole trees exploded in the heat of the blaze and its crackle and roar drowned the screams of men broiled inside. Six thousand Peers watched silently as their enemy was consumed.

But Kleomenes, true to his word, turned away from his nice warm fire and watched the sun set over the sea.

Λ

Sixteen

Dienekes picked himself off the ground and snorted. Sand, snot, and blood shot from his smashed nose. He'd already been thrown twice, once more and he'd lose the bout. Tellis was stronger, but that wasn't why he kept winning. All the boys liked the taste of victory, but win or lose, it was the fighting itself that Tellis reveled in. Combat brought him to life. He'd easily outmaneuver boys stronger than himself, use false leads to bait faster boys into making mistakes. Try to go under him, he'd go under you. Try to go over, and he'd go over you. As Dien had been made to run, Tellis was made for the melee. Not since before their basic instruction had anyone in Disappointment been able to beat him, only take longer than others before they inevitably lost. Only Aristaios gave him a challenge but even then only on stubborn grit, not technique or acumen. Dienekes, however, never lasted long.

He landed flat on his back.

"Like losing, do you?" Tellis gloated, putting a foot on his friend's chest.

"Gives me time to collect my thoughts." Dienekes wheezed. Tellis extended a hand to help him up, but Dien waved it off and rolled onto his side. Their new eriene was busy haranguing Pigfat and Asslicker so he had a moment to rest. Polygonos was less attentive than their former instructor. With Thrasilaos on campaign, the boys felt as if they'd been on vacation. The replacement's whip didn't even draw blood. But all good things come to an end.

Dien, with his ear to the ground heard the rumble. He looked up and saw a column of scarlet and a dust plume rising behind it. He almost called out, but realized the sooner they were reunited with the returning soldiers, with Thrasilaos, the sooner the whipcracks would bleed again. He watched and waited for the others to see it on their own. Polygonos was last to notice, and he scolded the boys for their lack of awareness.

"Shame! Had it been an enemy phalanx, you'd have been caught naked over a chair!"

They quietly humored him micromanaging their march to the bottom of the acropolis where the road from the north met the city proper and the rest of the city's population had already congregated to celebrate the homecomers. They marched in time, taking the smallest steps they dared, edging toes out of line, knowing the failure would incite Polygonos to make them stop and start over. Despite yearning to witness the glamour of the Spartiates in rank and file, they knew the longer they milked the distraction, the longer their reprieve from training. At least until they were back with their original instructor.

News of victory at Sepeia had come days earlier, time for the poets and flute girls to write songs to laud their favorite champions. Verses contended in the streets, but Disappointment was certain that they heard snatched lyrics about their own teacher, Thrasilaos, infiltrating the enemy camp alone and they swelled with a confused and frightened kind of pride. The warriors left behind to defend the city clanged their knuckles off the armor of their returning friends.

You're lucky I wasn't there, or there'd have been none left for you! They cried.

And, Bring me an Argolid heart, did you? I'm hungry!

They'll let anyone go to war these days.

Now, I know you never would have survived a battle, did you sleep through it?

They were proud of their brothers who had fought and won. But each man who'd been left behind bore a quiet searing regret that they were not there to share the victory.

Sparta shunned the marble-columned grandeur of its neighbors, so the ephors waited to meet the procession at the crossing of two simple dirt roads, one from the north intersecting the "race-track" that ran around the city. Kleomenes drew his horse to reign and raised a fist. Behind him, six thousand shields locked into place. The ground shook, and the rumble echoed around the valley like thunder. Their spears pointed skyward. Anywhere but home, they would have been leveled down.

Kleomenes dismounted. A horse was a strange luxury for a king on parade, but no one said so. Kleomenes was king after all, albeit a strange king. Sometimes it paid to be strange, and he made a point of proving it.

The king bowed before the ephors, and Timoxenos, their foremost, garlanded his head with the victor's olive wreath. A moment of silence later and the king addressed his men.

"My friends! My brothers! You who have marched through the darkness and fire with me and stamped out the flames! Your duty, for now, is done!" There was a cheer. A king was a king, but there is no king like a king loved by his men. "Now go home and fuck your wives! Or I will!"

He shared their laughter as formation broke and he disappeared into anonymity in the opening throng. Husbands embraced their wives, lifted children onto their shoulders. Though internally they shared his jubilation, their king was a deviation from Lakonian stoicism. They did not shed tears of joy, they did not fawn over each other

∧

and cry about how much they were missed. Little girls did not shriek and cling to their fathers' legs as they would in other cities. A simple smile was a grander gesture here than scores of poetry from some other luxuriant corner of Hellas. In Sparta, happiness was humble. In Sparta, happiness was strong.

The broken platoons percolated through the crowd, groups metered down to meandering individuals. In the squirm of the crowd, Polygonos lost track of Disappointment. They might have been initiates of the agoge, but they had families too. Families in the crowd. Some more than others.

Dienekes spied Krateros passing the reigns of his king's horse to a squire, and Krateros had spied him back. The grizzled warrior's bearded mouth scowled, but his eyes glittered with mirth.

"Elafakia!" He harrumphed. "Where were you, scoundrel? We needed your speed to dispatch the cowards as they fled." He jostled the boy with heavy-handed swats to the shoulders. "Don't tell me you were here? This whole time? Hiding beneath your mother's skirts?"

Dienekes had grown, and was not pushed so far by his mentor's little blows as he once had been. Krateros noticed, but the boy did not. He was preoccupied, brimming with questions.

"What was it like?" He settled on. Krateros sighed, too big a question to answer. "Did you teach them a lesson?" Dienekes asked instead.

"One they won't soon forget." Another Spartiate appeared by Krateros's side, dressed and adorned the same as any of the Peers. "Dienekes, this is an old friend of mine. We have shared many battles, and," he laughed a little, "many late night arguments. He has been wanting to meet you for some time."

"The boy Achilles! An honor indeed. We have heard so much. We have met before, if you'd believe it. But you were still a pink little thing running about naked and eating flowers."

Dienekes was growing into a man, but he had not outgrown his propensity to blush and stare at his feet. He feebly shook the hand proffered to him.

"So shy!" Guffawed the stranger. "It's just as well. Stay meek and they'll never see you coming. Not like Krateros. He was once the fastest in Sparta, but now he hobbles like an ancient. His old bones wobble and his joints crack. He couldn't sneak up on an enemy if they were already dead!"

"This may be, but at least they still can't sneak up on me." Krateros laid his arm round the shoulders of his friend. "This one yammers like an Athenian woman, day and night, an entire army could sneak up his ass as long as no one interrupted him."

The stranger put on a wounded mask, clutched a fist to his breastplate. "It only hurts because it's true, Krateros. You know me too well."

"And for too long." They leaned on each other, reminiscing. "You admit yourself

Λ

that I was swift before age took me. But you, alas, have always been a chattering nonce."

"Such venom! You see how he abuses me? I need a champion to avenge my honor." He pretended to search around. "Ah, here! Thank you, little Achilles, for volunteering. I'm sure you will put Krateros sufficiently to shame. This one's my champion."

"What? Champion? Sir, I-"

"It's settled then!" He proclaimed to the crowd. "A footrace! The winner will be crowned victor by the king himself, and the loser will lick the king's bootlaces." A few in the rabble whistled and clapped, but mostly they groaned and waved him off good-humoredly. Clearly they were accustomed to his outbursts. It was uncommon, if not taboo, for a Spartan to be so boisterous. Dien found it warm. Charming. Right before he was struck by another thought.

The King?

The stranger looked back down at the boy, a startling shift in his pallor, shit-eating grin wiped from his face.

"They tell me you are called Weeper."

Dien was struck silent. His unfortunate reputation never failed to follow him around and kick him in the guts, even in the company of strangers.

"No, boy." The man saw the child crumbling in on himself and pulled up on his chin. "Not today. Today is a happy day. No time for shame. Come, there is something I must tell you."

Dien allowed the man to pull him closer. Close enough that no one else would hear the whisper in his ear.

"Sometimes," the Spartan hesitated. "Sometimes, I cry too."

Dienekes had no time to process the revelation before slender arms encircled him from behind. Dien recognized the smell, though he had not breathed it since the day of his abduction. Hyacinths and barley flour. He spun into her embrace.

"My boy." His mother squeezed him. "I should have known to find you in the company of rascals."

"Just like his father." The stranger beamed. "Though fortunately, his looks favor his beautiful mother." He extended his hands to her.

"Thank you, My King." She clasped his hands, and then Krateros' while the child below them reeled, struggling to swallow his heart. "I'm sure he would be proud to see his old friends watching over his boy."

King? Old friends? Dienekes choked.

"Us? Watching him? Quite the opposite, my lady. Only just now your boy was defending me from this degenerate's savage disrespects."

"Some things never change." Rhoda rolled her eyes.

Λ

"It was wonderful, to see you again, Rhoda. And you, son of Hegisistratos. But we have business to attend, and families of our own to see. Gods be with you." He clasped both of their hands again.

"And you, sir… my… your.. mm… king." Dienekes stammered. And the old man bent to meet his eye level.

"No, boy. You call me Kleo. Like your father did." And he turned to leave, but called over his shoulder. "And remember what I told you. Even tell your friends if you wish. No one will believe you." He winked and was gone.

Dienekes spent the rest of the afternoon with his mother, basking in all the little joys that he had forgotten. When he returned to the training camps, they whipped him bloody for dereliction of duty, and he felt not an ounce of regret. His heart was light and full. A new strength had rooted inside him, and he clung to it, let its burn keep him warm in his grave-bed at night.

The King cries too.

Λ

Seventeen

Disappointment was thrilled. At least as thrilled as they could be with fresh whip scars scabbing over on their backs. Today was the first day any of them would be allowed to wear the bronze. It had been dug out of ancient storages, green with tarnish and poorly fitted, but with the cuirass rattling on their chests, the twenty pound aspis hanging from their arms, their hearts gleamed even if their spears and swords were only sticks.

"Form up!" Roared Polygonos. Thrasilaos had returned, but responsibilities due to his promotions at Sepeia demanded his time be split between Disappointment and his blossoming command. The toll of leadership was plainly visible in the deepening furrow of his brow, and he was not withholding in taking his stresses out on the boys. They were grateful for the comparatively soft touch of his substitute.

The boys formed up shoulder to shoulder, and before they succumbed to the pride of imitating their nation's fabled phalanx, the whip snapped between their heads.

"I said form up!" Polygonos gave no further instruction, but cracked the whip at them indiscriminately as they winced and shuffled into other formations. They let themselves be shepherded into a new line, single-file front to back instead of side by side, but not until every boy sported at least one new welt rising on his uncovered arms.

"Good! You're learning! This is your line!" He shaped them into stance with his whip's long handle. "Knees lower." Smack. "Spear arm up. Higher!" Smack. "Shield in the back of the man in front. Now push. Hard!" Smack. "The enemy sees nothing over the top but your eyes, and you be sure they're looking into them when they die." He carried on until satisfied. "Now hold position!"

Thrasilaos and Krateros walked towards them across the training grounds. Polygonos strolled off to meet them, leaving Disappointment in stance. The boys trembled and burned, bearing into each other under the unfamiliar weight of the armor, thighs and arms burning to stay bent in the knee and raised at the elbow. The three adults talked at length, apparently oblivious of the struggling children until a spear sagged or a shield drooped and Polygonos would fire abuse at them while the other two chuckled good naturedly.

The sun beat drums off their helmets, cooking them slowly, but the boys held form while sweat poured into their eyes.

"Weeper!" Polygonos shouted.

"Huh?" Dienekes relaxed, let his shield drop, and the weight of the boys behind smashed him into Tellis's back. Dien spilled off to the side when Tellis turned and knocked his face on Maron's shield, which Maron dropped while he tripped over Alpheos's spear, and the bulk of Olympikos in the back drove the rest of the column forward into a pile.

The silence of their eirene as he watched them founder terrified them more than any threat he might have voiced. But Dienekes was saved the consequence of his blunder.

"The Weeper goes with the polemarch." Polygonos loomed over his squad. "The rest of you will explain to me what formation this is."

Dienekes only now noticed that neither Krateros nor Thrasilaos were in their usual bronze and crimson. They were draped lightly and barefooted.

"Leave the armor." Said Krateros. "You will not need it."

Dien was reluctant to remove the hand-me-down wargear despite the weight, but he connected the dots as he unlaced. Krateros's bad knee was wrapped. Thrasilaos had his hands chalked and his forehead oiled for pankration. They were going to the *gymnasion*.

"I didn't think he was serious!" Dien had to jog to keep pace with the long stride of his teachers.

"About our race? Well it is hard to tell when the king means what he says." Krateros laughed like he did, quiet and thoughtful. "But he meant this. We are to run against each other before the ephors."

Before the ephors? Dienekes was a mix of himself. Frightened and excited, elated and withdrawn. He could have voiced his thoughts if it were just he and Krateros, but the presence of Thrasilaos hung in the air like a noxious fume. He feared speaking his mind now would be used against him later in training. They walked in silence to a new set of training grounds. They made their way into the city proper where the choking dust of the agoge's trampled barren valley gave way to the simple beauty of Sparta's infrastructure. They kept to the outskirts of the city where the shouts and grunts of pankrationists could be heard outside the *palaistra*. They turned off the dirt road and onto a narrow walkway aisled with fig and olive trees that athletes plucked from as they pleased. Here Olympians trained. They tossed discs and javelins and each other, drilling and laughing in the fierce camaraderie that bred only fiercer rivalry. Sweat and oil permeated the air. A Spartan Peer stood a giant over other men, but here, Spartans stood as giants over other Spartans. Dienekes revelled as he watched them work.

Not long ago, the boy would have balked at the thought of racing his mentor.

Λ

Even without stakes, the pressure would have caved his gut into a tangle, but now… His legs felt strong, his lungs full, head clear. Krateros towered over him still, thighs as thick as the boy's chest, but the defiance he'd been told of had taken root and sprouted upward. Dien jockeyed foot to foot in his excitement.

"Get warmed up, I'll be back." Krateros went to speak with the ephors. They had been expecting him. Expecting Dienekes.

"On the line then." Krateros shed his drapings onto a bench and took his own place at the head of the stadium. Dien joined him, but another athlete hissed. He was still in his tunic. Champions of Hellas trained and competed without a scrap of clothing, the only way to ensure no one carried an unseen advantage. Nothing but the competitor and the ground he walked on.

The root of defiance was burdgeoning into something else as Dien threw his tunic on the bench. Krateros had his right knee bandaged. 'His old bones wobble and his joints crack,' the words of the king echoed in his head, and the sprout of defiance blossomed into the intuition his mentor had spoken of. Dien took his place on the polemarch's right side, deliberately close. He did not notice the hum of activity die around him as the other Lakonians paused their training to watch.

The official dropped his arm and their feet beat turf. Dien took three steps to each one of Krateros's, accelerating him faster off the start, but he knew the elder's power would overtake him at full speed. So with a hair's breadth of lead, he hatched his little intuition. He crowded into Krateros' path, a perhaps questionable but not illegal maneuver. Krateros had to adjust his gait so his long, loping strides would not crush the boy. His adjustments fell on his weak knee, the old injuries having to bear the compensated weight. Each time he adjusted he lost more ground, and mere seconds later, Dienekes crossed the finish line an arms length ahead. Krateros was well-known for his speed. The onlookers shared a stunned silence.

"Well done, boy!" The man shouted as he caught up to his student. Both flushed, but neither out of breath. But Di felt pangs of guilt catching up with him.

"We should run it again…" He fussed over the right words. "It wasn't right, I think I cheated."

"No, Di." The man bumped a fist off the youth's shoulder. "I saw what you did. It was clever. Unconventional, perhaps. But lately I'm learning much about unconventional victories. If you see an opportunity like that again, I say you take it."

"Hold!" A voice rang out from the other end of the stadium, as another runner jogged toward them.

"Echemmon! Good to see you, boy."

"Polemarch." The newcomer tipped his head with respect.

"I'm glad you're here. Dienekes, this little rat, if you can believe it, won the boy's sprint at Olympia four years ago. Only fourteen years old then, and the fastest child

∧

in all of Hellas. You'd do well to learn from him."

"Couldn't have done it without your advice, sir." The boy was gracious in victory. But Dien felt a stab of jealousy as he shook the stranger's hand, that his teacher was coaching others as well. He shook it off, and scolded himself for childish feelings. Spartans belonged to all of Sparta.

"Well, what can we do for you, Echemmon?"

"I'd like to race him." The young man did not beat around the bush, and Dienekes was suddenly a bundle of nerves again.

"What? Now? I don't think-"

"Wonderful, of course you can. Get back on the line and I'll watch the finish." Dienekes was coming up with excuses, but Krateros squashed them before they could be heard. "Just run, boy. It's what you're here to do. No tricks this time, though." He winked.

So Dienekes ran. And lost. Only barely, but he still lost. Mere moments after his first taste of victory it was bitterly rinsed from his mouth.

"Well run!" Echemon looked stunned, merely humoring him Dienekes was sure, and he mumbled back something unintelligible. But a row of other athletes had aggregated to watch, and they slapped Di on the back too.

"Dienekes!" Krateros' jaw hung slack. "I've never seen you run like that!"

"But... But I lost?" Echemon and his friends were broken up by their coaches and ushered back to training, but cast lingering glances at Di as they dispersed.

"So?"

Dienekes stirred but said nothing. Hot tears brimmed his eyes, but he blinked them away. He had not cried for a long time.

"Listen to me, you little shit." Krateros kneeled before him, his words contrasting the grin spanning his entire face. "That was the best outcome we could have hoped for." Dien neither believed nor understood, but allowed his teacher to explain. "Look at him. He's six years older and twice your size. Not to mention an Olympic champion. One of the fastest people in the entire world. He's been training years for this one specific race. Of course you were going to lose."

Dienekes felt the tears again. So everyone knew he stood no chance and had him do it anyway. He felt the butt of a joke.

"Yes, you lost." Krateros held up his hand. "But only by the width of my palm. And in front of the ephors, too? Elafakia, losing to Echemmon may be the greatest thing you've ever done." Dienekes sniffed. "Now everyone, everyone, will know that the Weeper matched the fastest boy in Sparta. This went far better than Kleo and I could have hoped for." This last bit confused Dienekes, but he could not ask for clarity with Krateros shaking him in throes of celebration.

"My boy... your destiny has just taken a very interesting turn."

Λ

492 BCE

Eighteen

On the same day that Dienekes learned he would be attending the Olympic games, he learned that Krateros would not.

They had been training together daily. Krateros, a former competitor himself, was in a unique position to supplement the boy's martial training with drills and techniques to grow his speed. While the other members of Disappointment had begun to bulk in the chest and shoulder, Di remained a thing of bone and string. This made him the weak link in their phalanx drills, and he was knocked down often, but even Thrasilaos seemed to spare him the worst of the rod. If the boy was to remain skinny for the glory of all of Sparta, then so be it. It was that, or argue with the polemarch.

Dien was devastated. He had taken it for granted that his mentor would be with him every step of the journey, but had at least grown in dealing with disappointments of his own.

"I am sorry to hear that," he said at the news. "I had been looking forward to spending this time with you." The words spoke themselves mechanically, dry like his eyes. He was learning.

"I had too, my boy." Krateros rested a massive palm on the child's head, engulfing it ear to ear. "Seeing you run at the games would have been one of my life's finest moments. Alas, there will be other games. When duty does not call."

"And where does duty call this time?" He asked, knowing that trainees were deliberately kept ignorant of war plans. Boys had much bigger mouths before earning their crimson than after, but still Krateros let secrets slip when it would do no harm. Not this time.

"Perhaps far away," he shrugged. "Perhaps close. But I'm sure you've heard by now of the Persian advance."

Dienekes had. He hooked his fingers around his mouth and gnashed pretend fangs.

"Clay-colored cannibals who eat babies alive. They wear cloaks of human flesh and gold rings through holes in their faces!"

"I'm glad to see you're not yet too old for stories." Krateros chuckled. "But in truth they are just men like us. They practice different ways, but are men all the same. With the hands and hearts and minds of men, and that makes them far more dangerous than any flesh-wearing monster."

"I'd rather face a clay cannibal than Thrasilaos any day."

"If I'm honest, me too. He's a hungry one, your eirene. I wouldn't be surprised to see him in a cloak of human flesh one day." They shared a timid laugh, both checking their shoulders to make sure he hadn't snuck up behind them. "I think that's how you win at Olympia."

"Hm?"

"Pretend Thrasilaos is chasing you." Dien might have laughed again, but drooped, thinking about being without his guardian at the games. "Fear not." Krateros could see right through him. "I will not be sending you alone."

He nodded down the dirt path to a Peer wobbling toward them on horseback. The man harangued his mount with word and crop, but it paid him no mind and walked under the olive trees hoping to scrape the rider off on low branches.

"Dienekes, I would like you to meet-"

"Here, boy. Help an old man down." The man threw his crutches at Dien, and fell with his whole weight onto the boy before he was ready, flattening them both to the ground. It was the crippled surgeon who had healed Di's broken hands half a decade ago. He laughed at his poor prank, spittling the helpless child with phlegm as his horse cantered off. Krateros rested a defeated hand over his eyes.

"Dienekes, meet my brother. Onesiphoros."

Λ

492 BCE

Nineteen

"I can't believe I'm not going with you." Tellis flexed his neck and punched his palms. Paced and kicked the dirt. Disappointment had risen before dawn to see off their runt before training began. "Name a better boxer, just one!"

"Thrasilaos." Maron said.

"That doesn't count!"

"But that's the kind of person you'd be facing. Big fuckers five years older than you eating meat three times a day? You'd get manhandled." Alpheos mimed breaking Tellis over his knee and then spanking him.

"If the ephors think Di can handle it, why not me?"

"Cause you can't touch someone in a race, buttbreath. If you could then Di would probably… well…" He shrugged. "Die."

"Only if they can catch me first!" Dien snarled and playfully shook a fist, which was snatched from him.

"Caught." Said Olympikos. The other boys circled and shoved him back and forth between them shouting.

"Birdfeed!"

"Pip!"

"Mooncalf!"

"Weaseldick!"

"THE HELL IS GOING ON HERE!?" The little mob panicked apart and Onesiphoros hobbled into their midst. His one cloudy eye scanned the terrified faces Disappointment crowding over the fallen Dienekes. "Oh. Of course. My apologies. You may continue." Laughing, the boys hauled Di onto their shoulders and spun him until he felt sick. The sun was rising, just cresting the peaks of Parnon. Polygonos and Thrasilaos materialized from thin air, as was their way. The boys lined up without being told.

"Left Testicle!" Thrasilaos barked.

"Sir!" Alpheos saluted.

"Front and center!"

∧

The twin sprinted to stand before his instructor, who flattened him with a kick to the chest.

"I said Left Testicle! You are the right! Left testicle, front and center!" Maron ran to obey and was likewise hoofed into the dirt. "On second thought I think you had it right the first time. But I forgot what I needed you for. I hope you learned something." The boys groaned on the ground. "Are you ready, Weeper? It doesn't matter, we leave either way."

We.

Dienekes gulped. Despite sharing the training fields with him, he had forgotten that Thrasilaos was coming. And of course he'd be competing in the pankration, fighting effectively without rules. But Di was happy to see that Echemon would be with them as well, especially since the former champion had aged out of the boys' bracket and they'd no longer be in contention. They had become friends in training, but Di had still not wholly swallowed the jealousies and intimidations the elder runner brought out in him. Three other boys whom Dien had briefly met would join them. A boxer, a pentathlete, and a hoplitodrome named Polymedes. The third fascinated Dien. The *hoplitodromos* was another footrace, much longer than Dien's stadion, as long as Echemon's diaulos of two *stadia*, but unlike the other disciplines all practiced in the nude, the hoplitodromos was run in armor. Di had raced Polymedes naked and won soundly, but when carrying the seventy pounds of bronze he could barely move. Polymedes practiced with an aspis in each arm and never put them down unless his mentor instructed. He bore the weight like they were feathers. For their eirene's amusement, Disappointment had once been ordered to test the shove of their budding phalanx by pushing against Polymedes, and he had folded them into each other all afternoon.

In his head, Dienekes understood why Krateros was not there to say goodbye, but in his heart he did not. There were cheering crowds and flower petals in the air when the small caravan left the gates, but they lifted the boy's spirits only slightly. He felt more fear than excitement, but of what he did not know. It would be the furthest he had ever gone from home, and his first time ever leaving Lakonia. There were no hands indifferently clutching his arms this time, but he felt the same as the day he had been dragged from his mother to the polis, nearly half his lifetime ago.

Λ

Twenty

Dienekes had not known Onesiphoros long before he came to love the old git. "Uncle Ono", he liked to be called. The grumpy, hobbling goat of a man was not nearly so old as he seemed, aged beyond his years by countless injuries in battle. At least Dien assumed it was battle, as unhealthy specimens were discarded at birth. Ono peppered the boys with stories on the long walk to Olympia that confirmed the suspicion.

"See here?" He brushed gray curls up the side of his head, exposing half an ear. Leaning out of his saddle so the boys could see while they ran circles around him. "Lost that bit in Mantinea."

"Against the Tegeans?" Dienekes prided his memory of the battles Krateros taught him. Training wasn't just for the arms and legs, it was history too. Knowing where they came from. Knowing what it all meant.

"Yes and no..." Ono chewed his lip. "The Tegeans were our allies in that fight. But a Tegean's wife bit it off when I told her I wasn't bringing her home with me."

"And what did you do?" Echemon stepped on Di's heels as they chased each other around Ono's horse.

"Nothing! Dunno know what I would have done, either. Poor bitch choked on it. Bit of a travesty all around. I was only halfway done, so she's turning blue while I'm still pumping. I suppose we'll never know if it was my ear or my cock that killed her. But the lesson is, you get more than you can chew of Uncle Ono no matter which end you bite it off."

The boys laughed, the men groaned, and Polymedes' mentor chucked a disapproving apple at the cripple, who caught it between his teeth in an uncanny display of dexterity.

"Very generous of you, Diagoras!" Ono munched. "I'll give it back to you when I'm done, though it might be a day or two. These old pipes don't run like they used to."

The man was immune to shame, so great were the strifes he'd endured. He continued.

"This one was alongside King Kleo when we first went to free Athens from the

Peisistratids, ungrateful hogs." He pulled his cloak up to show a horrendous white mass of keloids from ankle to knee. "Bastards had war dogs. How I got my first limp. A pack of 'em gnawed on me the whole battle through. Didn't get em off till a day later, but by then we'd become friends. They were good bitches though, not like the Tegean whore, so they came home with me. Their grandpups guard my daughters as we speak."

"That's actually true." Thrasilaos materialized beside the trail. He was spending the journey mostly out of sight, disappearing at will in and out of the thicket along the narrow Panhellenic roads. His intermittent appearances kept Di hovering on the verge of soiling himself. "Though it's hard to tell the girls from the hounds."

"They are all that beautiful." Ono finished the apple, core and all. He noticed how Dien had turned white after seeing the tumorous scars on his leg. "Oh, you cringe at that boy? Here's one worse." He wrestled belt and tunic away from his significant belly. His pasty flesh was puckered navel to spine by knotty, discolored craters. Forty, fifty stabs, maybe more. "This was the one ended my days in the phalanx."

"Where'd you get them?"

Polymedes and Echemon had stopped to marvel. Dien turned green.

"This one was at home. On my own doorstep."

The boys need not ask more. The fertile valleys of Lakonia had never been invaded, and they'd had no civil wars. For Onesiphoros to be attacked on his own soil could only mean one thing.

"Helots." Polymedes muttered, with his eyes glazed. It was an unspoken fear for Lakedaimon. Their slave class outnumbered the Peers by sometimes ten to one. Their way of life depended on the subordinated labor, but meant the nation was cursed by the constant threat of rebellion.

"Indeed. They leapt out of the dark on me with knives. I left a pile of them dead but they swarmed like locusts. I would have been done for too, if not for our Krateros." Dien's eyes widened. He'd never heard this story. "I should have died, but Krateros followed me home from the acropolis. He didn't know why, he told me later. Just a feeling. That he should look in on his brother's family before going home to his own. Can you believe it?"

Dien could. -Intuition- he whispered to himself.

"To this day I have nightmares."

"Of the helots?" Echemon asked.

"No boy. Of my baby brother. Never seen anything like it. He did not even draw a weapon before leaping on the wretches. Tore them apart with his bare hands." Some of Ono's tales were taller than others, but there was no taste of jest in this confession. "Before my eyes went dark I saw him rip the throat out of one and use it to lynch another from the small oaks. He was an animal, like the shapeshifting heathens of the

Λ

far north."

Krateros? Dienekes could not fathom. Patient, gentle Krateros with his wise words and laugh like a bell? Dien could still feel the weight of the man's warm paw on his forehead.

"There must have been a hundred of them, to bring down a warrior like you, Ono." Euneas the boxer was not above a little flattery.

"Not quite so many as that. But they do not attack unless in great numbers, so you must always be on guard. They fight like rats, hiding and sneaking. And if they are like rats, then we are wolves. We are their betters, we know it and they know it. But when enough rats bite on the face of a wolf, it's no big thing for one more to burrow their feated claws into its belly." With this he looked directly at Dienekes, who went cold. "And I've seen them kill far better wolves than I."

"I'm sorry, Uncle Ono." Di whispered.

"What? Nonsense, boy. You've nothing to be sorry for. But if you wish, you can make me a promise. All of you can make me a promise."

He was the center of the boys' universe now, all of them ready to avenge his wounds.

"When it comes your turn to join the Krypteia?"

They nodded along.

"You kill every last one you can get your hands on." Ono growled. The boys cheered, not knowing yet what they promised, but if it pleased their Uncle, then they'd do it, and happily.

The man was good for more than stories. It ate at Dienekes that he could no longer fight alongside his brothers, so he worthied himself by learning any other useful skill he could. He was better traveled than a cripple had a right to be. Spoke many languages, played many instruments, and was familiar with matters of state, both foreign and domestic. He turned the hands that had once so expertly taken life to preserving it instead, and learned the healing arts in as many Hellenic cities as would teach him. He had earned a seat as the king's own surgeon, and in his time by the king's side had adopted much of Kleo's strangeness. But like Kleo, Ono's reputation was powerful and earned him forgiveness for his frequent and shameless absurdities.

Ono plucked from the unassuming shrubberies by the trail as he rode and ground them around their campfires into aromatic rubs to soothe the trainees' burning muscles. He knew what vegetation was good for eating, which would make your breath sweet, which would make you shit your guts out, and one he said would stand your pecker so hard you could break a sword on it.

After two days walking, Euneas stepped on a scorpion. A Spartan on the warpath would have been expected to keep marching, and live or die as fate saw fit. But they were not on the warpath. The caravan agreed to halt while Ono treated Euneas, if he

Λ

could be treated. He was an Olympic contender, and it made no sense for him to be pushed at the expense of his performance.

"It's not so bad as it could have been, son." Ono told the boxer as he inspected the specimen, holding it by the tail. "These are not so fatal as others. The venom will cause you great pain, but if you are to die it will be from infection." The surgeon lowered the wriggling creature into his mouth, pinched off the stinger and crunched. He rolled the stinger between his fingertips till they were slick with venom and smeared it into the bags under his own half-blind eyes.

"What does that do?" Dienekes asked.

"Not much." Ono chewed. "In the absence of cuts or punctures, venom can be a lotion for skin and hair. Keeps me looking young and beautiful."

"And what does chewing the scorpion do? Does it make a poultice to reverse the poison?"

"No, just tastes good." Ono swallowed. "Nothing will reverse the poison now, but these-" he produced a waxy, stringy-leafed tuft of green from the collection in his satchel. "Once brewed, these will keep his fever down and help chase the ill humors from his blood. It helped save me after the helots got their digs in, so you'll be fine, Euneas. It's the worst tasting tea I've ever had, but it turns your piss bright green, so that's fun."

Euneas trembled and sweated the whole night through. When he woke, he was pale and fatigued, but hale. His mentor bid him ride on a mule for the next leg, but the day after that he was walking again, his color returned. The day after that, the caravan arrived at Olympia.

Λ

Twenty-one

The Alpheos River was the strongest in all Hellas. Seven tributaries surged together in one current just south of Olympia and served to feed and water the city. Representatives of the Hellanodikai, the governing body of the Olympic games, met the Lakonians on the bridge and escorted them through the city to their quarters.

Dienekes had never seen so many people. They crowded shoulder to shoulder on wide flagstone streets and could not walk their chosen path without first bustling others out of the way. Merchants sang their wares from the backs of carts and shop doors, while next to them beggars clamored for alms. Scantily draped women laced fingers over Polymedes' biceps, whispered things in his ear that made him blush, then scorned him when they learned he had no coin. The boys understood nothing. Commerce at home was not like this. Citizens and merchants took their place in the agora where they could sell and purchase wares, but in Sparta everyone was given a job to do and they did it. Here, where people were more inclined to choose their living, they had to loudhail it to the public to be found, and the resulting chaos overwhelmed Dienekes. He clung to Ono's saddle straps to keep from being drifted away into the throng. The old man noticed and nodded understanding.

"Yes, child. Good boy. Help keep the old fool from falling off his beast."

Their lodgings might have seemed barren to a boy from anywhere else, but to Dien they proved a confounding luxury. His bunk had a mattress stuffed with straw. On a small table in the corner waited jugs of water and weak wine, bread and cheese and olives. There were separate rooms and accoutrements for nightsoil, which Dienekes viewed with suspicion, if not fear. The agoge had accustomed him to squatting over holes he dug himself while being verbally abused from a distance. A boy relieving himself in comfort was an alien concept. He was grateful when Onesiphoros called him away for a walk.

They passed government atria, market squares, and complicated towering temples where people wailed to the gods and burned incense, clothing, and animals. It all washed over Dienekes, the magnitude of experience deafening him to its details. He was relieved when Ono pulled him down an inconspicuous alley that opened into a courtyard, conspicuously empty and quiet. His head swiveled, eyes wide, over the grid of lifesize bronze statues and greenery hanging between them.

"This is Altis." Ono answered the unasked question. "Olympia during the games is mostly a trash city, fallen to the debauchery and tail-chasing anarchy that 'free peoples' succumb to. It's the tourism they depend on, and they suckle greedily at the golden tit, not realizing how it weakens them. But this… This is the seat of their greatness."

They strolled past the figures of men posed in immortality and here and there Ono would stop and have his ward read a plaque while he coughed into his cloak.

"Hipposthenes and… and Hetoimokles? They were from Sparta!"

"Yes, yes they were." Ono caught his breath. "Eleven events between them they won. Over a hundred years later and here they are in all their glory. Not a day has passed for them. And look at this skinny bastard, like you. Chionis, who won six races. In a row, mind you. And Philombrotos who won the pentathlon three times. Don't see that often."

"What about him, he looks familiar."

"Yes, great likeness, isn't it? Though it would have been more true to form had they sculpted his head up his ass."

"Knew him, did you?" Dienekes giggled.

"Aye. And still do. That'd be our King Demaratos. Won the chariot race here only twelve years ago."

That tugged a chord inside Dien, to see a living man revered shoulder to shoulder with ancient heroes. Somehow, it made the new city seem smaller, winning the games more attainable. He'd been named a champion of Sparta, but had never yet imagined himself as a contender. It sank into him now; he was here to run. He was here to win. Staring into the lifeless bronze eyes of his king, the intuition raised in him out of order.

That could be me.

And then the defiance.

That WILL be me.

Ono read it all on his face and smiled.

Busy waking dreams filled Dien's head that night. He did not find rest until he gave up on the bed and soft linens, to curl up naked on the cold hard floor.

Λ

492 BCE

Twenty-two

The games were more than just a competition. They were a celebration of mankind, to find who among them stood closest to the gods they shared. Even wars between the states were abandoned, weapons thrown down and enemies embraced when it came time for the tournaments. No one dared break the Olympic peace.

The games themselves only lasted five days, but the contestants shared the sands of the gymnasion for an entire month beforehand. To train together, to share in their talents and to commune with one another in the sight of the gods, a festival of athletics to ensure that every contender was honed and ready to give his finest performance. Buffets and masseurs and baths were available to the athletes, as well as master trainers loyal only to the Hellenodikai so as not to favor any athlete's training over another.

Dienekes ate himself sick on the first day and learned his lesson, but continued to stuff his belly more full than it ever had felt at home. Thrasilaos caught him packing down lamb and fowl at a mess bench, and terror froze Di with food on his face and in both hands. He expected to be berated. He expected the whip, to be made to run for three days with no rest or sustenance, worked to death as an example for his gluttony in front of the fastest and strongest of Hellas. Instead, his drill instructor looked left, looked right, and slid the child another heaping tray.

"Eat at least as much fruit as bird, Weeper." He whispered. "Meat alone will make you sluggish." And he left the boy to his banquet.

On the sands of the gymnasion he did his best not to draw attention to himself. He failed. The youngest and decidedly smallest competitor, he turned heads by outpacing most of his trial opponents without effort. Only one he had to burn to keep pace with, an older boy from Orchomenos in Boeotia. But like himself, it seemed the Orchomenian was holding back. Asopichos was his name, and he too failed to remain inconspicuous. He laughed too loudly, and butted his nose in the business of others. Dien overheard viewers referring to the little Spartan as "second fastest", and it chafed him that they had already made up their minds. What was worse, even though he fell ever a step behind the backwater shepherd from the Achaean plains, he could not begrudge his rival. Asopichos was warm and cheerful and had nothing but encouraging words for his competition. Dien was starting to like him and hated it.

They ran yet more heats. All day, sprints after sprints after sprints only stopping long enough for the Hellenic trainers giving tips after each dash. Another boy stood out in the crowd, for his enormous size if not his speed, and was getting sick of losing to the unknown upstart- the one with the torn back whose face always seemed to hover on the edge of tears.

"What's he doing here anyway? Is he even old enough to race? Barely an infant, I could crush him in one hand." He must have been seventeen, right on the edge of competing in the men's games. He had been looking forward to sweeping the crown from children before aging up and back into mediocrity. Dienekes stared at the ground as he walked away, not knowing how to handle the attention. He was followed.

"Hey, Infant, little baby boy, are you all alone? Did you lose your parents? Or did they leave you here when they didn't want you anymore. Look at me runt, I'm talking to you." He snatched at Dienekes, who flitted away.

"Iatragoras, right? From Ithaka?" Asopichos strutted up. He casually plucked seeds from a pomegranate and popped them into his cheek. He didn't chew them. "He is a baby, I'll give you that. Is that why it hurts when he beats you?"

"We'll see who beats who in the finals."

"I've got a sneaking suspicion you won't be making it to the finals." Asopichos wagged a finger and kept packing juicy red seeds in his cheek.

"And what's that supposed to mean?" Iatragoras was losing interest in Dien.

"Well, I mean…" Asopichos gestured girthy loops around his middle with both hands.

"You got something to say, shepherd?" The bigger boy's fists balled.

"Yeah, I'm saying that you're the only one here who jiggles when he runs."

"One more word, Orchomene. I dare you." His eyes narrowed.

"Fat."

His fist knocked like wood into Asopichos's cheek and spun the boy in a limp circle to the ground. Iatragoras reeled to strike again, but officers of the Hellenodikai swarmed him like ants.

"You desecrate hallowed ground!" They roared, many hands pinning the Ithakan's arms behind his back.

"Is he dead?" Dienekes asked. "He's not moving…"

"No, it was nothing," said Iatragoras, immediately wide-eyed with regret. "Nothing, I swear, we were only playing. I barely even touched him!"

Asopichos stirred. He moaned pitifully, wobbling to his hands and knees.

"Are you alright?" A race official asked.

The boy hurled. A stream of crimson gushed from his mouth onto the sands. The Hellenodikai's private guards whisked Iatragoras from the gymnasion. He cried for

Λ

help, for pity, for mercy as they dragged him away and even his own trainers turned their eyes from him in shame, for drawing blood in the heart of the gods' own peace.

The shepherd spat out a seed. With their attentions focused on the Ithakan, none of the officers saw the Orchomene give Dienekes a sly wink and a pink-toothed pomegranate smile.

When the sun lowered, the athletes retired to the baths to scrape the sweat and grime from their bodies with the bronze strigil. The baths were usually public. But this month they were reserved for the Olympians, so Dien was able to find a chamber to himself until Asopichos stepped through the door.

"Oh." He said, seeing Dienekes flinch. "I'll find another room."

"No, wait."

Asophicos waited, but Di struggled for words.

"You... That... I..."

"Why'd I stick up for you?"

"Yeah."

"Well you saw the size of him. He could've killed me and you too."

Some Spartan you're turning out to be. Dienekes said to himself.

"And if I let him kill you," the Orchomene continued, "then I wouldn't get the chance. And that's what I'm here for, Spartan. To beat the best. To beat you. In the sight of the gods and everyone."

He stepped forward. Di shied away until the shepherd proffered a hand to him to shake.

"Enemies?" He said with a smile now pearly white, and another warm wink. Dienekes giggled. He shook the hand.

"The best of enemies."

Having made a spectacle of themselves in shaming Iatragoras, being the center of attention was no longer an option for either boy. There was no reason to hold back anymore. For the remainder of training, they both ran their hardest.

Λ

Twenty-three

The day had come. To his surprise, Dienekes began to hear whispers of a new champion. "Little Achilles" they called him. He had looked on the training grounds but found no new faces. Di asked Ono about the stranger on their short walk to the gymnasion, and the old man laughed till he coughed and had to find a place to sit and catch his breath.

"Tell me," everyone's uncle wiped his mouth. "At Troy. Out of all our heroes. Who was youngest? Smallest? Fastest and Fairest?"

"Achilles." Dienekes felt patronized, made to repeat common knowledge.

"Well? Who here is youngest? Smallest? Fastest and Fairest?" Ono plucked a twist of `hair from Di's crown and showed it to the boy.

"No…" Dienekes did not think of himself as fair; he had never looked in a mirror. But the tuft in Ono's fingers was yellow. With a pang he remembered King Kleomenes calling him by the same name on his return from Sepeia, but he had thought the mad king was only being… Mad. And there was the strange thing Krateros had said when he lost to Echemmon.

-better than the king and I dared hope-

"Did Kleo have something to do with this?" He felt silly asking, that a king of all Sparta might make efforts on his behalf.

"What? Crazy old Kleomenes? Spread whispers in foreign lands to his own secretive ends? What a ridiculous notion." Ono grinned like a cat. He had a special kind of lie that he told when he had no desire to be believed.

"But Achilles?" Dien faltered. It felt wrong to be compared to the undisputed greatest warrior of all time. He was the worst at arms in Disappointment by far, maybe the worst in the nation. They called him Weeper for a reason. "They've never even see me fight."

"Nor will they, boy. So let them make their assumptions. You are the fastest thing they've ever seen, so let them attach whatever story to it they want."

"But I'm not the fastest," he mumbled. "Asopichos-"

Ono's four fingers flew across the boy's jaw and smacked his soul out of his body. He would have fallen to the flagstones had the cripple's other hand not held him up by the tunic.

"Who is fastest." He pulled Di's chin to face him. And shook him when there was no answer. "Who is fastest?" He repeated while the child blinked away stars.

"I.."

"Louder!"

"I'm the fastest!" Dienekes shouted. Ono's face softened and he let go. In a glimmer of weakness, he straightened the boy's shirt and ruffled his hair.

"Yes. Yes you are. Good boy. Now go prove it." And he sent the boy off to join the procession of contestants for their consecrations.

The gates of Altis were clotted. Formless masses of screaming mouths and flailing arms threw flower petals into the air, blanketed the athletes' path with cloaks and palm fronds. Dozens of priests laid their hands in prayer on each and every competitor, anointed them with purifying oils, and walked them through corridors thick with aromatic smokes. The athletes made oaths on the altar to obey the laws of the Olympiad, honor the gods, and make their countries proud. Then from Altis, the Olympians marched as one to the tournament sands.

Organized by event. Asopichos and Little Achilles were crowded together by default. It did little for Di's confidence to stand in the literal shadow of the older boy, who was all smiles and waves. To his surprise, both Asophichos and his trainer, Simon, threw their arms around the little Spartan and wished him luck before parting to sit in the stands with their fellow Orchomenes.

Dien's eyes were still bleary from the halls of incense, so he did not recognize the figure looming beside Uncle Ono before the stadion entrance tunnel. And once he recognized, he did not believe.

"What are you doing here?" Dienekes marveled.

"I do believe I took a wrong turn." Krateros smirked at his protege. "How embarrassing, a polemarch wandering so far off his way."

Dienekes wrapped his arms around the general's waist. Krateros even hugged him back for the briefest of moments before pulling away.

"What about the Persians?" Asked Di.

"Fled." Krateros shrugged, but Dien's expression begged more. "A storm swamped their navy off the coast of Athos, and without support, their troops on land were scattered to the wind by the Thracians. They will come again, I am sure. But there is time."

Dien stuttered incomprehensible syllables. This was great news, but not near so great to him as Krateros at the games. If only his mother were here too, but women were not allowed to attend. Anyway, he had not seen her face in years.

"We only received the news yesterday, so I rode all day and night. So do me a favor and beat these poor bastards quick before this old man falls asleep, eh?"

Λ

Dienekes could only nod. His spirit soared so that he did not even feel the ground beneath his feet. He was barely aware of the first few heats, so quickly did they pass. And then he met Asopichos in the finals. Ten boys stood in a line, but eight of them were only there for show. Unlike the other heats, instead of a cheer, this one ended in quiet murmur. The Hellenodikai chewed their fingertips and argued. The boys had crossed the line so close together that neither could be discerned as winner. After a long consultation while Dienekes and Asopichos both choked on their hearts, an unprecedented decision was made.

Rerun the race. Just the two of them.

"Boy!" Ono snapped at Dienekes after the announcement was made. "Rascal! What are you thinking?"

"Nothing… I don't know…"

"Close your eyes and picture the race. What do you see?"

"Just me and Asopichos and the sand."

"There! That is your problem. He's in your head."

"Well, what am I supposed to see?"

"Nothing! You are supposed to see nothing!"

"I don't understand?"

"Dammit, boy! The loser sees the winner. But the champion, he sees no one. He is alone." Dienekes swallowed and nodded. "Good boy. Now run. This time, only you."

"I hear them calling you Achilles," Asopichos said as they resumed their spots on the line. "It suits you. But they call me Hermes. Let us see who is faster. God or Hero."

Euneas the boxer fought well, but lost early. Some suspected he had not fully recovered from the scorpion sting. Polymedes and Echemmon stormed their events by embarrassing leads, Polymedes even turning to blow a kiss to the next in line, for which he would later be whipped. Oinomaos took second in the pentathlon, but no honors are given to the runner up. Thrasilaos took the pankration, but his winning blow shattered his opponent's skull. He had broken no rules so would be spared punishment, but would be barred from competing in this discipline again. All their names would be cut into bronze and sung from the stands, but none as loud nor remembered as long as Little Achilles, youngest champion in the history of the Olympic games and the fastest boy in all Hellas.

Λ

Twenty-four

In the aftermath of his victory, Dienekes was treated like royalty. Once the wreath of olives crowned his head he couldn't go anywhere without being carried on the shoulders of revelers. Even Asopichos helped bounce him from the coronation to the banquet hall where he saw things he'd never imagined. Nearly naked youths chased each other with flogs while fat men singing in tubs of wine flicked coins at them. Dancers undulated to the music made by the bells on their hips and acrobats swung from a ceiling trapeze, low enough to drop grapes in his mouth. Tiny hip-high actors reenacted the events of the games, chariots pulled by dogs, flying discuses made of bread, and fighters dramatized on a central stage. At first Dien thought the players were children, but looking closer saw beards and fully developed muscles. Until now he'd thought dwarves were only a thing of myth. He noticed that Thrasilaos's final bout was not performed, for good reason. Thrasilaos himself was nowhere to be seen in the banquet hall, but Dien knew from experience that this did not mean he was absent. Normally the thought would chill the boy's bones, but not tonight. Tonight he drank from cups handed to him without asking what was in them, and sang the words to songs he didn't know with friends he'd never met. He was vaguely aware of Krateros, a softly smiling sentry in red and bronze leaning against a marble column, and very aware of Onesiphoros surrounded by young and old as he told outlandish tales of the feats of Dienekes that had never actually happened. Dien was awed but somehow not surprised to see the old cripple sitting with a beautiful girl on each knee, their arms around his neck. Dien let another girl try on his wreath and she kissed him on the cheek before scampering away with the crown. Tongue tied and blushing, he never would have seen his trophy again had his eirene not magically appeared in her path to make her return it before evaporating again. The man could hide behind a pine needle.

In the morning he had a screaming headache, and anything he swallowed came right back up.

"Stay away," he dry-heaved, crying into a pot when his stewards came to rouse him for the journey home. "I'm dying. It's the plague, I know it."

It turned out Ono had an herb for everything, even the plague. A few hours later on the road he was stable if still queasy, and his stomach only lurched when a passerby thumped him on the back for luck. Everyone wanted to touch an Olympic Champion.

Back in the palm of Taygetos, the Olympic outfit was greeted with the same fanfare as when Kleo returned from Sepeia. The Spartans were not unused to welcoming home champions of the games, but today held a special glory. Theirs was the youngest victor ever to win a wreath, and they cast off their austerity if only for a moment to lay their hands on him and bask in his glow. The kings were there. Demaratos loitered proudly with the ephors on a simple dais while Kleomenes sang and danced barefoot in the dirt with children. For an instant Dienekes was enveloped in the familiar fragrance of hyacinths and barley flower as his own mother found him, crying and kissing his face before the crowd carried him off again toward the ephors.

"I saw your statue." Di said shyly to the Eurypontid king when he was lifted by many hands onto the dais. "I didn't know. Till I saw your statue." Demaratos humbly inclined his head and smiled.

"Take off your wreath, boy." He said, and then, "No, boy," when Di tried to hand it over. "It is yours. Hold it up. Hold it up where everyone can see." He took off his own helmet, placed it on the boy's head and turned to address the crowd.

"Peers of Sparta!" He roared. "I present to you- THE FUTURE!"

The force of voices cheering nearly knocked the boy down, the valley engulfed in the echoes of twenty thousand shouts. One hand on his wreath, the other held aloft in the fist of the king, Dienekes felt, for the first time in his life, large. Kleo, Krateros, and Ono, arm in arm with Di's mother, bore the crush of the crowd against the deck of the dais and howled louder than the rest of the crowd combined.

He did not get to keep his crown. It was passed to his mother for safekeeping until he came of age, as boys in the agoge were not allowed possessions. And such was the adamance of the Spartan upbringing that his training resumed that very day.

His brothers in Disappointment were thrilled to see him again, fighting each other to be the first to get an Olympian in a headlock, yank on his nose, knuckle his forehead. They wanted to hear everything, particularly about the girls at the banquet, but Polygonos armored and formed them up before stories could begin in earnest. Still they whispered to him behind their shields as they drilled, their clumsy questions eliciting scandalous answers. The whip licked at Dienekes when Polygonos sensed their stifled laughter, but the afterglow from his reception dulled the pain and tales of his adventures leaked out despite the lash.

Thrasilaos refreshed Polygonos after debriefing with the kings. When he heard the children sniggering he whipped the other boys, not Dienekes, and their interest in his gossips quickly dried. But they had opened the floodgates. Consumed with his own glamours, he could not stop recanting, embellishing even, the strangenesses he had done and seen. They hissed at him to shut his mouth but he could not, and the welts on their backs counted the tally of Dien's boastings. Tellis in particular, nearest to Di, took the worst of the abuse.

"Enough!" Thrasilaos barked. "Your shield wall is hopeless. Your formation is routed." He kicked over Aristaios for fun. "With the phalanx broken, you fight man to man." He took their shields and paired them off. Maron and Alpheos took to scratching and biting each other. Olympikos's brute strength stalemated against Lysimichos's superior technique. Tellis circled as Di babbled about the outside world.

"Shut up!" Tellis lost his temper.

"What? What did I do?"

"Chatter! Like a little idiot girl!"

"Chatter?" Dien scoffed. "If you'd seen what I'd seen-"

"I don't care! Be a man and show me your fists!"

"I'll teach you to talk to an Olympian that way." Dien tossed his hair and thumbed his nose. "They called me Little Achilles." He heard how ridiculous he sounded, but his head had grown too large to care. He breathed on his fingernails and buffed them on his tunic. Tellis flattened him to the dirt.

"What was that for-" He rose and Tellis tackled him again. "Have you lost your-" Smacked down again. It took the taste of blood for Dien to come to his senses.

Tellis paced, snorting smoke. Di could smell the rage in his sweat, the frustration and jealousy oozing from the fresh wet rents on his back and arms. Tellis had trained just as hard for the Olympics and been denied. And now his friend had come back with head stuffed up ass and added injury to insult by getting him whipped for the grandiosity of another.

"Come, Olympian." He snarled. "Teach me a lesson."

Dien felt small again. Muscles snaked under his brother's skin that hadn't been there before the Olympic party had left. All the time Little Achilles had put into running, Tellis had been training to brawl. Dienekes could not win. His speed was barely saving him from snatching grasps, strikes at the face; one wrong move was all it would take. He sprawled to avoid a dive at his legs, but it was only a feint and Tellis yanked him to the ground by his fattened head and climbed on top.

"Yield." Tellis whispered, as his arm snaked around Dien's neck. "Yield!" He hissed, his grip tightening against Di's hopelessly prying fingers. Tendrils of black splayed at the edges of his vision. His mouth gulped for air it could not swallow.

There had been a time when this was commonplace for Dienekes. When his brothers would beat him down and choke him unconscious and he'd rise to do it again and again. But a moon had waxed and waned since then. His legs and lungs had strengthened, but nothing else. Unable to use his only skill, he panicked. He raised a single hand skyward with fingers splayed, the Olympic signal for surrender. The boys

Λ

knew the sign but none had ever used it, especially not where their eirene would see. Tellis relinquished his grip and Dien fell coughing into the dirt.

He felt the cold of a shadow cast over him. He tried to stand but Thrasilaos's sandal planted in his back.

"No, Weeper." The instructor whispered. "You surrendered. You will stay down." The Spartiate ground his foot in the base of the boy's spine and pulled his head up by the hair. "Remember this face, Disappointment. The face of failure." They stared in horrified silence at Dien's open-mouthed grimace as their master twisted his neck to the edge of breaking.

"A few weeks in Olympia and he has forgotten what he is. Was one taste of victory enough for you? Were you satisfied? Have you had your final triumph? Did you run until you ran out of fight?" He craned Di's neck a hair further.

"No!" The boy cried out. His feet kicked, his fingernails clawed ruts in the soil.

"What good is a gift if you only use it to flee?" He asked the boys, none of whom could find their tongue. "Victory on one day is worth nothing if you surrender the next. And surrender-" he let Di's face drop to the hard earth. "Is unacceptable. He may have proved himself in a far away land, but once is not enough. A Spartan must prove himself-" he hoofed Dienekes in the ribs to enunciate his words. "EVERY. SINGLE. DAY. What is it we never drop?"

"...Our shield." The boys muttered.

"LOUDER!"

"OUR SHIELD!"

"Weeper has dropped his shield today, and proven himself a slave. Not like a Messenian, something even lower. For a Messenian is born a slave, without choice in his standing. But this creature was born to the greatest of men and has chosen to be a slave. He has chosen to give in to his fear. He has chosen the path of the weak and the unfree and spat on self-mastery, the only currency possessed by Spartans. He has shamed his ENTIRE COUNTRY." The whole squad flinched when he kicked the boy again. "Were he a man grown he would be exiled with his face and head half-shaved so that all the world may look upon him and know him for a traitor and a coward. But a man he is not. Nor do I suspect he ever will be. And neither will you, with creatures like him to rely on. The phalanx is only as strong as the weakest man. His weakness is your weakness, his failure your failure. His surrender is your death. I'll not stand shield to shield with the like, and if I see it again I'll chase you all into the wilderness myself."

Thrasilaos glared at the boys in turn, each of them breaking and dropping his gaze to his feet.

"Enough for today. I'm sick of your stench. Go sit in your barracks and contemplate your worthlessness. You too, Weeper, but you do not walk like a man

Λ

walks. You crawl. On your belly. Like the vermin you have chosen to be."

Dienekes wallowed face down for days, scraping himself along to keep pace with his brothers on foot. He was not allowed to stand again until his arms and knees and belly were chafed naked of flesh, the muddy trail behind him scabbed over with blood.

Λ

Twenty-five

Demaratos and Kleomenes had put their bad blood aside. There was no love lost between them, but they shared a love of their home and a hatred for those who would levee threat against it. No matter how gently phrased the Persian ambassadors initiated their parley, the threat had been leveed.

There was some insult taken by the foreign diplomats that their meeting should be conducted out of doors and out of the city. The two kings and five ephors met them up the road to the north, well beyond the village of Pitana, out of view of their homes. No tables, no chairs, no hospitalities of water, bread or wine.

"In Sparta we are accustomed to the elements." Demaratos addressed the complaint. "If you seek comfort, you have come to the wrong place."

"Yes, I have heard of your disdain for luxury." The ambassador's accent was thick and saccharine, sticking like honey to the gemstones set in his teeth. "It is admirable that you sacrifice pleasures so. But perhaps we may still retire in private? To sit and talk where unwanted ears may not hear?"

"Perhaps you've also heard that we are all equals here." Kleomenes did not look at the foreigner. Instead he delicately inspected a beetle that had landed on his cloak. "We have no secrets from our peers, so no need for privacy. As for sitting..." He plunked himself down cross-legged on the ground.

"I suppose it matters little." The diplomat shrugged, scanning the emptiness of the road and the field. "Secrets or no secrets, there seems no one around but us to hear."

"You may not see them." Kleomenes smiled at his insect, crawling it from hand to hand. "But I assure you, they are here."

The Persian swallowed the sudden lump in his throat, but recomposed himself before he started to sweat. He snapped his fingers and pointed at the ground. Three of his entourage with eyes downcast shuffled to the spot. Two of them dropped to hands and knees, and the third sat on them facing away from the kings. The ambassador girded the flowing lengths of his robes and seated himself on the chair his slaves had become.

"Are you unconcerned with your own spilling your secrets?" Demaratos was suspicious of the ambassador's host of attendants, mostly pale and waifish youths.

"Show him." The diplomat flashed his jeweled smile and snapped again. All but a few of his escort opened their mouths for the kings to peer down gaping holes where their tongues had once been. "Nor can they read or write. So can tell nothing to no one." He smirked. "They make for very peaceful traveling companions."

Kleomenes resisted the urge to toss a pebble into a mutilated orifice.

"I come with gifts." The envoy changed the subject, and two porters naked to the waist but for delicate gold chains dangling from pierced flesh bent their backs over a gilded chest of offerings.

"You mean bribes." Demaratos rolled his eyes.

"Nay." The envoy's eyes narrowed for only a fraction of a second. "Gifts. Freely given. Without condition. As a sign of good faith in hopes of fortuitous negotiation between nations."

"Negotiation? What have you to offer us that is not already ours?" Kleomenes pouted when his beetle flew away.

"You are a pragmatic people, it is known. But surely you do not lack for imagination. I am in a position to make offerings guaranteed to exceed imagining."

"In exchange for what?"

"A simple offering of your earth and your waters. In exchange, the Shahansha, the king of kings, offers your wildest dreams."

"So if I give him his dirt," Kleomenes mused, "would your master, say… suck my cock?"

The envoy flinched, and his entire entourage gawked at the king, as did the ephors. Only Demaratos, rolling his eyes, was unsurprised.

"Is that a no?" Kleo looked hurt. "My dreams must be wilder than Persia's imagination. Pity." He scrounged in the grass for another beetle and came up smiling with a cricket.

"Perhaps you misunderstand." The ambassador cleared his throat. "Suppose it is true that you have here all you could want. Suppose that you really are so modest as to be satisfied with this… " He gestured about. "Scarcity. But if it is indeed your grandest desire, then you would still do well to acquiesce. Your compliance is the way you keep what is yours."

"This is how you negotiate in good faith? You offer nothing and make threats?"

"We offer peace." The envoy seemed to believe in his message. "If you could but comprehend the expanse of our world, you would understand that everything under the sky already belongs to Dareios. In his benevolence, he grants you this chance to become one with him, to keep your lands and your way of life. All we ask is earth and water, and then we may become family."

"Family? You wish to be my family?" Kleomenes shrugged. "My daughter is of marriageable age. But I'd lay wager that her cock is bigger than yours."

Λ

The envoy did not balk this time, merely shifted his focus to Demaratos.

"Wise king. Should you plan to resist, as many others have, you should know our armies are so vast that we could not even fit them within your borders without spilling miles into the seas. Your island would be crawled over as if by ants."

"Then so like ants will they be trod upon." Kleo gently pet his cricket.

"Please, friends." The ambassador massaged his brow. "Dareios does not wish to make enemies of you. It is his dream that all the peoples of the earth become one in harmony. I understand how his vision is difficult for you, we know how you bicker and strife with the other Hellenes. But can you not picture a world where all are one united in heart and deed? A world without strife? A world after war?"

Demaratos and Kleomenes shared a look. Neither spoke. The envoy continued.

"The greater measure of the other cities of Hellas already resent you. The Thebans, Athens, Argos…" He took special care to draw out this last name. "They are not your friends. You owe them nothing. When Athens attacked us, they drew your hegemony into a conflict not of your own making. For this you should desire revenge upon them. For the sake of your people, join with us and we will end the bloodletting together, and Dareios will reward your wisdom by placing you and your children at the seat of power in the Aegean."

"We are the seat of power in the Aegean." Demaratos growled.

"Yes…" The envoy hesitated, and shifted in his human chair. "Yes you are. Which is why it should be you to bring your Hellenic cousins to the right. If you accept our friendship, surely they will as well."

"Friendship on the threat of invasion is no friendship." Said Ilioneos, eldest of the ephors.

"The Shahansha will have what is his, friend. And his is the world, whether you see it or not. He wishes to embrace you as his children returning to him. Only when denied must he subdue with the sword."

"Then it's good that we are well-versed with the sword," said Demaratos. Kleomenes glanced at him with a surprised glimmer of admiration and his cricket hopped away.

"What endowment may I grant that would convince you of the king's love for you? For your earth and water alone, we can provide wealth enough to replace your wood and stone houses with palaces of gold. We hear you do not even have walls? How can you defend a city with no walls? For your fraternity we can give you walls of diamonds and pearls." He showed his teeth again, a practiced smile so that his gemstones glittered most.

"Other cities build their walls of stone. We build ours of men. They do not fall." The envoy took a breath but Demaratos silenced him with a wave. "We do not care for your bribes any more than your threats. You have nothing we desire."

Λ

"What about that which you desire to keep?"

"Meaning?"

"Your freedom."

"I've heard enough." Kleomenes sighed and stood, brushing off his cloak. He raised an eyebrow in question to his fellow king, who nodded reluctantly. "Seize them." He said to thin air, and thin air exploded. Thrasilaos and his men dropped the diplomatic party to their knees.

"Wait! Hold! Mercy, please!" The ambassador trembled. "We are sacred delegates! Protected by God! To harm us will bring his wrath!"

"Your god does not exist here." Kleomenes bent to draw up a fistful of soil and snatched the Persian by the neck. "You want water?" He spat in the foreigner's face. "You want earth?" He forced the dirt into the pleading mouth, kept his palm over, and pinched the nose shut with a thumb. The man struggled feebly for a long and tedious minute before he suffocated.

"Kill the rest. Except one. One of the tongueless ones. Send him back to Dareios and see if he can decipher our response."

Λ

Twenty-six

Dienekes did not know it, but his thirteenth birthday came and went. And his fourteenth. Despite still being starved by his overseers, his arms and chest had begun to thicken. The boys were trading in their sleep for food, sneaking out at night to catch and steal. Frogs, fish, chickens, lizards, sparrows... they swallowed anything they could put in their mouths, usually raw. They began to suspect the starvation was to encourage their sneaking out at night, to teach them stealth and self reliance. It worked. All the boys learned to come and go as they pleased but the twins in particular flourished in clandestine affairs. Tellis would distract a roomful of people with some charismatic foible, pretending to be lost or confused, while Alpheos and Maron came and went through the window with armfuls of stolen larder. They delighted in their little freedoms, somehow learning to enjoy life despite the oppressions of the agoge.

Dienekes won the stadion again at Nemea, Isthmia and Delphi, sweeping the Periodos, a feat accomplished by few. He had become something of a celebrity in the Peloponnese but still bore shortcomings in Sparta's martial ways. His renown on the racing sands earned him some forgiveness from the Peers, but Thrasilaos was quick to humble him on return from each victory and still made him crawl behind his squad until his front was nearly skinless.

His brothers continued their own training while he traveled, and he fell further and further behind at skill in arms. With his growth in height and stature they were no longer able to throw him around like a toy, but he still struggled under the weight of the bronze the others now wore as easily as a second skin. He had learned to accept the pain, to embrace suffering as the sacrifice demanded for victory. They still called him the Weeper though he rarely cried.

Disappointment sweltered in their secondhand panoplies under the August sun. At an oak grove north of the city, they pushed down trees in single file. Thrasilaos drove them with whip and word.

"Insolence!" He barked.

"Sir!" Tellis responded

"What is your deadliest weapon?" He punctuated each sentence with a whipcrack by his students' ears, daring them to flinch so he could punish them.

"My spear, sir!"

"Why?"

"My lance is long! My spearhead is sharp! I deal death from a distance!"

"Wrong and wrong. I pity your teacher. This is your weapon!" The eirene's arms spread, pointing to his students. "Your squad. Not the men beside you, but the men in front and back. Shield to spine to shield to spine to shield to spine. You push as one. This is called the othismos, and more than our spears, more than our swords, this is our weapon. We crush the enemy against themselves, knock them to the ground, and crush their skulls beneath our feet. More men of Hellas have been trampled beneath the Spartan phalanx than will ever be cut by our spears. Even then, the front of your lance is not near so lethal as the back."

"Should I hold my spear backwards, sir?" Tellis shouted. Thrasilaos punted him out of line. His link in the chain broken, the rest of Disappointment fell in a pile.

"The tip of your spear will strike a shield a hundred times for every thrust that rends flesh. But when you flatten your enemy with the othismos…" Tellis tried to rise, but Sharktooth stomped on his chest. The boy's ill-fitting helmet rolled off, and the teacher skewered it with the back end of his lance. Though blunted, the narrow iron butt cap punched clean through the bronze and pinned it to the dirt. "Did you think this spike was for decoration? It's called the sauroter, boy. The lizard killer. It is for smiting things that crawl. Let the enemy fear your sharpened blades in their ignorance, but it is by this piece that he dies."

He stopped abruptly, sniffed at the air, and ordered Disappointment to hide in a ditch.

A runner galloped towards them down the road. As he came into view, his unscarred flesh and short-cropped hair made it clear he was no Spartan. He bore no weapons. A messenger. Thrasilaos beckoned with a hand from the rocks and trees. First one, then three shrouded figures in filthy brown cloaks scurried from crevices too small to have been able to conceal them. They shared a brief word with the eirene before vanishing back into the landscape and Thrasilaos went to meet the messenger on the road.

"What the… how did… Did you see them?" Alpheos whispered to his twin.

"I did. They must be Krypteians."

The boys only knew of it through rumor, the mysterious final stage of their military education. The secret police of Lakedaimon, living a year in the wilderness as the eyes and ears, the cloak and dagger of their country, killing lions and bears and seditious helots to keep the peace.

Disappointment strained their ears to overhear the conversation with the

Λ

messenger, but Thrasilaos had taken care to meet him out of earshot. They spoke only briefly before Thrasilaos pointed him south and called his trainees from the ditch.

"Who was he?" Olympikos was dumb enough to ask.

"Who?"

"The runner? Where was he from?"

"I saw no runner." Thrasilaos smiled his pointed grin and uncoiled his whip.

The runner, Pheidippedes, followed the eriene's directions to the city, down the dirt road south, flanked by unseen ushers should he lose his way. The heads of state awaited him in their humble council chambers, alerted to his presence by whispers from the Krypteians. The king's stewards gave him water and wine before hearing his message, sympathetic to the distance he had traveled. He ate and drank gratefully, then as if waiting for someone, he loitered until urged to deliver his correspondence.

"I was ordered to speak directly to the kings." He inclined his head reverently, hoping not to insult. "Both kings."

"Which king do you seek?" Said a man indistinguishable from the others but for his despondence in a far corner. Though many red-robed Spartiates attended, none among them wore a mark of office.

"Kleomenes? Of the Agiad?" Pheidippides sensed he was being tested. "I was present at the exchange of the Aigenetan prisoners, only several months past. I met Kleomenes there. And you." He indicated Leotychidas, the new Eurypontid king, and bowed. "My deepest consolations for the," he swallowed. "...expatriation of your forebear, and my blessings on your succession."

"My thanks, messenger." Leotychidas nodded. "He speaks well. And true. I remember him. And I may say he conducted himself nobly on the occasion. For an Athenian." He winked at the messenger.

"Is Kleomenes absent then? My message is not complicated, I can trust it to be recanted in my absence."

"Kleomenes is dead." Said the speaker from the corner.

"I..." Pheidippedes struggled for words. "He was a legend." He placed a hand to his heart.

"He was also my brother." The man from the corner approached. "You speak very kindly of a man who attempted to seige your city. But you are right. A legend he was, for better or worse. He left large shoes for me to fill. My name is Leonidas."

"It is a heavy burden to bear... the loss of a brother."

"More than you know," said the new king. "The pain is deep. But I am fortunate enough to have nine thousand more brothers, and at least that many sisters who mourn him with me. We yoke our grief together. But now is not the time for eulogy. Your message, Athenian?"

Λ

Pheidippides took a deep breath.

"I will not waste words… Athens humbly requests your aid." A suspicious silence circled the council chambers. Pheidippides had anticipated this. The two nations shared a tedious peace at best. He continued. "We share a common enemy. An enemy who has already landed at the bay of Marathon. My people have already marched to meet them. It is assumed that should they take Athens, or any other city, that their incursion will not stop there. We have heard of how Kleomenes threw the Asian ambassadors into a well… And hoped that our differences are not so great that we cannot put them aside to fend off this invasion together."

Silence lingered. Both kings frowned.

"Your timing is regrettable." One of the ephors was first to speak. "Until the new moon, we abide the festival of Karneia. We are forbidden to wage war. To launch a campaign now would invoke the wrath of Olympus."

"I wonder…" Leonidas intoned. "If Dareios had landed on our shores, invaded our lands instead of Athens, would we still be refusing to fight?"

"A fair question, my king." The ephor admitted. "But perhaps it is our faithful observance of the gods' holiness that has kept us safe from such attack."

"Or perhaps it is simply that Athens was a much shorter distance to sail." Leotychidas grumbled.

"Regardless of our interpretations," the ephor was patient in his piety, but adamant, "it is not our place to question the laws of Lykourgos, or the ways of the gods. We cannot march. The threat of Persia cannot be denied, but the threat of Heaven's displeasure is greater still."

"The moon changes soon." Leonidas wondered aloud. "To march, even with many men is not an act of violence. It would not be so hard to leave now, maintain our observance of the peace, but find ourselves ready on the battlefield at the ending of Karneia."

"I do not believe the gods will be convinced by your semantics. They will not be so foolish to believe a battallion deploys for any reason other than war. Many other kings have slighted holy decree in such ways, and I need not remind that it was often at the cost of their kingdom. We must not march."

"You are all in agreement?"

The five ephors nodded.

"Then I fear our traditions must be upheld. My regrets to you, Athenian."

Pheidippides could not hide his disappointment, but would risk no disrespect.

"I understand." He said with a bow. "Thank you for seeing me. I shall return to my people with your answer."

"Wait." Leo knuckled his brow. "I shall walk with you."

"I fear that time may be too short, Lord King. I dare not linger."

Λ

Leonidas shrugged. He stripped down to his tunic and tossed his robes over the back of a chair.

"Then I shall run with you."

They turned no heads as they loped through the streets, messenger and king. Sparta was accustomed to stranger deeds than this from their royals. Pheidippides could not help but be impressed by Leonidas's condition. Though well past middle age, he bounded easily alongside the famed runner.

"You must forgive me." He spoke as they ran without a hitch in his breath. "I can speak plainly with you, as none will believe you should you repeat it. But I do not agree with the ephors on this."

"It is not my place to come between you, Lord."

"You have the gift of diplomacy, Athenian, but I'd ask you to speak plain with me as well."

"As you wish, Lord. I think the judgement of your councilman is… compromised."

"We are of a mind. He is burdened by superstition."

"And by the stick up his ass." Pheidippides feared he went too far, but Leonidas roared laughter.

"We are more of a mind than I thought." Leonidas sighed. "I would dispatch the men if I could, but I am only newly crowned. Our ephors are elected representatives and I as yet lack the clout to defy them openly without drawing the ire of my subjects."

"But they are still your subjects, Lord. Do the people not serve you?"

"That may be the custom elsewhere in the world, Athenian. But in Sparta, it is the king who serves the people."

They had reached the city's boundaries. Before them stretched the road by which Pheidippides had come.

"I leave you here, messenger. And though I must abide the ephors, for now at least, I will not dispatch you completely empty handed. Be patient. Stall for time as best you can. I must wait, but I promise you, the instant the new moon rises I will march to meet you with every able man."

"Thank you, Lord." They shook hands. "I shall do my best to not kill all the Persians before you arrive."

"You honor me, Athenian." Leonidas laughed again. "I should certainly hope some remain for me. It would be a terrible thing for the first mark on my reign to be known as Leonidas the Late. I will hurry. And I hope to see you there."

Λ

Twenty-seven

Dienekes had noticed girls. One girl in particular, and he did not even know her name. Disappointment had gone to the river after training, and a family was there drawing mud to fix their clay hearth. The youngest was singing. Her eyes met Di's and lit his insides on fire. Her mother and sisters saw and whisked her away, laughing at his stupor. Weeks passed and he still heard her singing in his head. Was it a smile he had seen? Was it a sneer? The thought tortured him at night. She had freckles. He counted them in his dreams.

Though young women were not subject to the whip and warfare the boys were, they were still heavily policed. He carried little hope of speaking to her in person, but that quieted neither his yearnings nor the jeers of his brothers on their way to hear the ephors declare this year's Olympic contenders.

"We could get you two together." Alpheos and Maron conspired. "Her to you, you to her, just name it. Nothing yet exists that the Testicles can't steal."

"Have you ever tried stealing a girl from her mother?" Her mother… Dienekes sighed. He had seen her face clearly. That was definitely a sneer.

"Can't be much harder than sheep or pigs. Remember that boat we stole? And that was just for fun."

"Yeah, and then you got caught cause you couldn't find a place to hide it. And I got punished for it." Thrasilaos had made all twelve of them return the boat together, which wasn't so bad. Except instead of carrying it, they had to roll it overland across logs. They also had to be the logs.

"Yeah, see?" The twins were incorrigible. "If you're going to get punished for it, you might as well share the spoils."

"Who said anything about sharing?" Dienekes swatted at them. He might have been faster, but he was still the least expert scrapper and they smacked him back twice each.

"If you're gonna steal a doe, grab me a brace. Not only will I share, but Weeper doesn't even know what to do with them." Olympikos made a vulgar gesture that Dienekes did not comprehend.

"I do so!" Di snapped halfheartedly, as he wondered what he actually wanted to do with her. The want had not taken form in his mind, only pulled at his heart. What would he do? He thought about stroking her hair, holding her hand, nuzzling his lips to her cheek, but those modest flaunts still felt like a violation. Even in his own imagination, he shrank from her.

"Enlighten us, Pigfat." Tellis was in a foul mood. "What is it you'd do with a woman?"

"Oh, it's easy, you just.. Uh.." He pantomimed a strange dance. "And then you have to… You know… with your…" He began to blush.

"Such an expert." Tellis rolled his eyes. "Sounds like you'd need your woman to be the man for you. Show you how it's done." Olympikos waved it off.

"You're just mad cause you know you're not going to the games."

"Well, for good reason! Every season they call the same six names. Why do we need an assembly if we already know who's going."

"Don't worry, they'll call your name this time." Di patted Tellis's shoulder until his hand was pushed away.

"No they won't," Olympikos laughed. "At least not for years. There's no boy's pankration."

"Well what about boxing? They pick Euneas every games and he always gets clouted by some backwater halfgiant." He raised his fists and shadowboxed Aristaios to his left. "They should send me, I'm too quick for a dumb ox like that."

"Not too quick for me, though." Aristaios bearhugged Tellis into the air, squeezing the air from his lungs.

"Not too quick for Euneas, either." Lysimachos knew that wound was still raw, but prodded it anyway. They'd all watched the older boy pulp Tellis for almost half an hour before Tellis' own mentor called an end to the bout. Despite the beating, Disappointment's defacto leader had shown no weakness. He fought hard and proud and refused to go down. Never let so much as a knee touch the dirt, but the result remained obvious. He waited until his squadmates were asleep that night before he snuck off to have Uncle Ono sew his busted brow and pull his broken teeth.

Eleven of them traded insults the rest of the way to the acropolis, and one stared wistfully at distant hillsides and wondered which of the little long-haired silhouettes there sang the song that kept him up at night. His mind wandered so until a racous cheer startled him back to attention. The names were being read.

"Thrasilaos, son of Adrastos. Wrestling." The crowd cheered again, especially Disappointment. At least today, they were proud to be terrorized by their nation's most decorated pugilist. The ephors had difficulty selecting which event to give him after he slew his last opponent in the pankration, but eventually concluded that he would be less likely to kill another in grappling than with his fists.

"Echemon, son of Korax. Stadion and diaulos."

Λ

"See? Same as every year," Tellis grumbled.

"Polymedes son of Menandros. Hoplitodromos." Tellis droned along with the ephor's decree, pausing for a cheer after each name. "Euneas, son of Tarchon. Boxing. Oinomaos, son of Helikaion. Pentathlon. Dienekes, son of Hegisistratos. Boys' stadion." Dienekes flinched a little. He had been hoping to run the boys' diaulos this year as well, though he would never admit it was just for want of more crowns on his head.

"Alright, that's all six." Tellis grouched. "Let's go back to getting whipped to death."

"Tellis, son of Demarmenos." The ephor continued. "Boys' wrestling." Disappointment went wild.

"Wrestling? Why wrestling?" Tellis, confused, mumbled to his himself while his brothers dogpiled on him. Just this once, Polygonos pulled them apart good-naturedly instead of with a flogging.

"I can't believe it!" Alpheos pulled at his hair. "Only seven Olympians in all Lakonia, and TWO of them are from our squad!"

"At this rate, we're ALL gonna be champions," said Lysimichos.

"Oh yeah?" Aristaios elbowed him. "What's your event, pulling cod?"

"It might be, pull mine once and it's like pulling six of yours."

Their laughter evaporated in the sudden presence of Krateros.

"Did you hear, Krateros?" Dien's words ran together in his excitement. "That's TWO crowns our squad's bringing back from Olympia! We'll be legends!"

Krateros managed a smile, but his brow frowned. "It's not wise to count our victories before they are victories."

"They might as well be, you've seen me run. Six times I've won the stadion! Six! And I'm only getting faster. And Tellis can't lose, you've seen him wrestle. Who can stop us?"

"Boys." Krateros addressed the rest of the squad. "Return to barracks. Give me a minute with my student." He waited for them to leave and picked his words carefully. "Your confidence is growing too great, son."

"But no one can beat me-"

"Victory one day is worth nothing if you surrender the next." It was the same words Thrasilaos scolded him with after his surrender to Tellis. Dien took it like a slap in the face. He remembered the Krypteians hiding by the road. Did one of them tell Krateros? Did Krateros see it himself? The boy boiled. For once his shame rose up instead of inward.

"I'm not surrendering, I'm running a-"

"Ego is surrender, Dienekes. Do you remember when you broke your wrists? Afraid of your own shadow back then, remember how timid you were? How frail?"

Λ

"Well I'm not weak anymore."

"Because it was feeling weak that made you strong."

"That doesn't make any sense!" Dien shouted. He'd never raised his voice at Krateros before in his life, and he stunned himself more than his mentor. The old oak had never treated his student in anger, but it was there, flashing hot behind his eyes. Di could feel himself being weighed.

"We will speak again later. On a day when you do not already know everything." And he left.

Λ

Twenty-eight

The Olympic caravan left the city before Krateros sought out his pupil again, and Dien was festering.

Being weak makes you strong. Makes no sense.

He kicked a rock down the trail while others sang along with Ono's raunchy songs. These same athletes and their mentors had spent enough time on the road together that it had begun to feel like routine. Except for Tellis who clung uncharacteristically to Dienekes, twitching with nervous excitement. Insolence was brimming with questions that Weeper did not care to pander to.

"How many people come to watch?"

"I dunno. Lots." Di kicked the rock.

"More than a battalion?"

"More."

"More than a brigade?"

"More."

"How many more?"

"I dunno, a lot more alright?" Dien snipped.

"What's with you? I thought you'd be happy about this." Dien didn't answer, only kicked the rock. "It's that girl isn't it. She's still in your head."

"Yeah." Dien lied after thinking about it. He had not thought about her since his last moment with Krateros, but seeing her in his mind again was a welcome distraction. Her face was burned into his memory, and conjuring it coated his insides in warm honey.

"What do you think her name is?" He asked.

"Ha. We could wonder all day at that." Tellis walked and talked softly, not his usual gregarious self at all, out of his element in the strange lands beyond Lakonia. "But the thought did occur to me... That she knows who you are."

"What? How?" Dien forgot about the rock.

"Your name just got yelled in front of the entire assembly. For the seventh time."

"So? She wasn't there. None of the womenfolk were. And even if she was it's not like she'd know which one was me."

"Well she might not know which one you were, but she still knows you. Heard your story from her father who knows how many times. You spend too much time away, you don't hear how people talk. They still remember the hip-high runt being hauled up on the dais with Demaratos four years ago. I bet she was there for that."

"Really?" Di hadn't considered it. He stopped. Tellis was following close enough behind to walk into his back.

"And you know what else?" He waited for Di to urge on. "What do people call you?"

"Weeper." Di said blandly without bitterness, having hardened to the title.

"Aw, yeah, sure I know you as that. The boys know you as that. Thrasilaos-" At the mention of his name, Tellis instinctively scanned their surrounds. Rocks and scrubby little trees. Their eirene was concealed in there somewhere with Polymedes, helping the boy train for his upcoming time in the Krypteia. Tellis lowered his voice even further. "Thrasilaos knows you as that. But that's just us and a few of the Peers. Hardly anyone. People still remember you as the little deer. And thanks to his stories," he nodded toward Ono who still sang, "the name 'Dienekes, son of Hegisistratos', is one and the same with 'Little Achilles'."

The sun was already high, but Dien felt it rising on him again.

"Do they really?"

"They do. Which means that your Helen knows you by that name as well. So she hasn't learned your face yet, but imagine when she learns that it was Little Achilles, youngest Olympic champion in history, going all googly for her at the riverbank."

"Well I can't just walk up to her and introduce myself like that." Tellis had forced a smile out of Di.

"Well why not if it's true?"

"I dunno, poor taste maybe. Besides, her mother isn't going to let even Little Achilles saunter up and make boasts. Not until he wears the crimson, at least."

"Then we'll do what the Testicles said. We'll steal her. Just a little."

"Just a little." Di snorted.

"And once she realizes who you are? She's as good as yours. What doe in their right mind wouldn't go gaga for the man who's won six Panhellenic crowns."

"Seven." Dien hissed it just to spite Krateros, who was absent the caravan.

Being weak makes you strong. Doesn't make any sense.

Little Achilles bounced along renewed, drunk on himself. "Hey, Euneas!" He called. "Isn't this the spot you almost got killed by a bug?"

With no injuries on the road, the party only took two days to reach Olympia. It was a hard march, but they were all hungry for what they came for. Tellis, wide-eyed, clung to Di through the jostle of the crowd just as Di had to Ono when he was twelve.

∧

It had not been so long that Di had forgotten the feeling. He laughed, but allowed his friend's thumb and forefinger to cling to his tunic as he led them to Altis.

Di showed his friend the statues as he had been shown. Chionis, Hipposthenes, Hetoimokles, Demaratos... Tellis laid his hands on one, a wrestler. One of the Hellenodikai nearby moved to intervene, but when he saw the boy's whipscars and the Spartan name on the inscription, decided to leave it alone. This was part of the Olympics after all, to get in touch with one's history. One's traditions. Of course it would be the Spartans who took the literal approach. Di and Tellis let themselves get lost in the courtyard, trying to speak to the statues of their ancestors. Trying to listen.

"Weeper!" Tellis shouted from across the courtyard and Dien snapped alert. It could have been minutes, it could have been hours.

"Yes, Insolence?" Di whispered. The shout had drawn attention. People were looking. Tellis pointed at the last statue in the last row, the most recent addition.

It was a young boy. Very young, polished until the bronze glowed gold. The pieces were sculpted absent their subjects, so there was no true likeness. With some deviations for height or bulk, the other statues were all the same manner of diadoumenos, idealized muscle-bound men with blank faces that remained anonymous without their inscriptions. This one alone was a small child. Even on its raised platform it stood barely taller than Tellis and Di. One arm stretched skyward.

"Youngest-Olympic-Victor." Tellis read the engraving slowly, emphatically. "It's you, Di." They stared in slackjawed silence. Both touched it to be sure they weren't hallucinating.

"Didn't realize you'd get one of these, did you?" The boys nearly leapt out of their tunics at the voice behind them. For all his coughs and crutches, Ono had snuck up in complete silence.

"I thought only champions of the men's games were memorialized," Di sputtered.

"It would seem otherwise." The cripple shrugged. "They are a bit behind. Apparently it takes longer to make a statue than it does to win at the games. I understand they will one day commemorate every champion. But this one..." He leaned in, gingerly running his hand over the bronze boy's face. "I imagine there are those who believed this one deserved a higher priority. Besides, you're so little, it wouldn't take much bronze."

When he withdrew his hand, the face bore a curly charcoal mustache. The boys laughed until they fell into each other.

"Krateros didn't want you to see this." Ono indicated the statue.

"What? Why not?"

"He thought it would negatively impact from your training."

"He worries too much." Dienekes started to sulk again.

"Well he's right. But what are we to do, throw a sheet over the thing? You've been

Λ

getting more than a little big in the head lately, rather embarrassing to watch."

"I have not!" Dienekes moaned.

"Listen to yourself." Ono poked him with a crutch. "All whining and back-talk. There was a time when you used to listen to the words of wiser men."

"Well how many wreaths have you won?"

"See?" Ono poked him again. "Full of snot. You forget how you got here. And who helped you along the way."

"Last I checked it was just me out there on the stadion. Alone."

"And wasn't it this old cripple who told you exactly that four years ago? In this very place? To shake the Orchomene out of your fussy little head? My how things change."

Dienekes bit his tongue and Ono's sage advices ricocheted off his perfectly armored skull. There was a molten metal ball coiling in his stomach and it got bigger each time he was lectured.

"Where is Krateros, anyway?"

"Oh he's probably around here somewhere." Ono shrugged.

"I heard he might not make it." The boys jumped out of their shirts again at the grumbling from behind. "He is a polemarch of Sparta after all. Many responsibilities." He was buffing the mustache off the statue with his cloak with a scowl.

Dienekes was elated to see him for the briefest of moments before remembering how angry he still was.

"Krateros." He stared his mentor directly in the sandals. "How are you."

"I have been worse. Come, there is something you need to see. Tellis, Ono will escort you to your quarters."

"I most certainly will not. Do I look like a handmaid to you?" Ono curmudgeoned and Krateros rolled his eyes.

"Tellis, you will escort Ono to his quarters."

"Oh, well in that case…" The cripple took the boy's arm with excessive force. "Gracious, my very own Spartan boy. I do hope this one is broken in." He winked and waddled off laughing at his own joke.

Krateros took his student a few decades back down the rows of idols.

"Read this one," he said.

"Phanas of Pellene," Dienekes obeyed. The coils in his gut heated, anticipating more unsolicited guidance. "Triple crown in the footraces."

"He won the short sprint, the long sprint, and the sprint in armor."

"So speed, endurance, and strength." Dienekes pictured himself, Echemon, and Polymedes in one body, and the combined attributes confounded him. "He must have done the events separately then? Over multiple games?"

"Nay. He swept them all in one Olympiad."

Λ

"It hardly seems possible." Dienekes tried to act unimpressed. "He would be as strong as a bull, but light as a feather on his feet."

"He was."

"None of this is written on the monument. How did you know?."

"Because I was there. I lost to him."

...That bastard from Pellene... The memory echoed in Di's head, from nearly ten years ago when he was taken for the agoge.

"They say no one else had ever outrun you."

"They say right. Until you at least."

Damn right I did, Di did not say aloud.

"So he really was that fast?" Dienekes still struggled to picture the sprinter who could also race distance in armor.

"Well...maybe. Maybe not. The statue certainly says so. But it's not the whole story."

"So what's the rest." The boy's stomach was magma. He had his own statue in Altis and everyone still treated him like a child.

"I was young and proud and stupid and so sure of myself that I bet him I could beat him handicapped."

"What does that mean?"

"It means that when we took our spots on the line, I took an extra step back. And instead of staging for the sprint, I stood up straight. Like this." He showed the boy; locked his knees, crossed his arms, and tossed his mane like a lion.

A single step would not seem like much from in the stands, but Dien had raced enough to know that it could mean everything.

"When we crossed the finish I was certain I was closer to him than when we had begun. But he still crossed first. One moment of pride and it cost me a crown of olives, and a place in Altis. In Immortality..."

Dien might have seen the truth in his mentor's confession if the lava in his gut not been whispering to him.

But I already have the crown

I already have the statue

I already have immortality

He said nothing.

"I know you tire of my speechmaking, but do you see, boy? Do you hear me?"

"Yes." Dienekes lied. "I understand."

Λ

Twenty-nine

"Asopichos, what happened?" Dienekes wheeled on him after a training heat.

"Oh, I just had to stop and tie my sandal." They ran barefoot. The only scrap of clothing in the arena were the leather wraps on the hands of the boxers. For the first time in years, Asopichos had not crossed the line on Di's heels. He came in a lagging third.

"Too bad they didn't have wings on them. It's looking like you might need them to keep up with me, *Hermes.*" Dienekes drooled the last word.

"Ha. Yeah. Right." Asopichos had been acting differently. His usual warmth and charisma had turned impatient. Distant. Everytime Dienekes spoke to him, the shepherd was quieter and more reserved. Sometimes he would change places in the training lines in order not to run a heat with Dien. In past games the two had made a point to run together.

"I think I'm in his head this time." Dien threw grapes in the air and caught them in his mouth in the quarters he shared with Tellis at dusk. Training was nearly over and the games only a few days away. "Poor guy finally realized he can't beat me."

"I dunno, mate." Tellis was moving his bedspread off the mattress to the floor, as Di first had.

"What do you mean, you dunno?"

"That other kid he came behind in your heat? I saw him beat that same kid in every other round. Maybe he's sandbagging you."

"Sandbagging?"

"Yeah, like pretending to be worse than he is?"

"What?" Dienekes had never considered it. "That sounds stupid."

"I've been doing it." Tellis shrugged.

"Why?" A grape bounced off Di's forehead.

"Lure your opponent into a false sense of security?" Dien stared at him blankly. "Well, like all my favorite moves, the ones I can do in my sleep? Underhook throw? Sprawl to ankle pick? The shepherd's carry? I haven't done them the whole month we've been here."

"Why not?"

"My opponents won't expect it when it matters. Takes them by surprise."

"Well that's different. Wrestling isn't running. We don't have *moves.*" Dien spat a cheekful of grape seeds out the window. "And it's not just the races either. He's acting different too. Hardly talks to me anymore. Like he's avoiding me."

"Of course he has. You've been kind of an asshole lately."

"Have not!"

"Krateros and Ono have been too soft on you. They tried to tell you too, but you wouldn't-"

"So you're taking their side now?" The magma in his belly turned red.

"Well yeah, but you're apparently too full of yourself to see that it's your side we're all still on."

"Then why are you all trying to tell me what to do like something's wrong with me?"

"Di, listen-"

"No, you listen! Not one of the three of you has won shit at any games. I've won six crowns, Tellis. Six! I think I'd know what I'm doing."

"See? That's just it, Weeper. We all know you've won. All of Hellas knows you've won. So why the hell do you feel the need to keep telling us about it? I've seen you training, it's like you're not even trying. You spend more time peacocking and posing for crowds than you do running the lines. It's not enough to win once, a Spartan must prove himself every single day."

"They built a monument to me at Altis. I am proven."

"And you've been an insufferable cock ever since you saw it. Krateros was right, I shouldn't have shown it to you."

"You're just jealous."

"You want to know the truth?" Tellis started out the door into the night. "I think all this fame is making you slower."

"Where are you going?" Dienekes hurled the rest of the grapes at him.

"To train." Tellis shouted over his shoulder. "Like a real Spartan."

Dienekes tossed and turned in his bed, the words of his so-called friends echoing in his mind as the rage in his ribs grew bigger and hotter. He managed to fall asleep after hours of thinking about the girl whose name he didn't know.

She knows my name though.

I'll show them.

I'll show everyone.

I'll give her a story worth hearing.

Λ

Thirty

Dienekes seethed. The rage in his belly grew each day in practice when Asopichos avoided him and again each night when Tellis left their quarters to pursue further training. He mostly avoided Krateros and Onisephiros, assuming they'd further patronize him. He skipped every other round of practice heats to lean on a bleacher and brood while chewing his thumbnail. He thought about the girl, and the stories she must have heard about him. Maybe next time he saw her, she'd be singing a song about him. The final races were the next morning.

"Dienekes." A quiet voice called from behind.

Weeper turned. A fat old man rested his elbows on the partition between the stadion and the stands. Di vaguely recognized him.

"Simon." The man extended his hand, introducing himself. Di took it cautiously. "Asopichos's trainer, aren't you?"

"I have that honor, yes." Simon smiled.

"Well." Di shrugged and kicked a pebble. "As much honor as can go to the runner up, I guess."

The man frowned, and though a long moment before speaking again.

"It's lonely at the top. Isn't it." It wasn't a question.

"What would you know about it?" Di was always on the defensive these days.

"I was a champion myself, once. More than once, actually." Simon laughed at the disbelief, plain on Di's face. "I know, I know." He patted his belly. "I do not look it. It was a lifetime ago. There's a statue of me in Altis, but it looked nothing like me even then."

"Stadion?"

"Dolichos. The race around the city."

Dienekes nodded. Depending on the host polis, the course could stretch anywhere from five to fifteen miles. The distance made it a difficult event to spectate, so it lacked the notoriety of the stadion, but Di still respected it as no small feat.

"People tell you about the glory." Simon continued, shaking his head. "They tell you of the worships that come with the crown. Hard to miss, really. The wreaths and garlands, the fame and renown. Poets sing about you, actors pretend to be you.

Strangers so much as hear your name and already they love you as they love their own family."

Di nodded again. Only that morning on the way from the dorms, women with their children approached him with heads bowed in reverence to touch his hands and feet and pray, hoping the gods' blessings might rub off on them as well.

"But that's only half of it." Simon glanced over his shoulder, then leaned in as if to whisper a secret. Di leaned in too. "They take it all for granted don't they? They think it's all rose petals and banquets. They think the gods chose us, and that's all there is to it. But only one who wears the crown knows the truth of it. For how could they understand? Fools, the lot of them, standing on the other side of the line as us, looking in but never standing where we stand. They could never understand."

"Understand what?" Di asked. Simon leaned in even closer.

"Understand how hard it is to be a champion." Simon stared knowingly into Di's eyes. The boy looked away, feeling exposed.

"It is, isn't it?" He gripped Di's shoulder, and Di put his own hand on Simon's as he nodded. The old man continued.

"It is a burden. A blessing too, of course, but there is such a weight to it that only we know, isn't there?" Di squeezed his hand, nodding faster. "After I won, it didn't take but a fortnight before my friends wouldn't look at me the same. Something in their eyes, I know you've seen it. They regard you with suspicion. With doubt. They begin to avoid you. Talk behind your back. Suddenly, they have nothing but criticism for you, even as you stand on top of the world. How dare they judge you?"

"Exactly!" Di hissed.

"Anywhere else in Hellas, songs of my feats filled taverns. Son of Hermes, they called me, and anywhere I traveled, the wine poured itself in rivers and the women were just as wet." Di blushed at that, and the face of the girl back home flashed behind his eyes. "I was a celebrity. Welcome anywhere I showed my face..." Simon wagged a finger. "Except in my own home. My friends rejected me. My neighbors shunned me. My young wife left me before she even bore me a child."

"That's horrible." Di scowled, knowing the same pain.

"I chalked it up to envy."

"It is!"

"Of course it is! Stands to reason, doesn't it? And isn't that always the lot of we who are touched by the gods' favor? It's as if their blessing and their curse is the same." Simon counted on his hand, "Perseus, Herakles, Theseus, Orpheus, even Achilles." He poked Di in the chest and winked. "For all their greatness, they lived such lonely, tragic lives, did they not? For all their fame, they were still alone. They had no one to understand what it was really like on the other side of that line. And that's what I kept telling myself, as everyone close to me turned their backs."

Λ

"What did you do then?" Di was almost scared to ask. As mad as he was at his friends, he dreaded the thought of losing them entirely.

"Well…" Simon chuckled. "I turned to wine. And I mostly wandered. I was treated like a king everywhere I went. As long as I wore the crown on my head. Never had to lift a finger or buy my own drink. People would fight for my company. Until the next Olympiad."

"Where you proved them all wrong." Di scowled.

"No. I lost. All the wine had made me fat. And I had been so assured of my own victory that I had not even trained. Not properly at least."

"Oh."

"The instant I was no longer on top, all those rivers of wine and women dried up. I was forgotten. People now found me tiresome. An old, washed up, gluttonous bore. Now as unwelcome on the road as I had been at home. Overnight, the galavanting hero became the wandering wretch. I soon found myself so destitute that I sold my olive crowns for drinking money. And when that wine ran out and I was forced to sit in sober squalor and shake my fist at the gods, I realized why the gods had cursed me."

"Why?"

"They didn't."

"What?"

"The Gods didn't curse me. I did that myself."

"I don't get your point."

"The fame, the gifts, the showers of praise. It doesn't last. It isn't real. The people don't actually love the champion, they've just caught some kind of fever that passes whenever the next champion is crowned. But I loved it so much that I let it change me. My head got so big that I couldn't even fit through a door. So accustomed to being worshipped that I began to think that anyone not kissing my ass was an enemy trying to bring me down. My friends told me I was being a horse's ass and I told them they were just jealous. But they were right. And I had to lose everything to learn that lesson."

Simon reached for Di's shoulder again, but the boy slapped it away.

"You son of a bitch." Di spat, surprised at himself despite his fury. He had never cursed an elder before. Or anyone at all. Simon looked hurt. "Did Krateros put you up to this? Ono? Is Asopichos so desperate to beat me that he has you slowing me down with your sob stories?"

"My boy, I'm just trying to keep you from making the same mistakes I did. I was just like you once."

"I'm not your boy." Di spat. "And I'm nothing like you. You're nothing but a fat old drunk, and your friends were right. You *are* a horse's ass."

Λ

"Di, please-"

Di punched the wooden slats of the fence, splitting his knuckle. Simon recoiled. Olympic officials turned their heads to him, suspecting a conduct violation, but Simon hurriedly waved them off.

"You don't call me that. My name here is Achilles." Di growled before stomping away.

Simon gave one last word of warning.

"Remember, *Achilles*. The greater the pride, the easier it is to wound."

Di stomped all the way to his barracks and stayed there for the rest of the day and night. Tellis did not come back to sleep there that night. Di did not sleep at all.

I'll show him. I'll show them all.

He took his place on the starting line, and made sure to not look into the stands where he knew Tellis, Ono, and Krateros sat. Asopichos tried to shake his hand and Di smacked it away.

He crouched at the signal, but something in his muscles resisted.

I'll show them all

He stood up. Back straight, knees locked, arms crossed and chin high as Krateros had posed for him in Altis. He smiled at himself, chin high in the air.

In his periphery, Krateros sprang to his feet. The polemarch stormed the fenceline and would have vaulted into the arena but for the half dozen race officials who leapt to restrain him.

"The fuck are you doing, boy!?" He roared at Dienekes. Di's grin split even wider.

The signal was given, and feet hit the sand.

Thirty-one

Thump...
 Thump...
 Thump…

"Boy." The voice came from a world away.

Thump…

Thump…

Thump… Dienekes bounced his forehead off the wall, shaking the wooden planks. Then again. Then again.

"BOY!" The voice shouted. Dien reluctantly turned his face to the stranger. "Do that somewhere else, child. We're trying to have dinner." The man leaned head and shoulders from his window into the narrow alley, nodding to his family inside. Di stared, his face a pitiful mask, silently begging for a scrap of recognition from the stranger.

You know me… Di thought without saying. You know my name. Say my name.

The man showed no understanding, only flicked his hand at Di, urging him away. Little Achilles had lost the race, and no one knew him anymore. Simon had been right.

The man shuttered his window. Di slinked further down the narrow alley, and to not disturb the family, bounced his head off the stone corner column instead.

Thump…
Thump…
Thump…

I can't go back, he thought. He had seen Krateros -the closest thing he'd known to a father- stomp from the stands and away into the streets before Asopichos had crossed the finish line. The polemarch did not stay to see the end of the sprint. His protege's insult was more than enough to drive him away in a rage, regardless of the race's outcome.

They're going to throw me out. They'll shave my head and throw me into the wild.

There were not many places in the world where an exiled Spartan was welcome, and he was not even a real Spartan yet. He was nothing. His brothers would be at the banquet now, where they would be all night. He could hear its music and laughter in his head as he wandered alone into the city to lose himself, loitering in the lengthening shadows and praying for the growing dark to open and swallow him whole.

Thump...

Thump...

Thump...

The stone chafed his forehead to bleeding. Tears speckled the dusty flagstones between his feet.

Another voice spoke from far away. Di was deaf to it until it prodded him sharply in the back.

He hoped it was bandits. Brigands and thieves descending on the lonely lost child whose knives would find him in the alley, and then he would never have to answer to the wrath in Krateros's eyes. Alas, he was only prodded again.

"Feeling stupid are we?" Ono jabbed with his crutch again. "Feeling sorry for ourselves? Did we ignore our elders and go make a fool of ourselves?"

"Leave me alone." Di whispered to the stone.

Ono struck again, with malice. His crutch hammered the inside of Di's knee and sprawled him to the ground.

"What's that, Weeper?" Ono smacked again. "Can't hear you, Weeper." Smack. "Speak up, Weeper." Smack.

Dienekes flailed against the blows. It wasn't the pain he lashed out against. It was the embarrassment at the tears squeezed from him by the abuse he hated.

"Leave me alone!" Di screamed, his voice cracking. "Leave me or kill me, I don't care!"

"You are not so lucky, Weeper." Ono raised a crutch over his head, winding for a harder blow. Di cowered beneath it and Ono laughed at his fear. The strike did not land, pulled short at the last second to hover in the fallen child's face. Di took the hint eventually. He wrapped it in a timid grip and Ono pulled him to his feet. Then smacked him again.

"Turn around." Ono ordered. Di complied, and the old cripple clambered up onto his back. "That's better. Now march, donkey." He swatted the boy's rump.

"What is this?" Di asked.

"Your little stunt seems to have irked our beloved Krateros, donkey. So much so that he left the city on my horse."

"He left the city?"

"On my horse!" Ono coughed into Di's ear. "And then this old cripple had to hobble through the streets to find you, little ingrate. So until he gives it back, you will

Λ

be my donkey." He switched Di's behind and the boy trudged faster. "See? Good donkey."

"What will they do to me?"

"That remains to be seen."

"They'll shave my head. I'll be exiled." Di voiced his fears aloud this time.

"Unlikely." Ono coughed.

"Why not? I shamed Krateros. I shamed Taygetos. I am no better than the rhipsaspia"

"If you were older, perhaps. But not yet. You are still a stupid little boy. Your mentors will bear the weight of your failures for now."

"Krateros will be punished?"

"He already has. In a few days time, all of Sparta will hear how far the Little Achilles has fallen. Krateros will suffer the whispers."

"He'll never speak to me again."

"Nonsense."

"He stole your horse to leave the city. He's forsaken me."

Ono smacked him again.

"You are beyond a shadow of a doubt the dumbest donkey I've ever ridden. Krateros left the city because he loves you. And a Spartan's love is far more unyielding than his shield."

"That makes no sense."

"Have you still not learned to heed your betters? Listen and do not speak."

"Yes, Uncle Ono."

Di was smacked again.

"I said do not speak!" Ono barked loud enough to summon a coughing fit. He wheezed and little pink flecks splattered Di's cheek.

"You will not know this, but Krateros is famed for his temper." Di listened, but did not believe. His mentor had always been so gentle with him. "He keeps the monster inside him well-bridled, but there is a monster in there nonetheless. Even his brother Spartiates fear him for it. I believe he left the city because he feared he might hurt you in his anger. You've seen his hands, he could crush you between finger and thumb."

"So I was right. He's done with me."

"DO," smack, "NOT," smack, "SPEAK!" He paused for another bout of hacking. "I said he loves you. He will calm. He will forgive. You will resume the agoge and the world will continue turning."

Relief poured into the little donkey, and his eyes streamed once more.

"I'll fix this then. I'll win at the next games. He'll be proud of me again."

"I fear that may not happen."

Λ

"But you said-"

"I said you will resume your responsibility to the agoge. Not the privilege of the games. The ephors will decide that. But fear not. If they deem you unfit to compete, then you won't be special anymore. And what a burden that is, no? You have not fallen so far as to not be redeemed, and the wisest of our kind all still remember the times when they too fell. There is still a place for you in the phalanx if you earn it. Even if you never race again, this will be how you yet serve. Oh." Ono snorted and swallowed. "Your friend Tellis won at wrestling. Be sure to congratulate him."

Dienekes fell in line with his other competitors on their way out the gate. Tellis greeted him with a somber hug, but no one spoke to him. Only days ago, strangers fought each other to touch his hand in the street, but no one recognized him anymore. He was just a boy carrying a cripple on their long walk home.

Λ

Thirty-two

A year passed. For his failures, Dienekes was barred from the next games at Nemea. He had expected no less. When Tellis's name was called at the acropolis, Disappointment did not cheer. Dienekes appreciated them sparing his feelings but their sentiment went to waste. He was not saddened by his exemption. He felt nothing. He was broken and knew it was his own fault. He had tried to walk the path of a god and having reached too far, crashed into the sea on broken wings. His glory stripped away, he forgot his own wants and embraced his place in the phalanx, reducing himself to a spear and a shield.

Disappointment forgave his sins quickly. It did not hurt that he shared surprise meals with them. All of the mentors snuck food to their squires, but the consistency with which gifts of wrapped fruit or still warm meat were found where only he could have found them was uncanny and enduring. There was no mistaking them having been meant for him, always garnished with a hyacinth blossom. Of all the boys, only he had come from the south end of Amyklai, the stretch known as the Hyacinthian Way. A clear sign. Krateros was too old and too busy to deliver so many parcels, and leaving flowers was not his way. The polemarch must have dispatched an aid for the purpose.

Tellis won at Nemea, his second crown. He told Dienekes about how he saw Asopichos win by fathoms and misinterpreted his friend's silence for bitterness. Dien was not bitter. He did not care. Shame left no room for other emotions. His mind and body were surrendered to the agoge, no longer aware of his pains or the passing of time. Sharing the secret care packages with his brothers was the closest he came to joy. Only Aristaios declined his charity. Though he thanked Di for the offering, he preferred to kill or scavenge his own sustenance.

At dawn, twelve boys- nearly men- ran in single file. They slogged in full-armored panoply with a heavy skin of water each. Over seventy pounds of iron, bronze and hide hung from their backs, and still they were denied sandals. Only the crisp fall air brought them a measure of comfort. Their objective was fifty miles away before the succeeding dawn. No punishment was threatened if they failed. Disappointment had grown beyond threats, beyond failure. They rasped low hymns to keep time as they trekked. They did not stop to rest until their water skins ran dry. Pain can be overcome, thirst cannot.

"Stack!" Tellis barked when they reached a high knoll in the rolling hills.

Thrasilaos had taught it as a humiliation device, but as their unity as a team congealed it became an exercise in vanity. The twelve formed themselves into a pyramid, each layer standing on the shields of the boys below. Dienekes, no longer slight but still the smallest, capped the tower and shielded his eyes from the sun.

"See anything?" Tellis called from inside the construct.

"A stream. North-Northeast," Dienekes called. "We're lucky dogs. Closest bend minutes at a run."

The pyramid crumbled.

"Olympikos. Lysimachos. Aristaios. You're our strongest." Tellis delegated, the others trusted him to speak for all. "So you three run down and fill all our skins. I'll watch from the trail so you oxfarts don't get lost."

"So you lot put your feet up in the shade while I prepare your majesty's drink?" Pigfat mostly joked.

"Exactly. But lucky for you, there's nothing to stop you from cooling off in the stream while you prepare my libations. Which is also good for me, cause you stink like burning sewage."

"The armor smelled like this before I put it on, I swear." Neither boy was wrong.

"Alpheos, Maron." Tellis wasted no more time on banter; there were still leagues to cover. "Armor off, and into the bushes with you. Find me something to eat. Something light, I don't want to puke it up again in an hour. The rest of you, into the shade as Pigfat ordered."

There was no shade in line of sight to the stream, so Tellis paced alone in the sun while he watched his crewmen traverse the ravine. It took only minutes but with his pulse high and senses twitching, it felt like days. He was pleased to see his boys submerge all the skins before succumbing to the temptation of submerging themselves. He didn't want to drink their sweat.

"Nikomedes, Damiskos." Tellis said when he saw the flagons pulled up full. "Sing me a song." They obeyed without question and their brothers below followed the voices back to the trail. "Testicles!"

Alpheos and Maron sprang into view the instant their name was called. They brought nests of bird eggs, a few handfuls of berries, and a clutch of edible greens. Aristaios added a small haul of minnows he caught using his tunic as a net. They shared the proceeds equally and slurped the eggs raw, the fish whole, and munched the greens begrudgingly.

"No! Wait!" Dienekes smacked Alpheos in the back of the neck, making him spit out the berry he popped in his mouth.

∧

"What for?" Alpheos was loathe to waste food. He brushed dirt off the berry and tried to eat it again.

"Onesiphoros eats those when his philosopher won't speak." Di caught himself using Ono's own slang.

"And that means?"

"It means they make you piss out your ass." Tellis laughed. He too had learned Uncle Ono's old man idioms on the road to the games. "No berries then." He swatted Maron's cupped hand and the rest scattered into the air. "Unless someone's backed up... we have work to do, Spartans."

"Have you heard the crickets?" Alpheos asked Tellis while he helped the twins buckle their armor back on.

"Crickets?"

"Crickets, birds, anything."

"What's your point?"

"You can hear them up front, to the sides, not to the rear."

"Yeah, they go quiet when we pass."

"Exactly. If you listen close you can hear them start back up behind us when we're gone. And then they go quiet again."

Tellis stopped lacing Maron's armor.

"We're being followed." He chewed his lip.

"I think so," said Alpheos. Maron nodded in agreement.

"Probably just Thrasilaos." Dienekes assumed. "Make sure we're not slacking."

"Or Krypteians. For the same reason?"

"Likely." Tellis grinned bitterly. "But whoever it is, let's see what they're made of. Weeper takes point. Set a pace you don't think they can keep. Twins, each of you take a flank, see if you can get a look at them."

"Death by running. Hooray." Olympikos groaned, still dripping from the stream.

They crushed a mile, two miles, five miles, pacing just shy of a sprint and straining their ears for the tells of creatures in the brush over the jostling of their gear. A bird whistle keened from ahead at a bend in the well-beaten trail. It was Maron, leaning breathless on his knees.

"Saw..." He gasped. "I...saw one."

"Who was it, then?" Tellis asked, splashing water from his flagon on his friend's face. He did not believe that Thrasilaos would have given himself away so easily. That someone else followed was a mild relief, but Maron's eyes bugged on the edge between worry and fear.

"Illyrian." Maron waved his hand in front of his eyes, indicating the style of open-faced helmets worn by other Hellenic nations. "Illyrian..." he gasped again.

"What does that mean?" Lysimichos asked.

Λ

"It means they're not Spartan." Tellis said. "Whoever is following us is not Spartan. Not a friend."

"Then we fight." Aristaios said. The others nodded assent. They were hungry for it.

"How many are there?" Tellis asked. Maron shrugged, but Alpheos burst from the other side of the trail. He still had his shield, but was bleeding from the hand that no longer held his spear.

"Twenty," he rasped. "At least." Dien reached for the wounded palm but Alpheos brushed him off. "It's not bad. And I got him worse."

"What's it matter how many there are?" Aristaios puffed his chest out. "We are Lakedaimonian. Twenty? A hundred? I say let them come."

"No." Tellis shook his head. "We run."

His squad gawked at him.

"Don't tell me Insolence is… afraid?"

"Don't be stupid." He closed his eyes and turned his thoughts into words. "If they're this far inside our borders then they're good. If they're good, then they're not stupid and it would be stupid to invade with so few. So there are more of them. Probably lots. And if the polemarchs knew, then they'd already be routed. It is possible an army of enemy soldiers are on our soil and we're the only ones that know."

"An army? Get past the Krypteians?" Lysimachos was skeptical. None of them yet fully understood what the Krypteia was, but rumors of them being Sparta's border spies were hard to ignore.

"We can't know what we don't know." Tellis admitted.

"But if there are invaders, then we know they need to die." Aristaios was ready.

"No! Listen! If we stand and fight, and they kill us, then their secret is kept. We have to tell someone before they can do what they came for. They've got us cut off to the south, so we complete our mission. There will be Spartiates and runners at the rendezvous. First we blow their cover." He sighed. "Then we kill them."

"I'll stay behind." Dienekes said.

"What?"

"I said I'll stay behind." The idea came unbidden from his lips. It made sense. "Whoever they are, they have no trouble keeping up. It's only a matter of time before they run Pigfat, Asslicker, and Thumbsuck into the ground." He indicated the three who had fetched the water. They frowned but did not disagree. "I'm the fastest." The first time he uttered the phrase without bragging. "So I lag behind. I'll be the lamb for the wolves. When they catch up I'll put the burn on and make them chase me back south. Hopefully give you enough time to make the rendezvous."

"What if they catch you?"

Dienekes shrugged and smiled in spite of himself.

Λ

"Then I'll cry on them."

It was a good plan. Di kicked himself for coming up with it but kept a brave face as his brothers thumped their fists off his cuirass and left him on his own. He followed at a slow trot and listened for the soldiers he could feel creeping up behind.

Λ

Thirty-three

Horses. Dienekes cursed at himself. Fucking horses.

He expected men chasing him on foot but dove for cover when he heard the trample of hooves. Not even he could outrun a horse.

"He's here!" Cavaliers called to each other, tracking him from the saddle.

"It's only one!" Shouted another. "He's mine, the rest of you stay on the others."

Fuck.

And just like that his plan was ruined. Horses and trackers. Not playing fair. Dien did what he had to do.

"It'll take all of you to catch me, you whoresons!" He threw his spear at the closest soldier and it sank deep in the neck of his mount. Horse and rider went down together. The stranger's spear fell close enough for Di to steal it before barreling into the wilderness, screaming as he went.

He zigged and zagged, roaring at top speed to draw attention before silently doubling back to harass them from the sides. He stood little chance of killing his pursuers but could at least keep them from following his friends. He targeted their horses and hamstrung four before he got careless and rounded cover into a shield that knocked him to the ground with stars in his eyes.

The soldier could have finished him then but postured instead, allowing Dien to regain his feet.

"Who are you?" He asked. "What do you want?" The soldier only grunted. His helmet was open in the front like Alpheos had said, but he wore a cloth mask over his nose and mouth. The eyes were strangely familiar. "Alright fine then. Don't talk. Just die." Dienekes thrust with his spear.

The stranger dropped his own spear to snatch the haft of Dien's and wrenched it away with ease. He was enormous, freakishly roped over with muscle that Di only now noticed once his own spear hung leveled at his face.

"Alright then, asshole. Tell me how you like this." Dien feinted. When the enemy raised his guard, Di spun on his heel and bolted, leaving a trail of incoherent obscenities behind him.

He ran for minutes, long enough to forget his plight and fall into himself. His legs beating along below him calmed his mind and he went to that wide euphoric place he frequently floated to in training. The feeling had grown alien now that he trained weapons more than speed. He slowed to take stock of who or what to stab next. Less his spear, he drew his short sword, his xiphos. Lakonian swords were half the length of other hoplites', and mothers told their sons it was because they liked to get twice as close.

Dienekes turned and his eyes bulged. The giant stranger was still right on his heels. Where Dienekes flitted and weaved through the small trees, his pursuer trampled them to splinters.

FUCK.

Di panicked. He hurled his sword. It stuck hard in the soldier's shield. The invader paused to gawk at the blade quivering in his hoplon and Di took the chance to lunge inside the open guard and slash his small knife twice across the broad chest. There was no breastplate, only tunic, and it wept red. The soldier recoiled long enough for Di to escape again, cursing himself for throwing away his last real weapon. Though he couldn't resist a glimmer of pride at the sound of it sticking fast into oak and bronze. Tellis would never believe it.

The stranger continued chase, but the Spartan could hear him flagging. His breath came in hoarse, heaving coughs. But a hulk like that moving so quickly… Di remembered Polymedes and the hoplitodromos, how the older boy who raced in full armor had been able to push all of Disappointment over at once. Remembering this, he regretted the loss of his sword even more. Nearly a year had passed since he last saw Polymedes, but he could tell that this soldier was easily bigger. He could hear horses on his flanks where the ground was flatter and the brush thinner. It was only a matter of time. If he was to be caught, he decided to be caught on his terms.

"Come on then!" He wailed to the sky and his voice cracked. "I'll kill you all!"

A horseman calmly walked his mount through knee high shrubs to face the boy. He inclined his head but not his weapon. Curious, but not threatened.

"What are you waiting for!" The little Spartan foamed at the mouth, ready for blood. The fingernails of his empty sword hand dug into his fist and drew blood from his palm. "How many? How many of you die today? Let's find out together."

The butt of a spear brained him from behind, and Dienekes fell into darkness.

"What is your name." A fist cracked against Dien's head and he slumped sideways to the ground. Two pairs of hands pulled him upright. "What is your name." The voice said again, and Dienekes took another punch.

Think. Weeper. Think.

There was a sack over his head, so he could see nothing. Instead he tried to decipher the memories of fleeting glimpses of his captors through the trees. They all

Λ

wore masks but there had to have been other tells. Rough hands continued to beat him, rough voices asked questions. He pushed the abuse from his mind. It was nothing compared to what Thrasilaos had put him through.

Think!

They rode horses, and well. So they couldn't be helots in stolen garb. Thessalians? No… Thessaly was allied, and were furthest north in Hellas. They had only just sent envoys asking for aid against Persia.

What else.

They used long swords. Spathas. Thebes? Thebes used spathas and it was rumored they had not exactly met Dareios's proposal with resentment.

Some wore a linothorax, considered a lesser protection than the bronze breastplate Sparta's men wore, but still the possession of professionals. There were symbols on the armor. The winged feet of Perseus, medusa's severed head, an old dog lying down… Lightning fired in Di's brain and connected the dots. Painted on the shield of the giant that nearly ran him down, battered and faded but undeniably there with Di's own xiphos jutting from it… a big red Alpha.

Argos.

Chills ran through Dien. The ghosts of Argos had come for revenge.

"What is your name." They punched him again. The blows were still mostly ineffectual, but Di would admit he was starting to develop the beginnings of a headache.

"My name is Kleomenes." He spat.

His captors paused for a moment. There were whispers. And then they struck him again.

"My name is Demaratos." He mocked them each time they cracked his cheek. "My name is Leonidas. My name is Leotychidas. My name is Anaxandridas." The sack in front of his mouth was soaked through with blood. "My name is Achilles."

They hauled him to his feet. He fought as they dragged him forward, but the ropes binding his wrists behind him held fast. They threw him face down and pinned him with their knees in his back. He smelled smoke. The bronze of his breastplate warmed. The sensation distracted him from spewing insults and when his armor heated past the point of burning, he screamed. He could hear his own flesh sizzle. They had pinned him down on their campfire.

"Some Spartan." They laughed and pulled him off the coals. "So they do feel pain."

Dienekes promised himself he would not cry out again, no matter what they did to him.

It was getting cold. The sun must have gone down. His brothers should have made the rendezvous by now, which meant he'd be getting rescued any minute now. He clung to the hope as he was punched and kicked and beaten with sticks for the rest of

Λ

the night. No one bothered to ask him any more questions.

Thirty-four

Rescue did not come. The Argives slept in shifts so one would always be awake to beat him. They knew what they were doing, too. They hit him in the thighs, arms, chest, the edges of the face, but avoided his belly and joints. This way no bones would be accidentally broken, no organs ruptured. Dienekes could suffer like this for an age and not die. They were only softening him up.

The sack was yanked off his head. They'd turned him toward the east and the morning sun on his aching eyes burned worse than the blisters on his chest.

"I've got a surprise for you, Achilles." An Argive approached with a leather cup brimming with water. Dien's mouth lolled open in spite of himself. "Oh? You want that? It's fresh from the spring… so nice and coool…." He poured it out on the rocks between Di's knees. "That's not your surprise, boy. This is." The Argive grabbed him by the hair and twisted his neck to see another boy dragged into camp and thrown on his face.

Aristaios

"Friend of yours?" The Argive taunted Dien, hovering so close that the cloth of his mask fluttered against the boy's swollen face. Sunlight glinted off the hydra sigil on his helmet, another symbol of Argos. "I asked you a question." The Argive spun Di's jaw with the back of his hand, but went unanswered still. "No? Not your friend? So you won't mind if I…." He went to Aristaios and put a knife to his throat. Di choked. His mouth opened and closed. Aristaios stared him down and shook his head.

Say nothing, he mouthed. Di whimpered and tugged at his bonds.

"So he is a friend." The knife was sheathed. "Then where are my manners, he must be welcomed." The Argive took the end of a stick from the fire, and slowly rolled its smoldering tip across Aristaios's forehead. Dienekes shuddered to watch, but his companion did not blink. Aristaios stared back at the Argive, his eyes burning hotter than the brand.

Another soldier entered the far end of camp with a boy over one shoulder and another under the opposite arm. He dropped them limp to the ground and helped himself to water.

Euanthes. Anakreon.

Dien was no spy. He had neither taste nor skill for deceit and succumbed to the urge to crawl to his comrades. Aristaios shook his head as Di lay his body over theirs to check for signs of life. His hands were numb from their binds and he could feel no pulse, but with his ear to their lips he could hear weak, scraping breaths.

Alive he mouthed to Aristaios, who glared at him.

No weakness. Ari mouthed back. The skin on his forehead was already peeling away.

"Don't you fucking touch me!" Five of the outlanders had Tellis pinioned between their spearheads, using the points to corral him up the trail. He had been stripped of his armor and his clothes, but his arms and legs were unbound. He lashed out any way he could, kicking, gouging at eyes, trying to wrestle their spears away. Every time he moved on one soldier, the other four pricked him with their lances. It was a game to them. His naked body bled from dozens of shallow stabs while they mocked him.

"Yeah, laugh, cockbreath. Ha-fucking-ha. Feels good? Yeah? Enjoy it while you can, assface, cause you won't be laughing after I RIP YOUR FUCKING LUNGS OUT!" He turned. "Dienekes!"

Aristaios groaned.

"So that's your name, then." Said the Argive that Di had come to think of as their leader, the one with the hydra blazed on his helmet. "Dienekes. Sounds familiar."

"If you've hurt him, I'll kill you!" Tellis pointed a finger. Hydra waved a hand without looking and an Argive bounced Tellis's own breastplate off his skull. He fell to the ground.

Over the course of the morning, all twelve boys of Disappointment were dragged into the Argive camp in various stages of injury.

"You won't get away with this." Lysimachos growled. "The Peers will be looking for us. And they'll find us. You better pray you're not here when they do." His hands and feet were lashed to a stave on the shoulders of Argives like a stag slain in the hunt. Olympikos was carried the same way, only unconscious.

"Is that right? Who exactly is looking for you?" Hydra asked as he adjusted a spit of game hanging over the fire.

"You'll rue the day you learned the name Thrasilaos!" The other boys flexed at their restraints, shouting without words for their friend to stop talking. He did not. "The High Polemarch of Sparta himself is mentor to one of ours. Tell him, Dienekes!"

"Shut the fuck up!" Aristaios nearly broke his own wrists trying to break his bonds. The other boys shouted over whatever else Lysimachos tried to say. They quieted when an Argive, the giant who had chased Dien, put a knife to the eye of Euanthes where he still lay unconscious.

Λ

"I like this one," said Hydra. "He is helpful. Untie him. Give him food and water."

Lysimachos finally bit his tongue. He rubbed his wrists when they cut him free and did not touch the meat offered out of solidarity to his brothers. But to his shame, he could not resist the water.

The Argives put Disappointment on a rotation of torture. Eleven boys watched while the twelfth was beaten, burned, and cut. The questions were vague, simple, easily answered. But no one said a word.

Dien tried to form a plan of escape, but watching the Argives flay narrow strips of flesh from Tellis' back proved too much distraction. When Tellis passed out, they moved on to Anakreon.

"It'll be alright." Dienekes whispered to the body of Tellis after their captors had lashed them together. "We're gonna get out of here. Thrasilaos will be here any second, we just have to move when he does. See that one?" Dien looked at Hydra, eating and joking and quaffing watered wine while his subjects did the interrogating. "He's the leader. So when-"

"No." Tellis was still limp in the body but his voice was strong. He was faking. "That one's the leader." He slowly uncurled a finger to point to the far end of camp, at a figure Dienekes had overlooked. He wore a mask like the others, but his shield and armor were uniquely unadorned. Of all the Argives, he was the only one who had not performed some task, the only one who had yet to speak. More importantly, no one had spoken to him, as if they were under orders not to. When soldiers passed him, they went three paces further away from him than they had to, as if they were afraid. Hydra must have only been a patsy.

The questioning went on until the sun touched the horizon in the west.

Menalkas was dragged flaccid and bloody to the end of the line and tied to Euanthes while Olympikos was taken from the front.

"Enough." Hydra licked his fingers after his fifth or sixth meal that day. "These children, sorry fighters though they are, have earned my respect. I do not believe they will talk. We've wasted enough time. They die now." He drew his spatha and moved on Olympikos. "Starting with this one."

"No!" Lysimichos screamed. "Wait! Don't kill him." Hydra hesitated, the tip of his blade shaving the small hairs from Oly's chest. Lyso's words came up all at once, a frightened vomit. "We were sent for training fifty miles north of the city, where we were instructed to watch a Messenian revolt be put down." The other boys were too spent to shut him up this time and they hung their heads, ashamed of him. "We're alone. There would have been Peers at the rendezvous, a whole company, maybe. But I don't know who, or where they are now. We're not soldiers. Just recruits. Trainees. Please. We're not important. We're nobodies. Don't kill him. I'm sure they're looking for us still, if you let us go then maybe you can still escape, but if you kill him, then

Λ

our fathers and brothers will hang your entrails from the trees. Please. Let my friend go. Spare his life and your own."

No one moved. Hydra let his sword drop. Rather than satisfied, he seemed disappointed. Sad. The Argives looked at each other clumsily and gradually all turned to the unadorned man in the back, the one Tellis took for their commander. He rose slowly. As he approached the boys he removed his helmet and his mask.

It was Thrasilaos.

Λ

Thirty-five

"**T**raitor!" Tellis burst to his feet. His rage blinded him to the humiliation of his nakedness, to the dozens of small stab wounds in his flesh. "Traitorous backstabbing pigfuck!" He charged headlong at the eirene, who knocked him back to the dirt.

A sad sigh worked its way through the Argives, who were not Argives. They removed their helmets, and the scarves underneath that obscured their faces. Hydra was another boy of Sparta, Dienekes knew his face but not his name. The hulk who had chased him through the bush was the hoplitodrome, Polymedes.

Dienekes gasped. Each of the boys was a year ahead of him in the agoge. These were the Krypteians. Their faces hung heavy with the weight of conscience. Tellis still spat and screamed, kicking helplessly at Thrasilaos from the ground.

"Think, boy. Shut up and think." The captain bent and severed the cords on the boy's arms. The sudden freedom stunned Tellis into silence. One by one, all of Disappointment were cut free, but somehow their release was more frightening than captivity. The faces of the older boys were linen-white. They shared uncertain, darting glances. Something had gone wrong and they were afraid of what would come next.

"Lysimachos." Thrasilaos said quietly, using the boy's real name for the first time. He unbuckled his armor and let the Argive trappings fall from his back. "Will you stand for your punishment? Or will you remain on your knees."

Wordlessly, the boy stood. His legs trembled visibly but he did not beg. He blinked, and Thrasilaos was inches from him. A sword glinted in the captain's right hand. With his left, he snatched Lysimachos by his dusty black curls.

"You betrayed your people, Lysimachos. You caved under the questioning of the enemy. You surrendered your honor and your duty. Capture can be forgiven, but capitulation cannot. You are unworthy to wear the mantle of Sparta."

The blade flashed. Dissapointment, paralyzed in fear and confusion, cried out as one.

Blood splashed against the earth.

But only a drop.

Matts of tangled ringlets fluttered down, Lysimachos bled from his roughly shaven scalp.

"The laws of Lakedaimon demand your death. But your failure was in fear for your friend. You surrendered not to save yourself, but to save him. It is still cowardice, but not the worst of cowardice, so I grant you this one final mercy." He grabbed Lysimachos by the chin and the sword flashed again. The patchy fuzz that would one day have become a beard fell away. Thrasilaos stepped back and inspected his work.

Half the boy's head and face had been clean-cropped. Even one of his eyebrows was shaved off, the mark of a traitor. An exile.

"Your hair will regrow in time. But for now, even outsiders will look upon you and know your shame. Hear their whispers of scorn and be reminded of your failure. It will be your last deed in Sparta. As far as Lakonia is concerned, you are dead. Leave and never return. Take this sword. Carry it, or fall on it. The choice is yours. You are no longer of Sparta. Your life, and your death, are now your own."

Disappointment stared in open-mouthed horror, the realization not yet set in. Thrasilaos addressed them as he turned to leave, but refused to look at them.

"For the rest of you, this trial is over. Remember what you have learned." He gestured to the supplies around the camp. "Eat the food, drink the water, and for the gods' sake, clothe yourself, Insolence. Say your goodbyes to your fallen comrade. You number eleven now. Be back in the shadow of Taygetos by dawn or you will be counted among the dead as well."

With that, and without any further ceremony, he straddled a horse and rode away. One by one, the Krypteians melted into the scenery. Polymedes hesitated, his eyes mournful.

"Dienekes…" He whispered, met with Di's hateful glare. "I didn't know…" He mumbled as he backed into the thicket and out of sight.

In his heart, Di knew it was not the hoplitodrome's fault, but for now he was too angry, too shocked to spare Polymedes any grace. When their captors had all left, Lysimachos began to cry.

"I'm sorry…" He sputtered. "I'm so sorry… You were right. I should have listened. I let you down."

His brothers crowded to him, put their arms around his shoulders. Even Aristaios draped a hand around the nape of his neck. None knew what to say, so they said nothing and held their brother till his tears ran dry.

They restoked the campfire, passed around the water, cooked and shared the meat the Krypteians had caught. Still none of them spoke, only stared at Lysimachos until the sun went down.

"Remember that story?" Lysimachos eventually rasped. "The one your mother would tell us?"

"What?" Tellis shook his head.

"Not you." Lysimachos smiled weakly.

Λ

"I do…" Olympikos admitted. "I remember that she told us, I mean… But it's been so long, I've forgotten so much. I remember a boat."

"The Argo." Lysimachos's sad smile widened. "Tell me what you can? Please? One last time?"

Olympikos tried, stumbling over the words. Where his memory ended, Anakreon's began. Then Alpheos and Maron took a turn. They went around the campfire, and together they remembered the voyage's exploits and the strange places seen around the world.

"That's what I'll do then, boys. I'll find a ship. It's not over for me, I will find a ship and I will see the world. And I'll see you again." Lysimachos stared into Olympikos's eyes, the other boys ignored. They never knew that the two had known each other before the agoge. They never spoke of it, for fear that Thrasilaos would separate them. "Remember me, brothers. And when you see me again, I will have such stories for you." Fresh tears boiled in his eyes. "This is not the last of Lysimachos. Now leave me. It's getting late, and you have your own destinies to follow.

They helped Lysimachos into a full panoply of the stolen armor and yoked him with as many of the remaining supplies as he could carry, their final gift. Each embraced him in turn, Olympikos waiting till last. He broke down in the arms of his friend, bawling and refusing to let go.

"It's my fault." He sobbed. "You did it for me, I should be leaving, not you."

"It'll be alright, brother." Lysimachos lied as the other ten members of his squad fought to wrestle Olympikos away. "We will meet again."

They had to carry their big brother back to Sparta. So overcome with grief that his legs were unwilling or unable to walk. He did not regain his strength until the capital was in sight, and he uttered not a word for weeks.

Λ

Thirty-six

"**D**id you know I was an Olympian too?" Onesiphoros coughed, weak and wet, laid on a rough wooden table. His lips were glazed red. His tongue snaked over his chapped mouth and for a moment the taste of blood pulled him lucid.

"You were?" Dienekes could not even hear his own voice though it echoed in the dark. "No one told me." He took off his undyed roughspun cloak and threw it over the old man to stop his shivering. It was not cold.

"I was." Uncle Ono's eyes opened just long enough to wink at his boy. "A champion too. No one before or since has matched my feats." His hand rose and his fist clenched around a phantom victory. "Nor will they ever."

"Were you a wrestler? A boxer?" The medicine man had been iron-hard as a cripple. Dienekes shuddered to think how tough he'd been when he still had both legs and lungs. His brother had been swift, and even in his hunched decrepitude, Ono's physique remembered the days he could have lifted Krateros over his head. "Hoplitodromos?" Dienekes guessed.

"Nay. Perigonimopoio."

"I do not know this event." Dien shook his head. Certain games cycled in and out of contention, if they were too dangerous or obscure.

"You start at dawn and..." Ono's chest rattled and red mucous splashed over his chin. "He who impregnates the most women before sunset is victor." He smiled through the pain and Di cleaned his face with a rag wet from the basin over the hearth, which burned to keep the cold man warm.

"On second thought," Dienekes laughed despite the tears still wet on his cheek, "I do remember that statue at Altis. But I didn't recognise it through the pile of shrieking women on top."

"That's my boy. That's my boy." Ono's eyes rolled in his skull. He tried to lay a clammy palm on the boy's shoulder and missed. Di caught it and placed it on his crown and the thick fingers laced into his curly blonde locks. "You've grown so much." The old man's paw studied the length of the boys ringlets, which had been allowed to grow just enough to signal the boys' approach toward manhood. "But still so far to go."

"I'll make you proud, Giatros." Dienekes forced himself to remember the weight of the hand on his head, as heavy as it was when they met when he was only twelve.

"You already have, child. As proud as I am of my own sons." Ono's lips cracked in an upward rictus again. "All ten thousand of them." His ribs trembled, something inside of him writhed. He choked down his coughs, and his voice came like the grate of stone on stone. "Though if I could do it again… Have one wish granted." Ono clenched his jaw against another upward surge but the blood came out of his nose instead. "I wish I could have seen you race again, Little Achilles. One last time."

Di's heart broke. No one had called him that since his loss at Olympia. He would have shrunk to the floor had another strong hand not clenched his shoulder and held him fast.

"Baby brother…" Ono smiled, his teeth pink and filmy. "Baby brother, where have you been. Mother was worried."

"She may rest easy now." Krateros stepped all the way into the infirmary. He took the warm cloth from Dienekes and wiped his brother's face.

"I told you, Stratos." Ono said, wagging his finger to an empty corner of the room. "I told you he'd be here. Kleo will be along soon then too. Krateros never strays far from his Kleo."

Di looked at the polemarch, confused. Krateros shook his head knowingly.

"We should take you to your wife, brother." Krateros changed Di's now sweat-soaked cloak on the cripple for one of the fresh ones he had brought. The brief moment Ono spent uncovered set him shivering uncontrollably. "You should be with your children. In your own bed at home."

"This is my home." He struggled to control his bouncing chest. "Ever since the dogskins gutted me. You know it."

"Truth." Krateros nodded. "You've hardly spent a moment in Sparta that wasn't in this infirmary. Or the king's."

"Aye, baby boy. They may have taken my legs, but this is how we yet serve. You see me, Dienekes? I'm not useless. I can't fight but I'm not useless. This is how we still serve." A coughing fit nearly lifted him off the table. Di stroked the old man's head, trying helplessly to ease his convulsions. Sheaves of grey hair came away between his fingers. "Besides…" Ono rasped when his chest calmed and he hooked his fingers in the neck of Krateros's cuirass. "Would you want your children seeing you like this?"

Krateros did not answer.

"I was just telling him that he should race again." Ono kept talking to the empty corner. "It was beautiful, it was. The little deer, look, he's nearly a man now. Antlers and all." He tugged Di's hair again.

Λ

"My racing days are over, Uncle." Dienekes leaned over the dying doctor, using his face to fill his view, but Ono craned his neck around, still speaking to a ghost.

"You hear how he shirks his destiny, Stratos? Your hear how humble your boy?" Your boy? Dienekes's blood chilled.

"He was not always like this, let me tell you." Ono's eyes wept even as he laughed, his nose bled freely. His cough snapped like the breaking of twigs. "He flew too close to the sun, as we all did once. But he'll learn again. He'll learn his strength again."

"Rest, brother." All the rags were dirty with blood and soil, so Krateros dripped watered wine into his brother's mouth with the corner of his cloak. "You will need your strength."

"Oh, baby brother, always telling me what to do." Ono motioned for more wine. "I'll wait till Kleo arrives, then I'll rest. He'll be here soon. Stratos said he'd be here." He pointed to the corner again.

Dienekes shivered.

Your boy

His eyes burned questions into Krateros, who seeing this only held up a finger and mouthed a word.

Later.

Dienekes felt ashamed. A man was dying, his man was dying, and he could still only think of himself.

"Little Achilles. Promise me. Promise me and your father…" The old man's grizzly mitt clenched at the air. The flesh of his palm and back of his knuckles depressed as if grasped by an invisible hand.

"Promise us that you'll race again. For Sparta."

"Uncle, that's not up to me. I am but a soldier. My days of-"

"Hush, boy, don't make me whip you on my deathbed."

"You're not dying, Ono. Not tonight." Though Di knew it to be true he could not yet bear to hear it heard aloud.

"Be brave, it comes for me, not you. Twenty years it's taken, but that helot's knife got me in the end. I've been a walking dead man most of my life, but you're still alive, son. And you have a gift. It won't do to keep it locked away. You must give it. Give it back to your people. So promise me."

"Ono, I-"

"I almost forgot." Ono's quaking fingers fussed with his iron ring. With Krateros's help, it came off, and the old man patted it into his brother's fist. "You'll know who gets it next. But I would like it to be the girl."

"What are they for?" Dienekes asked, wanting for anything to keep his uncle talking. "What does the ring mean?"

Ono stared through him.

Λ

"Oh, look!" The doctor's head lifted from the bench, and nodded to the door and smiled like a child. "I told you he'd be here. I told them you'd come. It's been so long, Kleo, I've missed you, old friend." He said to the air as his one eye closed. "Tell us where you've been."

Λ

Thirty-seven

"Your brother would have frowned on this." Leotychidas could not help looking over his shoulder as he entered the chambers of the Agiad king.

"The two of us in the same place, you mean?" Leonidas tugged his beard and did not lift his eyes from the wooden tablet on the table, a message carved into a layer of wax. His wife, Gorgo, sat on the arm of his chair and combed oil through his thinning hair. She had ground fine soot into the ablutions to blacken the gray. It was not for him, her husband was not vain. It was for his men, so they would see their warrior king was still young and virile.

"Yes. The two of us in the same place. And so often."

"Is there something you're afraid of, cousin?"

"I understand the precaution is predicated in wisdom, not fear. Knives are everywhere. But you would know better, I wasn't there."

"Perhaps," Leonidas looked up then, "had my brother been as wise about his wine as he was about knives, then we would not be having this conversation."

"Was I summoned to be patronized, or do we have business." Leotychidas was the senior king of the two, but found himself in the shadow of Leonidas more than he liked.

"Business." His single muscular finger flicked the tablet across the table. "What do you make of this?"

"It's a message…" The Eurypontid lifted the wooden slat. "From Demaratos? I thought he had Medized."

"One can hardly blame him. Deposed under false charges by his own people? I would be angry too. And he would hardly be accepted elsewhere in Hellas. He went the only place he had left."

"To the court of our enemies?" Leotychidas scowled. "I'd fall on my sword before I'd turn traitor."

"But perhaps he hasn't. Turned traitor, I mean. Read the tablet again."

Leotychidas obliged, and snorted.

"It seems Kleo is not the only one taken to drink."

"I thought similarly. But read it once more. The script is not impaired. Neither words nor characters appear befuddled by wine."

"It's just a diary. He talks of what he eats each day. Who he talks to. The names of the horses on his chariot? Does he think we care the color of the Persian pot he pisses in?" He threw the slate back to the table and it clattered onto the floor. Gorgo knit her brow at him before picking it up herself.

"I knew Demaratos well. He was not a graduate of the agoge, so would never wholly be one of us. But he tried. He would not compose himself like this. Sending a vainglorious itinerary of consorts given and baskets of fruit…"

"Maybe the dotings of foreign royalty have softened him."

"I have another suspicion." He waited for Leotychidas to raise an eyebrow. "I think it is a code."

"A code?"

"A hidden message."

Leotychidas said nothing, but rounded the table to where the Agiad king sat with his wife. Their three heads bent over the message for a long while, scrying for patterns or symbols out of place.

"I was taught to march, not spy and riddle." Leotychidas stomped away, exasperated.

"As was I, Your Majesty." Leonidas said with a smile, soft enough not to offend. "But I must learn to be other things for my kingdom. Though I learn not well enough, apparently." He too pushed the message away.

"Well if at first you don't succeed…" Only Gorgo maintained interest in the tablet. She picked it up and paced with it.

"…Try again?" Leotychidas attempted to finish for her.

"No, cousin." She smiled. "Reconsider your strategy. A knife flickered into her hand from thin air- she was the daughter of Kleomenes after all. She scraped the blade over the wax with vigor.

"Woman, what are you doing!?" Both kings lunged at the tablet but she flitted out of grasp.

"Do you think me a fool, husband?" She chastised him. "If you love me, you'll trust me." She batted her eyelashes, mocking him. The two reluctantly acquiesced as she destroyed the message. "Besides," she said, "I already made a copy." The two exhaled relief.

"It's trouble enough to have a wife." Leonidas grumbled to the Eurypontid. "But to have a wife as clever as her is like-"

"Here is your hidden message." Gorgo, pleased with herself, presented the tablet. "See? Reconsider your tactics. You can thank my father for that one. He used to write to me this way."

She had cleaned the wax from the tablet. Beneath it, Demaratos had used the tip

Λ

of a knife to gouge rough Doric letters.

They are coming

Beneath the words was a map, crude but recognizable. The land of Lakedaimon was cut deepest, little stars for the cities of Sparta, Athens, Thebes, and others. Two arrows, one red ran west and down through Thessaly. The other, blue, followed it along the coast.

"So it seems Demaratos has not medized after all." Leotychidas grumbled into his fist. "He took great risk sending us this."

"Indeed." Considering the message, Gorgo stood strangely calm. "But not so great a risk as Xerxes."

"And how is that." Asked the Eurypontid.

"Because Demaratos only send us letters to be read." Leonidas smiled at his wife. "But Xerxes himself comes to die."

Λ

Thirty-eight

Dien moved his feet but could not feel them. The sun stroked his back but he was unaware of its warmth. There was singing that he could not hear. His brothers respected his space, assuming he was lost in grief for his uncle passing in the night, but they were wrong. He had not yet fallen into the pit of despair, but teetered with his toes on the edge. He felt nothing.

The boys stopped in file beneath the steps of the Temple Artemis with its unadorned stonework and simple Doric columns, flanked by the squads who shared their age. Despite their discipline, whispers skirted through their ranks.

"We are gathered today to give thanks for the bloom begotten of winter," the paidonomos, officer in chief over the agoge, recited from the top step. "...for the creatures born in darkness who will rise to see the summer light. Persephone has returned to her home in the clouds and brought with her the sun."

"Di, look." Tellis elbowed him in the ribs, his eyes dazzling.

Weeper studied the stairs and counted wheels of cheese, platters of sliced roast and bowls of fresh fruit, cups of honeyed water and watered wine stacked into pyramids, bouquets of smoked fish on spits dripping butter. The display was distinctly unspartan, but Dien could not clock its strangeness. He gazed past the spread, not at it, still lost in the back of his mind.

"Today our sacrifice is not one of abstinence, but abundance." The paidonomos lost control of the smile he was trying to hide and beamed at the boys, approaching down the wide stairway with his arms raised. "As you have been deprived, today you will taste fortune. As you have suffered, today you will taste reprieve. As you have starved, today you will feast. Future men of Sparta, I bid you, fill your eyes and your hands and your mouths. Come and take, this bounty is for you."

A gasp susurrated through the small crowd. The men of age who knew the secret laughed into their shoulders as they watched the boys weigh their suspicions. Many times the trainees had been taunted with reward only to have it traded for the whip when they reached for their gift, but hunger is stronger than reason.

"Fuck all." Aristaios broke rank first, sparing only the slightest glance toward their eirene, to see if he would be resisted. Thrasilaos did not move. Did not even look. Everyone watched his tentative steps towards the banquet, some followed.

"Look at that asshole," Maron nodded toward the paidonomos, his arms still raised. "Look at his stupid face. Something's wrong." But he too could not resist creeping towards the food. Only Dienekes had not moved at least an inch. He watched birds fly over, returning from their winter in Africa.

Aristaios touched a wheel of cheese with a finger before picking it up, as if it would spring some trap. The boys held their breath as they watched him take a bite, greedily gnashing through the rind. When nothing happened to him, they all surged.

And the paidonomos lowered his arms. So began the festival of Artemis Orthia, the best kept secret of the agoge.

Hundreds of screaming boys, naked but for masks and painted head to toe in red ochre, streamed from the doors of the temple and down the stairs. Each of them carried stout birch rods, some carried two, and they used them with abandon on any who did not flee from the bounty.

Aristaios did not run, but stood his ground. One fist on his cheese, and the other cracking the faces of assailants, he was instantly surrounded and clubs rained on him. Alpheos dragged Dienekes away by the arm as a stick missed his temple by an inch.

"You're supposed to be the runner, dammit. Run!"

Still not lucid, the fever in the air at least brought Di into his senses if not his thoughts. He could hear his own laughter even if he could not feel it coming out. His legs came to life and in a burst of speed, returned the favor, dragging the twins and Tellis and any other brothers who grabbed on. Blows hissed through the air behind them, snagging their tunics but not their flesh.

The temple lay some distance from the city, on the banks of the Evrotas, and when the red-clad attackers had fallen out of sight and the sounds of fighting were a faint echo, the boys found themselves a couple hundred yards away on the outskirts of the village of Limnai.

"Hell was that?" Olympikos panted. Bent double, he was the only one out of breath.

"He's dead! He's dead, they got him, I saw it!" Menalkas shivered. Not for fear of the sticks, but in shame for having left his brother behind.

"It'll take more than that to kill Aristaios." Damiskos peered around a corner, keeping watch. "And we're going back for him." He paused. "We are going back for him, right?"

"Shut up, I need to think." Tellis crouched in a gutter.

"We're going back for him, right?" Menalkas parroted.

"Yes we're going back for him, shut up I need to think!" Tellis chewed his thumb. "Alpheos, Maron, I need eyes. Climb up on the roof... Oh. Good." The twins were already halfway up the walls of some Spartiate's home.

Λ

Dienekes remembered only one detail.

"Polymedes." He said to Tellis.

"What?"

"Polymedes was with them."

"How do you know? They had their faces covered. Isn't Polymedes in the Krypteia now?"

"I saw his scar." Dienekes drew an 'x' over his heart.

"You're sure?"

"I'd know it anywhere. I gave it to him."

"So the Krypteians are back. It must be them in red. Gotta say, not a good look. Testicles, report!"

"They're mostly staying by the temple. They're chasing away anyone who comes close, but they don't go far before returning to the steps."

"Guarding the food..." A hungry smile waxed over his lips. "A game then. This should be fun."

"Fun? Hundreds of Krypteians beating us with sticks and you call it fun?" Menalkas rolled his eyes.

"Twelve years with Thrasilaos and you're afraid of a couple boys with switches?" Anakreon prodded him. "What's the plan, Insolence?"

"I'm thinking... we'll need a sack. A couple sacks. And some cord. Lots of cord. Maron, do you think you can steal us a few-" Two coiled lengths of sisal rope landed on Tellis's head.

"They looked useful!" The twins apologized from above before jumping the two stories down and rolling.

"Can you get on the roof of the temple?" He asked and the twins looked insulted. "Ok, you get on the roof of the temple with one of the ropes. Pigfat, why are you naked?"

"You said you wanted a sack." Olympikos held up his tunic. With the sleeves and neck knotted, it was indeed quite a large sack.

"Oh. Wonderful. I guess." Tellis gingerly took the sweat-soaked tunic and gave it to Alpheos. "Euanthes, Xiphilinos, you help the twins onto the roof, then help load the bag. The rest of you are with me. No time to explain, but you'll see when we get there. Except you, Weeper. Remember the last time you decoyed for us?"

"Yeah?"

"Well don't get caught this time. Here we go boys, time to get fat!"

They found Aristaios in a ditch diagonal to the temple yard, happily munching his second or third cheese wheel despite the countless bloody and swollen stripes across his body.

Λ

"You're back!" He said jovially, mouth full of food. "I was gonna wait for you, but I mean, come on. How can I resist?" He waved over his shoulder. They took turns checking the view over the ditch, watching boys chase each other back and forth, alternating screams of terror and mirth.

"Alright, then." Aristaios forced the rest of the wheel down his gullet and swallowed hard. "You girls ready for the next round?"

"Yes, glad to have you back," Tellis punched him warmly in a spot with no obvious bruises. "Here's the plan-"

But Aristaios was already gone, howling like an animal towards the steps and snatching at the banquet, impervious to the blows cascading down on him.

"Dammit! Go! Go now!" Tellis pushed everyone in their respective directions. "Di, get to the top of the stairs, quietly. When they're done with him, make yourself as big and loud as you can, then run back through here. Not too fast, though. Make sure they're tight up on you." He waggled the rope. Di had no idea what that meant, but shrugged and trusted his brother.

He plucked a cluster of grapes from a basket as he sliced up the temple steps unnoticed, stuffed them all into his mouth and pulled out the stem like a herring bone. The guards were frenzied and disorganized. Aristaios was hard to ignore. He danced through their beatings, laughing with red in his eyes and holding a leg of lamb like a woman and ripping off hanks with his teeth. With him drawing so much attention, Di had time to stuff his cheeks to bursting with another stem of grapes before Anakreon leaned his head around the corner where Disappointment waited.

"Dienekes! Tellis says do it now!" He hollered, loud enough for the whole courtyard to stop and stare at Anakreon. And then they looked where Anakreon was staring. And there was Dienekes alone at the top of the steps with his mouth full.

Big and loud Tellis had said.

Di puffed out his chest and roared. Or tried to. Instead he choked out a wet sputter with little chunks of fruit in it, then coughed up a little more when a seed caught in his throat. No matter. It had the desired effect. A hundred naked warriors charged him with their sticks.

Dienekes almost didn't make it. Three, four whacks glanced across his back and he ran the last short length up a wall and off of shoulders to keep the crowd from closing him in.

"Now!" Tellis had tied his rope to a post and Disappointment yanked the tripwire tight when Dienekes passed. Rows of boys lost their feet and the fastest in front were buried under the crush of their brothers swarming behind.

"Back to the temple!" Tellis shouted, throwing Di a fallen stick and taking two himself. "We'll hold them off!" He leapt on top of the groaning heap and labored about with his switches. Kicking and swatting and yelling curses, refusing to let the

Λ

tangle of boys unknot. Olympikos, Anakreon, and the others piled on. They relished their reversal of fortune, not knowing how long it would last.

Dien saw Alpheos and Maron leaning over the temple cornice, lowering their rope with Pigfat's shirtbag attached. Xiphilinos and Euanthes met him below it and stuffed everything they could reach inside.

"No! No! The cheeses!" Xiphilinos yelled at Dien, who was shoveling in bread and smoked fish.

"Wha?" More food fell from Weeper's mouth.

"The cheeses!" Xiphilinos threw a pomegranate at Di's face. It hit. "Forget the other stuff, just grab the cheese. They'll keep. They'll last." His eyes bugged out at the revelation. "We can save them for later!"

The cheeses then. They'd never had a larder before. They felt rich.

"It's full! Climb up! Lets get out of here!" The twins called down.

Euanthes wasted no time. Xiphilinos was short after, but Tellis's blockade was failing. Dien watched the heap capsize under his brother's feet and swallow him up. An instant later it surged back across the courtyard for him. He picked up another stick and swung wildly to keep the mob at bay while Xiphilinos scurried to safety. Dienekes screamed the only words in his head.

"Those are my cheeses!" His arms whirled like a hurricane. "I'M SAVING THEM FOR LAATERR!"

He could hold off a few at a time, but he was surrounded now. They snatched his sticks. Only a matter of time before he was overcome.

"I"m up! Grab on!"

The bag swung out over his head. He did not think, just leapt. His fingers closed around the roughspun wool and both he and it lurched upwards as his four brothers above heaved him hand over hand to safety. He hadn't felt this alive since he was twelve years old, coming home from Olympia. Again he was presented proudly for all of Sparta to see, only instead of holding the hand of the king at the gates, he dangled before the Temple of Artemis from a sweaty bag of stolen cheese. Even the guards he eluded could not help but laugh at the spectacle.

"And let that-" He could not resist a gloat. "Be a lesson! In DISAPPOINTMENT!"

The bag ripped. Dienekes fell back into the hungry red crowd amidst a storm of cheeses.

When it was all over, the guards gave Di and his squad back their little larder. The whole sackful, and then some. They remembered their turn in the festival a year before, though it seemed longer. It was theirs after all, the paidonomos himself had said so. But they made certain that Disappointment paid the price for the goods. With their hides.

Λ

Thirty-nine

Thrasilaos tapped his foot, scrutinizing his squad in file. A pair of helots flanked him, eyes downcast beneath dogskin caps and arms laden.

"Strip!" He ordered.

The boys dropped their weapons, their armor, their tunics. Thrasilaos snapped his fingers and the helots trotted from boy to boy, dropping a rolled bundle of wool at each of their feet.

"Look, what bounty." Thrasilaos smiled, licking his pointed teeth. "Behold the treasures Sparta endows. I still find you unworthy, but alas, Sparta is generous to a fault." Each bundle was a single overlarge bolt of thick undyed wool, a small knife wrapped inside. They were the first possessions the boys would ever call their own. "For the next nine months, the cape will be your blanket, your clothing, your rope, your shelter. Make it a cloak, a tent, wipe your ass, cut it into breeches, or a fancy dress to entertain your boyfriends. Twist it up and hang yourself, I don't care." The eirene spat. "The knife is a knife. If you still don't know what that's for, do us all a favor and die now."

The boys tried clumsy ways of draping themselves, all more or less kilting themselves for now, using the cord from the bundle as a belt.

"Good. Yes. Modesty first, budding into womanhood as you are. Do you know where you're going?"

Disappointment said nothing.

"Of course you don't know. You're idiots. But fortunately you have me to fill your heads with wisdom. You are going into Messenia."

This is it. The boys trembled internally. The legendary final trial of the agoge. Krypteia.

"You will sleep by day and walk in the shadows by night. You will abide in holes. Like vermin. And like vermin, you will not be seen, living under the nose and between the feet of men. For the next nine moons, you will have no roof over your head, no hearth by your side, no company, no help, no supplies, no contact with Lakonia. Whatever you cannot make with your own hands, you will go without. You will eat lizards and grass. You will drink piss. You will have no name."

The boys shivered with excitement despite the warning. They all itched to prove themselves.

"Do you understand?"

"AU!"

"Then we march."

Thrasilaos led them out of the city on the road. Once out of sight of Sparta's invisible walls, he drove them into the bushes. For several days they followed him, creeping from shrub to shrub, avoiding even their own countrymen and never speaking a word. They wove mantles of rushes and reeds so as to lie still and become bushes themselves. A Spartiate runner stepped on Maron's hand when he wandered off the road to take a piss and never knew. Once the messenger passed, Thrasilaos grinned ear to ear and slapped the back of Maron's head and almost smiled. It was the closest thing to a gesture of pride that Disappointment ever saw from Thrasilaos. They camped without a fire.

Then one morning in the heart of Messenia, the subjugated territory where they cultured their helots, Disappointment woke and found their eirene missing. Their Krypteia had begun.

The boys initially huddled together in their confusion, eventually going their separate ways, little by little. It would be easier to stay hidden as one and not eleven. Though they were still unclear on their mission, and reluctant to leave their companions, none wanted to risk disobeying an unspoken command and forfeit their Spartiate status. The loss of Lysimachos was still raw in their minds. They had come twelve years too far not to earn their crimson and bronze.

Aristaios left first. The other boys turned around once too long and he had gone. Olympikos went second.

"I won't say goodbye," he said. "Cause it's not. It's not goodbye. We'll be seeing each other again soon enough. And then we'll be men." He pounded his chest with a tearful smile and turned his back on his brothers.

The rest factioned. Euanthes, Xiphilinos, and Anakreon wandered away and back a few times before diverging. Menalkas and Damiskos left together. Dienekes remained with only Tellis and the twins. They huddled around a buried tunnel fire, barely warmer than a fistful of candles, but they dared not make a larger one until they better knew their surroundings.

"We're leaving tonight." Tellis said gravely.

"Alright." Dienekes had expected this. "Where are we going?"

"Not you." Tellis shook his head and pointed a finger at Alpheos, Maron, and then himself.

"Fine." Dien grit his teeth. "Where are you going."

"Into town."

Λ

"To look. To listen. To steal." Alpheos' gaze dropped from his brother's. "Other things."

Dienekes need not ask why they were leaving him. He could see the hunger in their eyes. A hunger for things he did not share the taste for.

"We'll be back. Soon." They assured him.

"Not here." Said Di.

"No, not here. You'll have to keep on the move. For now. But we'll find you."

"I'll have to come with you eventually."

"Eventually." Tellis nodded. "But we have all winter. No need to rush into things that can't be taken back."

A scream of agony sliced through the hills before being cut abruptly short.

"Sounds like someone's rushing it." Dienekes shivered.

"What do you think it was?" Maron asked.

"An animal. Someone fell in a hole. Cut themselves shaving." They grinned nervously at each other.

"If I were a betting man…" Alpheos ventured. "I'd say Aristaios found his dinner."

"You think he'd eat a helot?" Dienekes genuinely wondered.

"They're livestock. Why not." Maron shrugged.

"But they're people."

"If we've learned anything in the agoge, Weeper," Tellis put a hand on Di's head.

"It's that there are people, and then there are Spartans. Our time in the wild will decide which we are."

Dien nodded and wished his friends well as they left him alone on foreign soil. Their feet made no sound as they slipped into the moonless dark.

Λ

Forty

Dienekes did see his brothers again, and sooner than he expected.

"You know how to heal this, right?" Maron asked, dripping blood from his forearm. "Ono taught you the herbs?"

"Well time heals better than I." Dienekes inspected the wound. "But it's shallow. I think I can help."

They rinsed the wound with water and wine boiled in a stolen clay pot, dripped oils from selected plants into the gash, and sewed it shut with a sharpened thorn and a thread plucked from the hem of his cloak. Maron laughed through the pain.

"You'll have to stay with me. If I don't oil it a few times a day it will fester."

"You can't give me some to take with me?" Maron frowned.

"What do I have to put it in?"

"Stay." Tellis interjected. "For now. And we'll steal something for you to carry it in."

"How much more can you take? I thought we were supposed to go unnoticed." He squinted at the things they had brought him: whetstones, a mortar and pestle, full wineskins, a few sacks of grain and strips of salted meat and the clay pot. All stolen.

"It'll be fine," Alpheos shrugged. "We... uh... don't leave witnesses." Dien's spine chilled. Their Krypteia had been underway for less than two weeks and his brothers were already taking advantage. "Stay." Alpheos nudged Maron. "Help him get set up."

"Set up for what?" Dienekes asked, suspicious.

"Look at what you did for his arm. It's like it never happened." It was an exaggeration. The wound was still an angry swollen rift pinched reluctantly together. He'd only stopped the bleeding. "There will be more. Accidents, animals, uppity Messenians... We'll need an apothecary."

Dienekes wanted to argue, so as not to encourage their recklessness. But the idea sat well with him.

"A healer..." Dien rolled the word around in his mouth. He had never considered the thought but could almost feel the proud phantom hand of Uncle Ono weigh on his shoulder. "A healer."

This is how we yet serve.

Tellis punched him in the knee as he chewed a strip of cured beef.

"Looks like you just became the most important member of Disappointment."

"Most Disappointing." Di smiled.

"Yup! You're not useless after all."

Dienekes insisted that Maron stay for two weeks for his arm to heal. So he stayed for one. He took Tellis's suggestion and helped make Dien a functioning apothecary, a little witch's hovel excavated from an abandoned rabbit warren where he could brew his potions and say his magic words, Maron joked. The entry ways were barely wider than their shoulders and hidden under ghillie matts they wove from living plants. It even had the smallest of hearths inside with baffles over the chimney to break up the smoke. It was the warmest, happiest home Dienekes had had in almost thirteen years, so long as he minded the snakes and scorpions.

Maron did not share the sentiment. When he didn't have his hands occupied, he stared wistfully out over the distant valleys where he knew his brothers hid, wishing he was with them. Dienekes nearly asked what it was the rest of their squad was up to, then decided he would rather not know. Not yet.

Weeper saw his brothers nearly as often as he liked, though always under unfortunate circumstances. His healing arts were clumsy at first, but his fingers rapidly gained grace. Piecing the injured back together gave him purpose in a small way like winning olive wreaths used to. Not complete, not accomplished, those feelings were fleeting, but worthy. He began to pray to Ono like others prayed to Artemis Orthia or Zeus Agamemnon.

Apollo Ono…

Di's prayers were answered. He remembered the most fleeting advices the cripple had given him on the Olympic trails. The old man haphazardly sharing trivia years ago was saving lives today. The others traded Di's skills for goods stolen from the villages or game they'd caught in the bush. Dienekes did not lack his own hunting skills, but unlike the other Krypteians, he needed to stay put so the injured could find him at their need. He had shortly picked his little hilltop clean of food.

Boys from other squads came to see him too, over the months. Eventually he was seeing more he didn't know than he did. They stayed with him however long it took for them to be able to sneak back off in the night, never long enough for Dien to be satisfied in their recovery. He caught scrapings of their stories, and finally learned what his own eirene's promotion after Sepeia had been.

Kleomenes had given Thrasilaos clandestine command of the Krypteians. He had been whipping Disappointment into shape by day and putting down Messenian rebellions by night. He sniffed a rumor that Tellis and the Twins were taking orders

Λ

from their old sergeant directly and almost felt jealous that Thrasilaos had not come to speak to him as well. Then he remembered that he didn't even like Thrasilaos and pounded a poultice in his stolen mortar until he no longer felt silly.

It became apparent as autumn turned to winter that only one member of Disappointment had not come seeking Di's help. He asked his other patients about Aristaios, but they had neither seen nor heard of him. This concerned Dienekes, but Aristaios had always been a loner. And an exceptionally tough one. He'd never asked for help, and always refused it when offered. Dien envied him. Sitting alone in his burrow, he thought about all the help he'd had over the years. Krateros, Onesiphoros, Tellis, the Twins, even King Kleomenes, apparently… How he never would have accomplished any of his feats alone, however few they were. He wondered what it was like for Aristaios, to be enough all on your own.

A twig snapped by the door to his cave. Krypteians moved silently. They did not snap twigs.

He switched knives. The one given to him in the city was kept sharp and clean for surgery on his friends. He'd have to use a different blade for fighting Messenians. Their blood could not be allowed to pollute Spartan purity.

He slipped headfirst out a back entrance to his warren, but no sooner did the cold winter air strike him than he was clubbed on the crown of his head.

He woke disarmed and surrounded, hands bound behind his back. He had been trained for this. He didn't panic. He lay still with his eyes shut and ears open.

"We have to kill him. He'll tell the others and we'll be found out."

"And what do you think the others will do when they find him dead?"

"We'll hide the body. Or tear him up, so it looks like a lion got him."

"And what good will that do? Can you hide all our tracks, too? Because their weasel noses can sniff us out. They're probably watching us now. Lion or no lion, we'll still be blamed when he's discovered missing and Messenia will bleed for it. Lakonia punishes a hundred innocents to get to one criminal."

"We can just let him go. Cut his bonds and leave. He hasn't seen our faces. He probably won't even remember anything."

"Are you daft? He's the one we came for. He's the one who keeps stitching them back together. Why did you have to hit him anyway?"

"He came up out of the ground! I didn't know it was one of them!"

"Well what's done is done. You've attacked a Spartan. There's no way he'll help us now. Kill him before he wakes up. I'm not sure those bonds will hold him."

Strangely, Dienekes had not yet considered trying to break free. He tested his bonds as much as he dared without giving himself away. The leather cord felt frail, he could snap it. But he waited. He wanted to hear more.

"We can still ask. And if he says no, we kill him."

Λ

"He's not going to help your daughter. She'll die of the fever just like my wife and sister. He wouldn't have helped us anyway, especially not now that you've assaulted him. I never should have agreed to come. He'll think we're rebels. You have to end him. Then we go home and hope they don't come looking for us. We can't be out here any longer." Any helot off of their allotted kleros at night was subject to criminal prosecution and assumed seditious. The punishment was death.

"What about the body? You said-"

"We'll tear it up. Make it look like an animal did it. Hurry up, finish him."

"Why don't you do it?"

"Me? You started this! Now finish it!"

"Fine…" Reluctant footsteps padded to Dienekes.

"Bring me to her." Di sat up and the Messenians around him nearly died of fright. The one closest fell backwards and dropped his knife.

"Kill him now!" Their ringleader shouted, and sidled behind the others to cower. They brandished farm tools with violent intent. Di counted six, there were probably more.

"I will heal your daughter." Dienekes spoke directly to the one who had struck him. The one who would have killed him in his sleep.

"He lies!" Hissed another. "They all lie!"

"Do you swear?" The father whispered. "That you'll not hurt her?"

"I swear." Dienekes nodded gravely.

"How do I know you won't turn on me when I cut you loose?"

"You're trying to save your family. Your blood. I too would go to great lengths to protect my blood, so you have my sympathies. Besides." Dienekes shrugged and snapped the laces that bound him. The helots recoiled and swung their hoes and picks. "Peace." Dienekes stood and brandished his empty hands. "I heard you talking. You came here in good faith, in desperation for your kin. I surprised you. It was a misunderstanding and I hold no grudge."

Still the helots bristled behind their farm tools.

"Surely you saw inside my shelter. The herbs and tinctures. I am not a surgeon, but I manage. I can heal your daughter. This is why you came isn't it? The others may leave. Take me to your daughter, and we will all forget after that you visited me at all."

He held his hand out for the father to shake. The helot, trembling, took a step. As he reached his fingers toward the Spartan, a javelin erupted from his neck. Dienekes was too surprised to react. The shadows came alive and closed around the slaves before the carotid spurt from their first victim had splashed across the Weeper's face.

"Got here just in time, didn't we?" Tellis grinned, driving a sharpened stick into the back of a fallen Messenian. His smile glittered silver-white in the moonlight against

Λ

the coal soot that blackened his face and body. The twins threw their cloaks over the heads of two more helots and slit their bellies. Another pair of Spartans, whom Dienekes had treated but did not know, swung fire hardened clubs sculpted to an edge to break bones and sunder skulls. In seconds there were eight bodies on the ground, only one remained. Surrounded, the sniveling helot leader clutched his rusty sickle as if it would save him.

"This one we'll take back to Sharktooth for questioning." Insolence licked his smile the way Thrasilaos had always done, and the Weeper saw in the moonlight that some of Tellis's teeth had been likewise filed into fangs. The slave's eyes bulged. He put the sickle to his own neck.

"Wait." Dienekes tried to place himself between predator and prey as they jockeyed around him in an anxious dance. The helot scampered for his life. The Krypteians were merely playing with their food. "He doesn't know anything. He's not a rebel. I heard them talking."

"A ruse, Weeper." Alpheos snatched at the sickle and laughed as it hissed through the air, inches from his fingers.

"No, that one only wanted to help his daughter." He pointed and sighed at the corpse with a sharpened sapling through its throat. "It's why they came to me. They knew I was a healer."

"Oh, is that right?" Maron kicked the slave in the back and circled to kick him back down when he rose. Another move learned from Thrasilaos. "Trying to kill our surgeon? Hit us where it hurts, eh?"

"No! Never! I never did-" A slingstone smacked the dogskin in the mouth, he fell to the earth weeping and bleeding, teeth broken. One of the other Krypteians juggled three more stones, ready to throw. His name was Lagos, their hunter. Dienekes had sewed him back together twice already.

"Just listen to me!" Dienekes put his back to the servant, made himself as big as he could. "I heard everything, it's not what you think."

"Oh is that why they knocked you on the skull? I can see the blood, Weeper. Tied you up?" Tellis motioned to the marks on Di's wrists from the bindings, the broken leather thong on the ground. "You gone native, Di? What's wrong with you?"

"No, they didn't... well they did... but-"

"Liars!" Dien turned to face the scream from behind him. "Liars!" The helot screeched as he raked the sickle across Di's chest, opening him from the left shoulder to the right hip.

He watched the wound trickle slowly at first, then flood. Another moment and his whole torso was wine-dark with blood. He was unaware of the twins slicing around him to tear the Messenian apart. Di pressed his fingers to the wound and flesh yawned open at the touch.

Λ

"It's not that bad." He said to Tellis, who gawked in horror. "It's not that bad," he said again, as blackness crept in the corners of his eyes. "It's not that bad." He said, and collapsed.

Λ

Forty-one

He woke intermittently. He was being bound in a stretcher made from his cloak. He was being carried. He was being laid by a fire.

A fire? Who lit a fire? Bad idea. Someone might find them.

Hands shook his shoulders as dawn crept up in the east.

"Dienekes, wake up. Damn it, Weeper. Tell us what to do. How do we fix you?"

"It's not that bad…" Dien reassured them before passing back into black.

Searing pain woke him next. His hands lurched to his chest, but his wrists were lashed to his gurney. He bit into the stick tied between his teeth. Alpheos poured boiling wine into the rift in his chest and Maron followed with a glowing red knife to burn the wound shut. This stopped the bleeding.

The pain kept him awake that day. Still weak, but able to sit up and speak. The gash was not deep, but long. The flesh was already purpling under the surface, his blood pooling under the burns. But he had felt worse. He did what he could to clean it and help his brothers with their more superficial cuts. Then the fever took him.

He saw Ono. He saw Kleo. He saw his father, whose face remained in shadow. Lions the size of mice and mice the size of lions spoke to him alongside dead kings, but he could remember their speech no longer than it took for them to speak, except for one voice.

"…see you run again, boy." The phantom cough rattled in his ears. "…Race again, one last time."

The others sheltered him under leafy branches so he would not be found when they had to leave his side. He shivered and burned in his sweat-soaked cloak, alone. It was the dead of winter and they had to throw a second cloak over his head to keep the damp from freezing to his brow.

Through the leaves he saw the sun spin around him on a wheel.

Day-night-day-night-day-night.

He was occasionally aware of a Krypteian cleaning his wound, dripping water on his tongue. Small morsels were pushed between his lips and rough hands worked his jaw to chew for him. He feebly swatted them away. Later, boys fearfully asked his advice. How to heal, how to cure. Someone was hurt, he could tell, he needed to help them. It was his job. He tried to rise and was pushed back down.

"This is how we yet serve." He groaned.

"Is it this one? Is this the herb?" A verdant bundle waved in front of his blind eyes.

"No…" He whispered, recognizing the plants by their smell. "The one… The one that turns your piss green."

Day-night-day-night-day-night.

"Race again… one last time…."

Bitter tinctures were poured down his throat. He soiled himself. He shivered so fiercely that he felt his bones knocking together. More bitter tinctures, more spinning of the sun, more green piss.

Day-night-day-night-day-night.

And then his fever broke.

He had sweltered so long in delirium that clear senses felt wrong. The smell of meat and smoke in his nose was pungent and nauseating. As alien as the feeling in his fingertips. The crackling of a nearby fire in his ears, the warmth of the sun on his face through his bracken shelter, all were forgotten sensations he had to decipher. The pain across his chest had not subsided, but it felt good. It felt right. It grounded him to the here and now, an anchor by which he reacquainted himself with his faculties. The pain became his compass.

He turned his head, and through the side of his shrub-tent saw Tellis, grumbling to himself while he clumsily pounded a poultice into Dien's stolen mortar. A long afternoon shadow crept up behind Insolence. Then two, then three long shadows, looming closer. Tellis, cursing into his concoction, did not see them. They held knives.

Dienekes did not feel himself silently rise from his mound of weeds. There was a job to do and his body did it unbidden. There was a clear question and a decisive answer, no room for doubt. The three Messenians fell to the ground with their own small blades inside of them. Only then did Tellis turn.

"Dienekes! What are you…?" He saw the bodies. Saw the blood. Saw Di's chest heaving from the brief burst of effort. "Oh. So you had it in you after all… In broad daylight, too? They're getting brazen." He nodded, then reached over his small fire and pulled a roasting spit from its braces. "Here." He held a crispy fowl to his friend. "You must be hungry."

Dienekes was famished.

Λ

Forty-two

Krateros rose before dawn, as was his custom. His wife still slept, along with the rest of the city, save the sentries and the eirene. He dressed and drank his fill of water from a basin in the corner, the only furniture in his bedchamber beside his bed, and performed his morning ablutions from phials of oil on the basin stand. Olive for purity… lavender for serenity… hyacinth for wisdom… mint for vigilance… He combed them through his hair and beard, massaged them into his face and chest, lingering on his sore neck.

Helots silently padded in and out to lay a modest breakfast spread in his dining room. More olives, cheese, boiled eggs and a strip of beef… He paid the slaves no mind. They had brought him more than usual, which he would not have bothered speaking on, but they had brought him wine as well. Krateros had openly abstained from wine since the death of Kleomenes. The smell alone plunged him into melancholy. These were not his usual servants, his household knew better. The realization snapped him from his morning fog. He drew a small knife from a sheath hanging round his neck, a keepsake from his fallen king, and stalked down the hallway to the courtyard where his outdoor kitchens were.

Whispers cut the crisp autumn air.

"When do you think he'll notice?"

Notice? Notice what? The wine? Was it poisoned? Krateros sneered.

"He's old. It's early. He's not expecting us. Keep it together."

"But he will notice, won't he?"

"Eventually. He's a polemarch for a reason."

"I just hope that moon was full. It's so hard to tell some nights. One sliver of waxing off, and the ephors will have our asses."

"We went when we had to. Another night and he would have been looking for us."

Krateros lunged through the threshold to the courtyard and shouldered into the four conspirators. With a single sweep of his oaken arm, he tossed three to the ground and slammed the fourth to the wall. His fist bunched the Messenian's roughspun tunic around his throat, and the tip of his small knife drew a drop of blood from the helot's chin.

But it wasn't a helot.

"Hello, Uncle." Dienekes grinned at him from beneath a dogskin cap. The other three rose tentatively. Their chests shuddered, timid laughter trying and failing to rise after the old man knocked their wind out. All four were members of Disappointment, disguised and dog-skin hooded as slaves.

Krateros sheathed his knife, and struggled to conceal his joy at seeing them well.

"Good. You're back. Well done. Come. Sit. Eat with me. I'll have my servants bring more. That is, if you've left them unharmed…."

Λ

Forty-three

Their stunt did not go unrewarded. Creeping past all the citizen-guards of the polis was no small feat, let alone infiltrating a polemarch's own chambers. Their success was mostly due to the twins' expertise, but all four were credited. Spartans were not keen on gossip, but some news begs to be spread. They had been selected for the hippeis, the elite personal guard of the kings. Only the three hundred most formidable troops of all of Sparta's soldiers were tapped for the honor. They would have to complete the final probationary period of the agoge before being officially instated, but their pride was no less for it. They were home.

Even greater than the joy at their selection was that of being reunited with their brothers. Boys peppered back into the city over the next several days and into the next weeks. They resumed barrack life, eating and sleeping and training together, but they had no orders but to keep themselves clean and well-behaved. Training resumed, but more out of habit than edict. Some visited the homes of their birth, but most of the returned recruits spent their hours near the entrance to the city, standing by ready to smear a rough and rowdy welcome all over the boys coming home behind them. It was an infectious jubilation. Perioikoi dropped their duties to join Disappointment and other squads in celebrating the return of their own, boys they did not even known, but who had known the same struggle. They were of one blood, one family, even if they did not know each others' names.

Two weeks passed and the full moon had waned to half, nearly all the boys were home. Dienekes and his friends were sharing fruit and loitering in view of the road when Thrasilaos materialized in their circle. Di choked on an apricot. After everything they had been through, the man was still a menace. Instead of the standard crimson cloak over his shoulders, Thrasilaos wore a lion skin. Dienekes still looked for the whip tucked in his belt and sighed relief when he did not see it.

"Good. You're all here. Come. You are to receive your mess assignments." He said, and walked away.

"What? No, we're still waiting on Aristaios." Tellis, ever the leader, would wait until all of his squad had come home.

"No we are not." Thrasilaos did not break stride, forcing them to follow to continue speaking.

"He's here then? I never thought we'd miss that big bastard coming in. You remember the time he-"

"Aristaios is dead."

Disappointment did not speak. Did not breathe. Thrasilaos turned back with an eyebrow raised in challenge.

They had spent thirteen years with him, they could read his face when he wanted them to.

You're soldiers aren't you? He thought to them.

Soldiers die.

"How?" Tellis eventually asked.

"Infection, it would seem."

"Infection?" Dienekes was astonished. Until now he'd half believed that Aristaios couldn't die at all, but succumb to fever? To sickness? He had been so strong.

"I found him curled up in the skin of a lion. This lion." He brushed a hand over the hide on his shoulders. "I found the site where they fought. Aristaios killed it with his knife. He lived long enough to skin it and eat its heart, but his own wounds were too severe. They festered and he died of rot."

The late spring air chilled. The birds stopped chirping. Disappointment now numbered only ten.

"Come on then. Your assignments await. Or shall I stroke your hair while you cry." Even for Thrasilaos, that was cold. One of his own wards was dead and he gave no sign of caring, even sported Aristaios's own kill like a trophy. The old hates Dienekes harbored for Sharktooth had softened, forgotten during his time in the wilderness, but now returned inflamed.

Worse than the hate, was the guilt.

Infection!?

Dienekes could not swallow the thought.

I could have healed him. Why didn't he find me? Did the others know? Did they tell him about me? They must have, everyone else knew, why didn't he come for help?

And then he remembered. In all the time they had known each other, Aristaios had never asked for help. When it was offered, he refused. He might have been the strongest of them, was easily the toughest. He could do alone what took the rest of them working together to accomplish. And that was why he died. He had chosen to be alone. No matter how strong, no one man was stronger than the phalanx. Each man had to make their own contribution to the whole and let his brothers' strengths fill his weaknesses.

This is how we yet serve, whispered the ghost of Ono. Promise me... A forgotten purpose woke inside him. He had debts to pay.

Λ

"Thrasilaos, where is Krateros?"

"Attending business above your rank, I'm sure. I'm sure he'll come coddle you when he is finished."

Dien outpaced his once drill sergeant, turned to block his path, and spat through clenched teeth.

"I asked you a question, Spartan."

Thrasilaos smiled hungrily at him, lifting himself to Di's height to put his nose to the boy's in provocation.

"You defy me, Weeper? It seems I gave the name of Insolence to the wrong child."

"You're not my eirene anymore, Spartan. Answer me or I will find him myself."

"Your orders may pass through me, little boy, but they come from the state. Abide them or find yourself accused of treason."

"So be it. If you won't help me, then I shall speak with the state myself." Behind Thrasilaos, Dienekes saw the jaws of his nine remaining squadmates drop in terror and awe. The traces of pride and admiration in the blank of their stares egged him past the point of no return. He pressed a finger into the man's breastplate. "And you, killer of slaves, murderer, sneakthief, beater of helpless children," Di swallowed hard, steeled himself. "Can go fuck yourself."

He jogged away before his once master could retaliate but not so fast that he might seem to be fleeing in fear. Which he was.

"I will find you, boy. There is unfinished business between us, son of Hegisistratos!" The threat, or the promise, followed Di as he scampered towards the capitol hall.

By a stroke of grace, he found Krateros descending the sandstone stairs between obligations.

"My boy, my PEER!" Krateros knocked Dien's handshake aside and embraced him. "Are you not meeting your new mess? What brings you to the-"

"I need a favor." Dienekes interrupted.

"I suppose it would depend on the favor." Krateros said after a moment's hesitation, but Dienekes knew the man. The gleam in his eye showed that he already agreed.

"I need to speak with the Ephors. I have a promise to keep."

Λ

Forty-four

"This is… Unusual." Klytomedes, eldest of the ephors, regarded Di with polite suspicion. "But the polemarch assures us of the validity of your petition. What is your query?"

Dienekes did not waste words on introduction.

"I wish to resume my place as a runner in the Panhellenic Games."

The five ephors exchanged passive glances. Some shared whispers and small nods.

"It is my understanding that your restriction from the games was punishment for behavior unbefitting a Lakonian. You shamed your country. Do you dispute the justice of your sentence?"

"No, sir. It was fair. Merciful, even. I was young and stupid and succumbed to hubris. I allowed myself to be corrupted by the glamours of victory. I used my gift to pursue personal glory before honoring my home. I turned my back on those who had helped me, who had put their faith in me. I wallowed in my pride and forgot the tenets of our people, and I failed in the sight of gods and men."

"So…" The ephors wavered but remained patient. "Why should we reward this character by allowing it to retake the position it once disgraced?"

"Because I have learned. It has taken time, but my selfishness has been tempered by the death of friends. My pride-fogged sight has been cleared by the patient guidance of my elders and betters." From the corner of his eye, Di wondered if he saw Krateros blush. "I understand now that no victory comes from me alone. I am nothing without my comrades, without my ancestors. No matter how potent my individual skill, I stand to achieve nothing without standing on the shoulders of the giants who walked before and beside me."

"And now that you have grown you wish to redeem yourself in the stadion?"

"I do. But not for myself. For the nation. I have been given a gift by the gods. It is my duty to give that gift back to Sparta by showing our combined might at the games. I have learned that it is not my speed. It is our speed. I am but one link in the chain, one shield in the wall. This is how I yet serve."

"You speak like a poet, Spartan." Noikodos, another of the ephors furrowed his brow at Di. "You have indeed shown growth, and the sentiment is not lost on us. But we have other runners, runners who have not shown disrespect on the hallowed sands. You won many wreaths, but the decree at your failing was to bar you from the games for life. You had your time. It is now theirs."

One of the hippeis guards standing silent sentry in a shadowed corner stepped into the light from his post.

"Sirs." He said. "If I may speak..."

"You may not." The ephors were surprised at this breach in protocol. "It is not your place. Return to your station."

"I will hear what he has to say," said a Peer seated on a bench to the side with the ephors' attendants.

"Very well then." Klytomedes acquiesced, wagging a finger at the guardsman. "But know that this will not do in the future."

Di looked closer at the Peer who spoke, who had evaded his notice till now. He realized the only rank the elder council would have deferred to was a king. On his second glance the resemblance to his elder brother was clear. This was Leonidas.

"Speak, Spartan." Said the king.

The guard came to stand by Dienekes and removed his helm. It was Echemmon. Dienekes's heart leapt.

"I am one of those other runners you mentioned. And though it has been my privilege to serve my country in competition, and I have wreaths for the diaulos, I have not won the stadion since the same time Dienekes has ceased to compete."

"Well then neither of you should race, it would seem." Noikodos was growing bored. "We are many thousands, it should not be so hard to find another."

"With respect, Sir, I do believe it will be. I have returned defeated for years, it is true, but I have at least proven to always be second fastest in Hellas, with third trailing by a distant margin. As I am always second, the same man is always first."

"We have more important matters to attend than a footrace, gentlemen, if we could-"

"Let him finish." Leonidas again interrupted Noikodos. Dienekes suspected that Leo pressed the issue just to raise the stuffy old man's ire. "Who is this man who beats you?"

"He is a shepherd from Orchomenos. His name is Asopichos."

It had been an age since Dien had heard the name. A rush of emotions welled in him, memories of the happy times they shared, regret at the friendship he had soured. All the more reason to return to the games. He owed his old friend an apology.

"I am one of the few to have had the opportunity to race both Asopichos and Dienekes. And it is my judgement that of the two, Dienekes, the little deer, is the faster."

"Is there no one else who can beat the Orchomene?" asked Leonidas.

Λ

"I do believe that Dienekes is the only one who can. But you don't have to take my word for it. Dienekes has already beaten him. Six times, if I do recall. I would gladly step down from racing the stadion if it meant that he would take my place." He looked to Di, his eyes glittering.

So filled with gratitude was the Weeper that he nearly lived up to his name.

"If I may speak as well?" Another guardsmen stepped from his post. Noikodos wrung his hands and shook his head, but allowed Leonidas the chance to answer.

"Gods, you're a big one, aren't you?" Said the king. "Speak. But be brief or you'll give my ephor the fits."

Dienekes recognized Polymedes before he removed his helmet. No one else in Sparta shook the ground when they walked. He did not stop at his helm, he removed his breastplate as well, and unlaced his tunic to bare his chest. A knotted cross of scar tissue snaked over his engorged muscles.

"Dienekes gave me this scar when I was a soldier of the Krypteia, and he was just a boy." The ephors and the king looked back and forth between the hulking Polymedes and the scrawny Weeper. "I wore no breastplate for no Argive piece would fit me. But I had a sword, a spear, a shield… And Dienekes had only a small knife." Even Noikodos seemed impressed by this. "He doesn't look like much. And he's a bit of a whiner. But none of that matters when he sets his mind to a mission. When you throw him into the fire, he shines."

"It's settled then. Throw him into the fire we shall." Leonidas clapped his hands once. "Thank you Echemmon, thank you Polymedes. You may return to your post. Dienekes, son of Hegisistratos, you will compete in my name at the next games. Bring me a seventh crown."

"Thank you, King Leonidas. I will not let you down." Di forced himself to keep his composure until Krateros had escorted him down the steps and out of sight where the two exploded, laughing and howling and shaking each others' shoulders.

For you, Ono. For you, Lysimachos. For you, Aristaios, he thought.

Breathless and redfaced with triumph, a sudden wonder needled into his mind.

"Krateros… How did Leonidas know my father's name?"

Krateros's lips moved, but no sound came. He struggled to find the words.

"I will tell you, young ingrate." Thrasilaos appeared in his way, never failing to make Di's pulse race. "I told you we had unfinished business."

Λ

Forty-five

"Come along then, Puddles!" Kleomenes shouted over his shoulder. "I'm getting thirsty!" The boy with the wineskins jogged closer but Kleo urged his horse a midge faster each time he came within reach of the king's outstretched hand.

"Nearly had it that time. And they tell me you're swift? Stratos, what do you call a swift puddle?"

"A stream? A brook? Can't say for sure." Hegisistratos waited on his own horse at the top of the next rise. "But I suspect we'll soon find one between your feet once my boy brings you your drink."

The king guffawed.

"I wonder how you'll tell us apart after." Kleo allowed the boy to catch up but clung to his hand and spurred his horse again, forcing the child into a run.

"Continue to torment my protege, my king," Stratos rolled his eyes at his liege, "and I will allow him the same privilege toward you. And call him by his real name if it please you, his eirene is not present."

"Forgive my addled memory, child. Remind me what your mother called you?" The boy mumbled something unintelligible. "Speak up?"

"His name is Thrasilaos. He is shy, and we are working on that. But you'd never know it to see him in the ring. He fights like an animal."

"Good! You can be my bodyguard." Kleo slapped his own neck and showed Thrasilaos the bloodspot of biting insect smeared on his palm. "You can see I have no shortage of enemies here. How did you come by the name of Puddles?"

The boy mumbled inaudibly again, staring at the ground.

"It was the first time he tasted the whip." Hegisistratos spoke for him again. "He wet himself."

"Ah." The king nodded, sipping a wineskin. "Did you scream?"

"No, sir." The boy managed.

"Did you cry?"

"No, sir."

"Did you fall to the ground?"

"No, sir."

"Only pissed yourself?"

"Yes, sir."

"Then your name is a mark of honor then, boy. Wear it proudly."

"Honor, sir?" Thrasilaos hazarded a glimpse at the king before averting his eyes, as if the king were the sun and too bright to look at.

"Yes, boy. I was exempt from the agoge, like all royal firstborns. But as a child I once ordered a slave to whip me. He struck me well. I did not piss myself. But I screamed, I fell to the ground, and I very nearly cried."

"Why, uh. Why he... you..." The boy seemed ever tongue tied.

"Why order him to whip me?"

"Yes, sir."

"Because I was curious. So bear your name well, Puddles, it shows you are stronger than the king."

"A king. Not the king." Hegisistratos reminded him.

"Don't you worry, Demaratos is loathe to let anyone forget him. He had the nerve to tell me about his own Olympic victory for the hundred thousandth time when he found out I was coming. Told me to say hello to his statue, can you believe the cunt on him? I'll wipe my ass on it, hallowed ground or not."

"As far as I know, he is our only king with an Olympic title." Onesiphoros shrugged, riding his own horse behind Thrasilaos.

"That's because there's no competition for being handsome." Kleo beamed back. "Even still, chariots? What kind of Spartan races chariots. It's the horses doing all the work. Thessalian horses at that. It stinks. Posturing and privilege."

"A son of Anaxandridas speaks of privilege? Spare us..." If Hegisistratos rolled his eyes any harder, he'd have sprained them.

"I still lead my armies from the front. Can he say that from his chariot? And how many times have I challenged him to single combat? And how many times have I gone denied? Wrestling, boxing, wooden swords... he clearly fears me!"

"I think he knows you fight dirty." Ono suggested.

"Pankration then! That's nothing but dirty fighting. Boy," he craned in the saddle to look at Thrasilaos. "If you ever fight the pankration, remember to bite. Nobody seems to bite in pankration. Wasted opportunity to fight without rules and not bite."

"Not everyone is as unconcerned with honor as you, Kleo. Nor as ready to spill blood." Hegisistratos's tone indicated he spoke from memory.

"This one is!" The king winked at Thrasilaos. "I can see it in his eyes. There's a beast in him, clawing to get out. Besides, honor only serves to get good men killed. Don't worry, Puddles. They can keep their honor as long as they have us to do their dirty work." He took another drink.

∧

"Thrasilaos, come." Hegisistratos dismounted at a crossroads. "Take my horse for me. I need to stretch my legs, and it's time you've learned to ride."

"Perfect. Teach him at your leisure, we will camp here tonight." Kleo dismounted his horse as well.

"Here? This is no place to camp." The shoulder of the road was scant and they were barricaded on either side by dense foliage. A narrow pathway led through the thicket to a clearing where many had camped before, but it was not what Hegisistratos would have considered a defensible position. "And the sun is still high. Only King Kleomenes would take the long road to Olympia and still make every pleasure stop."

"Patience." Kleo stretched, cracking his legs and back "Your council is wise, but you do not know all. I suspect we will be receiving visitors tonight."

"Your secret keeping makes it harder for me to do my job."

"Ease, brother. You've only just been tapped as Polemarch, no need to carry the whole world on your shoulders yet. We are still in Lakedaimon, our enemies here are little more than biting flies and things that crawl."

"And seditious helots." Hegisistratos glared into the thickets on either side of the trail.

"As I said." Kleo growled. "Biting flies and things that crawl." He settled himself on his back, one wineskin in his arms and another for a pillow. "Axe! Sickle! Make me a fire!"

Two dark, hairy barbarians casually emerged from the foliage, spooking Thrasilaos and the caravan's horses. Ono cursed a tirade, barely clinging to the saddle. They ignored the boy and the cripple, but shushed the animals with gentle hands despite the protests of startled Lakonians.

"Leave them be!" Kleo shouted, wine spilling from his mouth down his front. "They are friends! And good with horses. At least they should be. What use is a Skythian who doesn't know horses..."

"Bah!". One of the foreigners spat.

"You couldn't have told me your barbarian friends were coming?" Hegisistratos helped Ono to the ground from his saddle straps, still cursing. The healer had not yet well adapted to the loss of his legs.

"How did they do that?" Thrasilaos, wide eyed, asked his mentor. "They came from nowhere."

"They're hunters. Men of the wild. Sneaky bastards, in other words. They'll teach you if you like? They may look like filthy centaurs, but don't be fooled. They're my sworn men. The powers in Skythia are now... Shall we say, tentative? So they reasoned they were better off with me than to see how the cards fell at home. Their kinsmen would flay them if they ever tried to return." He winked at Hegisistratos, who knew well enough that Kleo was hiding the whole truth. "Dishonorable as I am, You can

Λ

trust them. They can understand our language, but seem to have no desire to speak it. So good luck deciphering their garble."

"Pbbbbbth," one of the bearded Tartars blew a raspberry at the king, who chuckled.

Thrasilaos begged his mentor with a gaze.

"It could be a useful skill." Hegisistratos pondered. "I suppose I can teach you to ride any day, and you only have this little time with Kleo and his… friends." He eyed their leather and fur with suspicion until one of the two approached him and aggressively stuck out his hand to shake. They had met before, and Stratos was reluctantly learning to value their presence. He had a hard time not respecting a man who could stare him down. "If the king says it's alright, then I accept." He shook the hand. "Your Krypteia will come soon enough."

The Skythians, Axe and Sickle as Kleo called them, took a giddy Thrasilaos into the wilderness. But not before whistling for a third to come from the bushes. A young man, barely older than Thrasilaos materialized just as his elders had. A bow and a quiver of arrows hung on his back. In each of his hands was a rabbit.

"Ah, Shukxa, my boy!" The king clasped the youth's hand in both of his grizzly mitts. "Men, meet Shukxa. He is the nephew of Axe, or Sickle, I forget which. Maybe both. But he's a good boy. And clever too. Perhaps even more clever than I." Kleo's eyes misted wistfully. "His mother certainly was."

The young man built a fire while the king made himself comfortable and sang raunchy songs with Ono while the rest of the Spartans struggled with idleness. Some bathed in a stream down the hill, fished or foraged for food, but all of them save Puddles resented the downtime.

The sun fell, night came, and voices worked their way south on the road.

Kleo heard them first, he had been listening.

"Brother! I knew he'd be coming this way." He wobbled to his feet and drunkenly barreled toward   the torchlight of the newcomers. "Brootherrrrr!"

"Kleomenes?" Said a confused voice in the dark.

"BROTHERRR!" Kleo hugged Leonidas around the waist and swung him into the air.

"Hold! Hold, dammit!" Leo fought down to his own feet and punched his brother in the cuirass. "Bastard!" He hissed. "I told you, not in front of the troops!" Before embracing his brother back and stopping to punch him again. "Gods, you reek of drink. There are children present, have you no shame?"

"Well had you not been so damn slow on the road I would have had less time to imbibe, wouldn't I? Krateros! You're here too! Happy day!" He hugged the captain off the ground as well, though with greater difficulty. "Come! Sit by my fire! Eat! Drink! Tell me of your travels. How long has it been? Is our baby brother here too?"

Λ

Kleomenes called to the rest of the convoy. "Kleombrotos! Are you here? No? Not here? Shame. I've missed him even more than I missed you..."

"The fire is too high." Stratos grumbled.

"I am an old man." Kleo kicked another log onto the coals. "My feet get cold."

"You're telling the entire world we're here. All the worse now that you've sent Leo's guard away."

Other than the princes, polemarch, Skythians and surgeon, only seven Spartiates remained to escort them. And Thrasilaos.

"Let them come. If they are friend I will toast them. If not, then they shall learn why we call baby Krateros the Wall."

"You flatter me, Lord." Krateros hid a smile.

"Of course I do. You're entirely too terrifying to risk being anywhere but on your good side." The king burped.

"Oh, then by all means, ingratiate yourself."

"The Peloponnesian Punisher! The Terror of Taygetos!" The king burped again. "Bearstrangler! Boarbasher! Merchant of Murder! Manripper and Red Right Hand of Hades!"

"Did you just make those up?" Stratos asked.

"Aye. And I wrote songs to go with them. Would you like to hear?"

"Please, no." Leo interrupted.

"Kleombrotos always liked my songs." Kleomenes pouted. "Especially the one about the Olympics trials where Krateros scrubbed the wrestling sands with your face."

"If I recall correctly," Leonidas glared, "He did the same to you."

"I must have forgotten to include that verse."

"Should a poet not tell the whole truth?"

Kleo shrugged. "Indict my creative license when you're the one writing the songs, little brother."

"Is it true? What they say about you?" Thrasilaos, still bashful, asked Krateros as he refilled the captain's cup with water.

"What is it they say?" Krateros raised an eyebrow.

"That you killed a hundred men in one night. With your bare hands."

"No, boy." Krateros shook his head. "They were not quite a hundred. And they were not men."

"Biting flies and things that crawl." Kleo growled, suddenly hateful.

"Biting flies are not to be underestimated." Ono grumbled sourly. "They can still cost a man his life. Or his legs."

"Enough." Hegisistratose rose. "I will not have my student's head darkened by

∧

your black fantasies. Come, Thrasilaos. I wish to bathe. You will show me what you have learned from the Skythians."

"They call this the nightstep."

"I thought they didn't speak?"

"They don't. Shukxa translated."

Hegisistratos splashed around in the shallow stream like a child, blowing bubbles and squirting water through his fist.

"See, your your arms when you walk, twisting your spine. Right leg, left arm, left leg, right arm..." Thrasilaos demonstrated the technique. "But if you step without twisting, and reach with your feet instead of striding...Right arm right leg, left arm left leg... the weight your toe before your heel..." His movements were still awkward but the Skythians standing by nodded approval.

"It looks slow." The Polemarch frowned.

"It is slower, yes. But it is stealthy. Silent. And you can adjust your step after taking it. No more tripping or bumping in the dark."

"An assassin's trick." Hegistratos bordered on disapproval.

"It has other uses." Thrasilaos admitted. "Once I show my brothers, we can steal enough food to get fat!"

"I'll pretend I didn't hear that."

"Hear what?"

"Cheeky bugger." Stratos squirted a jet of water at his pupil. "Don't let the others hear you being so familiar. They will expect me to flog you."

The Skythians chuckled at this.

So they did understand Doric. Stratos confirmed in his head. The one called Sickle smiled horribly. His teeth had been filed into pointed fangs. At least Stratos assumed they had been filed. He was not convinced a Tartars wouldn't be born that way. He was not fond of foreigners. Even moreso, he did not like that he was growing fond of these foreigners, pointed teeth besides

The wind changed. The Skythian's snapped their noses up, sniffing the air. In the bushes surrounding, the chirp of crickets stopped short.

"Boy, my shield." Krateros was on his feet.

"What?" Thrasilaos hesitated.

"My shield, boy! Now!"

Λ

Forty-six

A nimals and men howled in the thickets to either side of the water trail. Stones and sharpened tools fell on them from all sides. The polemarch had no time to dress, so he abandoned his armor, snapped up his squire and ran. Thrasilaos couldn't breathe, clenched so tight to his mentor's chest. His arm burned protecting both of them with the heavy shield, and in his other arm he clutched what little of his master's wargear he had the time to grab. The Skythians stayed behind to cover their escape. By the time they made it to the others, there was already blood on the ground.

A crowd of helots ransacked the abandoned campground. They fought over the arms and armor of two fallen Spartiates. They held iron and bronze trophies over their heads with the dismembered limbs of hoplites still strapped inside. They devoured sacks of rations, drank or poured out wineskins, and tried to steal the horses until they realized Spartan horses fought back. Anything not of immediate value was piled on the now raging bonfire. Through the trees, Thrasilaos could see them dancing in its flames.

The princes and their Spartiates had retreated to the small clearing at the trailhead to the river. The four remaining of Leo's escort clogged the entrance with their shields. The bravest of helots taunted them and threw stones and hatchets, but stayed safely out of reach, knowing the guard would not leave their king to fight back.

Behind the bodyguards, Kleo and Krateros shouldered Onesiphoros, his broken legs dangling. The surrounding thicket was dense, but not impenetrable. It thwarted the bulk of the rebels from advancing off the trails, but a few daring Messenians needled their way through the tangled grove to dive at random into the clearing and make themselves a hero.

Leonidas stalked around his brother, killing the would-be assassins as they came.

"Two princes in the same place, Kleo!?" He roared. "This is your folly!" He pointed a dripping spear at his king.

"I told no one. Who else could have known?" Kleo mumbled, dissociated by guilt. He gawked at the distant red soup that remained of the two who had already died saving him.

"You're not the only one with spies, Kleo." Stratos put Thrasilaos down beside them and strapped on the swordbelt and leather skirt the squire had salvaged. Then took his white shield. His grieves and sandals had been saved too, but there was no time to assemble them. "Grab a weapon boy. You're going to be blooded today."

Thrasilaos scanned the ground and reached for a javelin. It was once a hoe or a spade, heated and beaten into a killing point. A brown hand grabbed his.

"No." Said Shukxa. "No room for that. Stay small. Stay quick." He handed Thrasilaos a blade from his own belt, as long as a xiphos, but curved wickedly forward. "Have you killed a man before?" The boy asked. Thrasilaos said nothing. "Well. Let's hope you develop a taste for it. And quickly."

"We can't escape by road," Stratos took stock. "There are too many. And there were more at the river."

Thrasilaos's eyes widened when Stratos turned away from him. Darts and crude arrows jutted from his muscled back. More slits wept red where javelins had penetrated and fallen out. The squire had protected their front with his master's shield, but the master had protected the squire with his own flesh.

The two Skythians retreated up the path from the river. Bows in hand, they took turns firing on their pursuers while the other dropped back and turned to cover the other. Sickle was bleeding. Axe was bleeding badly. They shook their heads at Stratos. There would be no escape that way either.

"Hades!" The polemarch roared. "We'll have to fight. No choice. And we'll have to fight on their terms."

"Isadoros escaped on horseback to warn the guards on the road." Said Krateros. "They can't be far."

"They could be hours away by now." Stratos grimaced.

"Or only minutes."

"Then there is hope."

Stones and sharpened sticks hurtled at them at random from the darkness. Thrown from inexpert hands, most yawed to strike flat or missed their targets entirely. Crooked arrows fired from makeshift bows twisted in flight and veered wildly from their mark. Though the missiles themselves were mostly futile, they threatened overwhelming numbers.

Enough insurgents had gathered on the road to brave a rush at the four hoplites in their way. They swung wildly with picks and scythes, more a danger to each other than the Spartans who ripped them apart. The charge broke and fled almost as quickly as it had come, but the number of dead was barely a fraction of those still surrounding the Lakonians. More still crept from the bushes, but the dense foliage forced them to attack one or two at a time. Even so, they came as quickly as Stratos and Leo could kill them.

Λ

Thrasilaos wheeled on a rustling in the shrubs. He held his ground, the knuckles of both hands white around Shukxa's falcatta. The smiling helot held a bow. The arrow on his string was knotted and warped, but it wouldn't matter so near his target. He would have easily shot Thrasilaos before the boy could close the distance, but a spinning hatchet split his head like a melon before the bow was drawn.

"You can start helping any time now!" Shukxa barked, pulling his little axe from the helot's brains.

Thrasilaos swallowed his shame and pounced on the next to emerge. He and the helot teased and feinted at each other. It was the first knife fight for both of them. Spastic and graceless, less concerned with cutting than being cut themselves. Thrasilaos swung high-low-high, changing levels like a wrestler. His first blood drawn was tentative and shallow. Hesitant. More a question than an answer. The next blow was decisive. His falcatta plunged in the helot's mouth and out his neck.

"Don't think of it as a swordfight." Shukxa noticed his inexperience. "You're no good yet in a swordfight. But you're a brawler, no? So brawl. This-" he tapped the Skythian sickle-sword with an arrow. "Isn't a sword. It's just another finger. Fight how you'd fight in the ring."

Another assault bounced off the four guardsmen at the trailhead. No one attack would turn the tide, but each retreat left the Spartans bleeding from another superficial wound. And they were adding up.

"They know I'm here." Kleo said to Krateros. They each fought with one hand, still holding Ono between them. "They know I'm here. And they won't stop coming for me."

"That's it?" Krateros scoffed. "That's all the insight you have?" He swung at a rebel and missed, too encumbered with the surgeon to use his reach. "And they dare call you wise."

"Think harder, Spartan." Kleo threw a knife into the helot Krateros had missed. "They know where I am. They have me surrounded and will not stop until I am dead. This is their plan. So let's make it harder for them. Let's see what they do when they don't know where I am."

Without warning, he pushed Ono's weight onto Krateros and dove into the thicket alone.

His Spartans screamed after him, but he was gone. Only the Skythians dove into the bush behind him.

Λ

Forty-seven

With Axe and Sickle gone, it fell to Shukxa and Thrasilaos to guard the rear. They fought from the sides of the trail, dancing from tree to tree to avoid the barrage of improvised weapons. Shukxa drew arrows from his quiver a fistful at a time. Holding them parallel between the fingers of his off-hand, he could nock and draw one the same stroke to loose two or even three shots a second. He broke up their number, forcing the front runners to face Thrasilaos one at a time.

The pankrationist was barely aware of their presence. He let his training take over, mind becalmed. He was an Olympian, after all. Though absent, his eirene's voice barked orders in his head, walking him through the complicated maneuvers they had drilled into second nature. Thrasilaos executed like a cold machine, no different from fighting his brothers on the sands of home except for the blood splashing across his face. He would not remember the faces of the men he killed. He didn't even see them. Painted on the back of his eyes was the vision of the bloody barbs in his mentor's back. They were his fault, the cost of his carelessness. He would see that cost repaid.

Behind them, the Spartans cursed their king while scrambling for a way to protect him. They could hear him fighting and bellowing from one side, fearing the worst when he fell quiet, only to hear him roar back to the fight from the opposite flank. Disorganized as they were, the helots did their best to chase him.

"He's here! He's here!" One would raise their voice only to have it cut off at the neck. The mobs surged this way and that, washing up and down the forked roadways like water in the bottom of a bowl.

Occupied with the king, attacks on the clearing slowed to a trickle. Stratos raged harder at the lulls than he did the helots. They were helpless to defend Kleomenes from the clearing, but they could not follow without losing the only advantage they had.

The clearing began to fill with smoke. The bonfire had spread into the treeline. The late summer growth was dry and caught quickly. In minutes, the Spartans could no longer spot the helots' silhouettes through the trees. They saw only flames.

"They're trying to burn us out!" Krateros shouted.

"No they're not!" Kleo returned to the clearing, looking pleased with himself. He held a torch in each hand.

"You did this?" Leonidas was relieved to see his brother whole, but veiled it in anger.

"Let's see them sneak through the trees when they're on fire."

"And when the fire dies?"

"Let's hope I have another clever ruse by then." He tossed his two torches into the darkness at the opposite treeline to encourage the blaze.

The screams of broiling assassins widened his wine-stained smile.

There was a brief respite while the rebel ringleaders rallied their rabble.

"Put me down." Onesiphoros tried to pry Krateros off.

"But…"

"I said put me down, man. I'm already useless in a fight. As long as you cling to me, you'll be useless too." Ono broke his reluctant brother's grip one thick finger at a time and slumped to the ground. Krateros bent to pick him back up and Ono rang his helmet with a fist. "You've saved my life twice already." He coughed. "Go save someone else."

"With me, Krateros!" Stratos ended the discussion, knowing that Krateros could not refuse an order.

He bulwarked the path to the river between Leonidas and the polemarch, supported by Shukxa and Thrasilaos. Kleo and the Skythians joined the four guards at the trailhead.

"You want me?" Kleo dared them. "Who among you has the heart to kill a king? Show him to me! I am waiting!"

Knowing time was on their side, the ringleaders clamored to keep their horde in check. But the mob could not resist the king's challenge. They poured in force to the clearing. The hail of missiles stopped, all of their number devoted to the charge.

Finally, the bodies of the slain were piling. The Spartans held a precarious line on either side of the trap's fanged maw, but thrust out into its jaws with their spears and pried its bite back open. Between them, Ono calmly lit a pipe.

A sharpened shovel nicked the jugular of one of the four guards. He was a seasoned veteran and had seen countless die from a similar blow. Knowing he had only seconds to live, he barreled forward into the mob.

"TELEMAKOOOS!" He thundered his own name as he died so his victims would know their killer.

Helots were crushed before and beneath him, many more knocked to his sides. The Messenians turned their weapons on him, stabbing an already dead man and freeing his brothers to avenge him without resistance. Seamlessly, Kleo took his place in the line.

As they fought, the fire around them faded. The undergrowth had burnt away hot

Λ

and fast, but lacked the heat to immolate the trees. By Stratos's count, they had maybe halved the original attacking force, but they were still woefully outnumbered. They had only maybe minutes before the brushfire was spent, and nothing would stand in the way of Messenians pouring in from all sides.

Corpses piled high enough to break the rebel spirit. The Lakonians serenaded the escapees as they scampered, limped, or crawled away in pieces.

One man stood apart from his fleeing conspirators. He held the dogskin hat he had been forced to wear his entire life by Lakedaimon crumpled in his outstretched fist. He shouted to the meager wall of men."

"We want the kings. The rest of you… We don't care. Give us Kleomenes and Leonidas and you can go."

Shukxa answered for all of them by putting an arrow into his shoulder.

Thrasilaos saw Axe and Sickle glare daggers at the boy. Their ward hung his head. Thrasilaos had been given that same look a hundred times by his eirene for missing a killing blow. There would be punishment for his imperfection. If he survived.

"So be it." The helot growled. Ceremoniously, he threw his dogskin cap at their feet as the fire around them cooled to embers. "All our lives we have been dogs to you. Beaten and starved and whipped and caged- that is how you've treated your dogs. But we learned from you. We treat our dogs better. Now let's see how our dogs treat you." He put his fingers in his mouth and keened an earsplitting whistle. Shukxa's next arrow pierced the helot's whistling hand and pinned it to his face, but the barb did not reach his brain. He fell to the ground and kicked the dirt as his life drained in pink bubbles out his mouth.

More whistles piped up from the hills. The laughter of men boiled up around each signal until their laughter was drowned by the braying of hounds.

"Dark day." Shukxa mourned. "Dark day." He unstrapped his many quivers and let them fall to the ground. They were all empty. He checked the edge on his hatchet and caught Thrasilaos watching him.

"Is it really darker than any other?" Said the squire, trying to be cavalier.

"Yes." Said Shukxa bleakly. "On any other day, I do so love dogs."

"Head on a swivel, boy." Sickle had recovered Telemakos's shield and xiphos and handed them to Thrasilaos. "They come from all sides now." Thrasilaos took the aspis but not the sword.

"I think I like this one better." He hefted the twisted falcatta. The Skythian smiled.

"Keep it then. Live, and it is yours."

Hunting hounds galloped through the dying coals, too swift for their feet to burn. They attacked Ono first.

"Save him!" Stratos ordered Krateros.

Ono had brought many a man back from the brink of death. If any number of

Λ

them were wounded in his defense, he could put them back together. But if he died, they might all be lost.

He writhed, barely visible beneath a mound of them, his kopis rising and falling but striking nothing. Krateros cast aside his own blade for fear of striking his brother. With his bare hands, he twisted necks to or ripped jawbones from their skulls. They piled on him too, and though a pair or more hung from each of his limbs, he ignored them for the surgeon's sake.

Thrasilaos and Shukxa moved to his aid, but a fresh pack attacked them too. No longer hampered by bramble, Messenians followed their animals through the woods. The hoplites on the path had no choice but to retreat to the heart of the clearing.

Together they pulled the slavering beasts from their doctor. He was chewed to bits, but alive. His pipe still dangled defiantly from his teeth.

They circled their shields around him. The mob had them from all sides now, penned in by snarling wolfdogs and a hurricane of sharpened ploughshares. Only fear of Spartan steel kept them from closing for the kill.

"Think it's too late to sell me out?" Kleomenes joked. "Anyone want to trade me for your lives, now's the time?"

"By Hades, I'll give them both of us if it means you finally shutting the fuck up."

"You need to move." Ono tried to puff his pipe, but cursed when he found it had gone out. "Push where they are thinnest and break for it."

"We can't leave you, cripple." Said the king. "I'd have no one else to drink with."

"Don't worry about me." Ono grumbled. His strong hands girded dead dogs on top of his body until he was buried in mangey shag. "I'm already dead."

"Are we in agreement then?" Kleo asked. "Alright then. The surgeon is dead!" He shouted for the helots to hear. "We leave his corpse behind! Now on me!"

They surged into the crowd, but as hard as they pushed, could make little headway. There was no othismos with them circled, and hundreds of pounds of dogs viced the rims of their shields to anchor them in place.

Messenians recoiled from each lurch forward, dodging a hair's breadth from thrusting spears while the edges of the mob relocated to block whatever path they picked.

"We need a diversion." Stratos barked.

"I'm all ears." Said Kleo. His polemarch's face turned to stone.

"Listen to me," Hegisistratos continued, now to Thrasilaos alone. "No matter what happens, no matter what you see, you stay with the king."

"What?"

"Gods damn you, boy, listen to me!" Something was burning inside Stratos. Thrasilaos could feel its heat building. "You're part of the phalanx now. Your shield is their shield. You are a stone in the wall, and in the wall you will stay. Today,

Λ

tomorrow, a hundred years from now, this is your place and you will hold it until you die! Do you understand?"

"I understand" Thrasilaos's voice trembled, fearing what his promise meant.

"Good boy. Now make me proud."

Hegisistratos exploded from the shield wall. Helots scattered in surprise and he made them pay for it. His kopis split them open two at a time, but he was still only one man, and naked but for his shield and leather skirt. For each swing of his arm, there were ten helots to swing back. Scythes and pitchforks buried their blades in him even as their bearers were butchered.

"Now!" Kleomenes ordered, his voice cracking. The circle broke and ran for the trailhead, nearly empty with the rebels clustered into the clearing. Leonidas and Krateros shielded their rear, running backwards while the three hippeans plowed the way and the Skythians protected their sides. Few of the dogskins could follow, too preoccupied with avoiding murder by Hegisistratos. Those that did were meat.

The polemarch crashed into wherever the mob was thickest, sending them sprawling despite their numbers. The more weapons pierced him, the harder he fought.

Thrasilaos fought his way up the road with the others. Every fiber of his being demanded he go back. Harder than fighting the helots he was fighting his own body to not break his promise. He heard his teacher's voice over the din of dying slaves.

"FOR DIENEKES!"

They met salvation on the road. Isadoros had returned with the Spartan cavaliers from Leonidas's battalion. Thrasilaos and the escapees huddled in the middle of the road as reinforcements stampeded past on both sides. Not stopping for orders, they drove their steeds over to the rebellion and trampled it flat. Though according to their reports, by the time they arrived at the fork and the road, the killing was over. The horde of Messenians lay dead or dying. Survivors found at the scene clutched themselves in fetal weeping balls, or paced, shellshocked, staring with wide but unseeing eyes. Those not killed or cut by Hegisistratos had the ghosts scared from their bodies. Their hearts still beat, but their spirits were gone.

A red sun rose on the forked road. The survivors squinted their eyes against the harsh light. They did not want the dawn. The light, the warmth, felt like a lie.

"The boy will need a new teacher." Kleomenes said to the nine who still breathed. He had asked the hippeis for a private moment with the bodies after the graves had been dug. Five holes gaped on the roadside, though two had nothing but bone fragments to fill them.

"I will teach the boy." Said the Skythian. Either Axe or Sickle, it didn't matter

Λ

anymore. One lived, one would be buried beside Hegisistratos.

"So you do speak our language." Kleomenes half smiled.

"I have always spoken your language, King. But it is no longer humorous to pretend I do not." His fingers vexed the hard earth beside his brother's linen-wrapped corpse.

"A boy of the agoge squired to a barbarian?" Leonidas grimaced. "Lykourgos would spin in his grave. Never."

"His master bid me give him lessons only last night." The Skythian bared his pointed teeth. "Have you already forgotten?"

"To teach him assassin's tricks. For one night."

"I have more tricks than can be taught in a night."

"Teach him your tricks then. You have a prince's blessing. But he needs a Spartan to teach him to be a man."

"You say I am not a man?"

"I say you are not a Spartan. We come home with our shields or on them. You don't even carry one."

"I meet my enemy face to face, Spartan. I do not need to hide behind a bowl of metal."

"Enough." The ice in the king's tone could have frozen the burning dawn. "This is a funeral. You will show respect or I will dig another grave." He shamed them. The king lay his open palms on his polemarch's burial shroud. Fabric bunched under his fingers as thoughts raced visibly back and forth under his closed eyes. "We still live because of this man's sacrifice. But together, we have saved each other's lives time and time again in one night. The Spartiate phalanx will always be our might, but without the barbarian's tricks, it would have failed us. Hegistratos knew this, and died that this man-" he nodded to his foreign friend "-might live. We cannot ignore this sacrifice. We cannot ignore the will of Hegisistratos."

"Kleo, you can't mean-"

The king silenced the prince with a glare.

"I approve. Vadasz will mentor the boy. His skills are numerous, and his violence unmatched. I would wager he is as dangerous as even our Krateros."

The Skythian raised his eyebrows at the compliment, but then realized-

"You know my true name?" He asked.

"I have always known your true name, friend. But it is no longer humorous to pretend I do not." He turned to Thrasilaos. "You understand, boy? This man may be different from us, but he is to be a father to you now. You will learn, without complaint, everything he has to teach. And his... his son..." He said the word remorsefully, as if it pained him to do so. As if it was a lie. "His son will be like a brother to you."

Λ

"He already is." Shukxa put his arm around Thrasilaos. "It is like he says." The Skythian boy said to the child of the agoge. "We have saved each other many times tonight. We will save each other many times to come. I am sure." Thrasilaos had been taught Lakonian austerity, but in this moment at least, he lacked the strength to shoulder it. He put his arms around his new brother and hugged him back.

"Though your family has lost one of its number tonight," Vadasz put an arm around each of them. "It has grown by two." Thrasilaos turned his face into the barbarian's chest to hide his tears. "We will make you proud, king." Vadasz swore to Kleomenes. "We will make Hegisistratos proud."

"That's one order of business settled. But I have more to ask of you." Kleo steadied himself for a moment. He caught the choke in his throat before it could be heard, and pretended it was dirt he wiped from his eyes. "Stratos made many promises in his life. To me, to his country, to his brothers, to his wife… He kept them all. In having died for us, those vows fall to us to keep. I would have you swear them now. On this." The king pulled an axehead from his belt. He'd removed the handle and washed the blood from the blade. It was just a simple thing now. A rusted lump of ore for splitting firewood. "It could have been any number of blades that did the deed. But this…" He steadied his breath again. "This is the one that was pulled from his heart. We will pledge our oaths on this iron."

Thrasilaos had his hand on the relic before the king had finished his sentence.

"Anything" He whispered. "Ask for anything, King Kleomenes, son of Anaxandridas. Ask for the world and I will swear it. I am ready." He was done crying.

Shukxa put his hand on the squire's. Ono clapped his on theirs. Then the two hippeans, and slowly, Krateros, who still had not spoken, wrapped all their hands in his one giant mitt. Vadasz next, and Leonidas last. The prince squeezed the barbarian's brown hand. The Skythian nodded, knowing it was as close to an apology as he would get.

"Not you." Kleomenes told his brother.

"What?"

"I said not you."

"Hegisistratos died for me too."

"This is true. But you may yet be king one day. Your reign must be your own, and not beholden to promises made to the fool who came before you."

Leonidas hesitated. Had the king phrased it any other way, he might have braved disobedience. Stiffly, he removed his hand and rose.

"Don't bury him without me." He said, walking away. "And be quick about it. We still need to get the boy to the games."

Over the next hill, the hippeis mourned, too. They embraced Leonidas without pausing their funeral dirge. The prince added his voice to theirs, and tried not to

Λ

wonder what promises his brother dared ask for. Promises that he was not allowed to know.

Λ

Forty-eight

Thrasilaos finished his story. Dienekes struggled with the revelation, wrapping his head around the secrets kept from his youth.

"So that's why you filed your teeth."

"Sharp of you, Weeper. Yes it is. So that even when my hands were empty I would never be short a weapon."

"And my father was your mentor?"

"As Krateros is to you. And it was no accident that I became your eirene. I had no wish to care for children, and I'm sure you noticed that other eirenes bore the title for only a year. I was yours for all thirteen. This was to repay the debt I owed your father. Hate me for my part in it if you wish... but of my students, two are Olympic champions, and four have been elected to the hippeis. No eirene before me can claim the same."

"What about the two you left to die? The one whose killer you now wear as trophy?" Di knew he spoke in anger, but he meant it no less.

"Allow me to show you something else, Weeper."

Sharktooth tugged a leather thong around his neck, pulling a small hide pouch from beneath his cuirass.

"This belonged to Kleo. He filled it with the soil of Thyrea the day before he burned the Argives at Sepeia. It reminded him of our first failure to smite the medizers. He wore its weight to remember his duty to bring them down. Now I wear it to remind me of how I failed to support my king. How I stood by and did nothing while he succumbed to his madness and died alone."

"What does that have to do with-"

"Silence, brat. I will tell you." Thrasilaos teased the pouch open and reached two fingers inside and pulled out a thick curly lock of human hair. It was coated in the dirt of Thyrea, but Dienekes recognized it all the same, the clippings shaved from Lysimachos. "I carry many failings. Lysimachos neither the least nor the greatest of them. His treason was his own, but he would not have betrayed us had I taught him better. Aristaios as well. Had I humbled him then he would still be with us. This cloak you call a trophy? It is a cowl of shame. I will fight and die and be buried in it so that none will forget the boy I failed. He was strong. He could have been so much more."

Many things made sudden sense to Dien- how hard Thrasilos had been on him in training, how he had been taken protege by a polemarch, why King Kleomenes had secretly invested in his training... But the resentments he harbored for his treatment still lingered. He could not swallow his grudge. Understanding and acceptance were not the same, but he knew that he would not have become what he was without his tribulations.

"Disagree and cling to bitterness all you like. But you, Weeper, I did not fail. Nor did I fail in my oath to your father. So I no longer need to carry this." Thrasilaos handed his broad white aspis, his shield, to Dienekes. "This was the shield of your father. It is yours now, as he meant it to be."

A Spartan aspis usually outlived its bearer. It was common for a soldier to battle behind the same shield carried by his grandfather. Di felt not only the weight of the oak and bronze in his hands, but the burden of duty passed by generations.

"I have painted and repainted the four shields of his heraldry before and after each battle," Thrasilaos continued. "They look now just as they did when he last bore it. They represent his devotion to the phalanx. His duty to support the line, to protect his brothers above all else. That is how he lived and died. I heard your speech to the ephors. It was as though Hegisistratos spoke the words himself. Be proud. I know he would be."

"I don't know what to say." From the back, Dienekes could see where young Thrasilaos had carved his name on the leather lining inside the dome, and where old Thrasilaos had crossed it out and replaced it with a new name.

Little Achilles

"Say nothing. You are a Peer now. Let your actions speak instead."

Dien looked up and Kleo's assassin had vanished.

"I hate it when he does that." He shivered.

"We all do, my boy." Krateros patted his neck with a meaty palm. "We all do."

Λ

Forty-nine

ienekes felt like a boy again. The spring wind in the air and the agoge behind him sent a tingle up and down his spine as he walked with his brothers on the road to Delphi. He regretted missing his turn to paint himself red and guard cheeses on the steps of the Temple Artemis, but returning to the games was more important. He was going to see Asopichos again.

Tellis jogged up beside and looked up at him, which surprised Dien.

Since when have I been taller than Tellis?

"I think I remember the last time we were on this road together..." Tellis bit his lip, trying not to laugh before getting the words out. "You were all knotted up about that girl. And being a right twat about it."

"Good Gods..." Dien gawked. "You're so right! Did we ever even learn her name?"

"Her name? No. But after you came back defeated, I learned the rest of her pretty well." Tellis thrusted his hips.

They shoved each other back and forth arguing about who best pleasured the other's mother until they noticed the face of Thrasilaos edging into the space between them. He was no longer their drill sergeant, but his presence was still sobering.

"We are not in Lakonia anymore, ladies." They were passing through the Megarid, out of the Peloponnese and into the wider part of Hellas where the world took a sharp turn away from their traditional Dorian ways. "Others will see how you behave. Give them nothing to gossip about."

They walked in happy silence for a time after, but not even the menace of Sharktooth lurking off the path could contain them for long and Krateros eventually had to separate them. They traveled as competitors of the men's games now, and would no longer be afforded the leniency they ventured with as children.

...Until arriving in Delphi. They both knew the city, the streets and buildings that ran up and around Mount Parnassos, and knew where they were supposed to be and when. Krateros slipped them a few coins at the money changer's and turned a blind eye as they disappeared into the crowd. He considered warning them against thieves, but had nothing but pity for the fools who might try to rob Insolence and his Weeper.

Training began, and it was as if Dienekes had never left. The burn in his thighs, the rasp of arena dust in his nose, the scuff of powdered sand beneath his bare feet... he felt like he was home. He had grown so much that no one recognized him. No one remembered his glory or his shame. At least not until he was outpacing fellow athletes by fathoms at the finish. A whisper in the audience grew to susurrating thunder and onlookers sank their teeth into the rumor.

Little Achilles had returned.

His heart swelled to hear them whisper, but not his head. He had learned his lesson. He no longer basked in their praise, he was simply happy to be here. Only one piece was out of place. Though he looked, he could not find Asopichos. Even Tellis asked his friends among the wrestlers of Orchomenos, but they shook their heads and would not answer.

"Either he is here or he is not." Krateros shrugged when the boys mentioned it to him later, not entirely unsympathetic. Ever the true Spartan, sometimes his emotions were misplaced or more often not placed at all. It was cold comfort.

Di felt cheated without a rival to match him. He'd always had someone to challenge him into being stronger or faster. Now he was so alone out in front that other racers would quit their heats in resentment rather than run against him. His mere attendance winnowed the ranks of sprinters and for it he did not go without a sense of guilt.

"Pussies. Mooncalves. Doe-eyed grass eaters, the lot of them." Tellis propped Di up in their quarters at night. "What are they here for if they're going to give up before the race even starts."

More than once, Dienekes could have sworn he saw Simon, Asopichos's trainer in the stands, but the face turned and vanished each time Di tried to pull his way into the crowd. He must have been imagining it, seeing what he wanted to see.

As the final race grew closer, his excitement drained. There was no challenge. With no risk came no reward. The sixteen-year-old brat he had been his last time at the games would have langored, but the man he had become swallowed his ennui and forced himself to keep striving. The vision of the Orchomene crossing the finish line ahead of him four years ago was his only motivation, and he clung to it. As he clung to hope that Asopichos himself would appear.

He did not. Dienekes dug his naked toes into the grooves of the marble starting block, but before he could conjure the spectre of his old friend in front of him, it appeared by itself. A blue and silver shimmer in the air, smiling back. Surprise nearly cost Di the same step he had given up his last race as the official signaled...

Go.

Λ

His legs churned. The apparition dashed ahead, grinning at Di over its shoulder as it charged effortlessly out of reach, feet never touching the ground. Weeper galloped undisputed over the finish line mere seconds later but the shepherd boy kept running past and so did he. He chased it into the stands where he lost the vision in the laughing, singing crowd sawrming to lay their hands on him. The strangers felt miles away as they hauled him onto their shoulders and carried him back to the cheerfully baffled event officials to be declared victor. He scanned the crowd for the vision of Asopichos, disoriented and confused. He did not find that friend, but he found another.

"I knew it was you!" Di shouted, and fought his way back to the ground. He clutched the old man by the shoulders, embraced him like family. "I knew it was you!" The old man seemed surprised by the gesture, his own arms stiff by his sides.

"You ran beautifully, boy." Simon spoke low, with respect and water in his eyes. "You did us proud."

"Us? He's here then? Where's the scoundrel hiding?!" Dien raked the cheering mob with his eyes.

"Aye, boy, he's here. Not hiding, but he's here." A tear rolled down his grizzled cheek. "I can feel him."

"Feel?" No one else in the crowd shivered at the cold wind that struck Di. He did not need to hear it said to understand. The pain on Simon's face was plain. Di's muscles went slack, and the mob finally pulled him away from his friend's former trainer.

This was a new kind of loss. Ono, Aristaios, Lysimachos... He could honor their memory. His father's legacy he could still fulfill. But his debt to Asopichos he could now never redeem. The failure of a selfish and stupid adolescent would haunt the man he had become. He fell into numbness.

The race official held Di's victorious hand aloft, then his dissociated body was jostled by others to the bleachers where he sat quietly with glazed eyes beside his Lakonian comrades.

He stood when they stood, cheered when they cheered, booed when they booed, but it was empty mechanization, his soul numb. Tellis won pankration, Thrasilaos took wrestling, Echemmon the diaulos and Polymedes the hoplitodromos. Dien grasped with his heart to share their joy, but could not reach past his shock. His mind's eye saw only the silver-blue shimmer of the Orchomene's ghost. To never repay the respect he had sundered left a greater hole in his gut than the shame of his boyhood hubris.

This is how we yet serve

His beloved uncle's memory whispered to him as it always did, but in his grief Di could think of no way to serve the only champion that had ever put him in his place.

Λ

That time had passed and he did not even know when or how. A hundred questions gnawed ulcers in his chest.

The coronation ceremony that afternoon nearly escaped his notice. Stonefaced and shivering in the Mediterranean heat, Dienekes allowed himself to be wreathed, anointed, and showered in flower petals before skulking away from the festivities. Nervously fingering his seventh crown of olives, he attended the victor's banquet only long enough to seek out other Orchomenians and ask where he could find Simon. They were suspicious of the query, but relented and directed him to where they had been accomodated.

Dienekes heard the man before he saw him, through an open doorway in his quarters. Either for nerves, or as a vestige of his Krypteian training, he lingered in the shadows and listened.

Simon was consoling a young boy, who was a runner too. He had lost his heat in the stadion that morning. Dien's throat tightened to hear the boy crying and before his own tears could join them, he stepped into the light and knocked.

Simon first glared at the intrusion but surprise pushed the insult aside. He stood and smoothed his tunic, blocking Di's view to spare the boy the shame of a stranger seeing him weep, an embarrassment Dien knew too well.

"May I... have a moment?" Dienekes could barely hear his own voice.

"Of course. Jason..." Simon squeezed the boy's shoulder. "I'll be just outside."

Di and Simon wallowed in a pregnant silence outside the dorm.

"Gods, look at you." Simon measured the Spartan before him, looked him over head to toe and gripped the muscles of his arm. "Can hardly believe my eyes. All grown up. Become a true warrior then, have you?"

"A Peer." Dienekes gave a solemn nod. "But not a warrior. I do not yet share that honor."

"Someday. And all too soon, I'm sure."

Another pregnant pause. Dienekes could no longer bear not knowing.

"How did it happen?" Simon took a long quavering breath.

"That same honor." The old man thumbed his eyes. "He fell as bravely as a man can."

"Asopichos? A warrior?" It was a hard thing to believe. So bright and warm and smiling the child had been, it seemed a wrongness to picture him in the phalanx, heavy with the trappings of war.

"He had no love for it. But he did his duty. Orchomenos is small, our army pitiful. Our Archon turned over every rock he could find for advantage. To have an Olympian on his side? One blessed by the gods? Too strong a symbol not to wield." Simon shrugged sourly. "He named Asopichos his champion and put him on the front line."

Λ

"Who would want to fight Orchomenos? What could they stand to gain?" At home, Dienekes had heard talk of no enemy but Xerxes.

"Thebes. They demanded men and taxes of us to pad their war effort against the Medes.

Or on behalf of the Medes. Dienekes did not speak the bitter suspicion. Krateros had been mentoring him in politics now that he was a Peer and had warned how the Theban loyalty to Hellas had come into question.

"We resisted." Simon swallowed hard. "We resisted poorly."

"I am sorry, Simon. I wish I had known. I should have been there. I should have-"

"Bah-" Simon silenced him. "What could you have done? Come by yourself and died with us? Brought a Lakonian contingent and sparked war with Thebes? Nonsense. Thank you, boy. Truly. You are noble to say so, but such is the way of nations. They toss us about even less gently than the gods. Do not saddle yourself with blame that is not yours."

"But what of Orchomenos? Does it... does it still stand?"

"For now. But..." He choked. Dienekes put a hand on his shoulder, and Simon gripped his fingers and steeled. "People are leaving. Women and children and the men like me, too weak or ancient to fight... We are all that remain. I am old and childless so my loss is not so great as some. But Asopichos fell alongside his father, his uncles, his older brothers... His mother withered away soon after. From illness or grief, or both... I cannot say. That boy in there, Jason, he is all that remains of Asopichos's family."

"The child? The runner? He is...?"

"That is Asopichos's youngest brother. And aside from me, he is alone in this world."

Rage and grief erupted in Dienekes. His heart pumped magma. Red-hot tears boiled down his face and he stomped past Simon before the old man could slow him, into the room where Jason still silently sobbed.

The child tried to hide his face as Di knelt before him, but the Spartan grabbed him too roughly by the jaw and forced their raining eyes to meet. The child recoiled in terror. Dienekes in regret struggled to soothe him.

"I am sorry. I am sorry. I will not harm you. I promise. Please, I am sorry." Gently now, he stroked a palm over Jason's hair then took the boy's little paws in his fist. He had never realized how large his own hands had grown until holding both small hands in his single one. "Your brother was a friend of mine. More than a friend. He taught me many great lessons. I would not be the man I am today without him. You should be proud."

Jason nodded, but his sobs redoubled. Dienekes, helpless, let his gaze drop as he

Λ

grasped desperately for words. He saw the olive wreath, forgotten in his other hand.

"This…" He held the wreath up to the boy. Jason, realizing whose presence he was in, was stunned silent. "This crown. It belongs to your brother. By the rights of men and gods it should be his. So now…" He placed it on the boy's head. "It belongs to you."

Jason's eyes darted back and forth between Dien's, his jaw slack. He did not understand and no matter how hard he wished, the Spartan had no more words with which to explain. He put his arms around the child and together they cried until they no longer could.

Simon respectfully barred the door from the outside until Di, still breathing hard, kissed both the boy's hands and left the dorm.

"That was… I cannot… You did…" The old man was dumbfounded.

"Do something for me." Dienekes commanded.

"Anything."

"You leave for Orchomenos tomorrow?"

"I have nowhere else." Simon wrung his hands. Dienekes snatched them and closed within them the coins Krateros had given. None had been spent.

"When you return home, pack your things. Only what you cannot go without. You will need nothing else. Leave your village and travel south with the boy. Present yourself at the gates of Lakedaimon and tell them you were summoned by Dienekes and Krateros and Leonidas himself if you must. An escort will guide you down the Hyacinthian Way to the kleros of Rhoda and Hegisistratos. You will be given shelter and a bed and a new life."

"I… I…" Simon's face contorted. He tried to push the bronze coins back on the Spartan and said with sudden iron in his voice. "No. Not me. I will be no man's slave. Is that what you think of me? You'd put the boy in a dogskin cap? Shame on you, Dienekes of Sparta, shame on-"

"No. Simon. Enough." Dienekes shook the man quiet. "Not a helot. Not you. I'll see you bow to no man. Not now, not ever. You will live in the house of my mother, chief of our perioikoi there. Simon and Jason of Orchomenos will be counted among my family. And you and I together will train the boy to run until he is the fastest man alive."

Simon's lips trembled and he clutched his hands to his chest.

"I don't know what to say."

"Say yes." Dienekes hugged the man close and growled in his ear. "Say yes, or I will hunt you down and drag you to Lakonia myself. For Asopichos."

"The Gods smile on you, Little Achilles!" Simon shouted at him, shaking his fistful of coins as the Spartan disappeared into the night.

Λ

King Leotychidas paraded the victors at the entrance to the city as was custom while Leonidas stood nameless in the crowd as his brother did before him.

"Did you bring a seventh wreath for me, Weeper?" He said to Dienekes as the welcoming party broke up.

"A wreath?" Dienekes shrugged. "Nothing but twigs and leaves."

That night Dienekes, Tellis and Krateros were reunited with their mess. The Peers kicked their feet up on the wooden tables and a relaxing firelight cast upon the thick oaken beams of the hall. The wine ran sparingly and heavily watered, but the men still sloshed in their cups, drunk on victory. When the conversation turned raunchy as it always did in the later hours, a captain indicted the polemarch for having kept his eldest daughter in his own home for an unsuitable number of years after she had come of marriageable age.

"Is our general a jealous man? Does he intend to keep her to himself forever?" The captain himself had asked for her hand and been denied, and did not want to give insult by asking again outright, though the intent was plain.

Krateros shrugged off the question. The daughter of a polemarch was a fine prize, and he had been propositioned many times. His many refusals had gotten him accused in whispers of worse than jealousy.

"A man has to have standards." He shrugged. "And mine are higher than most. A strong arm, a clear head, and a brave heart are not to be scorned, but I have traveled far and seen much and grown more difficult to impress than that."

"What would it take, then? What feats must I accomplish before you will call me your son-in-law." The captain hazarded a smile.

Krateros took a long drink of water from his cup and refilled it, making the petitioner wait for his answer.

"Little Khloris is the light of my life. And I would give her to no ordinary man. I decided on the day she was born that her husband, if ever I had the heart to let her wed," he cleared his throat and the listeners leaned in to see how they matched his criteria, "must have a soft voice and a reluctance to use it…" The more boisterous Peers leaned back in a huff, disqualified. "He must be taller than I…" Half the room groaned and slumped from the conversation. "He must have hair of xanthos…"

"Oh, vanity!" A few men declaimed. Only a small fraction of Spartans were blonde.

"… And he must have an Olympic statue of his likeness in Altis."

Dienekes was drinking deeply when he realized he was the only man in Sparta that Krateros could have described. He spat out his mouthful of wine, drenching Tellis across the table.

A few short weeks later, he was married.

Λ

Fifty

Leonidas pulled his beard. To anyone else he would have seemed stone, but Gorgo knew his tells. She saw how the fingers of his left hand vexed splinters from the wood of his table, how his teeth chewed at the inside of his cheek.

"You've spoken to the ephors, then?" She had predicted their answer as well as he, but the conversation bore having.

"We do not march." It galled him to say. But she could see this was not all that weighted his drooping shoulders. She asked wordlessly. "Thessaly has fallen. Medized without a fight. The cavalry we so desperately needed now fight for Persia. Not to mention ten thousand men fled in a laughable defense."

"But Tempe was two months ago. You bear the loss still?" She deciphered his glare at her knowledge. "I have my own spies, husband." She shook her ringleted mane.

"Xerxes leads a massive train, and each tribe he conquers fattens his host. Such numbers slow his advance, but time works in his favor more than it does ours. The longer he marches the stronger he becomes."

"You are king." She reminded him, nonchalant. "And your men love you. If you give the order, they will follow. Head him off. Stifle his growth."

"I am but one of two kings." He was always the first to temper his own power.

"Leotychidas follows you as readily as your own guard."

"Enough, woman." The words were dismissive, his tone was not. He leaned into her as she sat in his lap. "You speak like your father. He ruled unhumbly."

"He did what needed to be done."

"Even he neglected to march during Karneia. I would not only be defying our elders and our laws, but our gods as well. Some of our men are more devout than others, and the muster would split the nation. If we are to face Xerxes we must remain united."

"And if we are to face Xerxes, we must march."

"With all of our men." He raised an eyebrow at her.

"Would the gods not understand forsaking their festival for the fate of our nation? If Hellas falls, who will remain to worship them?" She drank from his cup and grimaced when she tasted only water. She poured herself a cup of wine and because he was watching, cut it with water.

"Why don't you ask them." He grumbled. "And tell me what they have to say." She neglected to answer, fiddling with the iron ring on her thumb. It was too large for her other fingers.

"One of these days you're going to tell me what those rings mean."

"But you already have so many burdens to bear, my love. I would not saddle you with another." She kissed him. "How long do we have before Xerxes is too far to turn?"

"A month? If not hindered, will be in our laps before Karneia has ended. Even if we muster a sliver before the moon reaches full, we will still be invaded."

"You are certain?"

"Too certain."

Silence rang like a gong as they weighed their options, too few.

"What of our allies?" Gorgo asked.

"Those that remain loyal to Hellas are preparing, but the games loom. They are as reluctant to violate the Olympic peace as our ephors are to campaign during Karneia."

"Our enemy's timing seems too opportune to be coincidence. Do I sense the guiding hand of a deposed king in the court of Persia?"

"Demaratos? It is possible. But it was him that sent us the missive. Why should he aid both camps?"

"Perhaps his heart is torn? Or perhaps he would sooner draw us all out into pitched battle where he can see us slain, rather than fight the ghosts of an enemy hiding in rocks and holes."

"Xerxes is an emperor... he will know how to quell that breed of rebellion." Leonidas knew how as well, but would still prefer the Messenian thralls fight face to face rather than plot in secret. "Speculating on Demaratos does not solve our dilemma. Lakedaimon is the spear of the Hegemony, it is us who must lead, who must be the example for actions taken."

"And our laws say there can be no action."

"Exactly." He let his head thud against the back of his chair. "I do not resent my duty to this nation. But sometimes I resent that I must perform it alone."

"Oh, husband, silly boy." She slapped him playfully. You are not alone. Do not forget the twenty thousand men and women that yoke the weight alongside you. Lean on us. It is a lonely affair to lead, and it was that loneliness that undid your forebear."

Leo scoffed.

"It was drink that undid Kleomenes."

"You do not think it was loneliness that led him to drink?"

"He had Krateros. He had his Skythians. He had his pet Thrasilaos. He had our

Λ

brothers. He had me."

"Sometimes company is the greatest loneliness when they do not understand you, or you understand what they do not."

"Bah. When did you get so wise."

"It runs in the blood, great king." She kissed him on the eyes.

"Does it not hurt you to speak of your father so readily? It pains me."

"We weather the pain for the good of our nation. Wisdom ought not be forgotten, however uncomfortable the memory."

He frowned.

"Darling, you've given me an idea."

"Oh?"

"Perhaps not. Rather an idea of an idea."

"It's a start."

"Kleo never really did break the rules, did he. He plotted and schemed around the rules and into terms they did not govern. Found ways to do what was forbidden in ways law did not forbid."

"Looks like my wisdom is rubbing off on you." She smiled at him proudly.

"The law states that no army may mass before the passing of the Karneian moon."

"...But?"

"But a king may come and go as he likes."

Her eyes widened as she grasped his notion.

"And a king needs an escort…"

Λ

Part Two

Into the Fire

Λ

Fifty-one

An Olympic caravan had been assembled.

"But we're not to leave for Olympia for another two weeks..." Dienekes said to Krateros, who saw the statement for the question it was, and did not misconstrue it for disobedience as another leader might.

"We do not go to compete. There are other uses for Champions." Said the polemarch.

Dienekes thought achingly of Asopichos leading his Orchomenian brothers into battle, but counting his own contingent knew they had not nearly enough for warfare, even if each Peer were counted as ten men.

"Let Leonidas keep his secrets. The king owes us no explanations." Said Thrasilaos, who seemed always placed by the fates at Di's side. He never had been able to swallow his fear of Sharktooth, though the stress of his old teacher's presence was not intolerable if it meant standing next to the likes of Echemmon and Polymedes again.

"Kleo may have kept secrets for other reasons." Krateros frequently invoked his old friend's name despite how somber its mention made him. "But in this case, Leonidas simply has np time to explain."

"So he's explained it to you then?" Tellis asked. His closeness to Dien had made him something of a son to Krateros as well, but even sons are only afforded so many questions.

"As I said." Krateros mounted his horse. "We do not have the time."

As if to emphasize the urgency, each man in the party was given a horse to ride. An utterly unlakonian parade. It turned heads as they rode together into Korinth. Dienekes wondered if this was part of Leo's intent. The king had ordered them to wear their wreaths, not only when riding into the city, but into the council chambers as well.

It was a stuffy affair. Spartan politics were discussed in the open air of the acropolis for all to bear witness. Despite their assertions of democracy, the fattened elite deciding issues behind walls felt dishonest and sickly to the Spartiates.

Gifts were exchanged, empty rites of diplomacy abided, chanting and name saying and sacrifices… Krateros frowned with venom at the empty seats that would have been filled by representatives of Argos and Thessaly, and other states that had Medized. Delphi's space was also unoccupied. Their oracles had urged them to take a stance of neutrality, but their absence from the council was too strong a statement to forgive under the urgency of their mutual threat. Leonidas vehemently ignored the empty seats, unflappable in his purpose.

Themistokles, elder statesman of Athens, took the floor. Dienekes had missed the point where ceremony had turned to diplomacy.

"My fellow Hellenes." He said. "I will be brief, as we have much to discuss. Persia in the east is news to none here. Our allies across the Aegean have fallen. Our own Hellenic states to the north now number among the enemy's vassals. We do not convene to decide whether to launch a military response, but where. The Mede knocks on our very door. We can no longer trust the gates to hold. It is time to open the door and fight. We propose a defense to meet them in the north where they march. An allied army must be raised. Athens will see that the Persians are taken care of by sea."

"How brave you are, Themistokles," Patron of Korinth rose to speak. "To tell us where to deploy without you. Though Korinth agrees that we must fight, we expect that a northern campaign will bear no different result than the fall of Thessaly at Tempe. To mount a force, especially a large one so far from our homes, forfeits us the advantage. Just as you would meet them on the sea where you are strongest, we should meet them where we are strongest. Prepare our defenses here, dig ourselves in at the heart of Hellas, where we know the lands and rivers and the enemy does not. We make them come to us, and we make them bleed for every inch."

There was scattered applause and murmured assent to the claim, followed by others hissing and shaking heads.

"I appreciate your stance, friend," Themistokles responded, "but there are many of our cities between Korinth and the Mede, and do they not all feel the same of their home as you do of yours? We cannot all fight in our native land. A compromise must be found lest we one by one be conquered and added to their strength. Should we abandon the lands above to their fate while we wait for the very threat that takes them?"

Patron looked regretful. "I do not advocate the abandonment of any Hellene, but advise sacrifice for the salvation of all Hellas. We cannot expect to walk out of this fire entirely unburnt. If we must surrender certain cities so that their strength be joined with ours here, then I say it is a price well paid. I do not make this claim lightly and will also mourn the loss of the land of our countrymen, however brief that loss, but if they truly desire freedom from the barbarian, they will see the truth as I have laid it. As the forest springs anew from the wildfire, so will the northern cities be reborn. And I gladly pledge Korinth to the aid of rebuilding the poleis taken by the blaze."

Λ

Pheidon of Aitolia rose, incensed.

"It is hard to be swayed by your talk of freedom when you speak of my home being burnt. How can we be expected to forsake our homes for the defense of yours when you are so clearly unwilling to do the same for us?"

"It is not a truth I enjoy the telling of. But unless you harbor some miracle from me, we must accept the loss of some of our territories or suffer the loss of all."

Pheidon turned red and readied a shower of insults for Patron, but Leonidas stood before it could fall. Even if he had not inherited leadership of the Hegemony from his father Anaxandridas, his presence would still have halted tongues in their mouths.

"Brothers. We may bicker about what land to give, what land to hold, but this assumes we have the luxury of the enemy meeting us on our own terms. I do not believe it is our compromise to make. We must concede the possibility that the Mede has already made the decision for us."

Brows furrowed at him in silent confusion.

"At Tempe, when the Persians marched around the corridor through which we had hoped they would be channeled, he showed that he is not beholden to our choices. We can pick and choose our battlefields, our strongholds, our roads and river crossings, but the host of Xerxes is so vast, that he need not meet us where we like. He can simply…" He twisted a finger in the air. "Go around. Burn our fields and our villages and homes where they lie while we starve in the fortress of our choice."

"I assume you have a solution to this predicament?" Asked Themistokles.

"I hope I do. I'm certain you have all heard of the canal dug by the Medes through Athos?" Most had, but the shock of some made clear who did not. "No? Well, now you know. So much does Xerxes hunger for our subjugation that he has moved the very earth. And now, as we speak, he walks from that canal to us on a bridge made of his ships moored side to side. All the way across the sea."

"You propose to meet him on this... 'bridge'?" Patron seemed skeptical.

"Ah, if only. If I had my way we would be burning both his fleet and his army at this very moment. Alas, we are here talking instead. The first of their number will have crossed before we can ride out and meet them, but they will remain narrowed along the coast and we can disadvantage their numbers if we-"

"If I may speak?" Leontiades, a general of Thebes, rose from where he leaned on his knuckles. Leonidas gave him the floor.

"I am prepared for this to be an unpopular suggestion, but have we considered the notion of not resisting the Persian?"

Shouts rose against him.

"We came to say our peace." Leonidas quieted them with raised hands. "So by all means, let him." The glare he gave the Theban conveyed the disdain he did not speak. Leontiades pretended not to see.

Λ

"All the people of Hellas, men... women... children, we number barely a million. Xerxes has at least that many fighting men. And many millions more than that follow behind. We can between our nations call on, what, several tens of thousands of soldiers? While Xerxes, with the blink of an eye, beckons hundreds of times that many."

His audience scowled, but they could not deny his reason. He continued.

"Xerxes has proven magnanimous to his subjects. Cyrus, his grandfather and founder of their nation, set the precedent of allowing his people to keep their gods and their ways. What does he ask in return? A little tax? A nod to his banner? Is that truly a worse fate than war? War alone is a great enough evil, but we speak of war against the greatest army the world has ever seen!"

Shouts of traitor and coward filled the hall. The General shrugged and shook his head at their abuse.

"Leontiades speaks of war as a man who knows it well. I will give him that." Leonidas stared him down. "But I dare say that I know both war and freedom better than any man here. And I say that war is but a small price to pay for liberty, and that the loss of that liberty is a fate worse than death."

"Oh, come now, Lakonian. We are all familiar with the fatalism of your kind. Come back with your shield or on it." He scoffed. "But may I remind you that unlike yourself, the vast majority of our fellow Hellenes are not warriors born."

"Spartans are not born." Leonidas growled. "We are forged."

"Spare me your poetry, King." He tinged the word with insult. Kings were an antiquated notion elsewhere in the city-states. "I do not share your fetish for pain and violence. Were it only my life on the line, I would gladly lay it down, but it seems the rites of your Lakonian death-cult have blinded you to how the rest of our world lives. War might be your bread and meat, but to the rest of us, war means the death or displacement of thousands. Tens of thousands. Hundreds of thousands. Women and children and innocents whose only crime was that their King would not bow. I stand here every bit as free a man as you, Spartan, but as dear as that freedom is to me, it is not so great that I would not forsake it so that my children and my children's children might live. Patron spoke of sacrifice for the sake of all Hellas. So do I. If my choice were to bow to Xerxes, or see our people wiped from the face of the earth, I confess, I would consider it. "

No accusation of treason followed this point.

"General, I am confused. You call me a fetishist? Call us a death cult?" Leonidas made his way down the stairs as he spoke, pointing a finger and following it to his opposition "But clearly, it is you who has already resigned yourself to Hades. You have already decided that you will lose this war. So yes, I am blind to your way of life, I cannot understand your fear, your resignation, because -and look at our histories if

Λ

you need the proof- the eternal truth of Lakedaimon is that we are incapable of surrender. Death cult? Death Cult?! Nay! We are a cult of life! Each man is a temple and our freedom is our prayer. So I will fight from the front line with my own sword and my own shield for my freedom and for yours, even if you will not. No man, no fear, and no king with a million man army will take it!"

His fist punched the air and a cheer rang off the stone walls of the council-chamber. Leontiades, exasperated with the theatrics, rubbed his palms into his face.

"Yes, Leonidas. Your country has never lost a war. Yet. This I concede. But you have lost men. And you only have so many. Persia has no limit. It takes thirteen years to make a Spartan but Xerxes's hordes are birthing soldiers as we speak. We have never faced, never even heard of an enemy such as this. How can you be so certain of victory in defiance of all reason? You yourself said that Xerxes has moved the very earth on his campaign, in days no less. That he marches his army across a bridge made from his fleet? He would need more boats than we have men! His archers are so numerous that their arrows eclipse the sun. How can we hope to fight that? What sign from the gods have you received that says you can stop the turning of the world?"

"There!" Leonidas whirled and pointed at Dienekes and his peers in their seats. "That is my sign from the gods!"

"What? A dozen men?"

"Nay! A dozen champions! Every one of them an Olympic victor, carved into bronze and into history where they will forever stand at the temple of Altis. Between them they bear over a hundred crowns of victory. Over a hundred times that the Gods themselves have reached down and raised them over the strongest and fastest and most skilled in all Hellas. You desire proof that the Gods stand beside us in our time of need? Here it is. They have named us victorious before battle has even begun, for these are the weapons given to us by the very hands of Heaven and I MEAN TO USE THEM!" Leonidas roared. "Do not speak to me of the multitudes of men behind Xerxes. Men are cheap. Men are chattel. Men are frail and frightened and shit themselves as they flee. One million men, one hundred million men, I say let them come. I am unafraid." He gestured again to his soldiers, his Olympians. "I will meet them on the field with giants."

Cheers drowned out Leontiades as he tried to respond. The cheers redoubled in jeers and laughter as he gave up, surrendered the floor and resumed his seat.

Themistokles rose.

"Rousing, King Leonidas." He said, as he waved the council back to order. "Inspiring. Reminds me of your brother, he too had a way with words. But if I may. I would request to hear the champions speak on the matter themselves."

"Request? Nay, Athenian." Leonidas rumbled, his eyes hungry. "I insist."

"Very well then," Themistokles rolled his eyes, but could not hide his smile.

Λ

"Champions of Sparta? What have you to say?"

Dienekes froze. He had not been prepared to speak, had never addressed a crowd in his life, but it was not a Spartan's duty to be fearless, only never to show fear. Fortunately, of all of them, Tellis showed no hesitation. Dienekes was both surprised and not. He smirked in admiration at his best friend, his leader, always leading by example.

"Honored councilmen," Tellis inclined his head humbly. "It is an honor to address you. But this is clearly a delicate matter of state, and I am but a soldier."

Dien gaped. When had Tellis become a diplomat?

"I only know my home, and the roads to the games, so I cannot speak as to where or when a battle should be fought. Only that I will fight it wherever it waits for me. Aside from that, I can tell you a little of my brothers. Echemmon, here, who wins the diaulos every year. But more impressive than that, I learned recently that when dispatched to Messenia for the final stage of our training he had left his knife at home. So-" Tellis broke into a moment's laughter, his intoxicating smile was already infecting the crowd. "He ran all fifty miles home alone in the dark of night, fetched his knife, and then ran back to his deployment before dawn and his instructor was none the wiser." The crowd chuckled slightly. "This is Polymedes, our hoplitodrome, and I've seen him push oak trees down all on his lonesome, stand up, Poly." The hulk did as he was bid and councilmen seated nearby recoiled in fear at the size of him. "This is Thrasilaos. He's won crowns in boxing, wrestling, and pankration, and even more frightening than his fighting is his stealth. He can choose to be invisible in an open field in broad daylight. A killer born. He was my instructor, and I still have nightmares from it but he taught me well. And just look at those fucking teeth. I can't think of a single man, even among Spartans, who isn't scared to death of him. Even our King." Leonidas nodded vigorously, begging yet more laughter. "Our brother Aristaios once killed a lion with his bare hands. And my best friend in the whole world, his name is Dienekes, I think you will have heard of 'Little Achilles'..." A gasp of recognition circled the rotunda. "Not only is he the youngest Olympic champion in the history of all history, but... Well, I'll just let him tell you himself."

Tellis pulled Di to his feet and took his own seat before Di could object. There he was, standing alone, all eyes on him and nothing to say.

"Well... I... uh..." He took the wreath from his head and fumbled with it between his fingers. "Everything Tellis has told you is true. So I suppose I will tell you the truth as well. Yes, if Leonidas points to battle, we will go to it singing, and Yes, I am the youngest champion, but..." He took a deep breath. "But that doesn't feel very important. It once did, but it's just a race. I've won... how many crowns? A dozen?" He looked at Tellis who nodded proudly. "A dozen then. But none of that matters. I am but one man and running a race will not win this war. I am nothing by myself. My

∧

strength comes from the line. From my brothers who stand beside me. I would die for them and they would die for me. We've done everything together and always will, and they say we are all of us equals, but I have to be honest, because in Sparta we aren't taught how to lie…" He hadn't meant it as a joke, but the crowd laughed again. They found his nervousness, his humility, endearing. "I might be a champion, but of all of my brothers, all of the men of Sparta who have stood by me and raised me up…. I am not their equal. I would count myself the last and weakest of their number. Without my brothers I am nothing."

"I don't understand…" Themistokles's eyes narrowed. "Are you telling me that a twelve time Panhellenic victor, the youngest Olympic victor of all time, is the weakest man amongst all the Spartans?"

"Yes, sir." Di nodded. "So weak, in fact…" He let a baffled smile wrap around his face. "My brothers, they… they call me The Weeper."

"Apologies, once more, please." Themistokles blinked. "You? You are the weakest of your kind?"

"I am. And proud to be so, sir."

"I think I am beginning to understand…" Themistokles turned his attention back to the Lakonian King. "I see where your confidence comes from, King of Sparta, if this is the least of your number."

"Yes, Athenian." Leonidas beamed at Dienekes, his eyes burning with pride. "Yes he is. As was his father before him."

"Then I believe I speak for the council when I say we are convinced?" A chorus of agreement rang. "Then this place you spoke of, where the Medes are to be narrowed. Does it have a name."

"Yes it does," said the king. "They call it the Gates of Fire."

Λ

Fifty-two

On the road to Olympia, Dienekes and Tellis behaved themselves for a change, though Thrasilaos's self-proud smirk made them want to act up just to spite him. For once, their minds were not fixed on the thrill of competition. The threat of Xerxes was too near for them to consider much else. There were scouts of the Hegemony watching every road and port from the eastern coast of the Aegean, all hoping that some thorn in the boot of Persia would impede their progress. But the Hellenes were learning that a machine so large does not slow. It would crush its own kind in its chosen path before allowing its stride to fall behind the pace demanded by their god-king. Spartans on the road and at home, hungry to defend their kind, did their best not to speak of their ill portents, but the truth hung in the humid summer air louder for all they tried to ignore it. For all of King Leo's talk of giants, Hellas held little hope without their crimson and bronze sentinels to vanguard their combined forces. Persia would arrive before the end of Karneia.

Weeper and Insolence were also both expecting their firstborns, and both were dreading that their child would be born in their absence. A man was not allowed the comforts of life at home until he reached thirty years of age so their daily lives would change little if at all after the birth, but they were proud of their wives and their future children and desperately wanted to be there to help bring them into the world. The notion of fatherhood was a warm one, even if its practice was carried out by the state. Dienekes was still growing accustomed to the aura of his father's white shield, but the thought of an heir to pass it to made it feel all the more lively in his grip. Men may be washed away in the ebb of time, but their shields remained through the ages. He dared to hope his grandson would carry the shield of Hegisistratos as well.

A grandson.

The weight of the thought caught Di by the throat. He still felt like a boy himself. Time was passing whether or not he noticed it.

"I know that look, little oak tree." Krateros sidled along Di on his horse, passing a waterskin down the line. They did not usually eat or drink mid-march but Krateros made exception to keep his troops in top form, whether they marched for battle or for games. Dienekes drank enough to wet his thirst but not quench it before passing the skin to Tellis. Comfort was ever the enemy, vanquished by moderation.

"What look...?" For only a moment Di pretended as if his mentor could not see right through him but could not hold out against his knowing smirk. "Tell me, then. Old wise oak." He joked. "When did you finally feel like you were no longer the sapling?"

"We learn much from the trees." Krateros leaned back in the saddle, thinking of other things as he spoke in riddles. His sixty-first birthday was approaching in a matter of days, marking the end of his military service. A strange calm had enveloped him in the days leading up. "The wood of a tree is hard, much harder than our flesh, but still they bend in the winds and high waters so they do not break. They reach boldly up to heaven's light, but also root themselves deep in the dark earth in depth equal to their height. They bear many children, even if only a few of those children are hardy enough to take root. If they lose a limb, or many limbs, they do not cease to strive and the branches that remain are stouter for their absence. But most importantly, until the day it dies, a tree never stops growing."

Dienekes looked at him puzzled.

"I'm sorry, but I don't think you answered my question."

"Didn't I?" Krateros raised an eyebrow.

"Then I'll ask plainly. When did you stop feeling like a child all the time? When did you begin to feel like a man?"

Krateros soaked smugly in his secret before sharing it.

"Never, my boy." He said. "Never," and galloped away.

The caravan arrived early at Olympia. All the contenders were veterans of the games and festivities, they needed no orientation so were given freedom to wander, to rest, to train, to bathe, or feast and frolic as they liked. Of course they all elected to immediately dive back into training. All except for Dienekes, who wanted a quiet word with Hermes, patron and namesake to Asopichos. The wing-shod god had his own temple inside the city gates but Di felt more comfortable praying outside, to the gods themselves rather than lifeless statues of their likenesses. Hermes was the god of roads and travelers among other things, and there was a strong northerly wind. Tellis kept him company and they sat in their armor on a hillside below the city until dusk. As the sky turned purple to the west, Di took a leather purse from his belt and carefully poured a mound of gritty, yellow-gray soil into his palm. Tellis asked without speaking.

"Simon gave it to me." Dien answered. Simon had quickly become indispensable in Rhoda's household, and was waiting hand and foot on the very pregnant Khloris at this very moment. Dienekes was grateful for having him. "He brought it from Orchomenos. From the grave of Asopichos. He asked me to scatter it at the feet of his statue in Altis."

Λ

"...Are you not?"

"Well I was. And I suppose I still am. But you feel that wind, surely it will carry some there." Dienekes stood, and sniffed the dirt. It was poor stuff. From the land of shepherds and wanderers, not like the rich black turf of his own home. "But at the feet of a single statue? No. Asopichos was too big for that. He is the stuff of legend, Tellis. Bested little Achilles at his own event." He and Tellis shared a sad little laugh. "I will scatter it here. And it will dance through the air over his statue, over Altis and Olympia, the road that brought me here, and with any luck, the wind will carry some home to Orchomenos. Somehow it still seems not enough, but I think better than at the feet of a single idol."

He swung his arm, and the breeze arced the soil away into oblivion.

"No wonder you're such a poor soldier." Tellis put an arm around him. "You're a poet born."

They heard no sound, the crickets behind them went quiet.

Someone is coming, neither of them had to say.

There was no cause for alarm, no reason to suspect the Olympic peace violated, but they were still graduates of the agoge. They crouched behind their shields, suspicious of the road that seemed empty, and the nature around that declared it was not. They struggled to see in the changing light.

It was a lone runner. A soldier. Another Spartan.

"Pantites!" Tellis called from the roadside. He was a former Olympian himself, had traveled with them to the council in Korinth months prior. "What news?" Tellis asked happily at first, excited to see another of their own, but the words soured in his mouth. It was unlikely the news was good. Especially if a runner had been dispatched to catch them so soon.

"Leonidas has called up the guard." Pantites was hardly out of breath.

"We march then? At last! We give the Mede his war!" Tellis's excitement was not for blood, but for duty. To finally face the invader who threatened his home, his wife, his child to come.

"But Karneia... It has not ended." Dienekes wondered. "The ephors have sanctioned an army?"

"We do not call an army. Only the guard."

"How strange," said Tellis, but shouldered his gear to obey. "And we only just arrived..." He appeared to be caught between the two things he loved most; the Olympics and war, though he had not yet tasted the latter. "Oh well. Let the Korinthian have his wreath this year."

"No, not you." Said Pantites, who seemed preoccupied.

"But you said the guard? I am-"

"Yes, Tellis, I know who you are. This is a new guard. A new three hundred. Only

Λ

men who have sired sons."

"What?" Tellis fringed on anger. "I lose my place in the guard because my wife hasn't whelped yet? What sense does that make?"

"I do not give the orders, merely carry them."

"From who? The polemarch is here."

"Easy, brother." Dienekes, confused as well, calmed his friend. "I'm sure there's a reason. Perhaps it's a concession so we can get those two new wreaths, eh?"

"No, son of Hegisistratos. You are coming."

"I am? But I thought you said…" Realization struck him like a hammer. His legs nearly gave out.

"Yes, Weeper. Born only moments before I departed."

"…my wife?"

"She's fine. Happy. Healthy. The child is strong."

Tellis, his anger forgotten, hugged Di around the waist and spun him through the air.

"I'm an uncle!" He screamed. The two roared and pounded each others' breastplates until Pantites bored of it.

"There is time for this later. I must tell the others. Echemmon. Polymedes. Thrasilaos. They are summoned as well."

"Thrasilaos has children? Gods, can you imagine?"

"Focus, Spartan." Pantites snapped at Tellis. "Where are the others. We are to leave exactly now."

With Dienekes still in shock, Tellis directed him to the gymnasium, where he knew his fellow athletes would be. Pantites directed Di to remain there, to be collected on their way back out, and ran to deliver the rest of his message.

"A son!" Tellis shouted when he was gone. Again they cackled and beat each other on the bronze. "A son!" Tellis yelled again for his friend, who still could not find words. "Wait, wait, wait, I'm the godfather, right?"

"MMffison…" Dienekes garbled.

"Is that a yes?"

"Ihavvason." Di was turning green.

"That's a yes. I heard a yes. I'm the godfather."

Dien grabbed his friend by the collar suddenly.

"Tellis, I need you to do something for me."

"Name it. Name it. I'm your son's godfather after all."

"When my son enters the agoge… You will be his mentor."

"Dienekes…" Tellis grinned so hard he feared his cheeks would split. "Son of Hegisistratos, you are going to turn me into the Weeper. Yes I will mentor your son. On one condition. You have to mentor mine."

Λ

"Of course. OF COURSE!" They embraced again until a thought struck Dien. "Wait, wait, what if you have a daughter?"

Tellis thought for a moment.

"Then you can teach her how to cry!"

Pantites returned at a trot with the Olympians in tow. Tellis and the polemarch would be among the only Spartans remaining.

"Take no prisoners!" Tellis shouted to Dienekes as he pulled away.

"And you kill that Korinthian!" Di shouted over his shoulder. "Oh! And if you make it home before I do... Tell them to name my son Krateros!"

Λ

Fifty-three

They caught up to their comrades the following day, all three hundred guardsmen reunited. They broke to forage and refill their water at a spring.

"Did you hear?" Dienekes shouted to Alpheos and Maron, wrapping his arms around them. "I'm a father!" They did not take long to find, despite sporting the same regalia as every other hoplite. After years of drilling together, he could tell either twin's gait from another Spartiate's at a distance.

"Of course you are. It's why you're here." Said Alpheos, glumly.

"If only he could have come a day later." Maron gave Di a sympathetic pat on the shoulder.

"What's it matter, a day sooner, a day later. He's healthy and strong. All that matters." Dien's eyes watered with pride.

"And not bad looking either. I saw him myself." Alpheos nodded. "A good man to lead the family."

"Absolutely! But all in good time. They'll still have me till he's grown."

The twins shared a look.

"...Yeah... Of course they will."

"Any word from my mother?"

Another look.

"With your shield or on it." They said after a pause.

"That's it? My firstborn arrives in the world and that's all she has to say?"

"She's a Spartan woman. She has a job to do. Come. We are also Spartan. With a job to do."

The whole precession walked beneath a shadow. Dienekes could not fathom why. They had trained their whole lives for battle, and many of them had already seen it and come home victorious. No one was more ready. He had seen soldiers march off to war singing, he did not know what was so different about today. He could not stop thinking about his son. He was ready to fight, to win, and to return home to that shining little face. He imagined it looking like Khloris. He imagined it looking like himself. He liked it better looking like Khloris.

"Strange." Polymedes said to no one in particular, passing around waterskins that hung off his broad back by the dozen. "In days as dark as these, it is only the Weeper who smiles."

Around nightfall the party was overtaken by a rider. Dienekes cheered when he recognized Krateros blister past them at a gallop, but no one else harked. The polemarch, now effectively retired, dragged to a stop in front of Leonidas, forcing him and the entire column to a halt.

"Not a word?" He bellowed at the king, for all to hear. "Not a word!?"

"You are no longer polemarch. No longer a soldier." Leonidas levied his palms.

"Well I most certainly was when you gave the order, wasn't I?"

"I do not know what order you speak of."

"You march to battle and do not consult your most trusted general? Your most trusted friend?" He dismounted his horse.

"Friend, I believe you have me mistaken. Karneia has not passed. We may not war. I am merely out for a walk."

"With three hundred elite warriors?!"

"Is it not commonplace for royalty to travel with a bodyguard?"

"It is not commonplace for YOU to travel with a bodyguard!" Krateros stabbed a finger into Leo's cuirass. Any other king would have shouted treason. Leo only smiled.

"Would it make you feel any better if I told you I consulted no one?"

"What, you hatch this scheme all on your own?"

"To be honest, it was my wife's idea."

"Bah! Kleomenes and his witchery haunts us still. What did she call it, a sacrifice?" Krateros paced and spat venom.

"A necessary sacrifice."

"Necessary to leave all their wives without husbands? All their children without fathers? To waste the greatest of our number, for what, for a story? To give the poets a song to sing?"

"Yes." Leo confessed with bold face, and Krateros stared at him shocked. "And no. Look." The king pointed to the moon, nearly full. "But a sliver remains and this nonsense superstition will no longer bind our hands. The full power of Lakedaimon will be unleashed. And in that time, all of Hellas will have heard of the impact made by but a fraction of a fraction of our number. Every son of the Mediterranean will stand united behind us and the Mede will have more than he bargained for. Because we bought them the time to rally their forces."

"You mean to make yourself a martyr?"

"Can you think of another way?"

Krateros paced and kicked the earth and grumbled under his breath before speaking.

Λ

"Fine. Then I come as well."

"You are no longer a soldier. Your service is up. Go be with your family. They need you."

"And your family doesn't need you? Your people don't need their king? My son-in-law is here, my best friend is here, my brothers, my people- my family is here. My service is up? Then I am a free man. No longer beholden to you. Free to choose my life and my death."

"Only men who've fathered sons were called for this campaign. You have many beautiful children, all daughters."

"Would you have me rush off and whelp another heir, then? You think me siring a son will turn the tide in this war?"

"Krateros, please. If not that, then Sparta will still need your guidance as ephor."

"An ephor? This is their fault! Their decree that brought you here, that launched your damn-fool suicide mission! We could be marching with ten thousand men if they would put reason before superstition. The moon can no more stop us than it stops the Persian. We are fighting men, Leonidas. I am a fighting man."

"Not anymore you're not."

"Am I not? Then show me, King. Stop me yourself." He stepped back and assumed a fighting stance. "Beat me, and I'll go be an ephor of Lakedaimon. But we both know I'll throw you just like I did when we were boys."

"The guard numbers three hundred."

"Three hundred and one!" Krateros roared, but remained coiled, ready to strike.

Thrasilaos apparated at Leonidas's side.

"Is it true? That he can beat you?" Asked Sharktooth, only half interested, smiling when he heard the grinding of Leo's jaw.

"Yes." The king confessed.

"Then let him come. We will need him. Every second will count." Thrasilaos polished his fingernails on his lionskin cloak. "Or fight so he can trounce you. I would very much like to see that before I die."

Leo took a breath and turned to his men.

"You heard the polemarch." He roared. "Three hundred and one!"

Now every Spartan cheered. All but Dienekes. He heard every word clearly, but their meaning he could not, would not fathom.

"I'm sorry, Di. We all knew. We thought you knew too." Alpheos put a hand on his shoulder.

"It'll be alright, Di. We're all in it together. For honor. For Hellas. For home." Maron took his other side.

Martyrdom?

Sacrifice?

Λ

Suicide mission?
He would never lay eyes on his boy.

∧

Fifty-four

L eonidas marched them slowly, fed them often, made them stretch and drink their waterskins dry twice as often as they needed. The helots carrying supplies for the short journey felt their loads soon lightened. There were no supplies for a return journey.

Dienekes imagined the weight of his infant son's hand in his own as they marched, painfully aware of how each step took him further and further from his child. But he did not falter. No Spartan faltered. Each of them had a son of their own, some more than one. They pooled their grief and lashed it to each other, braided it into strength.

Their march took them past Argos, whose people were scarce and scattered and glared from a frightened distance while whispering curses under their breath, too cowed to shout them. Those not old enough to remember the last Spartan visit had been taught to fear and hate the crimson cloaks by those who had been there.

Korinthians, who had heard of the Olympians at the council, lined the road to scatter flower petals and praise over the Lakonians. If Dienekes's thoughts had not been so far away, he would have heard his own name chorused in their songs. Many of his peers were as lost in their heads as he was, many more sang along and smiled at the Korinthian girls who garlanded them, never having felt more alive. They felt like dancing, and they would have if they were any other soldier. But a Spartan does not break rank, for pleasure or for pain.

At Thebes, they were met by an army.

"I remember parting poorly with Leontiades." Dienekes slipped from his fog. "I had not thought it was so poorly as this."

"Look closer." Alpheos told him, but Dien could not see what the twin did. "Just watch." He shook his head at his brother's ignorance.

"It's only…" Maron counted quickly. "Four hundred men. A pitiful force. And their people are still in the fields, the city gates are open. This is not a battlefield."

As they approached, Di could see for himself that the soldiers wore their shields strapped to the backs of their linothoraces and had driven their spear points into the dirt. Supply wagons flanked their force. Some of them waved.

Leonidas called his men to a halt and approached the Thebans alone. Leontiades strode away from his cohorts to meet him. They spoke little if at all, but they shook hands, the general's hand clasped in both of the king's. When the Spartan convoy resumed its march, the Thebans fell in behind.

The Spartiates silently suffered for nearly a week at the tedious pace set by Leonidas. Their long legs would not have struggled to reach the muster point in half the time and still be rested. It was not their way to languish so, but the king tiptoed them to battle for more reasons than to preserve their strength.

Word was spreading.

The Thebans had been the first but others were not far behind. Tegeans, Thespians, and Korinthians, having seen the Spartans pass, rallied volunteers and added their strength to the Lakonian spearhead. Arkadians came in the greatest number, one thousand strong. Macedonian and Thracian refugees from the north, their homeland already ravaged by the Mede, added the remnants of their demolished armies. Pantites had been dispatched ahead to tell the citizens near the gates of the days to come and on the arrival of the allied forces, contingents from Phokia and Lokris stood ready to join. The mere three hundred soldiers that left their homes behind a few short days before had blossomed into over six thousand ready warriors.

"It's because of you." Krateros whispered to Dienekes as they embraced their new friends. Dienekes's expression bore disbelief. "You and your dozen wreaths. Touched by the Gods. You give them hope."

Soon after the Hellenes had dug in, the tip of the Persian horde spilled out past the Asopos River. Their numbers swelled to bursting on the banks of the Spercheios as they disembarked. They already numbered in the tens of thousands and miles of men followed with no sign of stopping. Leonidas called a war council at a short stone battlement. Standing outside of arrow range but in plain sight of the barbarians to the west, he dared them to come. He made sure his Olympians were there. As still and silent as their statues at Altis, but radiating an invisible fire.

"The middle gate, you called this?"

"Aye," answered Sebastos, the Phokian general. "There are three gates, rock outcrops where the pass constricts. And they have all seen battle before. This wall was built to bastion us against the horses of Thessaly. And now it guards us against a common enemy. How quickly history changes its mind."

"These fields here." Leonidas pointed west at the plain between them and the Mede. A hundred yards of dusty track stretched between steep hills to the south and the Malian gulf to the north. "They're too wide to fight on. Persia has far more men than Thessaly has horses. We cannot garrison that breadth. We will have to fight from behind your gates else be surrounded. So much for history."

"Let us hope that our enemy makes your same mistake."

"Mistake?"

∧

"We may not match a Lakonian in the field, but we are not without our tricks." Sebastos grinned. " You see the steam rising from the fields? We channeled streams down the hills from the hotsprings when you sent word of your plan. By nightfall the whole plain will be marshland. Let the bastards try to push against a phalanx when they're up to their necks in mud. They'll have to advance along the sea, where the ground is rock, or they will not advance at all."

Leonidas squinted at the bubbling soil and issued a single barking laugh.

"Well done. Then we will fight...There." He indicated the narrowest point in the shelf at the third gate.

"In front of the wall?" Sebastos was skeptical.

"Have you not heard, Phokian?" Leo rapped his knuckles on the breastplate of Polymedes. "We are walls."

"There are ways around walls." Krateros remembered the failed defense of Tempe.

"Wise." Sebastos nodded. "But fortunately few. The Anopaian way is the only other route from where they are to where we are. But it is only a goat trail, used only by shepherds. They will not know it."

"Too risky to leave to chance." Krateros shook his head. "Of his millions, Xerxes will have many scouts. Someone will find it." He cringed at the thought of breaking up their already meager force but there was no alternative. "It must be guarded."

"Agreed." Said Leonidas, and then to Sebastos. "This is your land. You know the hills. You and your men will watch the pass."

"Me? While the battle rages down here? Surely my men will be better use-"

"Yours is the largest force. Your marsh-trap will render your numbers as useless as it will the Mede's. Hopefully they will remain ignorant of your goat trail, but if not... I am comforted by the thought of them stumbling blind through the woods while harassed by a thousand men who know every tree."

"I see your reason. But perhaps if I left-"

"Thank you, Sebastos. Your swamp is a great gift, but your place is in the mountains now. The fight down here is mine. I will hold for as long as you can ensure no one sneaks up on me."

The Phokian nodded and left to mobilize his troops.

"Arkadians, Orchomenes, Mycenaeans, you have slingers, yes?" The three commanders nodded proudly. Their shepherds could knock the tail off a wolf at two hundred yards. Spartans typically scorned ranged weapons, considering them a coward's tool. The other officers chose to take their inclusion as a compliment, overlooking how dire the situation must be for Leonidas to welcome them into his strategy. "They will support my left flank from the wall to as far forward as the ground remains firm. I should not have to tell you not to get stuck in the mud Sebastos made us." The council chuckled softly. "Any archers we have will join the slingers, but keep

Λ

our javelins with the hoplites."

"And what of those hoplites?" Asked Kosmas, commander of the Tegeans.

"Our advantage is unfortunately our weakness, here." Leonidas had thought of everything. "As long as my hippeis holds the gate, there is no room to deploy another phalanx. So the remaining hoplite battalions will stand in reserve."

"Reserve?" Kosmas balked. "Thousands of men in reserve while only three hundred do the fighting?"

"If I had but the room to play you, I would." Leonidas smiled apologetically.

"I came to kill barbarians, Spartan, not watch someone else do it."

"There will be plenty for everyone." Said Demophilos of Thespia, as a squire whispered in his ear. "My scouts have just counted a hundred thousand men on the beach, and still more soldiers as far as they can see. There will be more dead Persians than the crows and sharks can stomach."

"Indeed, old friend." Leonidas and Demophilos had a history. The two had learned respect for each other on opposite sides of the battlefield, but in recent years enjoyed an enthusiastic peace between their cities. "Your seven hundred men will station between the rear and middle gates. Arkadians? You will cover Thespia's advance if and when it becomes necessary for him to take my position at the second gate."

"So I'm first in reserve?" Demophilos did not bother to hide his excitement. There was a reason the Thespians and Lakonians got along.

"Yes. You are first in reserve."

"He most certainly is not." Leontiades stood from his perch on the low wall. He had been uncharacteristically quiet throughout the meeting.

"Why not?" Said Demophilos.

"Because I am."

Leonidas squinted, regarded him firmly for a long moment before speaking.

"I spoke poorly to you in Korinth."

"You did." Leontiades affirmed.

"Is that why you're here?"

"You insult me further? That I would be so fickle to chase war to mend my sullied pride?"

"Then why is it you chase war?"

"I do not chase it, it has placed itself inextricably in my path. But now it's here I intend to face it down."

"You wish to be second into the fire?"

"Spartan, I would be first into the fire, if you would but step out of the way."

"You know I will not."

"I do know. So I will follow if I have to follow. But I won't follow him." He

Λ

pointed at Demophilos, who rolled his eyes. "I will follow you and none other, so my people will be able to say that it was I who killed the man who killed King Leonidas."

Leonidas, amused, chewed his cheek while he measured the general for another long moment.

"Thebes will be first in reserve, then." He conceded with a smirk. "But know this, Leontiades... I do not intend to give you that chance."

Λ

Fifty-five

For five days the Hellenes awaited their combat. For five days Persians continued to flood the Phokian shore. And for five days the invaders bloated to higher numbers than the Hellenic spies could count. Xerxes's war party was accompanied by butchers and bakers and smiths and engineers and masons and shipwrights and tanners and artists and poets and scholars. This was not an army, this was a city on foot, a larger city than all the poleis of Hellas combined.

Each day an envoy wearing gems and cloth-of-gold was sent to speak with Leonidas, and each day a different man stood in his place and answered.

"I am he! I am Leonidas!" An Arkadian in a seaweed robe and a crown of crabs greeted the ambassador with exuberance. The envoy suspected he was being mocked, but the diplomats of foreign powers kindly offering their governance are rarely met with less than disdain. He took his ridicule graciously.

"Absolutely! Earth and water! My fealty is yours!" The Arkadian gave him a cup of piss, and a bowl of shit.

"I, Leonidas, was blind before your gift of leadership, but now I see with opened eyes!" Exclaimed a Korinth on the second day, with his greaves and linothorax worn smartly backwards. His earth and water was a furiously writhing octopus covered in chicken feathers. When the envoy accepted the gift with resignation, the hoplite snatched him by the face and kissed him full on the mouth.

The men of Hellas began to lose themselves in the stillness. Waiting on the threshold of their own death, they gave up their sanity a little bit at a time, in order to keep from losing it all at once. Little windows to the underworld opened inside of them, and demons crawled out. At night, they danced barefoot in their bonfires and howled like beasts.

The third day's offering was a bundle wrapped and carried like an infant from a Thespian singing lullabies. The legate recoiled when he looked beneath the swaddlings and dropped it to the stones of the pass. A pregnant feral dog rolled out from the bundle. She had been cut and turned inside out. Her still living pups squirmed organ-red at the end of their umbilical tethers.

The fourth day, a Macedonian survivor wearing nothing but the slayed face of a captured Persian scout danced wildly and sang in rhyming gibberish. He was no longer tolerated after attempting to fornicate with the envoy's leg.

On the fifth day, the Persian flood from the bridge had slowed to a trickle, and Leonidas himself answered.

"Great King of Sparta." The ambassador was exhausted. "I will waste no more of your precious time. Xerxes in his infinite patience asks for earth and water. You will be named friends of Persia and raised to lord of all the nations of Hellas. Let us go together into this bright future and live forever in peace and plenty." He seemed to genuinely believe his words. Please his eyes begged. "We can be as brothers. Only lay down your weapons."

And Leonidas responded.

"Come and take them."

Λ

Fifty-six

Dienekes sat with Polymedes, Echemmon, and the twins around a small fire in the hills behind the third gate. Stomachs were full to bursting with water and meat, and still officers paced among their men and ordered them to drink from refilled skins. Battle might rage all day, but stopping would not be an option. They sharpened their already sharp swords, polished their already polished armor, oiled each others' already oiled hair. Di looked for anything that could occupy his hands and mind so it would not wander to his distant son.

They looked up as Kosmas, the Tegean commander, presented himself to them. A small, shifty-eyed Macedonian sauntered along his flank.

"I have come to meet the Olympians." He shook their hands eagerly. "Before they are all killed." He lingered on Echemmon. "Remember me, brother?"

"I do." Echemmon rose to embrace him. "You ran well."

"Not well enough to be remembered it would seem."

"Is that why you're here? To be remembered?" Alpheos drolled.

"Yes." Kosmas flashed a blazing smile. "That is exactly why I'm here."

"Sit with us." Echemmon invited them.

"You ran the diaulos?" Dienekes asked.

"I did. Always a step behind this lanky fuck." He punched Echemon's shoulder and pretended it hurt his fist. "Perhaps if my trainers used whips like yours did, you would have tasted my dust instead."

"Small price to pay for a statue."

"And women do love the scars."

They talked and joked and traded stories for a while, and Dienekes took a quick liking to Kosmas. He reminded Di of Tellis, who would be training with the other pankrationists now, perhaps the only Spartan Peer remaining to compete in Olympia. The other Laconians still there were boys, or had all been called away.

To their deaths Di thought bitterly, then banished the thought before the seed of treason could take root.

"Oi, Big Bear." The Macedonian spoke in heavily accented Doric and rattled a small leather purse at Polymedes to his left. "You play, Big Bear?" He poured dice from the pouch into his hand.

"I do not know how." Polymedes shrugged.

"Thats ok, Big Bear, I teach you, Big Bear. First I roll." He cast four dice. "Now you roll, Big bear." He held out the remaining dice to Polymedes who did not take them. Only raised an eyebrow. The Macedonian lifted Poly's slab of a hand, placed the weathered clay cubes on his palm and tilted it so they spilled out. "You see? Is not so hard. Look, you win this round, Big Bear. Now we play for stakes. We'll bet shoes first."

The Macedonian rolled again, and Polymedes humored him.

"See, Big Bear? You good dicer. You win again." He took the tattered leather remnants off his feet and tossed them into the Spartan's lap. "Now we play for shields." They rolled. "Oh, too bad, Big Bear. Tyche smile on me today. Is my shield now."

Polymedes shrugged and held his aspis to the little man, who licked his lips as he reached for it. He pulled, but Poly did not let go. The little man dug in his heels and heaved with his back to no avail. He propped a foot on Poly's breastplate and shoved against it with no more luck, eventually levering both feet against the breastplate. Sweat beaded on the Mycenaean's brow as he grunted but still the Spartan's grip did not budge.

"It is stuck, Big Bear!" He laughed with them, goodnaturedly. Patted the Spartan on the arm and said. "Is okay, Big Bear. I collect tomorrow when you die."

"When we all die." Kosmas corrected him.

"Yes, but I rich man when I die. Rich man with Big Bear's big shield. Come, now we play for helmet."

"Gambling, Polymedes?" Thrasilaos and Polygonos stepped from the shadows. "I shall have to tell the king."

"Will he forgive me if I give him the new shoes I won?" Poly dangled the rotten strips of hide from a finger.

"Likely. Leo always had a weakness for fine footwear." Polygonos said to nods of his peers.

Laughing, Polymedes flicked the sandals back to the Macedonian.

"The northerner can bankrupt you later." Said Thrasilaos. "But come now. You are needed." Then to Dienekes and the twins, "You are all needed."

"Then I am likely needed as well." Kosmas stood and dusted off the white of his linothorax. "Have my gifts brought to Leonidas." He said to his companion, who tapped his nose and turned to leave.

Wait!" Dienekes called to him and glared at the twins, who feigned ignorance until Di smacked Alpheos on his armored chest. "You heard? They bring us gifts." He growled.

Λ

The testicles grumbled and reluctantly tossed the northerner his bag of dice and another purse of belongings they had sleighted away.

"Oh, I see you now, Little Bear." He laughed and tapped his nose again. "Tricksy little bear."

A score of Peers surrounded Leonidas at the middle gate. They strapped extra swords to their belts and stitched narrow leather pockets into the bottoms of their shields to socket extra spears.

Leonidas saw the Olympians approaching and beckoned them to do the same.

"As many as you can carry without it slowing you down." He motioned to the pile of scabbarded xiphos and kopis on a sheepskin roll. "One sword rarely lasts a whole battle. And I'm afraid I won't have the time to stop and make you another."

Dienekes could not help but notice the number of blades already dwindling. There would not be enough to outfit all three hundred hoplites of the hippeis.

"There are so few…" He whispered to the king so as not to appear disobedient. "Should we not save these for the front lines?"

"Did Thrasilaos not tell you? You are the front lines." He laughed at the widening of Di's eyes. "Fear not, little brother. You are ready. I want my Olympians where every friend and foe can see them."

"I am not afraid." Dienekes spoke truly. "Only unworthy. You honor me."

"No, boy. You honor me." Leonidas took Di's white aspis, held it where they both could see and pointed at the four shields painted on it. "This is your father, Hegisistratos. This is your grandfather, Thersandros. They both stood beside me on the front in their time." Di's eyes widened further. He had not known. Leo pointed at the third and fourth shields. "This is you. And this will be your son, Krateros. You know why the four shields?"

Di shook his head.

"It was your father's way. And your father's father's way. Some men fight because they wish to kill, some men fight because they are told. Your father fought in order to protect his own. He had no love of bloodshed, but he loved his brothers. So his shield was worth more than another man's. As we call you Little Achilles, we called him the aegis. The god's own armor. I say there are not enough drawn here to do him justice, but alas I have not brought my paints." He laughed from his belly but sobered again when Di did not join him. "This shield has saved countless Spartan lives. Mine included, and more than once." Leonidas handed it back. "I suspect it will save my life again."

Dienekes sat, inspired, and quietly sewed his two leather sockets into his shield liner like the other men had done.

"No." Said Thrasilaos, peering over his shoulder. "At least twice that many. More

∧

if you can fit them."

"But the others-"

"Don't worry about them. We are doing things differently tomorrow."

"We?" It was the first time his old eriene had referred to them as such. We. Together. The same.

"Yes, We." Thrasilaos licked his pointed teeth. "You are my second."

Drums were beating in Di's head. His first battle in the phalanx would not only be in the front lines but he was stationed on the second row, directly behind the fiercest killer in all of Lakedaimon.

"You two as well." Thrasilaos said to Alpheos and Maron. "You are behind the Weeper. Wear many spears. Many Xiphos. No Kopis. Leave the choppers for the heavy brutes. We are not hulking sloggards. We are the serpent. We are fast." He relished the final word. "I expected to support from the cliffside by myself, but more important men than I have insisted that my Disappointments join me. So prove me wrong and try not to hold me back."

"Remember our squad name, Puddles?" Polygonos approached, bristling with weapons. He was on the line to the left of Thrasilaos. The spot would have gone to Pantites, but the runner had been dispatched to Thessaly to try and convince them to turn once more against the Mede.

"I do." Thrasilaos stared wistfully up, as if remembering fondly. "One of our unit was brought to the initiation with the flux, then we all caught it. From then on we were called "Nightsoil"."

"Wait... Puddles?" Maron asked.

"He pissed himself his first time getting whipped." Dienekes was delighted to finally tell someone that secret. The twins gawked in disbelief.

"I did. Caught me by surprise." Thrasilaos admitted. "Polygonos here was called Trumpet."

"I was. The first night I snuck out to steal food, I got caught."

"And what got you caught?" Thrasilaos egged him on.

"I was hiding in a bush when a few Peers walked by, and I was so nervous I couldn't help but play them a tune. On my trumpet."

Alpheos and Maron did not understand. Who plays music when trying to sneak? Polygonos clarified for them.

"I farted."

The Tegeans arrived with their wagon.

"I had intended to use these myself." Kosmas dragged a long bundle from the cart and tugged at its bindings. "But the king seems determined to deprive me of that chance. So they are yours now."

Λ

He kicked open the roll, unwrapping dozens of freshly forged spears.

"Something wrong with ours?" Leonidas asked.

"Wrong? No. But mine are certainly more right." He borrowed one of the Spartan lances and held it adjacent to one of his own, which stood significantly taller. "The Persians use spears only five feet long. Yours are eight. Mine? Ten. It was my little Macedonian friend's idea. He's full of clever little schemes. We had them made special for this little get together. See? The points are narrower and rounded on the back. So they can cut through their wicker shields and pull back out without snagging. Lets see how they reach us while we fuck them in the eyes with these, yeah?"

Leonidas graciously accepted and distributed them to his men.

"It's good to have friends," he said, leaning on the Tegean.

"Until they're all dead." Kosmas's shining smile widened each time he spoke of death.

Λ

Fifty-seven

D awn found the Spartan guard ready and waiting while the Persians bumbled into each other, struggling to organize their bloated ranks between the thicketed hills to the south and the cliffs over the sea to the north. The Spartiates waited with a smile, basking in the Thermopylaian steam, its warm vapors staving off the morning chill. There was no more tension with their hour arrived. They stood calm and alert, almost happy. They had trained for this moment their entire lives. There was not a soul on the field more ready than the Lakonian. His time had come. Kosmas, Leontiades, Demophilos, and others stood by. To show their support, wish luck, or to say goodbye. Any and all were the case.

"I thought you said you would deploy at the third gate?" Kosmas turned left and right with his arms spread. The well wishers stood level with Leonidas and his front line at the Phokian wall, the middle gate, nearly a mile from the narrow shelf that the Phokians helped prepare for them.

"I will." Leoniads responded, his gaze staying fixed on the distant enemy.

"Then I imagine there's a reason you're on the wrong side of the map?"

Leo smirked.

"I want to get a running start."

The stone path on the edge of Sebastos's swamp was only wide enough for five rows of hoplites to fit comfortably shoulder to shoulder. Polymedes took the inland corner, his bulk and overlarge shield intended to take the brunt of what the Mede intended to give. Another shield hung from his back should it be needed. In his shadow stood Echemmon, slight in comparison, but tireless and precise with the kill. Echemmon locked his shield under Krateros's, Krateros locked his with Leonidas, and Leonidas with Polygonos. Dienekes had found a new respect for Polygonos in the recent days, discovering his slack as a substitute eirene had been a ruse to make Thrasilaos appear all the more terrifying. Polygonos was every bit the hardened fighter his brothers were.

The hippeis usually deployed thirty or forty men wide, eight to twelve men deep. With only five men on the front, each stood bolstered by the combined might of over fifty elite Spartiates locked behind him. It should have been sixty, but the three hundred and one guardsmen lacked a handful of their full strength. Pantites had not returned from his dispatch to Thessaly, and two more had been struck suddenly blind with an unknown affliction of the eye since arriving at the pass. Krateros ordered them off the battlefield. Thrasilaos joined the front on the right wing, leading a scant sixth row whose toes barely clung to the cliff edge. Dienekes stood behind Thrasilaos, Alpheos and Maron behind Dienekes, and behind them no one.

"Are we supposed to push with the strength of fifty men? Just the four of us?" Dienekes asked.

"I told you yesterday we were doing things differently. Were you not listening?" Thrasilaos shook his limbs out and stretched, as if warming up for the Olympics he had been called away from, deviant to his fellow guards who stood at perfect attention.

"Did you not tell the boys your scheme?" Polygonos asked.

"I told the testicles. But the Weeper does better when thrown directly into fire. Telling him beforehand gives him time to fret and cry. Besides, you see how he makes me repeat myself?" Thrasilaos leaned on Polygonos to stretch his thighs.

"Expecting a soldier to follow a plan without telling them what it is? Curious strategy."

"Curious indeed." Krateros interjected. "But more curisosities have influenced Thrasilaos in his upbringing than the rest of us. And he knows Dienekes better than anyone. It's a gambit, but a gambit I trust."

"The first polemarch of Sparta laying a wager?" Leonidas laughed. "What a day indeed."

He knows Dienekes better than anyone.

It was a notion Di struggled to swallow, but it made sense. Thrasilaos had been an ever present nightmare in his periphery for nearly two decades. There was no telling how much time Sharktooth had spent spying on him in secret, which frightened him far more than the thought of a million Medes.

"They are moving." Krateros barked. The ranks beside and behind him socketed tighter together.

"Hold!" Leonidas gave the command superfluously, only to ready his troop for the second order. A cloud of shadow ascended from the Persian horde, climbing like a flock of birds before arcing back down. "Shields up!"

Leontiades, Kosmas, Sebastos and their agents dove behind the Phokian wall as arrows rained down around them. The volley bounced harmlessly off Spartan bronze, each soldier guarding himself and those to his sides. Except for Thrasilaos, who continued callously limbering up in spite of the shafts peppering the ground around him. He did not stop stretching when the other five ranks began to march forward, slowly droning the paian, their battle hymn. The column had nearly passed them when he turned to Dienekes.

Λ

"Forget the rest of the phalanx today. Think only of the four of us. There will be no time for orders. No time for questions. My actions are my commands. Do as I do."

Dienekes nodded. He felt strangely in his element. His place had never been in the thick of Spartan order, always supporting somehow from the side.

This is how we yet serve.

The main column broke into a jog, shields still linked together tight as scales on a snake. Each foot struck the ground in time, one stride, one unified step beating like a drum from beneath the earth in time with the paian. They did not hesitate to charge into the second volley of arrows that scattered pitifully against their shields.

A third volley struck to the same effect by the time Thrasilaos advanced. The main force galloped hundreds of yards ahead but Dienekes caught easily with his Olympic speed, the twins close behind. Arrows stopped falling as the Persian vanguard struggled to reorder themselves. Archers fled in panic with nothing to protect them from the charging hoplites. Medish infantry barely had time to jostle into position before red and bronze streaked past the second gate. Someone cracked a whip and the Persians, still disordered but now close enough for the Lakonians to see their sun-brown faces, shrieked forward. Most were mired in the Phokian marsh, but a ribbon of still thousands coursed along the hard rock precipice to meet the Spartans.

The front of the hippeis halted step, still singing their hymn. The five men in front leaned on the shields behind them for balance and the strength of nearly three hundred men in tow continued to skid them forward. They dropped as one into a low crouch behind their shields and hammered into the ragged barbarian charge.

Medes crashed over the wall of bronze like a wave. The weight of thousands behind forced the forerunners to clatter overtop Spartan shields where they were minced on short swords, or spilled to the sides to drown in mud and brine. The brunt of the vanguard caused no more damage to the Hellenes than the arrows had. Persians far enough behind to survive the initial collision, but close enough to see its devastation, recoiled in shock but the tide of the horde behind did not slow. Countless soldiers still clamored to the fray from the back, trampling over and tangling with their own. They mounded over each other, fell in helpless heaps where they lay their weapons outranged by the new ten foot Spartan spears. The Tegean lanceheads went to work hungrily, and rapidly transformed the pile of struggling Persians into a barricade of dead men. No Mede could show his face over the top of the growing hill without a spearhead diving down his throat. Their choice was to hesitate and be crushed beneath the boots of their own or go bravely, shredding themselves on the meat grinder of Lakedaimon. Hundreds died in seconds.

Dienekes slipped by his comrades up the narrow cliff edge and saw the mound of corpses topple up and over the phalanx's front ranks, burying them. The avalanche covered his king, his mentor, his fellow Olympians, the whole three ranks closest to the fight. With Medes scrambling down on the backs of their fallen the fourth, fifth, sixth lines of hoplites were too busy killing to stop and dig their leaders out. At least until Thrasilaos hit the fray in a red mist. He dismembered the Medes on his side of the mound of bodies and scaled to the top and stood alone, effortlessly dodging javelins and skewering anyone brave or stupid enough to meet him. The olive crowns on his helmet dripped blood.

Do as I do.

Dienekes and the twins joined him on the writhing mound.

"Break them up!" Thrasilaos shouted. "Throw their own spears at the middle to spread them out and leave the close ones to me! Stay low!"

Di and the twins gathered up the short-hafted Persian lances and threw them as bidden, killing as they could but still buying precious seconds when they missed. Thrasilaos ended the scattered few who made it within his range. The four of them stood alone against thousands, their own advance still buried beneath the first wave of dead. If the Persians mustered the gall to rush again now it would be over. Persian fear was the only armor keeping Disappointment alive.

"Leo was right!" Maron shouted to Dienekes, who could not stop throwing spears long enough to respond. "Olympian! Chosen of the Gods! They are here with us! See how the mudmen run from you?"

Maron was right. Dienekes could not peer over the bunker to throw a spear without the nearest barbarians flinching away and tripping up his fellows behind. Their cowardice spelled their demise.

"Enough!" Shouted Thrasilaos, jumping down from the ridge. "Back to the sixth!"

They followed and helped their captain kick, push, and drag their dead foes into the sea. They had guarded the mound for a minute at the most, but it was long enough. The front lines were wrestling free from beneath their dismembered enemies. Dienekes's heart sang to see Krateros roar upright, his Kopis pointed skyward.

"Back from Hades!" Leonidas bellowed beside him. Polymedes's shield remained buried. While Echemmon covered him the hoplitodrome hefted a corpse off of his aspis in each hand, hauled them up over his head, and threw them into the closest barbarians, sprawling them into the swamp to be picked off by Arkadian slingers.

The phalanx reformed, dropped back, and opened up. Tight formation with shields interlocked was best for defense, but not for killing, and killing is how battles are won. With space between the rows, the hoplites in front had room to fight freely without the risk of cutting their brothers and the Spartans behind could fit their spears overtop and in between.

Hind ranks passed fresh lances forward to replace the ones lost or broken. Not a

Λ

single Spartan had yet to succumb to the enemy and with their phalanx regrouped, their enemies flocked mindlessly to their deaths. Medish moths flew to their deaths in the Lakedaimonian flame.

"Keep them broken up!" Thrasilaos shouted to his little suicide squad, as he slotted them back on the right flank, the four-man sixth row. "Let them make it to us, but not together! Keep them scattered!"

It was simple enough. The wall of carnage propped between the armies forced the attackers to climb up on their hands and knees to summit the slope unprepared and in small numbers. They were easy pickings for the hoplites waiting patiently on the other side.

Thrasilaos himself danced recklessly in and out of the phalanx front, deliberately making himself a target and fooling Medes to chase him back within reach of his brothers' lances. He didn't lean into the press of Dien's shield like the other Spartans did, but used it as a backboard, bouncing in and out of the thickest fighting. Weeper watched in awe. No foe made it near enough for Dienekes to use his own weapons.

Perhaps it had been fear of his master that warped his perception, but he had never realized how small Thrasilaos really was. He stood nearly a head shorter than Dienekes and even slighter in build. His body writhed with tawny sinews, powerful for an ordinary man, but scrawny for a Spartan. He fought with alacrity instead of power, slaying more enemies than not without touching them, instead dodging smartly aside so they slipped off the cliff into the sea.

Thrasilaos did not even fight with a Lakonian aspis. His shield was tiny in comparison, gripped by a single handle in its middle rather than strapped to the full length of the forearm. Instead of blocking he would reach out to turn a blow, trapping an opponent's weapon to their own shield before sliding his xiphos over or under their guard and into their lungs. Over and over he taunted them, filling their field of vision with a sweep of his lion cloak and reappearing elsewhere, or baiting the enraged enemy to chase him before he blurred back into formation while his brothers ripped the pursuers apart.

"Is that the Skythian way?" Dienekes shouted over the clamor.

"No." Thrasilaos licked his needle teeth. Blood dripped down his chin. "Its *my* way." And he saulted off Di's white shield back to the killing.

Still the Spartans sang. This, among other things, set the phalanx of Lakedaimon apart from other poleis. They never stopped their music. Floutists droned on their auloi from the rear and each man too far to fight drummed spears on shields. Every voice rose in harmony for as long as the battle raged. The music of the paian kept them in rhythm, kept their movements unified, their minds and bodies as one. Spears splintered, swords shattered, Spartan arms did not tire. They drew their next weapon and kept the fight.

Λ

"Are you learning, Weeper?" Thrasilaos shouted over the melee. "Do you understand your place here? Good!" Thrasilaos did not wait for an answer. "Pay attention now, this is the hard part!"

He pounced back out into the foray, killed half a dozen men easily as plucking apples, and sliced back into the phalanx, but between the other lines this time and not in his station on the right flank. Dienekes, heart pounding, was forced to step forward and take his place.

"Get em, Achilles!" The twins cheered from behind. Their spears reached over his shoulders, killing even faster than his own.

Λ

Fifty-eight

The Persians retreated. Fields of bodies sprawled so thick at the king's feet that he could not see the rock beneath. He gave no order to fall back, so his men remained at the gate. He knew there were more coming.

"Look at them." He vexed at one of the dead with the tip of his second Kopis. His first had already snapped. "Rabble."

The dead soldier's shield was made of wicker, good for stopping arrows but flimsy against a trained combatant up close. Scales of crude iron mailed his chest, softer than Spartan bronze from a century before. The tunic and trousers beneath his armor were ragged, patched from many colors of cloth. He wore no helmet, only a felt cap. Rust grew like moss on his sword. The others fallen around him were similarly ill equipped.

"They're not even soldiers. Peasants in scavenged armor." Krateros waded with him through the corpses, dispatching those that still moved. "This one didn't even have a spear, just a sharpened stick. He was trying us. So many lost and only to test our strength."

Leonidas nodded agreement and asked.

"How many of ours dead?"

Krateros glanced at his men, no gaps in the file. All at attention except Thrasilaos doing calisthenics off to the side.

"None." Krateros's stoney face could not hide its relief from his old friend, who grinned back. Leonidas, normally sullen and brooding, had been smiling all his waking hours these recent days.

"Then I believe we have passed his test" he said. "But fear not. I am sure he prepares another. Perhaps I make one for him."

Some of the Hellenes in reserve visited the line to gawk at the immortal Spartans, and help them push bodies into the sea. Tegeans brought water, bread, and meat. The hippeis drank gratefully, but abstained from food.

"A full mongoose is a slow mongoose." Thrasilaos told Kosmas, declining as politely as Thrasilaos could. "A slow mongoose is a dead mongoose." Their helots brought them more black broth instead.

Kosmas raised an eyebrow. "What the fuck is a mongoose?"

"We'll meet the next wave further up." Leonidas declared. "I want more room to dance." The Arkadians and Orchomenes had been weaving little thatchwood bridges so their skirmishers could navigate the swamp and strike from far enough forward to support the Hippeis, but Leo wanted to be even further forward than that. Arkadia would have to sling from directly behind. The other advisors didn't like it, thought he would be too exposed, but who were they to tell a Spartan what to do.

Xerxes must have realized his arrows did him no good. He wasted no more that day.

"Now these are soldiers." Leonidas grunted approval at the column marching to meet him.

They did not rush forward or stagger back at random like the peons in the first wave. They maintained cohesion as they marched. They did not falter when Arkadian rocks rained on them. If a man fell dead beside them, they did not recoil in fear at his blood. They stepped over his body and marched on.

The hippeis waited for them boldly, several hundred meters ahead of the third gate, well within range of Xerxes's archers. The Phokian swamp would not protect their flank here, but Leonidas invited his enemy to try and take it. He would not be here long. They deployed in broad formation, eight men deep and nearly forty men wide.

Once in range, the Tegean spears cut through the wicker Persian shields like paper. The elite of Xerxes's horde fell in droves, unable to reach their enemy, but they marched on as automatons. Thrasilaos, back in his place at the head of the sixth line, repeatedly tried and failed to scatter their line or bait a chase for himself, but they were too disciplined. The moment one Persian was slain, another took his place. Their advance was slow, steady, methodical. They did not crash into their dead as the wave before them had, nor would they fall for a similar trap. Still bodies mounded.

"Withdraw!" Leonidas thundered.

The ranks of the Spartans dashed from the line of scrimmage, but only a few metres. The Persians in front hustled to catch what they thought was a retreating enemy only to expedite their own impaling. The Spartans held their new position until another ledge of carnage had formed, just high enough to struggle stepping over. Leo did not want another wall. He wanted his foe to keep coming.

"Withdraw!" The king shouted again. "Let them count their dead before they join!"

They killed another few hundred, then gave up a fathom. Killed another few hundred, then gave up another fathom. With so many hurdles obstructing them, the Persian advance was slowing. But it never stopped. These men had come with purpose. They did not scream when they died.

Λ

Kill another hundred, fall back. Kill another hundred, fall back.

The Medes tried everything they could to reach past the Tegean spears. They threw their own spears, their axes, some tried to fire their bows from the battle lines, but had to stow their shields to do so and died all the easier for it.

Kill another hundred, fall back.

Had the Persians rushed instead of marching in time, then the width of their battalion could have surrounded Leonidas and his men. But even at their tedious, measured approach, the hoplites were slowly being engulfed. Their retreats came quicker and left fewer dead.

Kill fifty. Fall back.

Kill twenty. Fall back.

Kill a dozen. Fall back.

The terrain behind them narrowed. Their formation was too wide to continue retreating. The left Spartan flank scissored into the main group a row at a time. In a practiced motion from left to right, the exposed line merged with their neighbor, doubling its length, then folding the excess onto the rear. The Tegean spears had been depleted. The fighting was closer now, some Spartans left with only their swords.

Kill. Fold. Fall back. Kill. Fold. Fall back.

The hippeis slotted together seamlessly, squeezing through the gate while the bulk of the advancing forces were trapped by their numbers against the steep thicketed hillside. Perhaps a lone hunter with his wilderness expertise could have scurried through the brush, but for a soldier in full regalia, it was impassable terrain. They had missed their chance. Phokian slingstones and arrows harassed the barbarians from the cover of the hills, which they had no choice but to endure. Retreat was not an option until the thousands more behind were mobilized elsewhere. The only way out was to die.

The Spartans, braced in the sanctuary of the third gate, resumed their lethal math.

Kill a hundred. Fall back. Kill a hundred. Fall back.

Survivors had warned Xerxes's elites about the swamp and only a few dared to test it when their ranks spilled like ants onto the pass. Arkadian slingers were thrilled to rejoin the fight in earnest but this second wave, much more stalwart that the first, did not so readily scatter and die. Still, the stones combined with the tax of clambering over hurdles of fallen were finally breaking up their formation. Thrasilaos leapt from his post and screaming, went to work.

These unrelenting fighters gave Thrasilaos more trouble, he was only able to cull one or two at a time before slipping back between the lines of his own, but still he did the work of a dozen men. Keeping the enemy front out of unity meant the Spartans weren't fighting as much as simply tidying up. Dienekes had broken two spears, his third was seeing use, but still he studied his former teacher- how he could slip between

Λ

a Spartiate and their aspis so four arms fought from behind a single shield, how he would grab an enemy spear thrust instead of blocking it to pull its bearer onto the Lakonian blades, how he changed lines by walking or rolling over the shoulders and backs of his comrades while they laughed and cheered him on. They trusted him, they moved with him. Di had never seen a man so alive. This was Thrasilaos's home. If the phalanx was the wolf, Thrasilaos was the teeth.

Leonidas was the howl.

"Run!" The king commanded his men. "Full retreat! Back to the wall!"

Dienekes hesitated. He did not know what had gone wrong. They had been doing so well, but an order was an order. All three hundred Spartans broke formation, turned their backs to the enemy and sprinted for the middle gate, still maybe half a mile away.

The Persians roared victorious and galloped after.

Di felt his mentor's hand on his shoulder as they fled.

"Not so fast." Krateros advised. "You saw how they equip. A bow, a spear, a sword, an axe, all of them. Most have even more. They can't run with all that clatter."

"Isn't that a good thing?" Di asked. They were both trained sprinters, and could easily talk while outrunning their peers.

"No, boy. They'll never catch us that way."

"Isn't that the point?"

"No, dammit! We want them to catch us!"

As the Phokian wall loomed closer, Dienekes saw the members of the front line slowing, looking over their shoulders, falling back into single file. Echemmon dragged behind, limping, but Dienekes saw no blood. He was faking. Polygonos and Thrasilaos cackled wildly. Leonidas and Polymedes switched places from side to middle as the king trotted backwards, counting. The bulk of the hippeis wallowed, trying to tease the Persians as close as possible.

"What's going on?" Alpheos asked.

The wall was only fifty meters away now...forty...thirty.

"No time!" Dienekes responded, and he only had an inkling himself. "Just follow me!"

The back rank of the fleeing Spartans stopped dead and spun with shields raised. The rank after them turned on their heels and slammed their back into the shield presented, raising their own for the next rank. The Spartans stacked their phalanx back together in seconds, tight formation. With the rim of each aspis hooked under the rim of the aspis to the right, it did not matter how hard the Mede pushed from the front or the hippeis from the rear. Each pound of force only locked the shields that much tighter. Dienekes and the twins fell in behind Thrasilaos, stepping where he stepped. He did not rejoin the front line but vaulted over it, his feet finding purchase on the backs of his brothers. Disappointment followed, then Echemmon

Λ

and Polygonos too, not in the formation, but on top of it.

"Be a good little brother." Thrasilaos told them, his eyes wild and mouth foaming. "Try not to step on their necks."

Leonidas gave the order, and the Spartans pushed as one. Their flight had kicked up so much dust that the leading Persians in pursuit were dead before they saw the crimson and bronze monolith stomping back toward, and their charge crushed in on itself just as the wave before them had. The Medes were caught off balance, disoriented, surprised... They were dissected on Spartan blades, pulverized in the throng, or shoved off the pass to drown if they weren't first trampled by the leviathan of Sparta. The Spartans folded them over, and still they marched. Their muscles screamed fiery protest against the exertion of turning the horde, but they were accustomed to the strain. The trials of the agoge had demanded the same exertion every day for thirteen years, preparing them for exactly this. Pain was their mother. Through her they had been reborn.

The other Hellenes in reserve were just as confused as the Medes. The quickest witted, Kosmas and Leontiades, ordered their personal guards to support. Eventually the other regiments followed, squeezing as many troops as they could up next to the killing fields. Javelins, arrows, slingstones and insults hammered the Persians from beside and above while the anvil of Lakonia broke them from the front.

The corpse baffles Leonidas built of his dead enemies were all the harder to surmount when walking backwards, and the rear of the formation could not see the devastation they pushed their countrymen into. There could be no retreat.

A boyhood spent pushing down trees made a man who had no trouble pushing down other men. Three hundred of them could push an army.

The phalanx advanced, smashed like a battering ram through clay pots leaving nothing but shards in their wake. They need not bother to step over the piles of deceased, pushing them aside easily as a broom pushes dust. Polymedes pulled the extra shield from his back and carried one in each arm, angled into a wedge. Its point cut into the foundering barbarian horde, driving them aside or trampling them beneath, mutilated by the sauroteurs on the butts of the Hellenic spears. The phalanx became a blade and incised through the heart of the shattered enemy, the Olympians riding on top of it. One foot standing on Krateros, the other foot on the king, Dienekes drove his spear down from above. Thrasilaos, Polygonos, Echemmon and the twins did the same. Leo's words at the council rang in his ears.

Let them come.

I will meet them with giants.

Λ

The Persians were routed and the Spartans left the pass to the cheers of their allies. They held their heads and shields high, their bodies exhausted and burning though they refused to show it.

"So were you watching, Weeper?" Thrasilaos asked as they stumbled, fatigue threatening to put them on their knees. "Do you understand the role you are supposed to play?"

Dienekes refreshed in his mind the visions of the day. Supporting from the edge too narrow to field a whole column, dancing in and out of the lines where he was needed, pecking at the enemy formation to stack the odds for his brothers.

"I believe I do." Dienekes had learned much that day, his first day of battle.

"Good." Thrasilaos nodded and unfastened his lion skin mantle. He cut off Dien's crimson cloak before Di could object, let it fall to the ground, and replaced it with the predator's hide. "Then wear this. The Persians will think they fight the same beast. They will fear you."

"What? I can't fight like you. Move like you. If-"

"You will have to. Move like me. Fight like me. Be me."

"I can fight, I can do my part, but I am only one. With you and the twins we can-"

"You are not listening, Weeper. You have to be all of us tomorrow. Alpheos, Maron, Thrasilaos, and Dienekes…" It was the first time the teacher had ever said the student's true name. "You must be all four of us tomorrow."

Dienekes realized his teacher's meaning, but Thrasilaos said it anyway.

"Tomorrow. On the sixth line. You will be alone."

Λ

Fifty-nine

espite the day's victory, camp was somber and quiet. Not a single Lakonian had died, but to celebrate this was to ignore that the enemy's numbers did not seem diminished in the slightest. Mere hours after the battle, Phokian spies reported that the second wave, Xerxes's elites, had already replenished their copious losses and were positioned again to mobilize at their full strength of ten thousand. It took thirteen years to make a Spartan, and Xerxes seemed able to pull troops from thin air.

The spears from Kosmas had been depleted, and many of the Spartan spears as well. The other Hellenes pooled supplies to re-equip the hippeis at the risk of under arming their own. It begged the question, how long could this last?

"What's he doing?" Dienekes asked the twins, and pointed to where Thrasilaos sat out of his armor with a heavy blindfold over his eyes. Polygonos helped him blacken his body with dead coals.

"Must be going on a night mission." Maron checked the horizon. "Maybe an hour before sundown. The blindfold is to keep his night vision sharp." He'd used the technique himself many times.

"He said he wouldn't be with us in the pass tomorrow."

"Oh?" Alpheos and Maron shared a look.

"He said you wouldn't be there either." Dienekes tried not to accuse, but his meaning was plain. The twins shrugged. "When were you going to tell me? Were you going to tell me at all?"

"We do as we are told. Just like you. Besides, he had a point earlier. About throwing you into the fire."

"What is that supposed to mean?"

"You're a thinker, Di. Thinkers do better on the field when they're not... You know." Alpheos weighed his hands.

"Given time to think." Maron finished for him.

Dienekes grumbled. But they were right. He was already festering over why he hadn't been told, what they were doing without him. But to ask further questions would prove them right. He joined the other Olympians around Leonidas's fire and tried to think of other things.

"What tricks do we show the Persians tomorrow?" Polymedes asked his king.

"None."

"None?"

"We'll give the others a chance to fight in the morning. See who Xerxes sends against them. They'll be able to rotate units from the cover of the wall. We'll standby to step in at will."

"And then?"

"We'll fight plainly. They're not accustomed to fighting in a press. We'll squeeze them, and push them up the pass until they're choked off at the third gate." Leonidas seemed bored. "With so little room to move, our options are as limited as theirs. We can only run forwards and back so many times. We should assume he's caught on. Meanwhile he'll continue throwing troops on us for as long as he has them and it seems he will always have them. So any tactics we field would be more for show than lend to our success."

"What about Thrasilaos?" Dienekes asked.

"What about him?"

"Well not him exactly. But his ways. He fights out of formation. Crafty. Wants me to fight out of formation as well. It seems to work. There's got to be other ways we can out think Xerxes. Make our weapons, our men, last longer."

"That was precisely my point, Dienekes." The king stirred the coals in the fire under a another tripod of the infamous Spartan black broth. "Not only will they no longer fall for our traps, but whatever we do, they'll only respond by sending greater and greater numbers. The efforts of individuals, while valiant, will be unlikely to yield great effect. Unless you have a way of turning one spear thrust into two, we are only biding time."

"There must be something we haven't considered." Krateros said. "Short of hiding in a wooden horse. Do you think he's heard that story?"

"I will wait patiently for your report on the matter." The king dismissed the notion.

"Anaxandridas was known for his unconventional methods... His sons are known for their unconventional methods..." Krateros pressed the issue.

"I know what you're implying." Leonidas ruffled. "But I am not my brother. The agoge molded me into the same creature as you, so I doubt there is anything I know that you don't. Perhaps if Kleo were here, he would have some daring scheme to save us. But he is not."

"Well he is. In a way."

"Oh. I suppose if you mean...."

"Yes. Thrasilaos. Pantites. Polymedes. Dienekes. There are more. Their specialties

Λ

were all inspired by Kleo. He helps us still."

"Specialties?" Dien could understand why the others were mentioned, but not himself.

"You mean you didn't feel the invisible hand of the king pushing you along, Dienekes?"

He remembered the first wager, when he was made to race Krateros and was accepted into the Olympiad for it. Ono had said the name "Little Achilles" was first whispered in Olympia by Kleo himself in disguise. His ways were subtle for such a boisterous man.

"I felt it." Dienekes was thinking again, no matter how hard he tried not to. "But I suppose I understand what was different about the others he had a hand in. Thrasilaos learned to fight as a hoplite and as a rogue. And Polymedes... well... he's an elephant. I wonder what was special about me."

"Kleos."

Glory.

Di knew the word but did not comprehend its relevance.

"Think about it too hard and you'll hurt yourself. Trust that my brother could see it in a man, a spark, even before it had time or opportunity to ignite. He saw it in Krateros, he saw it in your father. He had an eye. And a mind for... manipulating... the things he saw." Leo's face turned dark. Too many memories.

"What happened to him?" Dienekes asked. The fireside went quiet, but Di couldn't leave it alone. "I remember him being king. Then suddenly he wasn't. No one talks about it."

"Indeed." Leonidas nodded to Krateros and rose to leave. "No one does."

The other Olympians left as well. Most of them would have been Spartiates of age when Leotychidas was crowned in Kleo's stead. Either they had already heard the story, or did not care to know. Krateros was left to tell Dienekes and the twins.

"Kleo was always strange."

"But the people loved him for it?"

"Some more than others. Mostly just tolerated him, for his strangeness always brought us victory. Until it didn't. There was a point where his curiosity deteriorated into madness."

"Have you heard how Demaratos was deposed?"

Disappointment shook their heads.

"The oracle at Delphi confided to the ephors that his birth was illegitimate. That his mother horned King Ariston with a foreigner and Demaratos was his."

"Then he should have been deposed. Shame on them." Alpheos was quick to judge.

∧

"So we thought. Until we discovered it was a lie."

"No..." Dienekes was reading between the lines.

"Yes. Kleomenes had bribed the oracle for false augury. Despite his fame with our people, Demaratos was always Kleo's first and loudest objector. He must have thought he could accomplish more unobstructed. He convinced the elders to instate his cousin Leotychidas instead."

"But what of Demaratos? Why wasn't he reinstated?"

"Well..." Krateros laughed bitterly. "His reign was defined by two things. His chariot victory at Olympia, and being a thorn in Kleo's side. He had no other accomplishments. Even before Dareios was making his way into Hellas, Kleomenes saw the signs and attempted to thwart it. Demaratos hampered him every step of the way. There was suspicion that he was sympathetic to the barbarian. A suspicion that was confirmed."

"He didn't..." Dienekes was confounded in all that he didn't know. He only knew Demaratos as the man who presented him to the people when he returned from his first games.

"He did." Krateros confirmed.

"He did what?" The twins were even more ignorant than Di.

"He medized. Ran straight to the lap of Dareios. Before Thrace, before Argos, before Macedon and Thessaly...The very first traitor to Hellas was a king of Sparta. We would never have him back."

"What did Kleo do when you found out about the bribe?"

"He was nowhere to be found. He was always a smart man, he must have suspected that he would be found out and left before the wind turned on him."

"So Leonidas took his place?"

"No. Not yet. We found him in Arkadia. Some of the Eurypontids believe he committed treason as well, trying to rally them to attack Sparta."

"But he would never do that..." Dienekes scowled.

"Oh, but he was. But he did not believe Arkadia would be victorious. He saw how the other nations bickered and backstabbed each other, while across the sea all of Persia marched as one under a single king. He thought Arkadia would lose, and become vassal to Sparta. Then Athens. Then Thespia. Then Thebes. So on until all Hellas was one nation. He saw this as the way to beat Dareios. Leotychidas and I were complicit to the scheme, though we despised it."

"That doesn't make sense... To fight Persia, he would have done exactly what Xerxes is trying to do. Conquer us all."

"Too true. Kleo realized this as well, and it tormented him. He saw no way of defeating Dareios without Hellas unified, and had learned from experience that diplomacy was not... reliable."

Λ

"But Arkadia didn't march?"

"No. Because who would risk a war with Sparta? And perhaps they could smell the ruse. We invited him home. The ephors scorned his actions but they could not defy the people's love for their king. But he was already too far gone."

"Too far gone?"

"Boy, does encouraging another nation to attack his Kingdom sound like the action of a sane man?" Dienekes kept his mouth shut. "He was in pieces, poor man. A muttering simp. Swinging wildly from joy, to anger, to sadness. Speaking to people who weren't there, ignoring those who were. And the wine. Always the wine."

"Is that why you don't drink it anymore?"

Krateros paused, glared, nodded.

"Why Leo doesn't drink either. The final straw was when he took to wandering the streets drunken and beating our own citizens with his staff."

"What sense is that?" Maron could not stifle a chuckle.

"At first I thought the same as you. His mind had come detached, but attacking our own... is it not a crude facsimile for the conflict he sought to sow in Arkadia? Sparta's way is war. In matters violent, we rise above. The harder we are struck, the stronger we become. So he struck us."

"Or he was just drunk." Said Alpheos. Krateros snorted.

"Or he was just drunk." The polemarch nodded, sadness in his eyes. "Leonidas thinks it was drink that undid him. It certainly did not help, but I have seen many men succumb to drink and it is not the same. Gorgo, his daughter, thinks it was loneliness, which is more likely. It is a lonely thing to lead. But Kleo loved many and had many more who loved him. I think Kleo's undoing was a greater power. Have you heard of Sepeia?"

"Yes! Where Kleo single handedly burned the might of Argos?"

"And what did he burn them in?"

Disappointment looked to each other, they did not know.

"There was a sacred wood outside of Argos that had grown there since before Herakles gave birth to our people. Not just sacred to them, but to all of us who follow the gods. As sacred as Delphi, as Altis, as the island of Delos, or Mount Olympos. The gods themselves walked there. And Kleo burned it down."

"They cursed him?"

"I believe they did. Sent the furies to tear at his mind till their talons left it in tatters."

"So what happened to him?"

"Spartiates in the street would not act against their king. They would take his stick if he swung it at them but they were used to his mania, they assumed he was illustrating some obscure idea as he usually did. Leonidas himself had to intervene. He and some

Λ

of Kleo's most loyal guardsmen arrested their king and stockaded him in a secret location. There would be no trial, no crime to answer for. They only intended to hold him. Sober him up. Speak to him. Decide what was to be done. He might have been a man deranged, but he was still a good king."

"Something else happened instead then?"

"Yes." Krateros faltered. His breath sped, a vein pulsed in his forehead. "A... a uh... While he was in bondage. A helot's knife found him in the dark."

"Tell them the truth, Polemarch." Thrasilaos stepped into the light of their dying fire and threw another log onto it. His eyes were still blindfolded, but he made his way around just fine without sight.

Krateros bowed his head and spoke no more.

"The part about the helot's knife is true. But it was no helot."

"An assassin?"

"In a manner of speaking." Thrasilaos stared at them through the blindfold. Waited for them to ask. "When a Peer feels he has failed his homeland, he falls on his sword. But Kleomenes had no sword, and dying did not come easy for one so strong. He still had his silver tongue, the devil. The details are infirm... but somehow the king found his cunning way out of his bonds, and convinced a helot to surrender his knife. Kleo took that knife, and flayed himself. When the guards found him in the morning, he was still alive. But not a ribbon of flesh remained on his body. I think he was trying to cut the demons out."

Dienekes was staggered.

"Do you think he succeeded?" He asked. "I hope so. He was always kind to me."

"We will be able to ask him ourselves soon enough." Thrasilaos, still through the blindfold, turned to the twins. "Come, Testicles. It is time."

They followed him into the dark, turning only to wave goodbye to their Weeper.

"We'll be seeing you tomorrow Achilles."

"But Thrasilaos said you'd not be coming."

They winked at him knowingly, which he loved and hated them for.

"We'll be seeing you tomorrow, Achilles."

Something changed in the wind. A smell. A charge. The flower of intuition bloomed. Di and Krateros were on their feet and running before they heard the screams. They were not the only ones. Sons of Lakedaimon flocked to the disturbance, spears and shields at the ready. Their vigilance was met with relief. The cries were not screams, but laughter. Some of the Lakonians had disturbed a hornet nest. They laughed at each other and themselves, and their brothers did too. Most walked away shaking their heads, some stayed to pinch the insects off their victims. Little red bumps were rising on half a dozen of them already.

Λ

"Come, little brother." Krateros said to Di. "All is well."

"No…" Di was not satisfied. "Something's not right…"

One of the Peers had a hornet crawl down the back of his cuirass. His hands fumbled to unfasten the armor. Brothers on either side of him thought it funny to grab his hands, keep the wasp in the backplate where it kept stinging and stinging and stinging. A hornet sting was no big deal for a Spartan. A tickle, nothing more. The three of them laughed and cursed each other.

"Is his prick bigger than mine, Agodias?"

"Aye, Nestor, and harder too!" Agodias struggled to free his arms. "And look how many times he can use it?"

"Good boy, 'Daios, wear him out!"

They laughed and wrestled and laughed. All a joke. All a joke until Agodias started to wheeze.

"Let him go!" Dienekes pounced and pulled them off. "Sit down, let me look at you."

"I'm fine, runt. Shove off." Agodias rasped through a sudden cough, and turned from Di.

"I'm a surgeon." Dienekes insisted. "Well. Kind of. Almost. Let me help."

"I said I'm alright. It's just a bee." Agodias choked. "Just a bee." He doubled over, held for a moment, then toppled all the way to the ground.

Di drew his knife and started cutting at the armor's leather ties.

"No time." Krateros stepped in and slipped a hand under each of the bronze plates. Muscles bunched and writhed in his arms and neck, his teeth ground. The bindings snapped. They tore off his tunic and the flesh below was feverish, bright pink and rashing over. "What's wrong with him?"

"I don't know." Dienekes rolled the man over and killed the wasp, but it was too late for that to matter. Agodias was choking. On what, they didn't know. The hands that still tried to push help away were ballooning into freakish lumps. His bloating tongue lolled thick out of his fattening face and foam flecked his lips. His eyes swelled shut. Breath jerked in short spasms, he could get air neither in or out. Agodias inflated.

"What sorcery is this?" Krateros growled.

"I do not think it is sorcery." Dienekes felt for a pulse and found it wildly erratic. "He can't breathe, maybe if I drain the fluid…" He guessed frantically, cutting superficial slits in Agodias's side, arms and thighs. They barely bled, even when squeezed. Desperate, Di picked out a vein on his patient's wrist and severed it. It should have spurted bright red but drooled molasses black instead. Di could no longer find a pulse on the wrist and could barely feel it off the neck, which was rising to engulf Agodias's ears and chin.

Λ

"His heart is slowing." Di pumped the chest with his arms, trying to move blood through the body. "Open his mouth, Krateros, try and get him air."

"I can't open it, it's too swollen." The polemarch's thick fingers were too wide.

"Pop his jaw out if you have to. He'll die if you don't." Krateros obeyed. Agodias mumbled protest before Krateros yanked the jawbone loudly out of place. Air hissed and gurgled inwards, but then the swelling filled even the new space made. Agodias's arms and legs squirmed feebly, and then stopped.

Dienekes kept pumping on his chest.

"It's over." Krateros sighed.

"No it's not!" Dienekes pumped harder. Ribs cracked.

"He's gone, son. You did your best."

"No, I can save him!" Dienekes swung his fist as hard as he could into the sternum. And again. And again.

"Enough." A hand caught his raised wrist. "Thank you for trying." Leonidas said to him. "But now we dig his grave."

The whisper spread like wildfire through the camp. A Spartan was dead. The susurrus tore through the Allies and the air turned cold.

Assassin

Poison

Witchcraft

Curse

Leonidas heard the voices and rebuked them. He would not let the omen take hold.

"Brothers!" He called to not just his hippeis, but to all the Hellenes. His voice echoed through the dark. "Let it be known! For all his millions! For all his swords and spears and spindles! For all his shining empire! All the hordes of Xerxes killed fewer men today than did a single biting fly!" Assent murmured up from his countrymen. "Tomorrow-" The king continued. "He kills just as many!"

Spears beat shields and voices rose, the Spartans buried their loss, and a single wasp buzzed onto Dienekes's face, stung his cheek, and flew away.

For the first time since the night before, he thought in agony of his son.

Λ

Sixty

The night before battle, commanders had bickered for who would be first in line the next morning. Though impressed with the Lakonian performance the day before, they were all eager for their own chance at glory. They diced at the wall for the privilege. Demophilos and his seven hundred Thespians were privileged to be first in line.

"Demophilos will start at the third gate and let the Persians slowly push him back to us here at the middle gate. Skirmishers to the sides, but none behind, the Thespians are too many." Leonidas drew plans in the dirt with a stick, but the rock-hard ground only yielded shallow lines. "The next two contingents wait in formation at the middle gate, and under cover of our missiles, the first phalanx will retreat behind the wall. The second will surprise from the left, and with the help of the third, will push them off the cliff and take position on the pass. The Persians are not accustomed to pushing together, they do not know the othismos." He meant the press of shield on shield between two phalanxes, where entire armies wrestled. "So our phalanxes will unseat them. Push them out to the edge of our slingers' range, then let them push you back to us. Be patient. We will field fresh troops several times each hour, a luxury they will not have. Driving them up and back the beach will demoralize and exhaust them. This is how we win today."

Kosmas of Tegea swatted his Macedonian as they left the war council.

"I told you to use the loaded dice." He scolded.

"I cheat already against Spartan Big Bear and you see what that get me." He ducked the back of Kosmas's hand and playfully slapped back. "Thank me, boss man. I get you next in line. You get your chance to die. We all get our chance to die."

"I'm not so sure, my little friend." Kosmas sighed. "Thousands of Persians dead, but only one Hellene. And killed by a bee? I fear we may yet make it out of this valley alive. What a boring story that would make."

At dawn, the Spartans waited at the rear of the allies. They were not included in the initial rotation, saving their strength for the second wave expected later in the day. The armies of four nations stood between them and the Phokian wall. Despite each cohort counting in the many hundreds of men, the phalanx patterns packed men tightly together, requiring much less space than their numbers implied. Battalions moved freely in the limited space. The Persians were slow to mobilize, so Leonidas left his own battalion to supervise the Thespians, Tegeans, Korinthians, and Mantineans smoothly rehearsing their transitions in the morning mist. Over two thousand men operated in perfect unity. Though he gave no sign of it, he was moved by the sight. If only their nations could cooperate this well when not fighting for their lives.

"I noticed you did not put my men in the rotation." Leontiades had sought him out.

"Nothing escapes your keen observance." Leonidas continued to watch the battle practice. Each rotation came quicker and cleaner, but would be a very different dance with men trying to kill them.

"Must you continue to mock me, Leonidas? I came here to die with you, I believe that commands some respect."

"One Leo to another, I advise you don't take it personally. I mock everyone." The king stepped down from the wall to look his ally in the face and put a hand on his shoulder. "But you are right. And I left you out of rotation for a reason."

"I suspected as much. But it occured to me that disrespect, or distrust, might be such a reason."

"On the contrary. I have been watching you. Watching your men."

"I assumed you had been watching all the men."

"Indeed. And I find all of them valiant, all of them worthy, but some of them more worthy than others." He removed his plumed helmet and scratched his greying hair. "Aside from my own men, the Thespians are the greatest fighters. But not by much, and they fight more as individuals than a whole. The Tegeans are fiery and bold, but too hungry for glory. They will put bravery before reason, and be unpredictable for it. The Korinthians are without obvious blemish, but unseasoned. However, your men…"

"…Yes?"

"They are hardened. Disciplined. They do not loiter or wallow. You brought me your best."

"They brought themselves. Every one is a volunteer."

"They honor me. All the more reason not to squander them. I have placed them at the back of the formation in the event the Phokians fail to defend the Anopaian Way. They are many, and they are in their own lands, but they are ordinary men. Not soldiers. If they are routed, then we will be pinioned by the horde on both sides. Should it come to that, I want the most experienced, most disciplined warriors fighting with their backs to mine. Your warriors are those warriors. We will make Xerxes taste

Λ

hell from both ends."

"Is this flattery now, Leonidas?"

"Is it working?"

"I'll tell you when we're fighting back to back."

Drums beat in the distance. Persia came.

"They look like the same breed of rabble from yesterday morning." Krateros grumbled to his king, having left their troops to watch. He could trust them to operate autonomously. "Does he expect a different outcome?"

"Perhaps he thinks we are too weary and wounded to withstand much more." Leonidas mused.

"Let us hope he maintains such misgiving."

The barbarians charged in a frenzy, but the last three hundred yards of their advance was blistered by missiles from the Hellenes. By the time their front runners smashed into Demophilos and his men, the flood of their stampede had been battered down to a trickle. Five rows of hoplites, each a hundred and forty men long, had little difficulty stopping their attackers in their tracks. Thespia was reluctant to fall back, eager to prove equal Sparta's performance, but they followed their orders and cut the Medes to pieces as they backed behind the wall to be replaced by the Tegeans. It was a long mile to march backwards, but much longer for the Medes. The retreat took nearly an hour and Persia bled for every inch.

At the wall, attackers trading blows with Thespia saw the trap open up before them. They dug in their heels, desperate not to follow the Thespians into the gate, but the weight of infantry pushing from behind gave them no choice. Hidden by the mountain's outcrop, the Tegeans to the side, and the Korinthians behind them, pushed the barbarians into the sea.

The Tegeans manned the pass with Kosmas at their head. He fought like Thrasilaos- in and out of his brothers on the line- though where Thrasilaos distributed death, Kosmas beckoned to it. He would hold his shield aside with his chest exposed to the enemy, his life spared over and over again as much by luck as the efforts of his comrades. They too were reluctant to fall back when they matched the range of the Hellenic missiles, but they would get another chance.

"They die like livestock!" Kosmas shouted to Demophilos, beating his chest after being relieved by the Korinthians. "Send me men! My conscience plagues me for slaughtering lambs!"

"They will come." Demophilos remembered the elite second wave from the day prior as he and his men shared dry water and dry rations to refresh the Tegeans. Combating them would be more difficult without the reach of the spears that were still breaking in battle.

Λ

Korinth was relieved by Mantinea, Mantinea by Thespia, Thespia by Tegea. They cycled seamlessly, each retreating from battle still itching for more. Men of Hellas were dying, but lost only a fraction of a fraction of the lives they took from the foe. The plan was working. Spirits were high.

"I'm starting to think we could win this." The Korinthian commander confided to Leontiades as the Mantineans resumed the field. But Leontiades had done the math.

"How many men have you killed today? Not your men, not your army, just you alone."

"Twenty? Maybe thirty?" The Korinthian commander shrugged.

"I lost count at fifty." Demophilos added.

"A hundred at least!" Boasted Kosmas.

"Only our front three ranks can reach the enemy." Leontiades watched the Mantineans with a furrowed brow. "That's fifteen men doing the fighting while the rest only push. For all our might combined, less than a hundred do any real killing."

"And we kill them so well!" Kosmas was not drunk on only battle, by now he was celebrating with wine.

"We do. We do. But to deplete the Persian force, and only then as many as we have counted, each of our men in front must kill three thousand of the enemy. Or die, and have the men behind kill that many. Even if we kill ten thousand a day, we will still be here fighting for another month, probably more. Tell me, Commander. Forget fighting. Forget war. How long does it take you to thrust your spear at the air three thousand times? And after, how tired is your arm? Can you even strike that many times?"

"Leontiades," Kosmas grumbled into his wine skin. "If my spear arm weakens, then I'll stab them with my cock. That sword never tires."

"Good." Leontiades snatched the flagon from Kosmas and took a drink himself. "Perhaps your loins will turn the tide. Perhaps your manhood is the weapon that saves us all."

Λ

Sixty-one

While the other Hellenes slaked their thirst for blood, the Spartans practiced. Dienekes familiarized himself to scurrying between the lines. He was not so small as Thrasilaos, nor as nimble, but he eventually learned to make his long limbs work the same by taking fewer, more precise motions. His brothers of the hippeis shouted encouragement and advice. They were more accustomed to this than he was. Nearly all of them having fought with Thrasilaos before, or one like him. Some had even served in Sharktooth's own special squads. For all the legend of their uniformity, the Lakonians delighted in surprise tactics and celebrated any creative ability that did not risk the fortitude of the line. Thrasilaos was hardly Lakedaimon's only wild card.

Dienekes had little success skirting beneath and between his brothers and their arms. He fared better after Krateros snatched away his helmet and chopped off the crest, but he still managed best rolling off his comrade's backs or leaping over top. The hippeis adapted with him. Their limbs were like stone to his touch, and he could walk on them with impunity. Their bent thighs, their shoulders, the crotch of their elbow... nothing budged under Dienekes, even in his panoply. He climbed around on them as easily as if they had been a ladder.

"Try again." Lagos called to him from the second line, tapping his shoulder where Dien had just stepped from. "Only jump this time. High as you can."

Dienekes obliged, and the half-crouched Lagos lurched upright when he felt downward pressure. The combined forced catapulted Di high into the air, more than twice as high as he could have by his own power. He stalled at the height of his jump, his limbs wheeling in surprise and he clattered hard to the ground. His brothers, laughing, picked him up.

"You know, you could have caught me." He said to the men who had instead slipped decisively out of the way. He forced himself to breathe evenly, trying to hide how the impact had knocked out his wind.

"Aye, we could have." Lagos winked. "But this was funnier. Again now. Off Polymedes this time, lets see how far we can launch you."

While the other men of Hellas made war, the Spartans drilled, their motions becoming seamless. They became as one body, one soldier, with Dienekes as the tip of their sword.

"Spend more time in the hind ranks." Krateros ordered. "They will have been telling stories at their campfires about the demon in the lion's cloak. So more than any of us, you will be a target. Too much time up front and a spear will find you. Drop further back, change lanes, then strike. Don't let them see where you're coming from."

They drilled and drilled and drilled. Some of the Hellenic reservists drifted to watch them rather than spectating the battle. The formula for holding the pass was working, a redundant mechanism. They knew how it would go, but this curious phalanx bouncing an acrobat off their heads? This was new and different. Some of them recognized Dienekes from the games. They rattled spears on shields and shouted the name they knew him by.

Little Achilles

Kosmas in particular took a liking to the new gymnastics. Out of rotation, he practiced the motion himself, ordering a clutch of his own men to be his springboard.

"Children's games." He told Leonidas after establishing a modicum of success. "It's great fun, but I hardly see much use for it."

"Fear." Leonidas educated him. "After Thrasilaos yesterday, they will wet themselves when they see that the lion can also fly. Dienekes need not kill so many men, his presence alone will torment them. Imagine how the rumors will spread like disease through their camp tonight, growing larger with each telling. This superhuman, this monster who can outrun horses, leap above the treetops, disappear and reappear at will, bringing death with a wave of his hand. They will believe him born of the Gods themselves."

"Ah, but Great King," Kosmas was only half sarcastic, "the mud people do not believe in our gods."

Leo's eyes narrowed with dark delight.

"Born of demons, then."

The sun hung at blistering height. A chorus went up from the line of battle. The first wave had been depleted and it's few hundred remnants scattered like a flock of starlings. The Thespians were holding the pass when the Medes broke formation, and they gave chase.

"Fools." Krateros muttered. "Did they not see how many times we smashed them after baiting pursuit?" He watched and counted, his eyes still keen despite their age, but no Thespians fell to the same trap. They hounded the fleeing Medes as far at the third gate, where they were turned back by a hail of arrows. Still howling, they danced their way back to their allies under the safety of their shields and were greeted with raucous acclaim.

Pipers droned, drums beat, singing and dancing broke out and wine was thrown

Λ

over the Thespians as they were hauled onto the shoulders of their allies.

"Enough!" Leonidas thundered, his voice flattening the revelers into silence. "Do you forget where you are?" His query echoed off the rocks unanswered. "Collect our dead. Push the rest into the sea. I want the road to my enemy cleared. More are coming."

Λ

Sixty-two

"Where is Little Lion Man?" Kosmas's Macedonian friend scurried alongside the Spartans as they marched into position. Scouts reported that the second wave had mobilized.

"Little Lion Man?" He called. "Heeere kitty-kitty-kitty! Big Bear!" He spied Polymedes at the front. "Big Bear, where is War Kitten? I have a gift!"

"Something for me?" Dienekes stepped from the shadow of his hulking friend.

"I do! I do! I-" The Macedonian stopped short, shot a curious look at Di towering over him. "You grow Little Lion Man?" He accused. "Much taller today."

"No, that was-"

"Skinny too." He pinched the muscles of Di's arm, which was indeed slight for a Spartan, but still considerable for anyone else. "This long skinny lion is the one with the jumping, yes?" The rest of the hippeis continued marching past.

"I suppose-"

"Of course you are the silly jumping kitten. Here. I make." He held the bundle to Dienekes. "Kosmas make you gift? I make gift too."

Di unrolled the bundle from its foreign cloth wrappings, no doubt stolen from the enemy. Inside were two long leather quivers, also likely stolen, each packed with ten of what appeared to be grossly overlarge arrows.

"I don't understand, I am no archer." Di puzzled.

"No, silly jumping war kitten. Too heavy for bow." He nodded towards Polymedes marching away. "Unless Big Bear have bow. Big Bow for Big Bear. Is scary thought. Maybe is next gift!" The Macedonian drew one of the arrows from the lot as he rambled and handed it to Dienekes to examine.

It was certainly too large for a bow, and surprisingly weighty. The fletchings were a rigid fabric, presumably stiffened by the same hoof glue that some Hellenes used to make simple linen into battle-worthy armor. The head was narrow and sharp, but heavy, too big for an arrow and too small for a spear.

"Is taken from *gastraphetes*." The Macedonian said, noticing Di inspecting the iron tip. "Is like a bow that you pull with your feet, then holds own arrow back. Give thanks Xerxes has none, they cut through your shield like-" He flicked a fingernail on the rim of Di's aspis to make it ring and made a fart sound with his mouth. He looked embarrassed when Di did not laugh.

The shaft was a cut sapling, still green, perhaps the only part of the assemblage that had not been pilfered. The staves were cleverly worked and perfectly straight, tapering from thick at the tip to slim at the tail to be front heavy and so fly true. Each had a little bulge of waxed cord two thirds up its length to grip in the hand.

"These are for me?" Dienekes was honored.

"*Special* for you, Long Lion. I see you throw spears yesterday. You throw well. Today you throw these. They are small, is true, but if mudman hit with little little spear he still being big big dead."

Dienekes chuckled this time, to the Macedonian's relief.

"Thank you, friend. Tell me, what is your name?"

"Ah…" The Macedonian tapped his nose and toed the dirt. "Is not wise to give name when man of my job. Name make easy to follow and find." Dienekes understood, a gambler, a thief, perhaps more, he was likely a wanted man. "But since we friends now… You call me…" The Macedonian chewed his lip in thought. "Long Lion call me *Barbadoros*."

Dienekes smiled and slipped his arm through the quiver straps and strapped the new weapons tight to his back before hastening to catch his unit.

"Thank you, Barbadoros."

"Kill well, Long Lion." The Macedonian called.

It was a crude translation, but the little man's meaning was clear.

Barboradoros

A stranger bearing gifts.

At the Phokian wall, the Spartans waited. The stench of bodies was no longer ignorable. Even the high sea wind could not scatter its offense. Bloated purpling corpses mounded in the Phokian swamp, picked at by dogs and crows. The bodies dumped into the sea sank plumb to the bottom under the weight of their arms and armor, whether the wearer was live or dead. The water of the gulf was several times deeper than the height of a man so to be plunged into the gulf wearing plate or mail was a death sentence here. So many had drowned that when the afternoon light caught the murky waters just right, Dienekes could see where undersea currents had drifted Persian carcasses into piles tall enough to touch the surface. When he first arrived at the pass, he had wrinkled his nose at the stink of the hotsprings, but next to the rot of men, the stale belch of sulfur was a welcome perfume.

How many of them had he claimed? Which bodies were dead by his hand? Before this battle he had only killed the one helot as the slave snuck up on his friend. He hardly remembered it through the fog of fever, just as he hardly remembered the kills of the previous day through adrenal haze and the shivering screen of bronze and flying iron. Everything had happened so fast, he had to kill or be killed. There had been no time to think, but now, standing amongst the open air graves of innumerable dead, he had questions. Questions that he did not know the words to ask.

He thought of his friends as he slipped up the narrow ledge where he'd been stationed the day before. The presences of Alpheos and Maron were sorely missed. Tellis too. He even found himself wishing Thrasilaos still stood by his side.

"Up front!" Leonidas called to him. "Stand where they can see you."

Dienekes trudged a few fathoms ahead of his phalanx, staring down the oncoming horde. The elites again, they needed no whips to spur their advance.

"No, not like that." Exasperated, Leonidas pushed back his helmet and ran a palm up his face. "Would it kill you to swagger a little?"

"What?" Dienekes turned. "Am I fighting or flaunting?"

"Both, damn you!" Leonidas retorted. "Are you thinking again? Now is not the time!"

The hippeis split at the sides. It had become a running a joke, Dienekes the thoughtful, the dreamer, his head always somewhere else. Di could not help but laugh as well. Here he posed for his enemy, a scarecrow, pretending to be some glorious instrument of death, an immortal and unstoppable killing machine, while his own squad behind knew him for what he was... their laughingstock.

"Remember Olympia?" Krateros shouted from his place beside the king. "When you were sixteen and you gave the Orchomene the yard?"

"How could I forget?" Di grumbled. It was still his greatest shame.

"Go back there. Show me that boy. That insufferable cocksure toad. He fights Persia today!"

"What like this?" Dienekes strutted like a peacock to a chorus of jeers and encouragement from his peers.

"Exactly like that!" Krateros cackled.

The Persians were less than half a mile away now, and Di gave them his best show, flexing and prancing like an actor. He danced some of the steps Thrasilaos had taught Disappointment during the agoge to teach them how to move together.

You will be Thrasilaos tomorrow.

The words echoed in his ear and he obeyed. He bent and contorted himself on display for the enemy, limbering up just as his teacher had. He did not comprehend before how his brothers, or Kosmas, or Tellis could laugh in the face of adversity and death. But now, brazening himself before the enemy, making a mockery of both them and himself, he understood. He stood alone and exposed in the face of thousands being an absolute fool, and he was having *fun.*

A shadow shot skyward from the Persian ranks, only a few hundred yards away

Λ

now. The hippeis tightened together and raised their shields. Dienekes nearly did the same, but he heard the words in his heart again.

Be Thrasilaos.

Be me.

He left his shield hanging by his side and stared proudly up into the storm of arrows as it rained down. A single bolt whispered past his face and cut the edge of his ear. The rest bounced harmlessly off the rock around his feet or pattered off the bronze behind him.

"Yes, Weeper, yes!" Leonidas cried. The hippeis cheered.

"Achilleeeees!"

Dienekes choked. He had forgotten to breathe. He felt a hot sticky flood racing down his bottom half. Gasping, he inspected himself for wounds. There was nothing-nothing but wetness down his thighs, pooling between his feet.

"I fucking pissed myself!" He shouted to the line, his voice cracking.

"I won't tell if you don't!" Leonidas shot back.

Another volley leapt skyward from the oncoming Persians.

"That's enough, Long Lion!" Krateros called him the name Barbadoros had given. "Now disappear!"

Dienekes obeyed, arrows cutting through his cape as he dashed into the safety of the phalanx.

"The illusion lasts as long as they think you invincible." Krateros's voice boomed around Di as he jockeyed amid his peers. "So whatever you do…" More arrows peppered down on the hippeis. "Don't die!"

The barbarians slammed against the wall of Sparta. Blood soaked the ground black.

Kill

Drop back

Change lanes

Kill

Drop back

Change lanes.

His task did not require him to be more lethal than his brothers. Thrasilaos had already accomplished the hard part for him, he only need maintain the illusion. As long as the Persians were scanning for where the lion would next leap from, their focus would be torn from the swords and spears ahead. The distraction would cost them their lives.

"What are you waiting for?" A hoplite seven or eight rows back said to Di, his muscles rippled as he pressed his shield into the Spartan ahead of him. He still had the faculty to lean his spear against his shield and gingerly pat his own shoulder. "Hop on then. Let's give them a show."

Λ

Dienekes switched his spear to his shield hand, drew one of the Macedonian's darts from its quiver, stepped onto his brother, and soared.

He released the bolt at the height of his leap and buried it in a barbarian neck. Startled to hear the gurgling scream of one behind, the front rows of Persians turned and were immediately swallowed. A dozen men went beneath the phalanx in a single instant, to be trampled and pecked apart by sauroteurs.

Leonidas began to sing, and his three hundred chosen sang with him. Forward they marched.

Kill

Drop back

Change lanes

Leap

Each time Dienekes burst skyward, his enemy flinched. Not all of them, not even most of them, but the one or two that recoiled from him opened crucial gaps in their line for the Spartans to reach in and pick the braver men apart.

Leap

Drop back

Change lanes

Leap

Dienekes loosed more missiles, and as they hit their targets, he became a target himself. Persians from many rows back had restrung their bows to fire on him. He was bleeding.

An arrow had struck him just above the collarbone and passed out the back. Crouched in the safety of formation, he braced for the pain and stuck a finger into the hole to assess the damage. Muscle and bone were fine, only skin had broken. He might as well have not been hit, but the damage was done. Spartans had long held disdain for bows and catapults and devices that struck an enemy from a distance. If not propelled by the might of your own arm, it was a woman's weapon. Worse, a *coward's* weapon.

"You want to shoot me?" Dienekes became enraged. He changed lanes again, sprinted forward and hurtled off a peer into the air. "You want to shoot me!? I dare you!"

He didn't throw a javelin this time, only kept his long limbs neatly tucked behind his white shield. Arrows- *spindles,* he'd heard Leonidas condescend them- bounced off the far side. He leapt again and again, inviting any who would take their shot to do so. The first volley was maybe half a dozen shots, the second was ten, the third leap earned him twenty. A few more leaps and spindles jutted from his aspis like a pincushion, but the more men who stopped to fire at him, the fewer men there were to bolster the soldiers separating the archers from the hoplites. With no one to back

∧

them, the front ranks of Persians were toppled, then trampled. The men behind them, those who stopped to shoot at Dienekes, helplessly clutched their bows as the Spartans trampled them. Arrows came rarely after that.

Kill

Drop back

Change lanes

Leap

Dienekes had not yet exhausted his first quiver of javelins but already they had advanced far enough forward that he could retrieve his spent darts from the dead. Barbadoros was some kind of genius. With the heavy weight, narrow profile, and ruthlessly pointed tip, the darts sliced effortlessly through the enemy's wicker shields and even punched through their iron mail at close range. The stories were coming true, Dienekes could bring death with a wave of his hand.

The Spartan formation had been advancing steadily, but suddenly, without warning, it began to race. Their battle hymn, the *paian,* wailed twice as loud. Dienekes stopped to look behind as his fellows streaked by at nearly a run. His heart sang.

The Tegeans, discontented to let the Spartans hoard the glory, took it upon themselves to push the hippeian formation from the rear. Behind them, the Thespians followed suit. The Korinthians and Mantineans who were still willing and able attempted to join as well, but there was no more room on the pass. They rocketed forward with the combined might of over two thousand men. For every dozen Persians that were killed by a blade, a hundred were trampled underfoot. Bodies dropped beneath in such quantity that Spartan sandals hardly touched the ground anymore, stomping instead on the skulls of the fallen.

The Hellenes were still outnumbered a hundred to one, but it did not matter. The Asians each pushed as one man and one man alone while the phalanx was one beast united. However strong, no amount of individuals could stand their ground in the face of the *othismos.*

The Persians grew desperate. They tried to climb over top of the shield wall bearing down on them and were dismembered. Some tried to slink into the swamp but were mired and sniped by Arkadian slingers. Some, rather than be crushed by the Lakedaimonians, threw themselves into the gulf to drown. Some tried to fly as Dienekes had, hurling themselves over the line of scrimmage in a suicidal attempt to take a Lakonian with them. One leaper came plummeting down on Lagos, ululating with a sword in each hand. Dienekes, creeping up the ledge along the shore, was only barely in time to place the shield of Hegisistratos between the shrieking Mede and his target. The impact sent them both careening off the cliffside.

Di clawed at the cliff with his swordhand. His fingers snagged the ledge and gripped, but only barely. Below, the Persian clung to the rim of the shield with one

Λ

fist, and wildly swung his remaining sword in the other. Dienekes could not pull them both up, and he could not defend himself from the blade. He was trapped. Two, three times he wriggled out of the way of its slashes, each a narrower and narrower miss. A fourth blow nicked high on his arm. The cut was superficial, not deep but long, and blood coursed down his limb and slicked the bindings on his shield.

No

No No No

Dienekes forgot the Persian and squeezed as tightly as he could to retain the shield. Losing it was not an option.

Come back with your shield, or on it his mother had said to him.

Come back with your shield, or on it every mother said to their sons before battle.

It was no longer a matter of strength or will to cling to the handle, though. The blood soaked leather grip afforded no traction and the flailing Mede below wrenched it from his grasp. Dienekes watched in horror as the Persian plunged into the sea holding the shield of Hegisistratos.

Strong hands hauled him up the cliffside, set him down on firm ground, and moved on. There was still fighting to be done. But not for Dienekes. He had lost his shield, his father's ancestral shield. He scoured the waters for sign of it, but it had sunk beneath where he could see. He considered jumping after it, but knew he could not swim with the weight of his armor, and then Sparta would lose not only his shield, but his panoply as well, deepening his failure.

He was *rhipsaspia*. Dienekes sobbed. He was guilty of the greatest crime, the greatest treason a Spartan could commit. A hoplite is not a hoplite without a shield. To lose it is worse than losing life, to drop your shield is to sacrifice your own brothers. He could never show his face in the city again.

"Forgive me." He asked of the heavens. He knelt, hyperventilating on the ledge, and began to panic.

He thought of Krateros even now fighting on the front lines. *What would he say when he found out his pupil is rhipsaspia? Here where I was needed most? The great polemarch would die of shame. He would fall on his sword. So that's what I will do. I won't let them see me like this. I won't let them accuse. I won't live in exile and shame with my head shaved. I will be brave. I will take my own justice.*

He stood, drew his sword and placed its tip to his breastplate in line with his heart.

"I'm sorry." He whispered.

He took a deep breath, rocked once, then tipped forwards toward the earth.

Λ

Sixty-three

"Oi, Weeper."

The familiar voice snapped his focus. The xiphos skittered harmlessly off bronze plate and his hands caught his fall against the rock.

"Must you always be so dramatic?" Thrasilaos bobbed his head up over the precipice, one hand clinging to the ledge with his feet propping him out from the wall. He was naked save for a dagger on a swordbelt that fastened a breechcloth around his loins. Seawater soaked him head to toe.

"I... I... I lost my..." Dienekes shuddered, eyes full of tears. He could not say the words.

"Yes, I saw. Shameful display. You dropped that too." Thrasilaos nodded where the dagger fell.

Dienekes picked it back up and gave a solemn nod, angling its tip up under his cuirass to slit his belly.

"Oh, fuck off with that nonsense." Thrasilaos rolled his eyes. "You think you're the first piss-ant to drop a shield?"

"It is said-"

"I know what is said. Worry about that later, there is still work to be done."

"How do I fight without my shield?"

"You start by picking it back up." Thrasilaos swung his free arm up and dropped the heavy hoplon at Di's feet, still dripping from the sea. After an awestruck moment the Weeper whimpered gratitude and scrambled to pick it back up.

"...How will I ever repay you?"

"I'm sure I'll think of something. In the meantime we forget it happened at all." Thrasilaos coiled himself into the cliffside and kicked off, arced backwards and diving into the gulf without a splash.

As Dienekes buckled his shield back into place, he watched the shadow of Thrasilaos cut beneath the water where it was joined by two more. They swam past the line of scrimmage under the Persian forces and began to climb. It was Alpheos and Maron.

The three scuttled silently up to the top of the rock face, counted wordlessly together, and erupted simultaneously over the ledge. They snatched a soldier each and dragged them off the cliff. Six bodies crashed into the water and only three re-emerged.

They struck repeatedly and at random. Sometimes pulling Persians down to drown, sometimes drawing their dagger and scything at ankles. Sometimes they burst from the surface of the water and hurled a scavenged spear. Each time they exposed themselves only long enough to strike once before they sluiced back into the safety of the dark waters.

The Arkadian and Orchomene slingers balancing on their makeshift swamp bridges took advantage of the disruption and concentrated their fire on the affected lines. Xerxes's elite could not protect themselves from harassment to the sides and still fend off the onslaught bearing down their front. The Persian ranks buckled. Dienekes rejoined the fray.

"Hold!" Krateros thundered, and the command echoed back to the hundreds of rows of hoplites, the longest phalanx the world had ever seen. The othismos had reached the third gate. To advance further would leave their flanks vulnerable. They would hold here until the end, whatever the gods deemed that end should be.

With the Spartans no longer advancing, the Persians did not need to resist the constant forward push. They could use their bows again. Spindles hissed from the ranks beyond the reach of a spear and ricocheted off bronze. Dienekes bounded off Lagos again, put a dart in a Median officer and landed on the unyielding back of Polymedes.

"Poly!" He shouted in surprise at the big man's shoulder. An arrow sprouted from the joint.

"What? Oh." Polymedes had not noticed. He reached to pull it out.

"No, leave it! You'll just make it worse!" Di swung his shield in front of Poly's face and two more arrows thunked into it.

"Ha!" The big man barked. "A souvenir then!"

Dienekes leapt away and disappeared among his brothers. An arrow meant for him whistled through the vacancy and found its way in the eye slit of a Spartan helmet further behind.

The battle dragged on and none could account for the passing of time. Hours blurred into instants. Dienekes had exhausted his javelins, throwing Median spears off the ground instead. The strength in his legs had long since faded, but he did not allow himself to slow. There were dead Spartans on the ground now. The othismos had stalemated at the pass. The phalanx held firm, but its parts were too fatigued for complex maneuvers. They were just as locked as the Mede.

Dienekes landed from a vault, forcing his legs to hold him in defiance of searing cramps.

He heard a voice from the hills, barely audible. He rolled over one line, then another, then another, to the far left flank of the formation. It called again. He stuck a finger in one ear and craned the other to the steep slope.

"---Strange gifts from above!" The voice yelled. "Strange big heavy gifts from above!"

Dienekes puzzled for a moment, then the flower of intuition bloomed. He recognized the voice.

"Fall back!" He screamed to his brothers, tugging his empty hand against their brawn. "Fall baaaaaack!"

Krateros took heed and echoed the order. The phalanx lumbered slowly for all the hoplites stacked behind it, but they managed to pull from the pass. Persians swarmed to fill the open space as a low rumble shook the ground.

"Fall baaaack!" Dienekes continued to shout. The rumble grew to a roar, drowning out even the screams of the dying, the clatter of iron and bronze.

Rock and scree cascaded down from the thicketed hillside. The rolling stones fell so large and plentiful that entire trees were ripped up and into the tumble. Xerxes's elites filling the gate were swept off the edge or buried beneath it. Most of the damage was done in an instant, but rocks continued to fall. The two armies made space on either end, hesitating to see who would be the first to round the obstruction.

"You are many welcome!" Barbadoros cackled unseen from up the slope.

The Spartans heard whip cracks on the far side as the avalanche trickled out. Persian hands swept rubble off the top. Any rock small enough to throw was thrown, anything not too big to push was pushed, and any Persian who showed his face over the mound was pierced by a javelin. Most of the impasse was too large to excavate under duress, but in less than a minute enough debris was cleared that a handful of men could charge around its corner or scramble over the top. They came slowly, each of the new vanguard finding a spear thrown into his heart. Until the Lakonians ran out of spears.

Leonidas gave the order to advance, to fill the gap between them and the obstacle. Spears or no spears, they could hold the barrier, but the rockslide had loosened more than boulders. The synchronized stomp of Spartan sandals was the final straw. Half the path ahead broke away in a crescent a fathom wide and two fathoms long. The ground beneath Leonidas's own feet crumbled into the sea.

Krateros dropped his kopis and snatched his king's wrist. The ground beneath the polemarch held firm and they danged together, exposed half over their death. Persians still crawling over the rockslide saw their opportunity and aimed to throw their spears.

Dienekes did not think, only reacted. He charged forward and put his foot onto Echemmon crouched at the right front, who lifted despite no warning. Di propelled

Λ

himself forward this time, not up, and spun to put his left side to the enemy. Median javelins bounced off his shield as he hurtled through the air over the crevasse.

His sandals scraped across rock on the far side and he nearly lost his feet. Cheers of gratitude chorused from his brothers. He had saved their king. Krateros hauled Leonidas back up onto the ledge and Polymedes, wide enough to block the remaining walkway by himself, enveloped them behind his shield. Dienekes allowed himself a moment's elation. It slipped away when the spear throwers advanced on him with axes drawn. More came spilling over the rockslide. The phalanx was packed too tightly to navigate the destroyed walkway, and from here, Dienekes could not slip back inside the fold of his brothers. Between a crumbling cliffside and a million Medes, he stood alone.

He drew his short sword and lunged at the first enemy. His blade pierced the wicker shield to draw blood on the other side, and Di kicked the wounded soldier backward into the others before their axes could fall. Arkadians could not angle a shot without the risk of hitting him as well, and the Spartans had no more spears to throw.

He killed them as they came, dodging backward in diagonals to lower the numbers of who could reach him, desperate to not stand where more than one axe could fall at once. Maron and Alpheos did what they could from the edge of the cliff, but the two of them unarmored and poorly armed could only kill so quickly. Medes continued to clamber past the barrier. There were too many for Dien to fight on his own, and their numbers only grew, rapidly filling any space he could use to avoid them.

Ululations rose from the Hellenic side. A figure all in white fell from the sky into the growing Persian crowd. He swung a kopis wildly, screaming to Zeus and killing any too slow to back away.

"Don't you dare die without me, boy!" Kosmas howled to Dienekes. Behind him, more Tegeans streaked up the vacant sixth lane to join their commander. Thrasilaos had climbed back up the cliff on the Spartan side and knelt at the edge for the Tegeans to bound off his back. One at a time, they vaulted the gap and slammed their spears and swords and bodies into the foe until no more men would fit on the tiny battle ground. Thrasilaos dove back down to rejoin the twins harassing from the water.

"Not a useless trick afterall!" Kosmas laughed to Dien, giving him a spare lance. He crowded the rockslide with the Tegeans and skewered whoever still tried to surmount Barbadoros's barrier.

"Enough!" Leonidas called, his phalanx reconfigured behind the collapse. "Save yourselves!"

The Tegeans with Dienekes backed away from the rockslide behind their own little shield wall and slipped one at a time through the narrow unbroken remnant of the pass. They splashed into the knee-deep mud of the swamp and slogged away from the fight while the reformed Spartan lines covered their retreat. As they passed, the

Λ

Tegeans gave the Lakonians their spears.

The rockslide and the collapse caught the Persian advance in a chicane. To reach the enemy, they had to swerve left around the boulders then right around the broken causeway. Choked into a bottleneck, they could only meet the Spartans one, two, no more than three at a time and so came as lambs to the slaughter. Persian leadership on the far side of the trap could not see the futility they urged their infantry into. Whips cracked, orders barked, and soldiers sprinted blindly to their deaths.

Morale blossomed in the phalanx. Fresh strength swelled in the arms and legs that only moments before had drooped dangerously beneath the weight of fatigue. The fight continued for hours. So many dead fell into the broken pass that their bodies piled above the waterline. Eventually the rush of troops between fallen rocks slowed to a stop. Hellenes held their ground in the lull, gasping for breath, ankle deep in blood, sweat and piss, waiting for more. Thrasilaos and the twins crept up the barricade and peered over the top, then turned, waving their hands. The Medes had retreated.

Hellenes filed back toward the middle gate to trumpets. The Tegeans, Thespians, and others screamed themselves hoarse in victory while the hippeis stumbled back to camp in hallowed Lakonian silence.

"I should have been a seer." Leonidas put an arm around Dienekes, who did his best not to let on that the weary king was leaning on him for support.

"What do you mean?" Di asked.

"I told you that shield would save my life again."

Λ

Sixty-four

The camps of Hellas revelled. Troops mingled out of regiment. Knowing no one's name and having no time to learn them, they only called each other brother. Wine flowed even among the Lakedaimonians, but while some sang in their cups others soured.

Eurymachos, son of Leontiades and second in command of Thebes, soured especially. The darker his red wine stained his teeth, the darker it stained his mood.

"Suppose we don't die here…" Said his friend Haimon. "Where do we go?"

"Better that we die here." Eurymachos replied, cutting his wine with water. They did still have a battle to fight the next day.

"You think?"

"We're traitors if we stay. We're traitors if we go. Either way, the stories and songs remember those who fight." Eurymachos growled as if he only half believed it.

"Who do you think will sing our story, then?" Haimon asked. "Not our own surely. If only to hide their own shame."

"Why did you come?" Eurymachos glared, trying to peer past Haimon's face for the flint of sedition hiding there. "We all volunteered. If you had doubts, why did you come?"

Haimon opened his mouth but was interrupted.

"Are you jealous?" Kosmas staggered drunkenly into the light of their fire. An enormous driftwood phallus was strapped bouncing between his thighs. Dithyrambos, a champion of Thespia, accompanied him.

"Jealous of what?" Eurymachos asked despite not desiring an answer.

"Yours is the only regiment to not see blood. Even these backwater Lokrians have tasted more glory than you." Kosmas poured a skin into his mouth, most of it dripping down his front.

"I came for reason. Not glory." Eurymachos poured his own cup into the dirt, the state of Kosmas drying his thirst for drink.

"Reason? Reason? What a horrible thing to die for. I'd rather die for poetry. Or a woman." Kosmas moved to sit on a log bench and missed, falling on his ass without complaint. Still he drank. "Or lots of women."

"So that's why you came?" Haimon extended the question asked of him. "To die?"

"Is there anything greater than to die in battle?"

"I think it matters some why the battle is fought." Eurymachos was sobering uncomfortably.

"Battles are fought for many reasons. Rarely are they for reason. I fight for the poets."

"You think they will remember you?"

"It increases my chances, certainly. No poems are written of old men who die in their beds."

"I might write one." Haimon shrugged.

"No one would read it." Kosmas dribbled more wine down his chin.

"What example are you setting, Tegean? Sloshed and wearing a fabricated member? This is no way to lead men."

"His men have come to fight." Dithyrambos broke his silence. "As have all the men here. As long as they do that, we will ask no decorum from men who only have a few more days to live."

"Is that how long you think we have left?" Haimon asked.

"Unless I kill them all tomorrow!" Kosmas burped. "And do not fear my wood. It's for the Persians, not you. They'll die faster if I wield two swords instead of one." He laughed at his own joke until he choked. "I heard a rumor..." He was suddenly serious.

"I'm sure you've heard many rumors." Eurymachos glanced at Haimon.

"I heard a rumor... That Thebes has already medized?"

Eurymachos scoffed and rose to leave, motioning for Haimon to follow.

"It is true." Leontiades stepped into the firelight from where he was listening.

"Is that why Leonidas won't let you fight?" Kosmas did not know when to leave well enough alone. "He thinks you are here to betray him?"

"Only Leonidas can speak for his motivations." Leontiades did not flinch. "But as for mine, I'm ready to kill any man who calls me a traitor."

"Are you not a traitor to your city then? If they have turned to Persia?"

"I gave my word at Korinth that I would support the decision of the Allies. I cannot help it if the city elected treason in my absence. This is your second and final warning. Any more mention of treason to me, and you will die drunk and choking on your wooden penis."

"Is that so?" Kosmas rose, wobbling, to the confrontation.

"You're forgetting something, Kosmas." Spoke Dithyrambos.

"My sword?" Kosmas extended a wavering hand to his friend.

"No, that you're a fucking idiot." He grabbed Kosmas by his strapped-on manhood and swung him to the ground with a thud.

Λ

"We fighting in the morning, Rambo. You and me." Kosmas mumbled into the dirt and fell abruptly to snoring. Dithyrambos patted his back sympathetically.

So you come for truth. A man of your word. You will be killed for your honesty when you could have stayed in the safety of your home.

"You think me foolish?" Leontiades said, still defensive.

"Perhaps. But moreso do I admire you. It is a rare man who would choose death before dishonesty."

"I am well known in my city. Many look to me for character. I do it for them, not myself."

"And what do they think of you now? That you have left them for a cause they abandoned?" Leontiades flushed red again at the question, but Dithyrambos raised his palms to pacify the general. "I do not mean to provoke. I am sympathetic to the plight of Thebes. Like your city, Thespia lies next in the path of Persia. It does not matter how long we hold them here, our homes will be sacked before our allies can fight again at the Isthmus. They will Medize or be destroyed."

"But unlike Thebes, Thespia chose destruction."

Rambos hesitated before answering.

"Yes."

"And what do you think of that?"

"I think that you and I are here. Men of our word. That is all."

"You find peace in that?" Haimon asked, ever the instigator.

"Look around you, fool. I found war." Rambos glared daggers at Haimon, who shrugged them off.

"So you came for Thespia. To fight for it before it is gone. Noble. You must love your city."

"More than you love yours, it would seem." He did not hide his distaste for Haimon, who responded in kind. The Theban bent to the ground to snatch a drunkenly discarded lance from the dirt but Dithyrambos was quicker. The Thespian jumped up and pinned the shaft down with his foot. Haimon drew a dagger instead.

"Enough." Leontiades barked. "Whatever our reasons for being here, it was not to fight each other. Drop your weapons, Haimon. And do not pick them back up till morning."

"You side with the Thespian over me? How many times have I fought for you-"

"Silence. I have heard enough from your poison tongue."

"I speak no poison, only truth."

"Insolence, then? So be it." Leontiades stepped forward and ripped the badge of office from Haimon's shoulder. "You've wagged your tongue too freely for too long. You are stripped of weapons and now of rank. If I hear you've spoken another word before sunrise, I will have you flogged. Out of my sight."

Λ

Haimon bristled with rage, but held his tongue as he skulked away.

Dithyrambos said nothing, only raised his cup in respect for the firm hand. The general still felt the need to warrant his punishments.

"Our mission here hangs by a thread. A whisper of sedition could end us all." Leontiades sighed to the Thespian.

"Personally, I think you all foolish foolish fools." Said Barbadoros seated on the back of a sleeping Kosmas. Both of the officers started at his presence.

"How long have you been there?" Asked Rambos. Barbadoros ignored him.

"Truth. Honor. Poetry. Home. Foolish. I come for the bounty!" He shook open his bulging sack. Golden trinkets clattered out, along with sweet pastries, steaming kabobs, and a tumble of ripe fruit. Rambos snatched up one of the morsels. He'd had little more than nourishing but unfulfilling military rations for weeks and was craving something sweet.

"Apples? Where did you find apples? Where's the closest orchard? Lokria? That's leagues away."

"Nay, there is orchard just over that way." Barbadoros pointed at the pass, to the Persian front. The others gawked, not understanding.

"They have… an orchard? But they've only been there for days."

"They carry it with them. Fruiting tree in neat little basket filled of dirt. Hundreds. Slaves pick up and move. Much clever." He crunched into an apple. "Mudmen have everything back there. Apples. Women. I see them building new boats on the beach like it no trouble at all. Clever mudmen."

The others looked at their feet. *Walking orchards.* Each day they discovered more and more daunting facets of this alien nation. Their soldiers might wither under the othismos, but they had enough boats to make a bridge from and enough manpower to dig canals in days and carry farms wherever they went. They were too advanced and too numerous. It was only a matter of time before the invaders innovated a way to deal with the hoplites. But adjacent to their apprehension, another thought dawned on the Hellenes.

"Wait… You were behind the Persian lines?"

"Yes?"

"But you are…." Rambos gestured to Barbadoros's complexion, his curly black hair. He was a strange little man, but he was decidedly of Hellas and not a mudman of Medea.

"Ah, yes, but is also Barbadoros. I sneak!" He laughed through a mouthful of apple and kebab. "But did not have need to after much long. They having all kinds over there. Tall men, short men, white men, black men, strange yellow men in funny headhat. No one pay little Barbadoros a look. Now I thinking for it, I even see man of Sparta talking to guards. Give orders like he in charge. How do mudmen get

Λ

Spartan of their own do you think?"

"Surely you are mistaken." Leontiades narrowed his eyes.

"Nay, Barbardoros eyes no lie. He look just like our King Lion. Tall, dark. All of bronze and red. I'm sure of him from Sparta. Nowhere else."

Dithyrambos and Leontiades shared a worried glance while Barbadoros munched happily.

"Commanders! You are needed!" Leonidas beckoned from the dark.

"Is there news?" Dithyrambos called back.

"Something is happening in the pass. They are building something. We don't know what." Demophilos answered from Leo's side.

"I come listen too then. My friend will have need to hear what is happens later." Barbadoros stuck an apple in the Tegean's mouth, patted his curls, and followed the others. Kosmas mumbled gratitude and chewed in his sleep.

Λ

Sixty-five

Dienekes cradled his battered body around a bowl of black broth, the vinegar, blood and pork a boon of restoration. His arms quaked to lift it to his lips. Even in both hands it felt heavier than his shield ever had. Lykourgan law mandated that no Spartan remove their armor when at rest on foreign soil, but after today, Leonidas granted them exception. He wanted them to recuperate unencumbered. They would never admit it, but even a Spartan body had its limits.

"Here." Alpheos slipped out of the bushes and threw half a roasted rabbit. "You need meat."

"You can still hunt? After today?" Dienekes asked around a mouthful of coney. Too hungry to pick bites, his teeth tore away muscle, tendon and bone. He chewed and swallowed indiscriminately.

"It wasn't us doing the heavy lifting." said Maron. "But if you're asking if we're tired…" He slumped over on Dienekes, pretending to snore loudly in his lap. "It was Lagos who caught it, not us. Genius with the snares.'" He gestured back to the bushes and another Spartan stepped through. Dienekes recognized him from the second line. They waved to each other, both their mouths full of rabbit.

"Sun is setting soon," Polygonos said, passing by. "Sharktooth wants you inked and ready by dark."

"Good Gods, not a moment's relief." Alpheos furiously rubbed his face. "If I didn't know better, I'd think we were at war."

"How does he do it? Fights all day, spies all night?" Dienekes wondered aloud. "Does he ever sleep?"

"Not since I watched your father die." Thrasilaos whispered from behind. Di choked and dropped his bowl of broth. "Someone's got to keep watch. And my eyes are best at night." He wore the blindfold again, and still made his way through camp unencumbered. "Come Testicles. If you're on time then you're late.

"I'm coming too." Di moved to stand, but his legs gave out. They held on the second try.

"Wobbling like a newborn colt?" Thrasilaos scoffed. "I think not."

"I can still outrun you."

"Perhaps. But can you outswim me? Outclimb me? Outsneak me? Outfight me?"

"I'll put it to the test."

"You'll do as you're told."

"If the twins are going, then I'm going too."

"You don't even know what we're doing."

"All the better." Di was not taking no for an answer. "Just throw me into the fire, right?"

"You're needed elsewhere."

"What, here? To leave my brothers to fight and die while I sleep? That is not our way, Thrasilaos. My eirene taught me better than that." Thrasilaos might not have been Dien's superior, but he was still a superior. Di wondered immediately if the jab had gone too far, but he did not rescind the slight.

Whip me then, he silently dared the captain.

Anything, even a flogging- *especially* a flogging- was better than sitting alone and thinking of the son he would never meet.

Thrasilaos simply smirked, and turned his blindfolded face to Alpheos and Maron.

"He's never let us down before."

"He might be a whiny shit, but he's always pulled through when we needed him. I trust him."

"So be it. You have the approval of an entire ballsack, Weeper. Try not to let it go to your head. Leave your armor. And your shield. Though you don't seem to have much trouble leaving *that* behind."

Di accepted the insult. An eye for an eye.

Thrasilaos led them in file back east of the pass and up a trail into the mountains near where the Phokians pitched.

"Do not look at their fires." Thrasilaos reminded them, Dienekes more than the others. "It'll ruin your night sight."

A small bivouac of Spartan shadows huddled further up the Anopaian way. Dienekes recognized every one as he moved closer. Krateros, Echemmon, Polymedes, Oenomias and Polygonos… Nearly the whole first two lines were present, and certainly all of King Leo's prized Olympians. Di's stomach boiled at realizing he was the only one uninvited. But he was here now and decided it better not to mention.

They pulverized charcoals in a tripod with a mix of oil and pitch, boiling the potion over a faintly glowing bed of coals that gave off heat without too much light. None of them wore their usual panoply, equipped instead with a pile of hoplons borrowed from allies or taken from the dead. The shields' original heraldry had been painted over with black.

"Don't get it in your eyes." Maron told Di as he caked himself with the black tar tincture.

Λ

"Why? What happens?"

"Just. Dont. Get. It-in-your-eyes. Savvy?"

"Oh."

The sun bled red in the west and winked out as they took painstaking hours to coat every inch of their bodies with the stuff, then their tunics, then blacked out the sheen on their blades. They wore no armor at the insistence of Thrasilaos. For tonight at least, it was better to be light of foot than protected. They left even their feet bare, not risking that the laces of their sandals snag an offending thorn and give them away.

Dienekes began to lattice bunches of twigs and leaves onto the loaned shield, to break up his profile like he had in the Krypteia. Alpheos stopped him.

"You'll snag. Make noise. This shield is the same size and weight as yours. Stick to what you know."

Thrasilaos, his blindfold now removed, came and went as he pleased until deciding the time had come, and led them a distance further up the goat path before veering sharply off. They were miles away from their camp, and from the field of battle.

"I cut a trail last night. But it's only wide enough for single file. Step where I step. Duck where I duck. Make too much noise and I'll kill you myself."

The path snaked wildly. It was slow going, but a straight cut increased their chances of being spotted. The near-full moon cast a silver glow through the trees, a double edged sword. Their way was illuminated, but if they could see then so could the Mede.

The treeline broke abruptly at a rock outcrop, a flat clearing that jutted over the battlefield below. An elaborate tent crowned the ledge, ringed by scores, maybe hundreds of guards. From down the hill came sounds of life, not the scratch of metal on metal that a war party resonates. It was civilization. The Spartans crouched at the edge of cover, out of earshot.

"Is that what I think it is?" Dienekes asked the twins, who nodded.

"See their spears? Almost as long as ours." Maron pointed. "They're called 'applebearers' for those big round counterweights on the butt. Personal guards to Xerxes."

"Why does he camp on the edge of his force? Is it not safer in the heart of his people?"

"He thinks himself untouchable. We are way over there, not creeping round to fuck him from behind. And he wanted a scenic view of the battle." Lagos answered.

"Yeah, a scenic view of us kicking his ass." Whispered Alpheos.

"Something is wrong." Thrasilaos hissed at them. "There are twice as many guards as last night."

"Have we been betrayed?" asked Krateros.

Λ

"Impossible." Thrasilaos shook his head. "I didn't know we were doing this until today, and told no one. Not even you." He winked at the Polemarch. "I'm going in for a closer look. Wait here."

He was not gone long, and returned from behind wearing strange Persian clothes and an embroidered sack.

"What did we learn?" Polygonos rubbed his hands together, ready for a fight.

"Not a damn thing, maybe he's just feeling skittish."

"He should be after the beating he's been taking."

"I did find a way to pull those guards away, though. I hope." Thrasilaos opened his stolen satchel to show a nest of carefully packed ceramics orbs. Each was corked. He pulled the stopper on one and held it under Krateros's face. "Remember that smell?"

"Naptha. Bastards. Did they plan to use this on us?" The Polemarch wrinkled his nose. "Are we going to burn him out?" asked Polygonos.

"No, there's no guarantee he'd fry. And it'd bring the whole Persian horde down on our heads. No. We burn *everything else.*"

He tore the eastern clothes into strips for wicking. There were six jars and ten assassins. Thrasilaos paired them off and took two for himself.

"One of you lights it, the other throws it. Immediately. Hold it in your hand and the flame will give us all away. Throw far. Try to hit something crowded. Meet back here and we'll see what they do. Do not look into the fire."

They spread out across the treeline to throw from different vantages. Dienekes was paired with Krateros.

"It's not because he thinks less of you, you know."

"What?"

"Why Thrasilaos didn't pick you for this mission."

"*What?*"

"He thought it was too risky. That the front lines would need you tomorrow, whatever happened tonight."

"Risky?"

"Yes. We came not knowing if morning will find us at the pass or in Elysium."

"Die today, die tomorrow, what's the difference." Dienekes growled.

"It is not when you die that matters, Little Achilles. It is how."

Naptha had soaked the wick. Dienekes lit it off a spark from his xiphos and Krateros let fly. Its cold blue light was barely visible against the flickering backdrop of stars. As Thrasilaos commanded, they did not watch for it to strike, but they heard it as they scampered to regroup.

Little red towers were cropping up in camp down the mountainside. People panicked. Thrasilaos grinned. He'd thrown his own grenades at the quartermaster's

Λ

tent he'd stolen them from.

"Cover your eyes."

They could see the light of the blast through their fingers as the supply tent was consumed by fire, scattering white hot tongues through the canvas village.

The desired effect was achieved. The greater number of applebearers were drawn from the royal tent to deal with the fires. The remainder was still too many for the Spartans to fight, but not so many that they should not be able to slip a knife through to Xerxes's heart. Thrasilaos readied to give the command to move in, but their target moved first. One of the tent walls blew out, and a chariot rolled out, thronged by guards at a sprint. The rest of the structure collapsed and a new fire caught from the censors and lamps burning inside. The guards outside followed the chariot.

"Something's wrong." Dienekes rasped

"You don't say?" Thrasilaos spat. "We follow. We have no choice. Go now."

A pack of shadows erupted from the treeline at a silent sprint, following the chariot up the only path wide enough for it.

"He rides away from his army?" Dienekes thought out loud.

"Kill first, Weeper. Questions later."

Di and Echemmon shot ahead of their group, their victims run through before they knew they were fighting. Polymedes swept between them and crushed a guard's throat in his fist. The Spartans leap-frogged over each other, silently picking off the units that trailed behind until Polygonos's sword found a liver instead of a lung. The man screamed. Dozens of his comrades turned to fight. Only a handful remained with the chariot as it clattered down the trail.

"Echemmon. Lagos. Dien. Go with Thrasilaos. The rest of you with me." Six shields hammered into place on either side of Krateros. "We'll hold them off."

Di could not bear to leave his mentor in the face of futility, but the Polemarch had given an order. Di flanked around the charging Persians, screaming as he went.

It is not when you die that matters. It is how.

Dienekes and Echemon thought they were alone in pursuit until Thrasilaos dropped from high in the trees ahead onto two guardsmen. He bore no more weapons, and before his squad overtook him, they saw him tear out the hapless Persian throats with his teeth. One of three archers on the back of the chariot sighted an arrow at Echemmon, but a stone whizzed through the dark and shattered the bowman's face. He slumped from the carriage. Echemmon nodded thanks to Lagos who was already reloading his sling while they ran. Dienekes dodged an arrow, snatched a spear off a corpse and threw it in the back and out the belly of another fleeing Mede. Lagos stunned one more with a slingstone to the spine. Thrasilaos burst off the trailside again and gouged his fingers through the eyes of the final guard until they clawed into brain and the man's spasms ceased.

Λ

The chariot slowed to a stop of its own volition. The two remaining archers dismounted and drew back their bows. The man, the king, driving the chariot girded his flowing robes and stepped down. His gold mask and headdress glittered in the moonlight.

"Four of us. Two arrows. We can get him." Thrasilaos gnashed his teeth. "On my mark."

But the king of kings himself stepped forward with a knife drawn and put it into his own archers from behind. Their arrows flew wild. Slowly, Xerxes removed his mask.

The Spartans stood immobilized by shock. It was not Xerxes.

"I did not wish it to come to this, my brothers."

"You do not call me brother!" Thrasilaos howled, so bewildered that even he stood his ground.

"Alas, bonds of blood do not break." Demaratos shrugged off his foreign robes. He still wore his Laconian panoply beneath.

"Take that off, traitor!" Sharktooth spat bloody foam.

"Is that any way to speak to the man who has only just spared your life?"

"Spared my life? We could have ended this! Tonight!" The Spartan captain screamed.

"Don't be a fool, Thrasilaos. You never would have made within a mile of Xerxes."

"I can go anywhere there is darkness. Does darkness not fall on your great king?"

"Not tonight, it would seem."

"It was you, all along. You told our people not to attack Argos even as they Medized. You told Xerxes about the road to flank Thessaly. You told him to march during Karneia! You stab us in the back and dare call us brothers!?"

"Wisdom is not always sweet, chosen of Kleomenes. You can fight and die with all our kind, or you can accept that the world has changed. The life you knew, that *we* knew is no more. The Achaemenids are here to stay. Join them in enlightenment or be washed away in their tide."

Dienekes had not breathed since he saw the man unmasked. His mind replayed visions of his own greatest day, when Demaratos had held his hand aloft before all of Sparta and proclaimed him the future. A single tear rolled down his cheek.

"This is my final gift to you." Demaratos spread his arms wide, bloody dagger dripping from one hand. "I have spared your lives spared tonight in the hopes that you may hear me. Join me. Join Xerxes. Join the world as it becomes one. You have fought well, but if you continue to resist, you will be swept away and forgotten. This is your final chance. Tell your king. Tell Leonidas. You will be met with grace. With mercy."

"I'll show you mercy." Thrasilaos rushed forward. Demaratos defended himself

Λ

with the knife but the captain had him disarmed and on his knees in an instant. "I'll show you mercy!" Thrasilaos's hands wrenched Demaratos's throat so tight that blood vessels burst in the traitor's eyes.

"Wait!" Dienekes shouted. He still choked on his boyhood memory. And regicide, even of a traitor king, was still a heinous crime in the eyes of the Gods. Dienekes did not want Thrasilaos to meet the same fate as Kleomenes. "Don't kill him…" For surprise or for something else, Thrasilaos listened. He released his grip. Demaratos, gasping, collapsed to the ground. The faintest of footfalls padded up the trail from behind. Four more Spartans joined them. Only four. Thrasilaos's eyes widened at the loss.

"Is he..?" Sharktooth stared at the shape of Polygonos, draped over the broad shoulders of Oenomias, who solemnly shook his head. Polymedes carried a corpse as well, a charred and smoking thing. Thrasilaos threw his head back and screeched. "The Weeper is right. Death is too good for you. Live with yourself, traitor. And let all who look upon you know your shame." He snatched Demaratos by his long black hair, plucked the fallen knife from the dirt, and put the blade to the nape of the king's head, just as he had done to Lysimachos so many years ago. When he pulled the blade, he shaved away more than hair. Demaratos screamed as he was scalped.

"There. I have something to remember you by." Thrasilaos tied the scalp to his belt by its bloody ringlets. "Now let me give you something to remember me by." He sunk his fangs into the once-king's cheek and tore away a mouthful. He chewed. He swallowed.

Voices and bootsteps clamored up the trail after them. The twins pulled on Dienekes.

"Come. We've failed. It's time to go."

Dienekes nodded and followed, falling in beside his friends.

"Wait… Alpheos…" Dienekes said as they broke into a gallop, falling out of memory and back into his senses. "Alpheos, where is Krateros?" They plunged into the woods, following Thrasilaos as he wove through the trees.

Alpheos did not respond. Did not break stride. His face like granite fixed hard on the moon-silver darkness of the forest. Dienekes turned to the other twin, who likewise ignored him.

"Maron! Where is Krateros?"

Λ

Sixty-six

I t was not yet light, but the eastern horizon glowed with the coming of day. Already the thousand Phokians were armed, armored, and ranked at their station. Their bodies and weapons were fresh and ready but their minds fatigued, wearied by the suspense of routine.

Sebastos paced feverishly, unbecoming of a general. It unnerved his soldiers. Nearly a week they had readied and rallied in formation near the summit of Anopaia, to wait for nothing. Runners sent daily for updates from the gates below had returned with uselessly vague reports, unbelievable tales of extravagant valor, or hadn't returned at all. Frustration through the camp was palpable. Each passing day mounted their tension as they listened to the distant whisper of metal on metal at the coast, barely audible at such distance, when it was audible at all.

"Flying lions, sorcerers hurling rocks, furies climbing out of the sea…" He grumbled to his second-in-command after dismissing his messenger. "What am I to do with these fantasies, Phillip?"

"Yes, I hadn't realized we were doing battle in a Theban play." The first captain smirked. He was doing a much better job of feigning warm humors for their men.

Sebastos snorted.

"Rations will soon be dwindling. We'll need to dispatch more foraging parties so we can keep the stores. But keep it quiet."

"Of course. The men in line will be bitter if they find out they didn't get to join the hunting trip."

No sooner had they mentioned hunting than did a storm of animals erupt into the clearing from the forest to the west. Rabbits, foxes, deer, boar, even several lions and a bear stampeded from the dense woodland and charged uncaring through them past the awaiting army. Many were lanced after the soldiers overcame their initial shock. They broke rank in pursuit of breakfast and waved their quarries aloft on spearheads, letting blood drip onto their faces as they thanked the gods for their gift. Suspicion did not set in until the parade had fled east, doubt creeping into the minds of the Phokians even as they butchered their kills. Sebastos was more aristocrat than veteran, placed in charge by family name without any proven military proficiency. But Phillip was a traveled man, he had seen the like before. Predators do not flee their homes without an even larger predator in pursuit. He did not wait for Sebastos to command, he gave the order himself.

"Form up!" He howled, his urgency bordering on panic. "Form up!"

Before the stomp of boots was in the ears, they felt it through the earth. A rumble that vibrated up their legs, numbing their feet and shaking their hearts before Persians spilled from the treeline. They were out of rank, each walking as their own man and ignoring the trail. Spread as they were, a hundred stepped into view at once and each subsequent step forward harkened hundreds more.

Sebastos counted their number for as long as he dared before admitting he stood in the path of annihilation. He trusted his men, they were drilled and trained and loyal but they were no Spartans. They would not hold for long when so dreadfully outnumbered.

"Fall back! To the summit!" He bellowed. "Reform in the trees, make them chase us. We'll fight as Leonidas does, where their numbers matter not."

Several of the junior officers hesitated, deferring instead to Phillip.

"But, sir…" Philip said, not wanting to disobey. He tried to contain the panic in his own voice. "Our mission is to protect the Anopaian way… If it is taken, our allies on the coast will be flanked."

The current Phokian deployment straddled the shepherd's trail, brazen in the Persians' path before it bottlenecked back down to the rocky ravine descent. There would be no access without battle.

"We'll be swamped! You would have all our men die at once? We can hold them much longer from the treeline. Just as Leonidas said, we will harass them from the trees."

"Sir, if we leave the objective unguarded-"

"Do it now!"

Phillip succumbed to his orders. He barked to his lieutenants who barked to theirs, and confused, the troops reassembled several hundred yards south into the trees and waited for the enemy to follow.

It could have been as many as ten thousand men who filled the clearing, and more cluttered behind them unable to assemble for lack of room. They ordered themselves casually in battle lines opposite the fleeing Phokians. A leader in extravagant garb bounced in a chariot to their front, his horses laboring to tug the wooden wheels across uneven ground. A distinctly not-persian footman trotted along beside, calling up to the rider animatedly. He had the dress and manner of a Hellenic shepherd, not of a polis but from one of the ruralities between. Sebastos's blood boiled to see a backwater traitor consorting with the enemy, but could do nothing from his distance.

The charioteer rolled to a stop and stepped down, appearing to argue with the

Λ

turncloak. Eventually he pointed and a small ensemble of runners jogged towards the Phokian assembly.

"Ready yourselves!" The general harked. He did not know what to expect from so few, but he would be accepting no parley.

Instead of engaging, the runners stopped halfway to the Hellenes and peered intently from under their hands. They shrugged, and trotted back to their lines. They briefly conferred with the shepherd and their commander until he swatted the air with a horsetail scepter. Archers drew back and rained arrows onto the shrouded phalanx.

"Shields up!" Phillip howled.

Iron barbs clattered off of bronze. Men crouched behind their hoplons as if waiting out the weather. More spindles fell in the first volley than there were soldiers in the whole Phokian contingent. Shafts littered the ground and pocked the trees. Sebastos listened for the cries of his men, already counting the dead in his head but there came no screams. The rain stopped, and still he heard of no casualty. The projectiles harmed not a single hoplite.

"You see how they waste their weapons?" He called to his troop, who cheered in return.

Another volley whizzed skyward, and laughing, the Hellenes crouched behind their shields again.

"Like children throwing snow!"

Their spirits were somehow higher now that they were under fire, rather than waiting in ignorance. Taunts and jeers and songs rose from their lines.

"What's the matter with you?" Sebastos asked Phillip at the end of the second volley. The first captain had gone pale as a ghost.

"All is lost." Phillip whispered.

"What are you talking about?" Sebastos scoffed. "Not a single man has fallen, they fight like cowards. They'll not pry us from these forests today." The general's chest swelled.

Phillip only shook his head.

"All is lost." He said again, and sat, laying his spear and shield on the mossy ground.

The Persian archers had unstrung their bows and reordered into marching file, no longer caring about the Phokians in the woods. They fell in behind their fellow infantry and tens of thousands of men casually funneled down the Anopaian way, the Phokians forgotten and ignored.

"What is this? Phillip?" Sebastos blubbered.

"They don't want us, you fool." He was too disturbed to dance around insubordination. He had witnessed the very moment that allowed the Achaemenids into Europe, the moment when their world ended. "They only care about the path.

Λ.

And you gave it to them."

"An entire army at their wing and they do not fight? Cravens! Why don't they come for us?"

"Oh, they will." Phillip droned, his face sagging with the weight of defeat. "I'm sure they'll be back to finish us off when they're done with the Spartans."

Λ

Sixty-seven

D awn had not yet come, but the death of Krateros had already sent shockwaves through the hippeis. Unlike the generals of every other polis, Sparta's polemarchs led from the front. He had spent his entire life distinguishing himself as the best and boldest of infantrymen. From his induction to the Hippeis of Anaxandridas at twenty years old to his death forty years later there had been no man who could match him, even among the Lakedaimonians. But it was no one man they had come to fight. Leonidas barely retained his composure at the loss of his best friend and confidante. Thrasilaos failed at it entirely.

The captain muttered incessantly to himself, oscillating between whispered recitation of Lykourgan law to screeching incoherently at the top of his lungs. The few who dared console him thought better when he gnashed his pointed teeth at them. His shins bled freely, skinless from kicking trees and stones in frustration. He scratched frantically at himself, vexing more blood from his forearms, chest and neck. Hanks of his hair came away in his fists. He howled. Finally, he sat himself on a rock and his rantings deteriorated into hysterical sobs. Tears spilled through his fingers as he held his face. Quieter and quieter his breath heaved until, exhausted, he slid sideways and limp on the ground into sleep or unconsciousness.

His brothers did not begrudge him his outburst. He had earned that much.

Dienekes, for once, did not weep. Not yet. There was work to be done. His bare fingers pulled to little effect at the harsh and rocky dirt beside two wrapped figures that sang to him silently in their forever slumber. Funeral pyres for the other Hellenes yet smoldered from the previous battle, but the Lakedaimons did not burn their dead. They buried them on the fields where they died.

"Krateros saved our lives." Maron whispered. "All of us."

"I've never seen anything like it." Alpheos choked on the memory. "He took them all on himself. There were dozens at least. The way he roared, I swear he killed men with his voice alone."

They sat in silence while Dien pawed at the grave. He eventually stopped raking at the earth to turn his stone-dry eyes at them, asking without asking for more, for some kind of closure on the life of the only father he had ever known.

"He was an animal. Something from hell." Alpheos took his cue.

"Polygonos died first. A lucky shot. Arrow in the eye. We were all together, shields locked, we would have fought as a line. But when Krateros saw Poly go down, he decided that was enough. He wouldn't let any more of us die."

"He knocked us all down. All of us. The old man sent Polymedes sprawling. Picked him up and dropped him on us and charged the Applebearers by himself."

"They ran from him. Could have been a hundred, but in the face of Krateros they scattered like mice."

"He caught them one at a time. You've seen him run. Not as fast as you but faster than us. He chased them like a hound and tore them apart. He broke his sword on the first man that dared to stand his ground, then killed the second with the handle. He just ran them down after that. Charged into their weapons, bowled them over and stomped on their skulls."

"He ripped a Mede's jaw off with one hand, Di. Then stabbed it through another man's neck."

"I've never been more scared in my life, Weeper. But I wasn't afraid of the Persians, I wasn't afraid of death."

"We were afraid of Krateros."

"Eventually his shield was too full of spears and arrows and axes to use anymore. He had to drop it. That's when the real killing started."

"He pulled their bodies apart, Di. With his own two hands he tore them to pieces. Shredded them like linen and used their bones as weapons against their brethren."

"If the Gods themselves had been there with us, they would have fled from him in terror. He's with them now, Dienekes. With the Gods in Elysium and I doubt a single one of them has the gall to look that man in the eye."

"They filled him full of arrows and spears till he bristled, and not a one would slow him down. He pulled iron from his own chest and killed them with it. They hit him with naptha and it only made him wilder. Burning and bleeding, he did not die. He became."

"A towering inferno. If he could have opened his mouth any wider he would have swallowed them whole."

"He kept calling something."

"Every second. He couldn't be silenced."

Dienekes heard the words in Krateros's own voice, though it was the twins who spoke them.

"I'm coming, Kleo. I'm coming, Stratos. I'm coming, Ono. Make a place for me, brothers. I'm coming home."

Λ

Dien's fingers scored the ground with such adamance that most of his fingernails had shorn off. He had forgotten to breathe.

"He killed them all. All by himself. His heart still beat in his burnt and battered body when we caught up."

The twins hesitated, shared a glance.

"His last words…"

Dienekes stopped digging and turned to them again, pleading with his eyes.

"Tell Dienekes…"

"Tell Dienekes that he…"

"That he's the big oak now."

Di slumped into the hole he had scratched from the earth, body balled up like an infant drowning in tears. The twins threw their red cloaks around him and the three of them wept into each other's shoulders. When their eyes dried, they dug the rest of the grave together.

Leonidas sensed a silent something in the bushes behind him. He spun on it with spear extended.

"Declare yourself." He demanded.

"You are impressing me." Barbadoras stepped from the shrubs. "Well done for you, King of Lions. To hear the creeper when he is at creeping."

"Barbadoros." Leonidas lowered his spear and inclined his head. "I hear I have much to thank you for."

"Perhaps you thank me in the later, yes?" He chewed on a fingernail. "For I have more gift to bring and this one not so shining as the others."

"What have you brought me?"

"Is not gift for you, brave king. Is gift for him." He nodded to the woods. "For surely, the Lion would have done the killing him if not brought by Barbadoros and his creeping."

Leonidas raised an eyebrow and Barbadoros whistled softly to the bushes he stepped from. Nothing happened. He whistled again, and jerked his arm as if beckoning a reluctant dog.

Out stepped a man. His skin was dark red-brown. His eyes were kohled and his clothing colorful. His hands were loosely bound. He wore the dead eyed look of the man who has given up all hope.

"A Persian." Leonidas remarked. "You are right. We would have killed him. Why should I not kill him now?"

"He bring message for you, great king. Have mercies. He good messenger, but the message bad."

Leonidas sighed. Stout as his heart was, he did not know if he could yet stand more bad news.

"In a moment then. Have him taken to my tent. I will be with him momentarily."

"Is important, great king." Barbadoros scratched at his forelock, but Leo dismissed him with a wave.

"Thank you for your counsel, Macedonian, but so is this."

Leonidas had distanced himself from the gravedigging so he could think but to little gain. His thoughts could not penetrate the static that occupied his mind. He, like Thrasilaos, had dared to hope the night mission would bring an end to this. Instead he had a friend to bury. He marched loudly, with purpose, to where the bodies lay. His brothers heard his footsteps and fell wordlessly in behind them. The graves were ready on his arrival. Dienekes, the twins, and the others gathered there stood as he approached.

He wished he could stand in silence, but that was not his lot. He swallowed and wrestled the chaos in his head to order. It was the king's place to deliver the eulogy for his sworn man.

"Thrasilaos should be here for this." Dienekes spoke softly and moved to wake the captain.

"No." Leo stopped him with an arm. "Let him rest. He has not slept for a week, and his efforts have just cost him both his closest friend and his commanding officer. If any man has needed the privilege of sleep, it is him. He has earned it."

Di's hands were desperate for action, so he would not be left to his thoughts. He and his friends put themselves to lifting the cowled corpse of his mentor.

Leonidas breathed deep, then spoke.

"Krateros in his lifetime did what few men before him accomplished. He did all what his world asked of him. Loved by many, trusted by all, he was quiet in word, noble in deed, and unmatched in fulfilment of his duties. The consummate soldier, he rose from the lowly beginnings we all share to become the right hand of not one, not two, but four kings, Agiad and Eurypontid both. It is on the backs of men like him that nations are built and it is by his example that the trail to all good things are blazed. We were blessed to share in his guidance, his friendship, and to stand in the shadow of his shield. He is survived by his many daughters, his only son-" Leo broke gaze from the grave to lock eyes with Dienekes, who nearly wept again. "-his grandson by the same name, and his many great-grandchildren to come. We were unworthy to stand beside him, but in our deeds yet undone we will earn the right to call him brother, and it will be him that welcomes us to the golden fields of Elysium. We do not mourn his passing, but rejoice in having been part of his life. A greater man there has never been, nor will there ever be. The world will never see the likes of Krateros again."

Leonidas dared not speak another word lest he choke on it. His men sensed this,

Λ

and wrapped his shoulders in their cloaks as another man stepped forward to speak for Polygonos. When that finished, they all sang the paian together as they buried their brethren one fistful of soil at a time. The sun rose in the east as it set on the First Polemarch of Sparta.

"Now…" Leonidas now fully composed, said to Barbadoros, stepping into his tent with his fellow commanders in tow. "What message does the Mede bring us."

Λ

Sixty-eight

Barbadoros translated with some difficulty, but there was no mistaking the defector's missive. They had been flanked. Persia had taken the Anopaian way. There would be no more defending the pass. Barbadoros bowed solemnly and left the leaders of Hellas to discuss their options.

"Forgive me for asking the obvious," Kosmas was still green in the face, eyes ringed in dark purple, but feigned composure nobly. "But how do we know he isn't lying?"

"Barbadoros or the Mede?" Asked Dithyrambos.

"Either?"

"Barbadoros is clearly a liar." Said Leonidas. "But he is our liar. I wouldn't trust his dice, his stories, or that he is even really Macedonian, but his allegiances are plain. He is with us. As for the Mede? It matters little. He may not have mentioned the Anopaian way by name, but he spoke of a goat path through the mountains. That is enough. With as many men as he has, Xerxes will find it if he has not already. We must decide on contingencies."

"Like what?" Asked Kosmas. "Which hill to die on? I rather like this one."

"That's precisely the problem. I would not have all of us die here." Leonidas stared with glazed eyes into space as his brother Kleo once did, seeing things the others did not. "It serves no purpose when every man who survives today will be another man to join the forces at Korinth."

"You would have us retreat? After all we've done here?" Even Leontiades scorned the thought.

"Not all of us. I will stay to cover the escape."

"Then I stay too." Kosmas demanded. "The poets won't sing your name without mine next on their tongues."

"I have no home to go to. I stay as well." Leontiades agreed. His son, Eurymachos, seemed less adamant.

Leonidas turned from them, palming his brow in an unlaconian display of distress. The moment passed.

"Sparta stays. The rest go. We've done our job and bought our cities time to muster, but now we are lost. I will not be responsible for the deaths of men not from my country. I am king of only one land." Dithyrambos and Demophilos stood to argue and he silenced them with a glare. "Tell your men what has happened and pack them to march. I will suffer no dispute. Don't bother to strike camp. It will take too long. Carry only the supplies you'll need for the journey home and leave the rest."

The troops nearly fell to riot when they received the order. Some were elated at the thought, having received new lease on the lives they thought were over. Some, like Kosmas and Dithyrambos, were bitter. After the blood and sweat spilled from their bodies into the ground, they had come to think of the pass as their own.

Spartans filtered through the camp to confirm the command and rout any taking too long to pack. Tents were to be abandoned, supply carts full of rations would be spoiled and poisoned so not to nourish the enemy, any weapons not on the belts or backs of their bearers were to be left to rust in the dirt for scavengers to pick through.

The Lokrians were first to leave. Their home sat less than a whole day's journey away, so they needed carry little. By nightfall they would have spread the word to their wives and children and overnight the polis would become a ghost town, its citizens scattered as refugees across Hellas. Armies with further to go took longer to prepare, but by midmorning the number of hoplites in the foothills had halved.

Some, however, neglected to pack at all.

Dithyrambos slouched on a rock, sharpening his sword.

"Thespian." He looked up when Leonidas addressed him, flanked by his Olympians. "Are you not preparing to march?" Rambos shrugged. Leo's eyes narrowed. "To disobey a superior officer is to invite death. Tell me that's not what you're doing."

Dithyrambos didn't have time to answer before the treeline to the north exploded with wildlife. The same stampede that passed the Phokians had made its way into the lowlands. The men still here revelled in the chaos in the same way their allies on the summit had, relishing the chance to spear game and distract themselves from the shroud of defeat hanging over them. Leonidas did not share their joy. He recognized the parade for what it was.

"See? I tell you is true." Barbadoros whispered to the king, standing in what had been empty air a moment before. Unlike Thrasilaos, no one winced at Baradoros's sudden appearance. He had become a welcome interruption.

"Yes, I can see." Leonidas watched without reaction as panicked boar shredded the forgotten tents of his allies, as stags leaped and dodged through laughing soldiers. Kosmas cornered a bear. Rather than kill it, he fed it a bowl of black Spartan broth and cackled when even it turned up its nose at the foul stuff. "It is how we hunted in the Krypteia. Ten of us would chase creatures from a larger tract into a choke where

Λ

two of us waited with spears." Speaking this, he now knew how his prey must have felt. He shook the dread thought from his mind. Unlike the beasts of the forest, he would stand his ground. "What's that you have?"

"Ah… is my own prey." Barbadoros unrolled the blonde hide in his arms, a freshly flayed lion skin. "Methinks is for your scary man." He hooked two fingers under his lips, miming fangs. "One for Leaping-Weeper, one for Sharptooth. When Persians seeing two where there were before only the one, then they are surely being piss themselves to death." The pelt was still stained with pink blood and dangled scraps of flesh. Leonidas grunted his approval. It suited Thrasilaos. "I am having more gift as well. For you, Genitals." He pointed to Alpheos and Maron. "Is too much for me to bringing my ownself. But I secret to you where I have hiding it." He bent toward their ears and whispered. The twins looked to Leo, who nodded, and they left to find their treasure. Dienekes moved to follow them but Barbadoros caught his arm.

"No, is just for them. Secret, secret. You taking this to your teacher." He held out the flesh-wet pelt. Dienekes sighed and accepted the hide. Glancing back after his friends, he saw they had already gone. Thrasilaos, for once, was not hard to find. He had not moved an inch from where he'd fallen spent the night before. He had missed his polemarch's funeral, and the burial of his best friend. The Weeper wanted to kick the sleeping form for the wrongness. Punish it. But he reminded himself of Leo's words and knew the rest was well deserved. In all the time Dienekes had known him, the king's assassin had never once shown weakness. To see him like this would have been disheartening if it had not been so surreal. Neither his eyes nor his heart could comprehend the sight of the Spartan captain limp in the dirt. Where a child might have sucked a thumb in their sleep, Thrasilaos's pointed teeth chewed the skin from his. Dried blood caked his lips. Dienekes could not bring himself to wake his former master. He unrolled the pelt, blanketed the sleeping soldier, and walked away thinking of his dead father, his dead mentor, his dead friends, and all those soon to join them. He told himself he'd cried his last, now carrying too many myriad pains for a man to digest, his stream of emotions dammed up by its own multitude. It was just as well he'd be dying soon, too. Then he wouldn't have to feel.

He returned to his King, who was losing his temper.

"Your orders were plain, Kosmas." Leo growled.

"And they have been fulfilled!" The Tegean commander had treated his hangover the hair of the dog that bit him. His color and manner were restored, albeit with a dark stain around his lips. "My forces have left the pass, see?" He pointed to his white-clad column marching southwest out of the valley. "Only I remain. I told you, King. I will have my verse in this song."

Barbadoros stopped short, trundling past with a handcart full of what had recently been someone else's belongings. "It saddens me to hearing this, brave Kosmas. We

Λ

have been companions long times and I shall be miss you forever." He wrapped his arms around the Tegean, his face pressed into the commander's breastplate. Kosmas laughed and patted the little man on the head.

"You will see me again in the sky, little friend." He said. "Though with your wily ways, I'm certain it will be many long years."

When Barbardoros backed away, there were tears in his eyes. He rummaged through his cart, chewing a quaking lip, until he brought out a flagon of wine and a cup. "Drink with me then, please please." His voice was soft and trembling. "My very very best drinking, I save it for special time. I hoped would be happy times, but friend is a friend if happy or sad, yes?"

"Well said, Doros." Kosmas was clearly moved. "You've been a true and loyal compatriot, and I have cherished every moment of our time together."

Leonidas twitched, clearly frustrated with the delay, but reluctant to rush the disbanding of brothers.

"I drink to you, friend, forever man for the poets. They will writing your songs, and Barbadoros will writing songs for you of his own, brave brave Kosmas."

"You honor me."

Kosmas drained his cup. He coughed and gagged at the sour swill.

Barbadoros smiled, and poured out his cup on the ground.

"You... You scoundrel! Brigand! Common backwater sneakthief!" Kosmas wobbled, his words slurred together. His bloodshot eyes wide with realization.

Barbadoros shoved him hard in the chest and the commander flopped backwards into the handcart, unconscious.

"He will being fine!" Barbadoros's eyes had dried, his scandalous smile returned. "I will taking to his men, but myself will staying here a little while yet. Call if you have needing me. Even if you will not seeing him, your friend Barbadoros is there."

And he trundled off, whistling away with his loot.

The remaining officers watched him in momentary shock.

"Should I drug you too, then?" Leonidas asked Dithyrambos, who still sharpened his sword, seated on the very same rock.

"If you must." Dithyrambos said with only a trace of insubordination, and slid his weapon into the scabbard on his belt.

"Soldier, I warned you the consequences of disobedience. Do you test me?"

"Insubordination is death, you said?" Dithyrambos stood, fingers fussing at the laces on his breastplate.

"I did."

"Kill me then." Dithyrambos stripped his cuirass and threw it down, his burly hands tearing away his tunic to expose the flesh beneath.

Λ

Leonidas hesitated.

"Kill me. Here. For all to see, so they will say that King Leonidas of Lakedaimon murdered a man in cold blood for sharing a like mind, a like heart, and a like will to not bend to the invader."

Leonidas drew his kopis. Rambos spread his arms to the side, and thrust out his chest.

"I scorn you, Spartan. You claim yourself king of only one land, but here you are demanding men of another country bow to your will under pain of death. It was a fool's errand to follow you here. You are no better than Xerxes. Did you think I fought for you? Under your banner? Under some delusional dream of Hellas united? I do not fight for Sparta, I do not fight for the Isthmus of Korinth, nor for the righteousness or freedom. I fight for my home. You don't understand with your home so far south, so far away from the threat. Whether or not I live to fight another day, my home lies next in the Persian path. With my home gone, what will I then have to fight for with my wife and children dead or displaced? At the council you spoke so proudly of freedom, the same freedom that to me you now deny. So do it. Kill me. And let history forever know that Leonidas is not a man of his word."

Leonidas chewed his cheek.

"Does this man speak for all of you?" The king gestured with his naked sword to the other Thespians clustered around Rambos. None of them had made any preparation to leave either. They did not answer, but rose one by one to remove their own breastplates and stand beside their captain. "So be it." Leonidas growled.

He stomped forward. Rambos closed his eyes and tilted his head back, ready for the blow that never came. Instead Leo drew the Thespian's sword, longer and broader than his own, from its sheath.

"This is mine now." The king rumbled. "And this," He slid his own Kopis into the empty scabbard. "Is yours." Dithyrambos, baffled, opened his eyes. "This is yours now also." Leo unclasped his crimson cloak and wrapped it around Rambo's shoulders. "I am not accustomed to being spoken to in that manner. But your words ring true, and remind me of what I had lost sight of. Your people and mine have long been allies, and now, in our darkest of moments you dare to stand with me again. You honored me with your courage and I spat in your face. My words spoken in haste are now regretted. Take this as my apology. If today you fight for Thespia, then so do I." Leonidas unfurled Rambo's silver-grey cloak from atop the pile of the Thespian's wargear and wrapped it around his own shoulders. "Today, Sparta and Thespia are one."

Unbidden, the Olympians beside Leonidas drove their sauroteurs into the ground, leaned their shields against their spears, and stepped forward with empty hands to wrap their red capes over the Thespians. The display drew attention. Those who had

Λ

not heard the argument only saw comrades embracing and exchanging robes. Moved by the sight, they took off their own cloaks and traded until all the Spartan backs were draped in silver. All save Dienekes, who still wore the lion, and Thrasilaos who still but slept.

"It is a wise man, a strong man, who can admit fault. Your people are lucky to have you." Dithyrambos ran his fingers along the hem of the scarlet wool.

"I am but learning." Leonidas accepted it as a compliment. "Unfortunately, it seems too late. The wisest man in Sparta died last night."

With the sudden ceremony completed, the parties returned to battle preparations. Leonidas visited Leontiades at the Theban camp behind the first gate. He was speaking with one of his officers- former officer. Hamon, the one who he had stripped of rank the night before, who seemed in exaggeratedly good spirits considering.

"Your apologies are appreciated, hoplite." The general said, though Hamon visibly winced at the conscript title, rather than his former honorific. "You wouldn't be the first man whose mind was poisoned by wine."

"Yes, sir, poisoned mind, sir. I was not myself." Hamon wore a shamelessly painted smile, brow peaked in theatrical remorse, head nodding like a chicken. "Your punishment was most merciful, sir. Drawing a weapon on a comrade on the eve of battle is a capital offense, sir. You spared me. I promise you it will not be forgotten." Hamon's teeth flashed through the apologetic rictus of his lips. "I look forward to the chance to prove myself worthy of your grace." His words dripped sacharine.

"You seem suitably humbled, soldier. And I grant that these are extenuating circumstances. But a warrior must be able to keep his composure in any event. I'll be honest, you've never been exemplary in the bearing or dignities of a warrior, but your record on the field speaks for itself. I have no regrets for having had your sword in my service. The men have been uninformed of your demotion, and I shall see it stays that way. Redeem yourself on the field today and we shall speak about reinstating your office."

A wave passed from one side of Hamon's face to the other, a glimmer of rage and rebuke. The possibility, not promise, of promotion after his certain death for the man that shamed him fell across his jaw like a hard slap. But he recomposed, painting his face placid and mooncalved again.

"You honor me, sir." He said. "And to this end, with no men of my own to command now, I am free to station on the line wherever you see fit?"

"Hm?"

"Then may I request that I be stationed on the front line. Next to you and your son, my dear friend, Eurymachos. So that if-" he stressed the word, " -if I die, I can hope that it is to save the life of the man who spared me when he should not have."

Λ

"You surprise me, Hamon." Leontiades nodded. "Request granted. Perhaps you have the dignities of a warrior afterall."

They saluted, and Hamon took his leave.

Leonidas coughed loudly behind the general.

"I hope you're not here to order me away again." The Theban general hailed him, quizzically eyeing the grey cloak. "I'd hate for first blood of the day to be between Hellenes."

"On the contrary, friend. I have been convinced." They shook hands. "Tell me what we have learned."

Leontiades pointed.

"They've built a wall, three, maybe four men high. Tall enough that we can't see down into it from the hills. Nothing impenetrable, mostly wood frame covered in canvas, and then more to the sides so we cannot see around from the swamp or the sea. It's no fortress, just a strange tent. Through the night and into the morning, they crept it forward an armslength at a time." The Persian baffle had scraped from the third gate to just past the Phokian wall.

"And I assume you've been making it difficult for them?"

"Like I'd miss that sport." Leontiades chuckled. "The builders are living a nightmare. My archers have killed dozens, and the Medes themselves whip to death any who refuse to risk our arrows. He rules through fear alone, this Xerxes. It will be his undoing."

"What are they hiding behind it?"

"Nothing yet, so far as we can tell. My spies have seen only more builders through the cracks. They seem to be keeping it empty on purpose."

"Well, whatever they plan on sending through it, it's nothing a Spartan phalanx won't stop."

Leontiades laughed again.

"Of this, my new friend," he said. "I have been convinced."

Λ

Sixty-nine

The morning sun had long since burnt away the morning mist. Each day prior saw battle well underway by this hour, but the Persians were biding time into their schemes. The helots brought by the Lakonians loitered mostly ignored at the northwest edge of the Hellenic camps. Many, if not all, had contemplated escape, but they were not people of the world. If their thrall's garb did not give them away, then their infantile bearing certainly would. Fear kept them trotting at the heels of their Spartan masters. They prickled in terror when Persian drums beat from the forest behind them and they scattered, screaming and wailing, into the protective arms of those who kept them as slaves.

"See me, Hydarnes!" Barbadoros screamed to the distant Persian commander from the top of an overturned wagon. "You remembering me, Hydarnes? I remembering you! Do the ghosts of my brothers and sisters haunting you? We will all haunting you forever, bastard whoreson for what you take from us! Barbadoros will haunting you till end of both our days!"

"The enemy of my enemy…" Alpheos mused. He and Maron had returned from their treasure hunt, but breathed no word of what the treasure might be.

"…Is a friend indeed." Oinomaos finished the phrase. The Olympians sat out of arrow range, but in full view of both the Persian elites assembling to the west and to the cloth and timber corridor stretching across the pass. Despite the proximity, they were in no danger yet. The enemy's multitudes would prohibit them from mobilizing effectively for potentially hours to come. Dienekes and his fellows watched, brazenly combing and oiling each other's hair while they turned up their noses at the slaves crowding among them in fear.

Hauling himself up onto a boulder a hundred yards away, Leonidas did something that no Spartan king before him had done. He addressed the helots directly.

"Do not run to us for succor!" He bellowed. "For you will not find it! These fields are naught but blood and entrails and my feet churn in its red mud no different from yours. If the craven in you begs for salvation then flee if you will. Turn to our enemies, or to the wilderness. But know that our foe does not hold you separate from me and their knives will water the earth with your bowels just as they would mine. Run for freedom and be hounded all your days by fear and destitution until the teeth of dogs tear you apart in the gutter with none but maggots to remember you. Or. OR! There may yet be a man among you. A man who craves to take the reins of his own destiny. Who has no wish to run and hide but to feel the weight of his own efforts in the turning of the world. If you are that man then I say to you that this is your day! Uplift yourself from the shackles bound to your birthright and take your place in history on a day that will be sung through all of time! Stand and fight! Take up arms and be remembered! Fight with me today, and die as my equal!"

The helots were too baffled and surprised to react themselves, but slowly took heart when the Thespians and Spartans cheered. Some of the Lakonians walked among them, knocking their dogskin hats to the ground, helping them collect weapons from the abandoned supplies and demonstrating the proper way to hold them. On any other day, the weapons would have instantly been turned against the Spartiate, but there was a magic in the air that stayed the hand of sedition. The devil they knew proved preferable to the devil they knew not.

"Equals?" Polymedes spat, watching with scorn as the helots received their first and last combat instruction. "He can't mean that."

"Maybe. Maybe not." Dienekes wondered himself, harboring his own share of venom at the thought. "Helots killed his best friend. Tried to kill him and his brother. I'm sure he has not forgotten. But a king makes sacrifices. Perhaps he thinks it is worth the foul taste of a lie in his mouth for the sake of a few more Persians dead." The slaves outnumbered the Spartiates three to one, but no one believed their presence would make a difference. They kept this detail to themselves.

While the Spartans calmly groomed each other, ceremoniously cleaning and donning their armors, the Thespians prepared themselves their own way. Chanting, beating their shields, they screamed into each other's faces and drummed themselves into a frenzy. Their seven hundred men would hold the western flank while the Spartans held the pass to the north and the Thebans stood in reserve to support where it was needed.

At least that was the plan.

"Something comes." Lagos's keen hunter senses prickled. He sniffed the air and his neck twisted in the direction of the Persian cloth causeway. His brothers knew better than to second guess him. They lifted their shields and marched without order into place. The Phokian wall had been taken in the night, the mouth of the tunnel opening just passed it. No longer would the phalanx have the swamp and the archers to lean on.

"Is it men? Battle engines?"

"Men, yes. But..." He sniffed again. "Livestock? Lots of it."

"I hope it's pork." Polymedes dared to dream. "We haven't had a decent roast since…"

"Since the Tegean squires cooked us a boar yesterday?" Dienekes joined them on the first line.

"Ah, but that was ever so long ago…" Poly licked his lips.

Leonidas fell in infront of them. Without being told, Lagos and Oenemias took the places that Krateros and Polygonos had left vacant. It was bittersweet for Dienekes. He lamented the loss of his brothers, but he had other brothers still to lean on even if he wished it was still his mentor standing in his place. They understood, knocking their shoulders into his and sharing a nod.

"We're still missing one." Lagos counted only five men where there should have been six.

"No we're not." Thrasilaos growled, shoving between ranks to the front. He wore his new blood-ragged lion cloak and inclined the shield of Hegisistratos toward Dienekes with a gracious nod. His eyes were still watery and unfocused, but aside from that he showed no signs of being worse for wear. His presence in the formation made the other Spartans feel all the more dangerous. Their strides lengthened and hearts rose. He shouldered Lagos out of the way, deliberately standing next to his Weeper.

Leontiades and his retinue saluted as the column, silver now instead of crimson, passed to form up at the pinch of the first gate, still at least a hundred yards from the Persian curtain. Well within arrow range, but arrows they did not fear, but something else caught the eye of Thrasilaos as drums began to beat on the far side of the partition. Men skirted in and out of the curtains, rushing and arguing, pointing and making last minute adjustments.

"No… no…" Thrasilaos mumbled. He recognized the lamilar scales of their armor and pointed helms, their bowlegged walk. "Bastards!" He cried. "Traitors! Scum of the earth! I'll butcher the lot of you and feed you to your stupid God-King, you craven, bitch-whipped, sons of dogs!"

His comrades looked at the captain in confusion. Only Leonidas understood, as he had been there when Thrasilaos had been bonded to their people. He was familiar with their strange raiment as well.

"They are Scythians." Leonidas told his men through clenched teeth. "Thrasilaos learned his strange ways from Scythians." He eyed his captain.

"My tricks won't work on them." Thrasilaos shook his head. "At least not all of them. And you can be sure that whatever's behind that wall, it's something none of us have ever seen before."

"Oh, good. I love killing new things," Lagos sucked his teeth.

The partition opened. Lesser men would have shuddered at what waited behind but the Lakedaimonians faltered not. Any fear they had left in them had been

Λ

swallowed back when their king made his pledge in Korinth. Rows and rows of heavy cavalry already trampled towards them down the pass. Beside and between the horses bounded trained leopards and panthers. At the head of the charge thundered a beast that could only have come from hell. It stood half the height of a horse and rider but carried nearly five times the bulk. Its hide hung in leathery folds looking like scalloped iron. A single monstrous horn jutted from the center of its face and the ground shook as it pounded toward them. No Spartan doubted that their number would be buried in seconds by the thousand horse charge, but none flinched. They would take as many Persians with them as would come. Shields slammed into place, tight formation.

"You said they won't fall for your tricks, Puddles?" Polymedes strode forward from his place on the line, standing upright and spinning his spear into a reverse grip, a throwing grip. "Perhaps they'll fall for mine."

"Poly, no!" Dienekes screamed, Leonidas screamed, Thrasilaos and Lagos and Echemmon and Oenemias screamed from behind their hoplons, but he was already gone. The giant hoplitodrome sprinted at the enemy with his spear arm trailing. He threw, and his javelin sailed into the chest of the alien ox-dragon's rider and out his back. The monster did not stop with its rider slain, but slowed, rearing and swinging its head as horsemen struggled to navigate around it. Still Polymedes charged. His empty hand drew his second shield from his back.

"How many men does it take to stop your army, Xerxes?" His brothers could hear the voice of Polymedes bellowing over the cacophany of hooves and shrieking Skythians. "How many men, Xerxes? Only one?"

"Only one!" Dienekes echoed, sudden tears streaming down his face.

"Only one!" Echoed Thrasilaos.

"Only one!" Echoed the whole of the hippeis.

"ONLY ONE!" Polymedes howled with both his shields raised and threw himself headlong into the stampede.

One instant he was there, the next he was gone, smothered under an avalanche of bodies. The cavaliers he struck flipped end over end. Riders were crushed instantly. Horses bounced and rolled, screaming in strangely human voices as legs and spines snapped. The ranks behind could only pile on, adding weight and chaos to the mountain of men and beasts.

Dozens of Skythians had been killed in a mere moment, hundreds more injured and taken out of the fight. Only one Spartan lay slain.

"ONLY OOOONE!" Screamed his brothers, mourning, celebrating, envying his heroism and hating him for leaving them behind. They would see him again soon enough.

Their first charge failed, the otherwise agile Skythian horsemen struggled to retreat down the narrow causeway to make room for infanty. Median officers whipped their footmen to task, berating them clumsily through the clotted ranks of riders. After the last two days of battle, there was no question what to do with the obstructions. The bodies of men and horses, living and dead, were thrown into the sea to make way for the second wave. The heaping carnage pulsed and swelled like a beating heart, showing that somewhere beneath it the horned behemoth still lived and thrashed.

The clash of steel and bronze could be heard from the east. The Thespians had met with the Persian elites.

"Fall back." Leonidas gave the order. "We will help Demophilos while the pass is blocked. Let the Thebans take their turn guarding the gates."

The Spartans turned their backs on the crumpled hurriedly pitching their wounded into the gulf. Leonidas and his two Lion-cloaked assassins stayed to watch the enemy struggle as the rest of the hippeis jogged past them. Laughing Theban skirmishers peppered the Medes and Skythians with arrow fire but despite the volley, a lone rider mounted the heap of dead. He rode a Medditerranean horse, smaller and more nimble than the Asiatic beasts the Skythians used. A surefooted garron that had no trouble climbing the mountain of flesh that writhed beneath its hooves. On its back was a man in crimson cloak and crest. Arrows bounced off his bronze. Painted on his shield was the likeness of Zeus and his eagle, the symbol of Eurypontid kings. A linen bandage covered the ragged wound on his cheek.

Leonidas felt his blood boil. His life was forfeit anyway, he might as well have the satisfaction of his own personal revenge.

"DEMARATOS!" The king roared, frothing at the mouth and charging just as Polymedes had.

"No, Leo, it's bait!" Thrasilaos called after him, but too late.

The trained big cats had stopped with the cavalry, but now they pounced at Leonidas. He dodged one leopard, and his swinging fist shattered the skull of another in stride. Theban archers honed in on him, sticking arrows in anything that moved near the king. Arrows ricocheting off him, Demaratos calmly retreated from the action to draw Leonidas further into the trap. The king surged up the hill of bodies and behind him, the hippeis dashed to catch up.

Λ

Seventy

D ienekes and Thrasilaos were first over the wall and they found the sky blackened with arrows. Diving behind their shields, they shouted to their king. Unable to peer out of cover they groped for him with their hands as they crept forward. Other Spartiates mounded the wall behind them and linked shields to protect each other from the barrage. Someone sounded the paian, and the rest joined in as they inched forward under enemy fire to find their leader.

"He's here!" Someone, anyone, cried, and the hippeis converged on his position.

He still breathed, barely- unfocused eyes darting blindly from side to side, mouth moving in the form of words but no sound. His body bristled with arrows, his shield and sword had been lost. One hand clenched the broken neck of a jaguar, the other held the sundered helmet of Demaratos. There was no other sign of the traitor king and the Spartans did not look for any as they hopelessly dragged their king to safety.

Persian officers seized the confusion to mount another attack and turned their infantry to the disorganized Lakonians. Some of the braver Medes got their hands on the king himself and his body was lifted off the ground, each side tugging with all they had to claim the prize. Losing his body was out of the question. Some Spartans even dropped their shields to desperately cling at him with both hands. Unprotected, arrows found them. Casualties mounted on both sides and the mountain of dead grew higher until a rush of Thebans scaled the bodies and returned fire on the Mede. They held the hilltop with bow and spear while the Spartans fled with their king on their shoulders. The enemies of Lakedaimon had finally discovered what it took for a grizzled Spartiate to forsake his discipline and devolve into a panicked animal.

The death of their King.

There was no time to communicate. The Spartans had to trust the Thebans to fulfil their duty independently as they rushed behind the Theban ranks with the men they had left. Leontiades did not need to be told what to do, he had been waiting three days for this moment. The Persians lacked the heart to pursue the Spartan escape under Theban arrows and under threat of the whip returned to clearing bodies. The Theban general addressed his phalanx where they'd held their reserve position as his skirmishers hurried back into place on his wings.

"Now, men. My men. The only brave men left in Thebes!" He had practiced this speech each morning and night in the privacy of his tent, surgically selecting the perfect language to raise the blood of his men, to fill them with the fire a mortal needs to charge bravely into death. He had already imagined the words chiseled in marble over his tomb. Words he was proud of, that he could die with the taste of on his tongue.

He took a deep breath.

And never let it out.

The gasp escaped out his back, air hissing out his lungs and bubbling around the dagger that Hamon slipped between his ribs from behind.

The general slumped to the ground and Hamon gave his own speech, graceless and to the point. His voice boomed over his dumbstruck countrymen.

"Have any of you asked what we're fighting for? What we have to gain? Our people have surrendered. Our entire city has surrendered. So some old man" -he gestured with his bloody dagger to Leontiades, red splattering the general's face- " gave his promise at Korinth that he would march with strangers, and you loved him and trusted him so you came to die with him. Fine. Lovely. Beautiful. Well he kept his promise, and now he's dead and in a fraction of a moment we all will be too." He threw down the knife. It stuck blade first in the soil. "Well that man over there-" he pointed to Xerxes past the enemy army, "-has told us time and time again that if we throw down our arms we get to see home again. So that is exactly what I intend to do. So unless you're all too proud to live, I suggest you follow me."

He turned and trudged towards the enemy lines that still bustled to clear the pass of corpses. The mound still heaved and shifted with the dragon thing struggling underneath. Hamon dropped his arms and armor as he went till he wore nothing but his tunic.

Eurymachos choked. He looked between his dead father and his best friend, the bloody knife stabbed into the dirt. Around him his own troops dropped their spears and shields, disrobed as Hamon had, and raised empty hands skyward in silent surrender. Eurymachos gawked, too stunned to move, until he was the last Theban who remained. He stared in shock and denial as all four hundred of his men gave up without a fight, and watched as uncaring Persian arrows rained down on them.

Λ

Seventy-one

S partan life, for all their courage, was founded on obedience. Without their king, they wallowed in loss and confusion. Some two hundred of them that remained crowded around his body as he breathed his last. They would have turned to a polemarch if one still lived but instead the absence of Krateros weighed down on them all the harder. They cast wanting glances around their number ready to follow, but searching for searching for who.

"Thrasilaos." Someone said.

"Aye, Thrasilaos." Someone seconded. He wasn't the most senior or the highest ranking, yet the choice was obvious. He was the most feared.

Nods and assent spread round the circle in consensus until Sharktooth himself spoke.

"NO!" He shouted so all could hear. "I do not lead armies, I kill them." He thought for a moment, knowing that his seniority demanded he give some solution, even if he wasn't it. "We have only one among us worthy to lead. The son of one polemarch, the student of another, the most decorated Olympian in our history, and the hand picked champion of not one, but two Agiad kings. We need not choose, for by his deeds, the gods have already marked him out for us." He stomped towards Dienekes and raised his once-student's sword arm into the air. "Dienekes, son of Hegisistratos will lead!"

All eyes of the hippeis fell on him.

Dienekes balked. His throat knotted at the thought of taking the place of Leonidas, the place of Krateros, and of Hegisistatos before him. He felt like he was stepping into a prophecy. And he felt like he would wet himself again.

"I can't..." He whispered to Thrasilaos.

"You can and you will." Thrasilaos hissed back. "I can't fight how I fight and lead at the same time. Besides-" he ran his tongue along his horrible fangtoothed grin, "it appears I am now again your commanding officer, so you will obey, you snivelling little shit. The last order you will ever receive. From me, or from anyone. From here til the end, you're in charge. Take command." His voice cracked as he threw his head back and howled. "Hail, Dienekes of Appia, son of Hegisistratos! Polemarch of Sparta!"

Swords beat shields and the men roared back.

"Weeper! Weeper! Weeper!"

Dienekes couldn't hear their chanting over the pounding in his ears. Still he felt like the little oak.

Fortunately, his men knew their place. With someone to rally behind, they abandoned their sorrow and let their training take over.

"Sir, Polemarch, Sir," Alpheos and Maron addressed their friend, using his new honorific with impish glee. "Permission to deploy our gift."

"Gift?" Dienekes hesitated, the last to adjust to the new hierarchy.

"Yessir, the gift from Barbadoros. We'll get it set, you just be ready to run when we say so."

Dienekes had no notion of what they meant, but he trusted the twins and even trusted Barbadoros, so he nodded. His brothers stripped out of their armor and scampered away with only loincloths and daggers. The rest of the hippeis waited for orders of their own. Dienekes took a breath and assessed the field. Knowing there was not a second to spare, he asked himself what Krateros would do.

The Skythians and Medes still wrestled to clear the pass, the presence of the Thebans only adding to their confusion. Arrows stopped falling on them when Persia realized their surrender, and though Dien's blood boiled for revenge against the cowards, there was no time to deal with them yet. The Thespians were faring poorly against the Asian elites to the west.

"You!" Dienekes pointed out the biggest, strongest looking helot who gripped a spear with white knuckles. "You now command your people. All of you at once, rush the pass and kill them while they open the pass. They'll shoot at you, so pick up Theban shields as you go. You'll have the advantage."

The slave hesitated, but Dienekes advanced on him with sword drawn and his conditioned obedience took hold. Helots differed from the men of Lakedaimon in every way but one- slave or Spartan of Lakonia, you obeyed or you died. Di gave the new leader one small courtesy, a sliver of advice.

"They will be occupied with moving the dead. You will not have to fight true battle, just harass them. So take heart. Throw spears, throw rocks, throw shit and bones and spit in their eyes if they get close enough. Whatever it takes to slow their progress. Do your job well, and I will see every one of you freed from bondage."

It was an empty promise, Dienekes knew, and the taste of it soured in his mouth. None of them would be making it home alive, but even the whisper of freedom could put iron in the backs of small men. Hope rippled through the helots as they gripped their weapons and advanced in resolute disarray.

"We rally to Demophilos!" Dienekes roared to his own, surprised at the strength in his own voice. Then he bent to close his dead kings eyes and lay his shield over his chest. It knotted his gut to leave the body here unattended, but further rites would

Λ

need to wait. Di trotted towards the fray and his men fell into step behind. They fanned abreast, slotting into a grid as they gained speed.

The Thespian phalanx held a half circle against Hydarnes. The rounded shape minimized their chance of being flanked, and forced gaps to open in the line of Persian shields where they impacted against the push of the othismos. Thespia held strong, but there is no true defense against such overwhelming numbers. Losses were great.

"Half our rank down each side." Dienekes called over his shoulder as he ran. "No formation yet. Strike, fall back, and strike again. Make them chase us. They can't fend off a skirmish and push Thespia at the same time."

"Au!" The hippeis barked their understanding.

"I'll take the left, you take the right." He delegated to Thrasilaos who prowled at his heels. "I want a lion-demon at the front of each line." He mimicked Barbadoros's heavy accent. "Make them to being piss themselves with fear."

The captain howled with laughter and galloped ahead, half the contingent following him.

Dienekes smiled himself as he and his half broke into a sprint down the left. Hundreds of feet pounding the ground behind him shattered his fears and apprehensions. He may have been the weakest man of Sparta, but now his arms and legs were other Peers and he felt their strength rising in him. Someone sang the paian, and all their voices joined him.

Such a small company moved almost entirely unnoticed, just over a hundred down each side. They crashed into the Persians sides without warning. The mudmen's death-wails craned the heads of their comrades and when shields turned to face the Spartans, Thespians spears found their ribs. From his chariot, Hydarnes could not see the cause of the disruption. He dispatched more regiments down the side to stabilize his ranks who arrived to see squads of Spartans fleeing with their backs turned. Heartened by the flight of their enemy, they pursued, and could smell victory thick in their nostrils all the way until the mouth of the ambush, where Spartan iron dropped them in their tracks.

Their wings protected by Spartan rearguard, Thespian morale soared. They employed a trick learned from their Lakonian allies and rolled their formation backwards in a fighting retreat, shortening the distance for the Spartan hit-and-runs and forcing the Persians to stumble over the bodies of their fallen.

Ten or twenty mudmen tasted iron for every Hellene that fell, but only the hoplites appeared to diminish in number. Asian elites still streamed from the mouth of the Anopaian way by the hundreds.

"It's time." Two men in Persian regalia materialized beside Dienekes as he readied another sortie down the Thespian flank. He nearly cut them down before recognizing Alpheos and Maron. "Order the retreat, the trap is set. Fall back to the king."

"Good." Di nodded, having no idea what he agreed to. "Go tell Thrasilaos." They sprinted off to the far flank and the new polemarch thundered to his men.

"ONE MORE PUUSH!"

They sliced up the side through the harried enemy. At the head of the charge, Dienekes broke off from his men, trusting them to operate in autonomy while he slid between the Thespians to their leaders in the front.

He could not find Demophilos.

"He's dead!" Dithyrambos shouted and made room for Dienekes to put a shield in his back.

"Who's in charge?"

"I am!"

"Give the order to retreat!" Di yelled over the clamor. "We have to clear the field!"

"Retreat? I thought Spartans never run away?"

"We don't! But we often pretend to!"

The command took some time to relay, the rear ranks needing to break from pushing before the front could escape. Dienekes helped usher them safely away.

So few left alive…

The sour thought penetrated his mind as he covered stragglers. Both nations combined, barely more than five or six hundred hoplites remained. And though the field was littered with corpses of Asia, their numbers appeared undiminished.

"Keep running!" He hounded Thespian and Spartan alike for nearly a mile to where Leonidas lay.

"What's the plan?" Dithyrambos asked him as they clumped together on the hilltop.

"I don't know." Dienekes confessed.

"You don't know?' Rambos echoed in disbelief as the Persian hordes reordered themselves to march in their full number.

The Polemarch had no time to explain. A white hot flash erupted from the heart of Hydarnes's advance. Tongues of red and yellow split off from it, licking from eruption to eruption and engulfing not just the forward troops, but the entire battlefield in a grid of flame. Ahead of the immolation, two figures sprinted, tossing little pots as they ran, at risk of being engulfed by their own fire.

"It's the twins!" Someone harked, and the hippeis watched with bated breath as the two fled from the inferno until it blasted them off the cliffs into the sea.

Λ

480 BCE

Seventy-two

Dienekes dashed to the cliff edge, Thrasilaos on his heels, and they scanned the water for signs of the twins.

"There!" Di pointed to a dark shadow sliding beneath the small waves until it dove out of sight.

"No..." Thrasilaos's eyes narrowed. "There." He pointed to a different spot further out, and two heads burst gasping from the surface. Thespian and Spartan cheered alike. Except for Thrasilaos.

"If it wasn't them... What was it?"

"It's bad is it what it is." Thrasilaos was already unlacing his armor, dropping his rancid lion cloak. "Look. There are more." Dien tried, but did not have the hunter's sight. "Unfocus your eyes. Just watch for movement."

That did the trick. Here one moment, gone the next, the gulf was teeming with long dark shadows cutting through the water like knives.

"Corpses?" Di asked, knowing it could not be. Even if the bleached and bloated carcasses littering the sea below weren't anchored by the weight of weapons and armor, they would not be swimming.

"Gods, Polemarch, have you never seen the ocean before?" Thrasilaos unstrapped his greaves. "They're like lions. Lions of the sea."

There were so many. Dienekes panicked for his friends.

"Swim!" He screamed to the twins, who were laughing and splashing each other as they kicked for the shore, happy to be alive. Not far now.

"Silence!" Thrasilaos hissed. "Noise excites them. So does movement. Splashing." He was down to a breechcloth and xiphos now, pacing the edge, counting the beasts, watching their angles.

"Well what else can they do?"

Thrasilaos grumbled unintelligibly.

"Damned if they do." He said. "Damned if they don't." Maron's head plunged suddenly underwater and Dienekes would have jumped in if the captain didn't snatch his arm.

"They just bump you first."

Λ

On cue, Maron came up sputtering.

"Fuck was that!" He coughed.

"Out of the water! Now!" Thrasilaos screeched at them, against his own advice.

They had reached the cliff face and began to climb, but the wall was much higher here than down in the pass, and earthen instead of rock. Clay and rubble came away in their hands, dropping the twins back into the sea. Dark grey fins crested the water in circles around them.

"Rope! Spears! Branches! Anything! Now!" Dienekes shouted to his men who, unaware of the danger to the twins, watched the Persians burn.

Dienekes dropped his own cloak and tried to tie its corner to Thrasilaos's, but the slime of the flayed hide was too slick to hold a knot.

One of the shadows turned from its wide arc around Alpheos and Maron. It jetted towards them in a straight line. Echemmon was running to them with a coiled rope abandoned from the camps, but he would not get there in time.

"Fuck all." Thrasilaos sighed. "I suppose it's as good a way as any. Two for one. A good trade." He looked into Di's eyes and laid a hand on his once student's shoulder. "It's been..." He didn't finish the sentence. Only nodded. Then dove.

He crashed on top of the charging shadow. Fins and limbs thrashed and Thrasilaos stabbed madly with his dagger before both beasts sank out of sight leaving nothing but a floating ring of foam.

Dienekes stared in shock. The twins still struggled for purchase. Another shape drove toward them but stopped halfway, jerked to a halt, and swam spastically away. A third was stopped, likewise spasmed, then sank. The waters darkened, turning slowly from blue-green to purple, then red.

Echemmon arrived with the rope, already uncoiled. Dienekes snatched and tossed it down.

"Grab hold!"

The two Olympians had no trouble hauling their unarmored brothers up until the cliff edge beneath Di's feet crumbled. Echemmon released the rope, dropped to his chest on the precipice to catch his new polemarch by the wrist and the weight of the twins dropping yanked the rope from Dien's hands as well. His friends splashed back down while he dangled.

Echemmon pulled at Dienekes, who yelled at him to stop.

"Just throw me a cloak!" He commanded instead.

Dien dangled the lionhide to his brothers, who still could not reach.

"Worst rescue of all time!" Thrasilaos resurfaced, spat a hunk of animal flesh from his teeth, and churned water towards the twins. He dove then surged up from beneath, raising both of them the last arms length needed to grasp the cloak. He did not see the shadows that followed.

Λ

"Now!" Dienekes yelled to Echemmon. Lagos, Oenomias, and others had joined them. With their combined strength, the whole chain lurched upwards, leaving only Thrasilaos's legs still submerged.

Something bit down on them. He screamed in anger and agony and the water ran redder.

"Don't let go!" Dienekes pleaded to him. But Thrasilaos smiled through the pain and repeated.

"Two for one. A good trade."

His hands released the twins.

The sea frothed as he tumbled down into it. Tails and teeth flashed in a gyre of frenzy. White foam turned pink.

Λ

Seventy-three

The foothills were a garden of searing red. Plumes of black smoke choked the pass and spilled like ink across the sky. The ocean beneath the cliffs churned and darkened, the foam of fresh blood washed away. White ash drifted between the waves like dirty snow.

Alpheos and Maron dripped seawater from their Persian garb beside Dienekes, who he stared disbelief into the spot where Thrasilaos had been pulled under.

"...They said no man could kill him..." One of them said.

"I suppose they were right," said the other.

Dienekes was deaf to both. His eyes had clouded over. Too many men, living and dead, too much smoke, too many graves too count. Darkness and fire were all he could see.

"How?" He asked. His sword arm stretched feebly to the fields of burning.

"Naptha," Alpheos nodded. "Barbadoros gave us Naptha."

"A cartload of it. We spread it about as best we could."

They had done well, infiltrated between enemy battle ranks and laid a grid of the caustic stuff, poured in thick lines across the turf or left to slowly bubble from cracked pots. More of the plains were left unburnt than not, the fire concentrated into stripes that split battalions into pieces and separated troops from their leaders. The Persian troops lucky enough to go untouched by flame huddled in frantic, twittering clusters. They were trapped in place until the fuel burnt away, choking on smoke and slowly cooking in their armor. Lagos and Barbadoros worsened matters by hurling more cannisters of the noxious oil from their slings. Explosions flowered where the little pots burst, and Medes threw themselves into the same flame beside them for fear of it falling on them from above.

Dienekes watched the fire, his mind somewhere else.

"Di." Alpheos shook his friend's shoulder. "Dienekes."

More voices joined his, Di hearing none of them.

"What are the Polemarch's orders?"

The helots ordered to harass the Medes at the gate had done work, but little. Bodies still blocked the pass, but the few Messenians that fought as bid were getting picked off. Most just shouted, brandishing weapons from a safe distance. Some fled.

The Weeper's gaze migrated to where Spartans regrouped around the body of Leonidas. They swore final oaths with their fingers pressed to his sun-warmed breastplate, kissed his ice cold hands. He heard the dead king's words in his head from only days ago.

Are you afraid?

"Yes." Dienekes responded aloud. "I am afraid."

I am too. But hold it. There will be time enough for fear tomorrow.

Di looked back to the enemy. Through a gap in the curtains of smoke, he saw clear across the fields to where he had camped the night before, the same low hills now completely under Persian control. The white shield of his father blazed like a beacon, marking the site where he buried his mentor. Captains drove on with their whips, crowding their troops to the edge of the burning barrier. The advancing infantry knocked the shield from its post. Their boots stomped the dirt of Krateros's grave.

Until this moment, Dienekes had never known anger. His blood flushed as hot as the smoldering fields.

"I'll kill them all!" He roared. His companions looked to each other, perplexed. Their commander still did not hear them.

Good, boy

The voice of Krateros whispered to him now, transporting him home to a hilltop at night, the grizzled old warrior imparting a lesson while a little boy ate a fistful of meat and tried not to fall asleep.

That is defiance. The green that shoots between the rocks. And what comes after defiance?

"Intuition." Dienekes said. The memory yanked at his heart. Tears prickled his cheeks. Dithyrambos said something far away.

Yes, boy. You're learning.

Now he heard Uncle Ono in his head. Laughing and coughing and spitting.

I know he grieve, he said. *But do not linger in your grief. Life goes on, and so must you. But I hope you have since learned to listen to you elders and betters.*

His finger itched around the ring Ono had placed there as he died. He stroked it with his thumb. His left thumb sympathetically stroked the ring on his other hand, the ring of Kleomenes. Then the long dead king spoke to him too.

In the face of a superior foe, always cheat.

"Always cheat." Dien repeated. His exasperated comrades shook him again.

The wind rose, and Thrasilaos's pouch of dirt bounced against his cuirass. He heard his eriene's voice join the chorus of ghosts.

Forget the phalanx. We are something else today.

Λ

The voice continued, overlapping with that of the Orchomenian, his friend, Asopichos.

We are fast

And then Asopichos alone, as bright and mirthful as he had been at Olympia.

Be faster.

The wind blew harder, as if stirred by the presence of the remembered dead. His cloak pulled at his shoulders in the gale. Lion hide slapped his legs, the lion slain and skinned by Aristaios during the Krypteia. Di remembered his words at their capture, bound and stake by Argives who were not Argives.

We all die, Weeper. You can die like a bitch, or you can die like a Spartan. Your choice.

A hard slap cracked across his cheek and he snapped to his senses. His empty sword hand clutched the shoulder of Barbadoros, who had struck him. They locked eyes.

"Are you being with us, Little Leaping Lion?"

"I am being with you, Stranger Bearing Gifts." Dienekes mimicked the Skythian's jilted speech with a savage smile. He raised his head and bellowed. "Hear me, Hellenes!"

His army, the combined forces of Sparta and Thespia roared wordlessly back. Their captains came for their orders.

"Archers of Thespia, what brave few who remain, join the Messenians. Shoot the Medes clearing the pass, and any Helot too craven to fight. They'll die by Persian arrows or by yours, but see to it that they fight."

"But they are just helots…" Alpheos whispered to him. "Do you expect them to make any difference?"

"Maybe, maybe not." Dienekes whispered back. "But we brought three helots to every Spartiate. At the very least, there will be nine hundred more bodies for the mudmen to clear before they can take the gate."

Always cheat. Di remembered Kleo again.

It was a black order, and Dienekes resented giving it, but he would face judgement for his crimes soon enough.

Barbadoros lifted the lion skin that Thrasilaos had dropped.

"Someone is to must be putting this on." He shook the dust from it. "For us, the fear of lionmen has being a great gift. The Persian heart will strengthen if it they are learning that their demons too can die."

"Any volunteers?" Dienekes asked.

"Lord Dithyrambos volunteers." Barbadoros spoke for him, and unlaced the suprised Thespian's new red cloak before asking permission. By now, everyone trusted Barbadoros enough not to question him.

Λ

Forget the phalanx. We are something else today.

"Forget the phalanx!" Dienekes parrotted his intuition to all who could hear. "We are something else today!"

We are fast

"We are fast! We are hunters! Our prey is trapped in the darkness and fire, so darkness and fire is what we shall be! Let our spears find them from behind, strike from the corners of their eyes. Fan out, dash in, and be gone before they know they are slain. We are all already dead men, are we not?"

Voices raised in unison. Spearshafts rattled on shields.

Dienekes did not know where his words came from. He had never been gifted with speech or charisma, but he was too deep in his intuition to question it. He let his teachers speak through him, their wisdom becoming his own.

"Then we shall behave as dead men behave." He barked. "We will fight like ghosts. Can you kill a ghost? Can you kill what is already dead?"

"No!" His comrades shouted back.

"Then neither shall we die!"

As the army roared to itself, Barbadoros advised Dienekes.

"It is a good to remembering. On long invasion such as this, it is being better to maim than for to killing. The screams of pain at night are to be haunting to the hale. And the army must still for to be feeding and healing the wounded. Their morale and their supplies are being deplete. And winter comes. They will be thinking of nothing but your torments as they wallow in the mountain snow. The dead are going glorious back to their god, but the still living? They are bring you as nightmares back to their home."

Dienekes nodded. He wanted them all to die, but he could be contented for now with their suffering.

"You heard the man! Do not take their lives. Instead, take their eyes. Take their hands. Take their legs and their scalps and ears so they may walk from this field forever changed. Leave them alive so they may tell their children the horrors that wait for them across the Aegean. Carve your name in their scars so their grandchildren will never leave their homes again for the fear of lessons Hellas has to teach them. We are not soldiers today. Today we are poets! Carve our song into the flesh of our enemies so that the world can look upon them and read what we have done. Write the song, my brothers, and we will be remembered for as long as men have eyes to read and lips to speak! Today, we inscribe our eternal truth!"

Dienekes gave the order with his feet, cutting off his speech by leading the charge.

"Now we hunt!"

His men, Spartans and Thespians alike streamed along behind. As commanded, they broke off into groups, then smaller hunting packs, then lone predators. Like

Λ

grains of sand on a beach, they scattered into obscurity, nearly invisible in the chaos. Thirsting for blood and glory they descended, howling into darkness and fire.

Λ

Seventy-four

Rows of burning naphtha vomitted clouds of oily smoke. The Persian elites under Hydarnes claimed to fear no man, but they fought each other like rats to avoid the fire fences splintering their rank and file. They crouched to breathe without the fumes inking their lungs, but the heat of the air still scorched their insides. Between the smoke above and the white hot light below, they were blind. Outside their purgatory they heared the roaring of beasts. Man, animal, or demon, they could not tell. But they could feel the hungry eyes and slavering jowls thirsting for their blood. They knew they were being hunted.

A spear incised from the corner of a flaming pen. Persians recoiled only to back into three more spears thrust from the far side. Braver veterans rallied their valor and charged through the inferno. Fuel splashed onto boots, the hems of robes and the wicker of their shields as they crossed over and they burst, immolated, from the other side. Comrades left behind were serenaded by their agonized screams, screams not cut short by the end of a blade. The Hellenes ignored the escapees and let them die slowly from their burns.

Captains penned in with their troops tried to beat the fear from their men and force a charge, but caught between a rock and a hot place, the soldiers quickly turned to cut their leaders down. Then they turned on each other for the meager right to stand furthest from the fire. The few survivors still composed enough to fight strung their bows to fire into the twisting shadows. They did not care that they were more likely to hit their own men than the enemy, but they could tell who caught their arrow by the cries. By now, the Persian had learned that, unlike their own, Spartans did not scream when shot.

Between the fire, the arrows, the whips, and the lances of Hellas, the foothills of Anopaia became a chorus of tortured ululation. Men in the thousands wailing to the sky, begging for the release of death. For once, the Spartans would not give it to them. They heeded the advice of their foreign advisor and aimed to cripple and maim. Their lance heads stabbed through feet and knees, careful to not strike the arteries that would bleed their victims dry. Pairs of hunters leapt off their brothers backs over the flames and onto spartan heads. They laid about with xiphos and kopis, only cutting off fingers and hands before evaporating back through the blaze. Their hair smoldered, their reddened flesh cracked and peeled, but unlike the Asians, their wool and leather did not burst alight in the furnace. Tempered to steel from the Agoge, they did not flinch when burned. Outside the gates of fire, the brothers took turns splashing jugs of water over each other to quench the heat gathering in their armor and steam hissed from their bronze.

Oinomaos hurled boulders into the smoke, and laughed at the sound of breaking bones. A small band of Thespians shovelled dirt onto short stretches of the fireline, making a small corridor for Persians to escape. As they fled, Alpheos and Maron knifed them in the heels. Dithyrambos plowed through the turmoil like a creature possessed, his lion cloak black with soot. When his spear broke, he swung the shattered haft like a club, cracking ribs and skulls. Echemmon and Dienekes hurled the Persian short spears back at their owners, dedicating each of their throws.

"For Polymedes!"

"For Krateros!"

"For Polyogonos!"

"For Sharktooth!"

"For Leonidas!"

When the naphtha burned away, the Spartans were gone, leaving nothing behind but the moaning of cripples and the stench of burning meat.

Their flesh was scorched pink. Breastplates bounced on chests that heaved for breath. They regrouped at the body of Leonidas and roared their victory to the sky. Whether Thespian or Spartiate, not a single one of them had fallen. Though one had stayed behind.

Focus, boy

A ghost whispered in Di's ear. He broke from revelling with his men and scanned the battlefield. Hydarnes's forces were shattered, would take time to regroup. But the Kissians and Medes on the pass had dug through the bodies barring their path. The last of the dead helots were being dumped like garbage into the sea and the few Thespian archers left alive either ran to rejoin the hoplites on the hill or were cut to pieces by enemy volleys.

"The pass is clear." Echemmon joined Dienekes. "They are coming."

"AU!" The polemarch cried.

His hoplites echoed. Red and silver cloaks mixed without rank or order, all of them now proven equals. Their shields rang off each other like gongs as they clamped into place.

"We will wait for them here, at the high ground." Dienekes addressed them. "Let them creep forward on the ends of their whips, listening to the songs of their dying and knowing every step brings them closer to pain and death! We will sing for them

Λ

too, won't we? Sing for them now and a hundred years from now, our paean will be the anthem of the terror that wakes their great-grandchildren crying in the night!"

They raised their voices. The oncoming Kissians shuddered when the sound hit them, doubt rippling through their ranks. Their captains' whips redoubled, but then rapidly died out. The march halted.

"What are they doing?" Lagos hissed through clenched teeth. He stood with Di and the twins, outside of the phalanx.

"They've stopped." Echemmon called from the shield wall.

"They're watching something..." Alpheos shielded his eyes with a hand. Each of the Kissians stared away to the south, where the last of the fires were being stamped out.

Following their gaze, Di spotted lone figure in the fields ahead of where the Persians struggled to regroup- a lone figure with a broken spear in a lion cloak.

"Dithyrambos?" Dienekes was as baffled as any of the Kissians. "What is he doing?"

"Does he think he can take them by himself?" Maron wondered.

"I wish I'd thought of that..." Alpheos frowned.

The Thespian captain raised his broken lance and shouted something unintelligible to the Persians.

"Quiet!" Dienekes ordered his men to stop the paean and strained his ears as Rambos shouted again. It was no tongue he recognized.

"What is he doing? Has he gone mad?"

"Truth being told truly..." Barbadoros said from behind. "Our friend Dithyrambos has always being one for the madness." His eyes hung wide and he chewed on a knuckle. Dithyrambos called out again.

"What is that? Is that gibberish?"

"No." Barbadoros's eyes were locked on the distant Thespian. "I taught him the words."

"Words? What words? For once in your life, speak plain!"

"It is being a challenge. He is for to the challenge of single combat."

"Challenge who?"

"Hydarnes." The name dripped like venom from his lips. He spat the bitter taste from his tongue.

"What? But why would... would he?"

"Without their numbers they have no advantage. Why would a commander risk fighting a hoplite one on one?"

"For pride." Barbadoros still stared without blinking at Rambos. "And for shame. Watch next. This is how he make Hydarnes fight."

Λ

Dithyrambos approached the Persian line and challenged again, and when he did so, he dropped his shield to the ground and left it behind. Again he challenged, drawing his xiphos to cut the ties on his linothorax. He challenged again and threw away his sword.

"Why haven't they shot him?" Lagos asked.

"Shut up and watch," spat Barbadoros.

With each taunt, he dropped another weapon or scrap of clothing as he marched on the Asian host. Should the archers fire, Rambos was hopelessly inside the range of their bows. He bore no armament save the broken lance handle. He wore no garb but the lionskin cape. Even his heavy sandals had been discarded.

Again, he challenged. He dropped the spear haft.

Again, he challenged. He dropped the cape. Arms spread wide.

"You seeing now?" Barbadoros said. "No leader of men can refuses the challenge of naked unarmed man without declaring himself being a weakling and a coward."

"This was your idea, wasn't it?" Dienekes asked the stranger. "You put him up to this." Barbadoros did not answer. He only stared. If his eyes opened any wider they would have fallen from his skull.

Dithyrambos paced along the enemy line, naked but unafraid, challenging over and over. The still living wounded nearest to him crawled to escape. He grabbed one, stole a knife from the man's belt and plunged it into his belly. The Thespian ripped and sawed with the blade for a long moment before reaching inside to the elbow. He grabbed hold of something within and wrenched away.

He challenged again, holding high the Persian's still-beating heart in his fist.

"He has insulted all of Persia now." Barbadoros muttered. "If Hydarnes does not accept, he is being finished. No man will follow him."

There was still no movement from the Achaemenid line. Dithyrambos challenged again, lowered the heart to his mouth, and took a bite.

A halfhearted cheer rose from the Asians as a six horse chariot clattered over the rocky ground from the back of their formation to the front. Many men rode inside it, archers and lancers and drivers. Only one disembarked before Dithyrambos before waving the chariot away.

"Is that him?" Dienekes asked. "He accepts?"

Barbadoros nodded gravely. A pulsing vein bulged in his forehead. His knuckle bled where he chewed it.

The two fighters circled. One bristled behind his shield with spears, axe and sword, the other naked and empty handed as the day he was born.

"We can't just leave him like that." Dienekes fumed.

"You must. And you will." Barbadoros growled.

"He'll be killed!"

Λ

"Did you not say you were all to be dying in this place?" Dienekes had no response. Barbadoros continued. "The Persians are to be holding at the line. So must we else we are forsaking the challenge. I have seen the both of them fighting. Hydarnes is fat and slow on his successes. The Thespian will be eating him for his dinner."

Still, Dienekes could not stand idly by.

"Sing!" he called to his troops. "Sing for Dithyrambos!"

The paean began anew.

The duelists tested each other, shifting and dancing, trying to bait a misstep. Hydarnes menaced with his spear, not attacking, only teasing. Rambos snatched for the haft. He missed, and his hand came away bleeding.

"Patience..." Barbadoros whispered into his fist.

Rambos backed away, arms stretched open and chest exposed. Hydarnes lunged. The Thespian snatched with both hands this time and locked in. With a quick turn, he levered the spear off the general's shield and disarmed it.

Dienekes and his Olympians cheered while the rest kept the paean. Di was surprised to see Dithyrambos break the spear over his knee and throw both halves into the Persian crowd. Hydarnes calmly drew another spear from the quiver in his shield.

Rambos dodged two more lunges before snatching the second spear. Instead of pulling, he pushed, driving Hydarnes backwards until he had to choose between releasing the weapon or being bowled over.

This spear, Dithyrambos kept, and he wasted no time attacking with it. He thrust along the center line, knowing that it would be blocked- counting on it being blocked. The spearhead drove into and out the back of the wicker and hide shield, lodging in the stiff woven lattice. He thrashed then, jerking in every direction until Hydarnes, overpowered, was forced to let it go. The general's hands flew to his belt, drawing his axe in a practiced motion but his counterattack was baffled by Rambos swinging the shield on the end of the spear like a hammer. It made a clumsy weapon, but it proved more difficult to avoid than to wield. After half a dozen blows, Hydarnes's hands were knocked empty. A half dozen more, and the general was knocked to his knees. The Thespian thrusted, and the Persian only survived my gripping the rim of the shield, the leaf-shaped blade stopping inches from his face. Rambos yanked away, freeing the spear from the wicker. Hydarnes spilled onto his back. The Thespian stabbed again, but impaled only earth when his quarry rolled away. He struck with such force that the spear shaft snapped.

Hydarnes found enough space to draw his sword, and swung wildly with it to keep the Hellene at bay. Rambos circled like an animal, growling and dodging just out of reach. One final insult at the Persian's expense, he threw down broken handle, facing the swordsman empty handed once more. Hydarnes responded exactly how the

∧

Thespian wanted, striking straight down on Rambos's head with all his strength. One arm went up and caught the blade mid swing on his bare arm, his other rose in a fist and smashed into the general's face. Stunned, he slumped to his knees. He sputtered, drooling blood and teeth.

Dithyrambos, still standing, turned to the Persian army so they could see him wrench the sword from where it lodged in his bone. He tossed it away and walked once around the writhing general before sitting on the enemy's chest and pounded like a gorilla with his uninjured arm.

"KILL HIM!" Barbadoros foamed at the mouth. "KILL THE SON OF A DOG!"

Rambos beat and beat until the barest scrape of life was left. It took all of the general's remaining strength to roll over and slowly crawl back towards his army, battered to the point of delirium.

Dithyrambos licked blood from the fingers of his wounded arm while his unharmed hand cupped his manhood and took aim. Roaring laughter, he pissed on the general's head.

"I SAID KILL HIM!" Barbadoros frothed and sobbed. Tears traced his cheeks. "END IT!"

Instead the Hellene stomped on the Persians hands. Kicked him in the ribs. Picked up a spear and drove it through his opponent's calf. He wrenched Hydarnes to his knees by the neck and with the general's own knife hacked the long hair and beard from his head before carving the symbol Delta into the Persian's chest. Delta for 'D'. 'D' for Dithyrambos.

Still the Spartans on the hilltop sang.

"KIIILLLL HIIIIIIIM!" Barbadoros shrieked so loudly, a blood vessel burst in his eye.

Dithyrambos let his broken and piss-soaked foe fall to the ground. He emptied his hands, once more naked and unarmed.

He spread his arms wide, and shouted to the entire Asian horde.

"I challenge!"

He charged.

A storm of arrows ripped through the air and into his body. The foremost infantry still ran from him, though he bristled arrows and poured blood. He fell to his knees, surrounded by enemies who fired arrows even as they fled.

"Cowards." He rasped as best he could, his lungs filled with iron. "Cowards all."

And that was the end of the Thespian.

Cheers and screams of mourning shook the air around Dienekes, but all he could hear was the blood in his ears, his breath rasping against the bronze on his face. The elites clustered around their fallen leader, bickering in clumps as his chariot rolled back out to claim him. Generals argued who would take his place. The Kissians and Medes at the mouth of the gates hovered in the absence of orders. They watched the discourse, waiting.

Waiting.

Dienekes threw his head back and roared.

"CHARGE!"

Λ

Seventy-five

Three hundred yards passed beneath him. He was in bow range now. Three hundred more remained between him and the enemy. Either direction demanded minutes of dead sprint in full panoply. The adrenaline that fueled his push has faded and without it his limbs were empty aching sacks of meat under the weight of three days fighting. He churned through the fatigue, no different than the final stretch of his childhood stadion, no different than any day of the agoge. This was his comfort zone, he realized with a sad irony. He had been afraid once, but once battle-whetted, he realized he had been made for it. Forged for it. His whole life had been battle. The acidic burn was a blanket of comfort, a familiar friend in the tides of foreign blood. As a boy with bandaged fingers, the pain in his legs and swollen hands had eased the pain in his mind while he was made to run the ridgeline, displaced with broken wrists far from his friends fighting in the valley of Taygetos. He focused on his tearing muscles to block out the strobing visions of the son he would never meet. He had been made to run, if it were running toward battle then so be it.

"THIS IS HOW WE YET SERVE," he screamed, though no one could hear.

By now the fall of arrows felt natural as spring rain. Sharpened spindles bounced harmlessly off his raised bronze. The mud below quickened to turf, turf to gravel and gravel to stone. He could see their faces now. He could count those he meant to kill. Fear in the eyes of the enemy renewed the power in his limbs.

Kissians and Medes buckled under threat of the single hoplite. They fought each other to escape his reach, less afraid of Dienekes than the cloak. They had seen how the last lion shamed their commander and none were willing to brave a similar fate. They turned their spears back on their leaders and comrades before daring to engage the demon at their front.

Dienekes, fastest man in all Hellas, had outpaced his fellows by a hundred yards. He was alone. Still they fled.

His short sword swung wildly, but cut only air. Though whips cracked from behind, no soldier drove forward. Rather than meet Spartan iron, the Asian infantry cowered in the swamp or spilled into the sea to drown. The Weeper met no resistance.

He carved hollows in the air and spalled off chunks of stone until his sword broke. Then he killed with the jagged handle.

"For Krateros!" He bellowed. "For my father! For my son!"

He threw his broken hilt and it bounced off a Persian's wicker. He plucked up a stone and hurled it between that same Persian's eyes and the man folded.

"For Thrasilaos!" He kicked. He punched. His blows caught shields or nothing, but still the enemy shrank from him, their terror killing more men than his arm could.

"Fight me!" He shrieked, his voice cracking. "Fight me like men!"

He dropped his guard, arms spread, exposing his face and chest.

Two Persian sergeants called his bluff and hurled their spears.

Di would show them how men died, without fear, without flinching. Overcome by the fever of battle, he dared their flying lances to pierce him.

They did not.

Echemmon flanked. The spears bent off his aspis and he hurled his final shaft back. No man died from his weapon, but three men died escaping it- two dragged to the bottom of the bay by the weight of their armor and one crushed under the feet of his own. Unarmed, the two Olympians reclaimed the first gate.

The Mede was forced to engage, if only from the crush of infantry bearing down the pass behind. The two runners joined shields, ready to fight with empty fists.

Alpheos and Maron skidded between their ankles with knives in each hand. Fighting like vermin, they bit and clawed at ankles and feet. Kissians danced to escape the short blades to have their skulls cracked by Olympian shields. Lagos joined them, his own iron long gone, and laid about with his loaded sling swinging like a mace.

The ground shook. Thunder drummed from below.

Dienekes dove left, knocking himself, Echemmon, and Lagos into the swamp as their battalion hammered in behind them.

Euneas had taken command of the phalanx with Di so far ahead. Shields were already locked, left under right. He led as he had fought in the Olympiad. Always outclassed in weight, he came from below. The rim of each aspis scraped the ground, the tops tilted back, his own strategy. Persians felt their legs break beneath them and their bodies forced over the bulldoze of singing hoplites. Few weapons remained to dispatch them. Those not trampled beneath Peloponnesian feet were torn apart by bare fingers.

Dienekes and his retinue pulled themselves from the mud. Lagos was already loosing stones with ruthless efficiency. Di and Echemmon followed suit with abandoned Asian short spears. He could see Alpheos and Maron through the legs of his comrades, dangling again from the cliff edge, reaching and pulling to feed Easterners to the sharks.

Λ

Slogging through the knee-deep muck, the Weeper could not keep pace with the phalanx pressing nearly to the second gate. He hurled spears over the formation of Spartans and Thespians, their traded silver and crimson cloaks now a uniform scab-gray from the soak of blood and dust. Both nations pushed as one. And as one, both nations sang.

From his vantage to the side, Di could see the rear ranks of Kissians break and run. The phalanx could push to the third gate, but only if they wished to be pinioned on both ends by the enemy.

Di knew he would die here, but was committed to taking as many as he could with him. That meant fighting on a single front. The moment they were surrounded was the moment their fight was over. He glanced to the north and saw what he already assumed. The elites had remustered without Hydarnes. A new leader rode in his chariot, flying a banner southward to reinforce the Medes.

"Fall back!" Lagos yelled from his side, anticipating Di's command.

"Fall back!" The order echoed through the ranks.

They scattered like deer. The minutes barreling toward the Kissians had felt like an eon, but their war-wearied legs carried them the same distance back to Kolonos hill in mere moments. In the absence of food and rest, victory sustained them. They rallied around the body of Leonidas, silent but for ragged gasps for air. Thespians and Spartans had lost another dozen between them, their lives traded for hundreds of the Mede.

Dienekes tried to hail his men, but breath caught in his throat. He felt himself fainting, fought it and failed. Strong hands caught him and steadied him on his knees as his vision turned black.

"Take your time." He heard Echemmon through the darkness.

"There is no time." Di hissed, his blind eyes turned to the voice. He could not see them, but he could feel the thousands of bootsteps through the earth.

"There is no time," he said again, as the first of the arrows began to fall.

Echemmon knelt to Di's level, his one shield guarding them both from the hail of barbed shafts. Quietly, one Olympian to another, he whispered.

"We have all the time in the world."

Λ

Seventy-six

The Weeper slumped, unconscious. But his Olympians held him by the arms so he dropped no further than his knees. They had watched him lead nearly every charge for days, first to the fight, last to leave, and running perhaps miles further than his comrades during a single engagement. They owed him this rest, and trusted he would need only a moment.

"Strange weather we're having!" Alpheos joked as another hail of arrows hissed down around them. They raised their shields over their catatonic commander.

"It's really not unpleasant." Echemmon mused. "You know, I always did sleep better with a steady rain beating on the roof."

"I hope it lets up soon, though." Maron frowned.

"What's the matter, scared of a little thunder cloud?"

"Oh, no, I just want to find my fingers before they go rank." The twin balanced his shield on his head like a hat so he was free to fuss with his hands.

"Your fingers?"

"Yeah... Silly really, but I can't for the life of me remember where I put them down." Maron waggled the digits on his right hand. Only the first two fingers and thumb remained.

"Looks like it'll get worse before it gets better." Echemmon snuck an upward peek. Every second, hundreds more bows were strung and added their missiles to the barrage. Arrows stalled and clustered at the height of their arc. At times, the streaks of black eclipsed the sun and cast the valley into an unnatural night.

"More." Dienekes mumbled.

"He speaks!" The Olympians leaned closer. They smacked his cheeks to no response. He smiled weakly, his mind in another world.

"Yeah, boss?" Maron stooped to his level, still balancing his shield on his head. "More what?" Arrows passed the sun again, blanketing them in darkness.

"More arrows." Di giggled, eyes closed.

"More arrows?"

"Ask them..." his head lolled. "Ask them to send more arrows."

His brothers laughed at his delirium.

"Why more arrows?"

"So we can fight in the shade."

Dienekes wobbled in and out of his body. One by one his senses flickered and failed, till his only awareness in the quiet was the scrape of breath in his ears. Then a voice.

What are you doing?

Though he blinked, squinted, craned his head, he saw no speaker. Waves of splotchy blood-brown tides rose and fell on all sides. Painted with the same mortal brush, the march of Persians was indistinguishable from the sea. As the voice spoke again, he materialized, standing on the ocean. A blue glimmer of a boy, an afterimage that Di could only see if he didn't look at it.

What are you doing, Little Achilles?

"Asopichos?" Di wheezed.

Who are you?

A blue shimmer tapped its foot, his toes clapping the choppy wave-tops. He shook his head in disapproval. Ripe olives bobbed from the wreath on his head. He ate one.

"Asophichos?" Di asked again, reaching out. A hand took it.

"No, Di. It's me. It's Echemmon."

"You haven't changed a bit."

"I should hope not." Echemon waved a hand past Di's unseeing eyes.

Asophicos tutted Dienekes.

"Who are you, Achilles? What were you made to do? Is this it?."

"I don't understand."

"Me either," said Echemmon, patting his shoulder.

"Dienekes of Sparta, you were not made to stand. You were made to run."

"I will not run away." Dienekes spat venom.

"That's a relief," Echemmon slapped Di's cheeks.

Asopichos shook his head again.

Do not die on this hill.

"What's he doing?" Lagos and the twins crouched beside.

"I think he's talking to old friends." Echemmon guessed.

"Now?"

"I think he's earned a minute." Echemmon sighed.

Do not die on this hill, Asophichos repeated.

"I will not run away!" Weeper growled.

Not away. Run toward. Run toward me and live another day. He waved his arm, beckoning Di into the sea.

Di mouthed the words again, lacking the breath to speak them.

Λ

Run, Little Achilles. Your task is not yet complete.

And he was gone. Dienekes fell back into himself.

He spasmed, snorting and gasping. He tried to rise and fell again. His brothers caught his flailing arms and held him while his strength returned.

"The Kissians are holding at the edge of bow range." Alpheos rebriefed him, pointing to the formations. "The elites hold the same distance south with a large detachment moving west. Archers and slingers are filing into the swamp, but moving slow. It looks like the other units are waiting for them."

The elites to the east hooked north, cutting off the way the Hellenes had come, the way their allies had left that morning.

"They're waiting until they have us surrounded." Dienekes was lucid again. "This fight is over the moment that happens." He paced, peering for a new way out. What he wouldn't give to have Barbadoros with another gift. "If we stay on this hill, we're dead."

"It was a good run, boys." Alpheos sighed with genuine pride.

"A hundred of theirs fell to each of ours." His brother smiled. "We'll be remembered."

Thespians began to sing and beat their shields, but Dienekes could only hear the echo of Asopichos scorning him for leaving his task unfinished.

"Shut up!" He screeched. "Silence, all of you!"

They hushed in surprise.

"Do you not see them still?" He impugned them. "Can you not count their number, still greater than the grains of sand on a beach? These are the men who will rape your wife and murder your children! They will eat the fruits of your lands, sleep in your beds, and erase your names from history while they piss on your grave. As long as one yet breathes, OUR TASK IS NOT DONE!"

The Olympians shared looks of confusion.

"Weeper, we're here to the death. We'll fight till it's finished. To the end."

"No. We don't fight. We don't let it finish. We don't let it end."

"Di, you're not making sense."

"For three days we have wracked them without mercy. For three days we have showed them such horror that they would sooner kill each other than fight us. All it takes for us to keep killing them and invading their nightmares is to get off this hill. We don't need to fight, we need to live!"

"Where do you expect us to go?"

Even as they spoke, the eastern Persian lines were hooking again, to completely encircle Kolonos Hill.

"To the sea." Di said on impulse.

"You want to fight them in the sea?"

Λ

"No, I want us to escape! We swim past their lines to the east, regroup near Lokris, and take to the hills. We are already ghosts to them, so we fight them like ghosts. We pick them off one at a time, steal lives in the dark of night. We will be stinging flies, biting at the eyes and ears of Persia until her whole wretched body succumbs to our pestilence."

"It sounds dishonorable." Grumbled a Thespian. "To be assassins in the night, we would tarnish the glory we've earned so for."

"Then you stay here with your glory. You can have mine too. I don't want fame, I want to protect my son!"

He struck a nerve in the crowd. That was the real reason they were all here. They'd seen enough blood to know that glory was an empty boast for stories to be built on. Warriors might sing of it in poetries and promise to bring some back for those they left behind, but it wasn't the warriors who wrote the poems and it wasn't the poets who did battle. It was the ones left behind they were fighting for, not songs. Glory was not for soldiers. It was for they who remembered them.

"How long do you intend to hunt them?" Asked a Thespian.

Di flashed an evil smile.

"For the rest of my life."

Murmurs shuttled up and down the line. Heads nodded or shook. Most of them looked dead already after three days of war, and stared mournfully at Di or at their own feet. They were tired. They hadn't the strength for another campaign. They had done what they came to do and were ready to die.

He would forgive them for it.

"We will hold them off while you escape." A Spartiate veteran bowed.

Though some began to remove their armor.

"If we are to move, we have to do it now." The Persian pincer was closing around the north face of Kolonos. "Who's with me?"

The Olympians hailed. A few of the other Lakonians raised their broken spears. Only two Thespians stepped forward. Di could not blame them. They were battlefield creatures, untempered by the Krypteia.

"Sure you're up for this?" He asked them.

"We are the sons of Dithyrambos." One spoke for both.

"Say no more." Dienekes laughed at his luck. "If you fight half so well as your father, we may yet win the day."

The volunteers would never don their armor again, so they cut their laces to save time. They ignored their shields. While swimming, an aspis was an anchor, and was too bulky and bright for stalking through the trees. Abandoning their shields meant abandoning their vows and their honor. They elected wordlessly to not speak of it, try

Λ

not to think of it, and leave the hoplons where they lay, resisting the urge to say goodbye to the heirlooms their grandfathers had carried into battles of their own. Holding it one last time risked not being able to put it back down.

Their wreaths, however, their braided olive crowns, they removed from their helmets and wore around their necks or bare scalps.

Euneas joined the Olympians to prepare, but Dienekes snatched the boxer's knife hand by the wrist before he cut his armor.

"Wait." Dienekes stared a thousand yards away.

"Yes?"

"I have an idea." Di gasped.

"And?"

"Wait, I'm still having it."

Patient, but awkward, Euneas let his commander grip his wrist while the thought congealed. Dienekes was nearly giddy.

"Your strategy yesterday… striking from below, pushing at the knees…"

"Oh, you liked that?"

"It was brilliant. So brilliant, that much as I want you with me, I think I need you to stay and lead the phalanx. I've got a plan, and it starts with you. We've got one more trick to play."

"I like tricks." Euneas flashed a broken grin. There were more teeth missing than Dienekes remembered. His face was characteristically battered, black eyes nearly swollen shut. Euneas may have never won a wreath but he never backed down either, despite always punching up to opponents twice his size. The other Olympians considered him no less of a champion. He'd never met a punch he couldn't take, even from them.

"Do you remember my first games? One the road… there was a scorpion?"

"Do I?" Euneas guffawed. His swollen mouth made his words sound wet. He picked up his shield, flipped it around to show his polemarch the back. A scorpion the size of a hand was painted above the grip. Dien ran a fingertip over it. The ink was raised, like it had been painted on top of itself many times.

"What are these marks?" At first glance like the scorpion walked on a bed of grass, but closer inspection revealed dozens, maybe hundreds of neatly tallied hash marks.

"One for every fight I lost." Euneas beamed with pride. "The first one here-" he pointed "-was to the scorpion himself. Without Uncle Ono, I'd have likely died. Or worse, given up. He stitched me up more times than I can remember. Inside and out." He tapped a finger to his heart, then to his head. "He never let me forget that it's our losses, not our victories that make us better men. Remember what he always used to say? What doesn't kill you…"

Λ

"Turns your piss green." Dien ran a tongue over his own smile and realized some of his teeth were newly missing too. Mention of Uncle Ono transported him to happier times. He could have spent the whole day reminiscing, but Persia still marched. He refocused. "So the scorpion. Hard armored front, occupies its enemy with a wide forward push from below. It controls the ground first, forces the enemy to either rise or retreat, giving openings to latch on with its claws. And then-"

"And then the stinger rains death from above."

"Exactly. Now imagine the scorpion is… bigger…"

The phalanx formed, and retreated to the north face of Kolonos, out of sight of the Persians awaiting command. Di suspected correctly that they would close any distance the Hellenes gave up.

No time for goodbyes, he gave the hippeis and their Thespian brothers a nod. As he turned from them, the hoplites broke into the paean. Two dozen dashed with him, only a few hundred yards to the sea. Euneas gave Di's first order, and he with the rest of the phalanx turned and ran south to the enemy. Two staggered walls pounded forward. The boxer with and the red-cowled Thespians in front, the Spartans in their silver cloaks behind.

Surprised at the sudden change in direction, Asia's northernmost troops ignored the few dozen unarmored escapees to pursue the hoplites. Archers launched a volley at the charge as it crested the hill, but the phalanx was gone before arrows peppered the earth in their wake. The Persian elites were hardened professionals, not conscripted slave-soldiers like the Kissians and Medes. Without the threat of Barbadoros's fire, they did not balk. They waited bravely for the Hellenes to smash them. They held even after shields had crashed together. The hoplites pushed with the strength of the othismos, but there were no longer enough of them to move a host outnumbering them by hundreds of thousands. Dozens of Applebearers were instantly crushed, but their line held.

Euneas gave Di's second order. The phalanx crouched. Still they pushed, but the first line raked their shields back so the rims gouged into the ground. Achaemenid shields were too tall, their iron-scaled hauberks too unwieldy to change levels with the hoplites. The Hellenes capitalized, diving like wrestlers to tackle beneath the waist so their slanted hoplons chewed into the Persians like a plowshare. Their balance broken, mudmen spilled over the bronze wall for Thespians to dismember with small knives and bare hands. Those not poured overtop found their legs broken off at the ankles and knees.

The phalanx advanced until it had surrounded itself within the enemy. When the last rows of Thespians were in striking distance they sang a new paean. The rows in front changed to their song to match, and when the harmony reached Euneas at the front, he gave the Weeper's third and final order, the scorpion's sting from above.

"Mayhem!" He roared, the golden light of Elysium already shining behind his eyes. "Give them MAAYHEEEM!"

The Lakonians in the second phalanx did not put their shields in the backs of their comrades. Instead of pushing, they vaulted. Their strides carried them across the backs of Thespians ready for the weight. The foremost hoplites lifted when the pressure came and catapulted the men of Lakedaimon over the heads of the Persian host. Screaming Spartans plummeted like rain, but in the air they transformed. Simple soldiers had burst into the air, but what came back down was Chaos.

Each man alone struck freely into the mudmen on all sides, filling their hands with stolen weapons and impaling the enemy on their own iron. Their dense ranks worked against them again. They tangled with their own, struggling to turn and face Hellenes from all sides as yet more crashed down on their heads. With the supporting files defending from within, their front buckled against the Thespians. When the red cloaks caught up to silver, the Lakonians remounted and hurled themselves again. The Hellenes scattered and exploded amongst the enemy like fireworks. They had all become the demon. Persia hallucinated a lion cloak hanging from every back and slew each other in panic.

Confusion and surprise had shattered the elite's formation. Officers could not give orders against what they did not understand. Every second they wasted in shock, dozens more were devoured by men become beasts.

Terrified that the savagery would reach their own, officers to the sides and rear ordered their archers to fire. Every able bow of Persia bent to launch poisoned spindles into the frenzy at the heart of their host. Commanders would sooner wipe out their own men than allow the hoplites to fight on. The storm of arrows did not stop until every man beneath it, Persian or not, was cut down.

The battle was brief, and the price of victory staggering. Units enclosed from the sides to finish off the wounded. Persians stabbed frantically at the corpses of their enemy, refusing to believe they were dead. Veterans of many battles sobbed, shellshocked, as they hacked Hellenes to pieces, fearing that if they stopped cutting the bodies would rise again. Archers retrieved arrows from the fallen, finding their own barbed points in the heart of a friend as often as foe. Unable to trust the men who could not defeat the naked and unarmed, or those who would order them to kill their own, many took their chance to desert before dust settled on the bodies.

It wasn't until silence fell that anyone moved to pursue the escapees. By then it was too late.

Nothing remained of them except a totem staked into the cliff from which they had plunged. Two broken spears had been hitched into a cross; from it hung a crude

Λ

scarecrow. A bronze helmet balanced on top, the demon's lion cloak tied around its neck. The breath of the ocean filled the pelt like a sail, and even now it taunted the Asians and soured their victory. For all their number, none were brave enough to approach it. They volleyed burning arrows from afar until it fell smoldering into the sea.

Λ

Seventy-seven

Dienekes half crawled, half floated onto the rocky shore, many miles east of where the vultures now circled his friends and comrades. Here and there the Olympians followed, each looking as bad as he felt. The shore met the water in crumbling hard-rock bluffs. There was no beach. They forced their broken bodies, fueled now only by will, to fall up the ledges one at a time to dry ground before collapsing. Most of them left scrapings of flesh on the sharp stone, some of them came only in pieces. An arm or a leg bobbed along behind the survivors while sea monsters fought for the rest. Alpheos wrapped a tourniquet around Maron's arm. Blood from his severed fingers left a trail in the water. Something followed the scent and bit it off at the elbow.

"It's only right." He smiled through the pain, white as a sheet. "It wasn't fair to the rest of you. The gods took mine to level the field." He vomited seawater and passed out.

"We need to find shelter." Dienekes rasped as they collected each other at the top. "They saw us jump. They'll be looking." Alecto and Lysandros, Dithyrambos's sons, were last on the bluff. It took all the Olympians to haul them up the edge. Daggers out, covered in blood not their own, they had stayed in the water to fend off predators while the others climbed.

"We have to get to the treeline." Dienekes repeated. "Take cover. That's an order, soldiers."

They collapsed in a heap, and slept.

They could not hope to fight when they woke. Their insides were sacks of broken glass. Colorful bruises erupted on more skin than not. Acid pooled in their muscles. The bottoms of their feet were black with pooled blood.

Dienekes led by example, too weak to speak, and they followed him like dumb beasts into the hillside where they foraged on grubs and worms and mushrooms. They sucked on moss for water or licked the condensation from a stone. Slowly, agonizingly, they stretched the feeling back into their tormented limbs. By noon, they could straighten their arms and legs. By dusk, they could stand. By morning, they were ready to kill again.

Λ

Seventy-eight

"We watch." Dienekes breathed. "For now. We keep them in the mountains as long as we can. Every second here is a second our brothers spend gathering the might of Hellas." He whispered no louder than the hiss of the rustling leaves they hid themselves in. They recoiled from the golden sunlight filtering through their thicket of cover. Forsaking its warmth, they moved only at night, sleeping or waiting out each day in a new nest of ghillied moss and mud and broken branches. They clustered in small groups of three, four, five… so if found, they would not all be lost at once.

"We are no longer men, so we do not fight like men. We died on that hill with our brothers. And you can't kill what is already dead."

They nodded, solemn, as they had when he last spoke those words. It was a balm over their shame. Shame at a word they all screamed in their own head, but none dared speak.

Rhipsaspia.

They had left their shields at the pass. Outside of pitched battle, there was no reason for them but vainglory and pride. But that didn't stop their left arms from aching at the absence, or their fists from clutching at phantom handles. They had left behind a piece of themselves- the biggest piece. In abandoning their shields, they had abandoned their vows. They had abandoned their sense of self. They were no longer soldiers. By law, they were no longer even Spartan. They had their reasons, and still believed the sacrifice worthy, but they did not regret that none would ever hear of this shame. The poets would say they were cut down at Kolonos. It suited the Spartans as well to believe that their bodies had died with the pride they left behind.

These were not hoplites, not even human. This was a congress of ghosts, a shroud of ghouls. The gates of Hades had opened and spat them back out as furies to deal the woes as had been dealt to them.

"Kill no one unless you have to. Let them think they are safe. Let them think that we have fled, or been taken by the sea and its many hungry mouths. We stay dead. For now…"

He spoke more for his own benefit than his ghosts', reassuring himself of his own plan, so that their commitment to duty not be overcome by his own ravening for revenge.

"When they believe their victory complete, we will turn it to ashes in their mouths." Though none spoke, he could hear, almost feel the hammer of their pulses rise. "Rest. Eat. Heal. We lack the numbers to fight them with weapons. So we fight them in their minds. We are nightmares lurking in the dark. We are the lingering shadow at the edge of vision that will not let them forget that they are unwelcome on this ground. They will learn that as long as they tread in the realms of Agamemnon, they will be haunted by its spirits."

They raided a small Lokrian fishing village for supplies. The locals had evacuated, leaving a ghost town with larders only missing what its people could carry on their backs. A detachment of scouts had taken up residence in the empty houses, but soot-blackened spectres choked the life from them in their sleep. Corpses were weighted with rocks and tossed into the gulf so as not to be found murdered. The ghosts ate as much as they could stomach from the raw meat of the scouts' horses, then dumped them after their masters. With any luck, their officers would think them deserted. Most of their victims in the first days were fugitives from their posts. Each lost Asian begged for mercy in a different language. Their empty hands trembled in the air and tears streamed on their cheeks, but none found mercy. One or two or a half dozen at a time, the Hellenes started collecting bodies faster than they could be hid. More came looking for the lost.

Whether the hunters tracked hoplite survivors or Persian deserters, Dienekes could only guess. But when he woke at midday to the braying of hounds, the distinction hardly mattered.

The stench of death had drifted and settled like snow on the foothills of Anopaia. The musk of rot was hot in the nose no matter what direction the wind blew it. But sometimes the stench of life was worse. Hunting dogs would have no difficulty sensing the sweat-soaked and bloodstained assassins squatting in their den of leaves. Even if the wind lucked their scent away from the dog-teams, they would never miss the noxious stench blooming from the rancid stump of Maron's severed arm.

Dienekes had done what he could, but without a fire, or a hearth, or freedom to forage, his efforts were symbolic at best. Pestilence had claimed the wound and kept Maron sweating, shivering, and pissing himself beneath their verdant shroud during the nights as well as days. Opening his mouth to drip-drink water from a rag was the most he had moved since climbing from the sea, not until howling of hungry Skythian curs rattled him from his fever dreams.

Λ

The ghosts traded panicked looks, their eyes speaking what they could not afford to with voices. Is this it? Do we run? Do we make a stand? Who of us escapes? Who will pay the blood price that others might live?

The dogs were close. If they hadn't caught the Spartan scent yet, they would have it in moments. Though he lamented that it be so soon, the order for the final charge hovered reluctantly on the tip of the Weeper's tongue. For once, hesitation saved him.

Maron's eyes burst open. Half an instant later, what remained of his body burst from their cover. The other ghosts latched to Di and Alpheos to keep them from following. No sooner had Maron dragged himself out of sight to the north than the hunting party appeared in pursuit to the south.

He tore off his bandages, leaving a trail of blood and pus as he half-sprinted, half-crawled away from where his brothers hid. As he fled, he realized that though each step carried him ever further from the death that followed behind, that same step brought him that much closer to the death waiting for him up ahead. To his fever-baked brain, nothing had ever been quite so funny. Beautiful, even. He was a warrior pinioned between the end thrust upon him, or the end of his choosing. Grateful for the grace to choose the latter, he threw back his head and shrieked laughter.

His brothers beneath their foliage and loam could hear his wild cackles over the din of dogs passing them at less than an arm's length. Lagos was splashed by a straggler hiking a leg on their hideout. A suspicious Skythian hunter poked into the mound with his lance from horseback. He stabbed Alecto twice in the side, but the Thespian never flinched. Maron bleeding and screaming through the forest turned the rider's head. He spurred his mount after his cohorts and never saw the drop of blood sliding down the tip of his blade.

In his spying, Maron had seen the witch-women and worshippers of Ahora-Mazda caterwaul their freakish warbling hymns around the fires of Xerxes. He ululated in their own voice, his siren song enticing them to quarry he knew they would never catch. He cast himself happily into oblivion, but his voice stayed in the land of the living to echo circles through the trees and mock the Skythians as his body sank to the void below. The hunters tracked his bloody footprints up to and off the cliff edge, and the tide smashing the bluffs below meant no one could have survived the plunge. But with his laughter still ringing in their ears, they wondered. None had seen him. None knew who they had chased. Had it even been a man? Perhaps a wounded beast? Or merely a phantom, a hallucination of war? They traced his tracks back to the den he had fled, but by then it was empty of all but more doubts.

Λ

Seventy-nine

The hunting parties forced their hand. They could no longer bide their time. Braving suicidal odds, they stole into the enemy camps one at a time. Lagos snared a pair of young swine and herded them frightened and squealing to turn enough heads for Di and Echemmon to sprint by unnoticed. Some Spartans lured sentries far enough into the woods to slip past, others simply killed the sentries. Lysandros and Alecto hid in plain sight, lying naked and limp on the piles of slain Hellenes where Xerxes demanded their bodies be mutilated and displayed. His own dead he commanded be buried or burned for the number of hoplite dead to seem greater than his own losses. Scattered among the enemy, under piles of refuse, soiled laundry, amongst livestock or as pretenders among the wounded and sick, the ghosts waited.

Alpheos disguised himself as a camp follower and wandered unmolested. As long as he carried water for their horses, fuel for their fires, and wine and fruit for the warriors, no one paid him a second glance. They drank and feasted with him under their noses. In the coming days, hundreds would fall inexplicably and fatally ill. Mystic physicians would call it ill humors, battle sickness, retribution from foreign gods. They would pray, make sacrifice, and believe themselves purified of the blight. But hundreds more would fall, eating from the contaminated bushels of apples that Alpheos smeared with the putrescence of decaying bodies. The wine and water, he hemlocked. He chopped their firewood from rhododendron and oleander trees, piled with twigs of azalea and belladonna. Persians breathed deep from the aromatic bonfires, unaware that the pungent smokes were poisoning their food and sickening their lungs. Many coughed themselves to death that night. Many more the nights after.

The Laconians had studied the guard shifts. Just before relief from duty, a sentry's head was most likely to nod. Eyes drooping for a moment too long invited a garotte to slip over his head and tighten till he jerked himself silently to death. His body was then tied upright to a post, his head surgically removed, and then fixed back in place on the neck with a short sharpened peg. One by one, the Hellenes turned the night watchmen into scarecrows of themselves.

The replacement sentries at dawn laughed at the laziness of their comrades, caught sleeping on watch. They took their friends by the shoulder to shake them awake. Their heads fell off instead. Horrified screams from the perimeter woke the troops in the barrack tents. As the village stirred, screams came at random from the encampment's center. Scant few lives had been claimed in the night, but many of those spared came to wish they hadn't. Screams from the garrison harmonized with those from the outskirts, as soldiers woke to find every other sleeping man's throat slit. Some survivors were too frightened to ever sleep again. A man can live longer without food than sleep.

Covered in the blood of their dead friends, men spilled from their quarters, shrieking of phantoms and foul spirits. Rumors flocked and grew on the wind, and the camp swarmed like ants. In the growing chaos, Alpheos sparked the fires he had prepared. Foodstores and stables burst into flame. Horses and oxen stampeded. Persians swarmed like ants to douse the flames and corral the beasts while Dienekes and his ghosts stole away.

More disorder than destruction, it did not take long for officers to restore order. They commanded those lost in the night be gathered with the other casualties and their deaths investigated.

The highest ranking among Xerxes's tacticians, physicians, and alchemists bickered back and forth about how and when the victims expired, who did it, and why.

Engrossed in their speculations, they did not see two of the dead and desecrated hoplite cadavers rise from the grave. Lysandros and Alecto had lain motionless for a day and a night amongst their dead countrymen. All day the sun had baked their skin crimson, and all night their dead kin whispered to them of revenge. The brothers filled their hands with stolen iron and charged.

The most trusted of the Shahanshah's advisors, the most feared of his commanders, trampled each other to escape the revenants. The sun had burned the brothers devil-red from head to toe, and in their fury there was no believing these were mortals. The God-King's counselors shit themselves under assault by demons from a realm beyond.

The sons of Dithyrambos died as their father died, naked and fearless. Hordes of Persia broke and scattered in their path. A chariot of terror drove before them and granted a strange invincibility. As long as none dared strike them, they could not die. They rampaged with impunity until distant archers buried them in clouds of flaming black shafts. The Thespians only succumbed once the weight of the arrows in their scarlet bodies was too great for their legs to bear.

The Persian mystics dismembered their corpses, wrapped the bloody shreds in sage leaf and silk and scrawled the wrappings with sigils and spells. Each morsel of man was packed in salt to the brim of a small urn and the caps sealed with molten

Λ

lead. The urns were loaded onto a sailing galleon with one mystic and enough slaves to crew it to the open ocean. Once beyond the sight of land, the mystic sang a final prayer and set the boat to flame. He burned and sank with the vessel, sacrificing himself to guard the demons, so their fragments would never be reassembled to visit evil on his people again.

Λ

Eighty

Their insurrection drove the Persians rabid. Commanders dispatched patrolmen on endless search and destroy sorties. The Achaemenids tripled every effort to hunt down the red hand responsible, be it deserter, assassin, or ghost of the vengeful dead. Mudmen, even among the immortals, no longer felt safe sleeping in their own tents. They moved their bedrolls as close as crowds were allowed to cluster around their religious leaders, that they might be sheltered in his holy aura while they slept. Many more didn't sleep at all, and preferred volunteering on hunts for unseen enemies over braving their own nightmares. Despite the need for fresh supplies, none bore the nerve to loot abandoned Lokrian villages. Houses were surrounded and put to the torch rather than risk springing a trap set by whatever imaginary devil lay inside. Oinomaos died in one such conflagration. He sat, breathed deep of the flames and let them consume him so the Asian might still blame spectres for their misfortune and not have the security of knowing their killers were flesh and blood.

Every shrub, every pile of leaves was suspect. Spears thrust into empty bushes. When blades were drawn back bloodless, unsatisfied Persians thrust them in again. Instead of searching a forest, groves of trees were leveled one trunk at a time. Pine thickets were perforated by volleys of arrows because a squirrel chattered too loudly. Every bird call was assumed an enemy agent. The invader went to war against robins and sparrows and vultures and stray dogs as if the wind, the rain, the land and all its creatures were the enemy. More deserted by the day, and many volunteered for sorties only for a better opportunity to abandon their post. Foreign soil beneath their feet, foreign sky above their heads, foreign sounds in their ears and smells in their lungs, they found no comfort day or night.

A dozen, maybe more of the Weeper's ghosts remained. He could not be sure, they had split up, operating as individuals instead of a squad so if one was lost, it was only one and no more. Any more attacks required a larger retreat, lest they be caught in the retribution at the edges of the ever expanding camp-city. His final order had been to disperse to the south and west. With the distance, they bought a day or more each to forage and recuperate, taking turns harassing expeditionary units or executing scouts. In the pass, they had paid in blood for every moment, every breath. Now time had changed her favor and the Spartans could do with her as they pleased. They could afford to be patient in their murder.

Dienekes found a lone quarry and stalked him for a night and a day to see if others would join him. Whether deserter or camp follower, he was Asian regardless. He was no regular, at least not anymore. His garb was a mismatch of light armor and stolen finery. His eyes were kohled, fingers jeweled, and hair in loose-spun Persian ringlets. The man looted with a merchant's tastes, selecting expensive and impractical wares over humbler goods and supplies that would have improved his chances of survival. He heaped his treasures onto a horseless wagon. Beneath piles of bolted silk and skeined wine, Dien spied Spartan hoplons. Polymedes's shield was apparent by size alone. Among those stacked above were the four-shield icon of Hegesistratos and the screaming Gorgon of Krateros. His shields. Rage overcame Dienekes. Roaring, he charged.

The Persian turned to face him. Rather than fight, he sighed. His brown shoulders slumped.

Di woke on his back. The sky spun above, the ground spun the opposite way below. Tinnitus rang in his ears.

"I was wondering when you were going to say hello."

If Dienekes wasn't so focused on finding his feet he would have noticed that the Persian spoke flawless Doric.

"Die, bastard, die!" Di frothed. He drew a sword from those pilfered on the cart. He slashed through his vertigo at the rippling mudman.

"You do not know me?" The stranger sighed again. A bolt of linen unfurled in his hands. "I am the being of insulted to." He drolled, sarcastic. The cloth flourished in a wide circle, filling Di's swirling vision. When he fell back to the ground, it bound his hands. "And after I am having give to you so many the presents."

"Give? You give nothing." His speech gone feral, barely intelligible, was less language than growling and gnashing of teeth. "The mudman only takes!" Wrestling against his bonds, he lathered. Prejudice was an alien concept to him a few short weeks prior. But by now, he hungered to kill anything with dark skin or almond eyes. Three days in the pass had taught him to hate.

"Don't bore me, little lion." The barbarian patiently unbound Di's hands, trusting his words to immobilize the Laconian.

"Little lion?" Di repeated, dumbfounded.

"Yes, yes, now he sees." The stranger rolled his eyes.

"Barbadoros?"

"Yes, it's me. Though I think now that name has outlived its usefulness. I should take another"

Λ

"But I never... you look so..." Di struggled to understand. "You look taller... and your accent! What happened to your accent?"

"A fake. Keep up boy. You were a fool to believe it in the first place. No one talks like that. Not even mudmen."

Di's skin crawled with questions. One squirmed out ahead of the others.

"Where are you from?"

The man who was no longer Barbadoros smiled.

"I am from everywhere. I am of Persia, of Athens, of Judah, of Skythia..." He gave the Weeper a knowing glance. "But first and foremost, believe it or not, I am of Sparta."

"Is that why you steal a wagon full of hoplite shields?" Di accused, still smoldering with fury.

"Oh hush, boy. I won Big Bear's shield fair and square. Though from the kindness of my heart, I will gift it to his son. As I will give yours to your son. He will have two to choose from. How blessed." The words themselves were grateful, but the way he said them was bitter and sad.

"You are going to Sparta?"

"Yes. You may come too if you wish?"

The idea wounded him deeper than any of the cuts or bruises on his body. He remembered the smell of hyacinths on the road to his home, the barley flour on his mother's hands, the son he had yet to meet. Every trauma-factured shard of his soul screamed yes, yes take me with you, take me home!

"No." The sound of his voice broke his own heart. "This is my place. This is where my duty lies."

"I had assumed. No harm in asking."

"Ha." Di gave a tragic laugh. "Yes, no harm at all." He told the shattered pieces of his heart.

"There are others here who may wish to join you."

"Others?"

Barbadoros whistled. A bridled mount thundered from the treeline.

"The dragon!" Di burst to his feet, dizziness gone. "You caught the dragon!"

"Dragon." Barbadoros scoffed. "It is no dragon. She is a rinokeros. The word even comes from your language. You may well have heard of them if Mother Sparta looked out into the world half so much as she gazed in. Do not fear. She is vegetarian." The beast nuzzled Barbadoros, mouthing at him with thick lips like bricks of leather until he unsacked a sweet smelling acacia bush and tethered it to a mount hanging from her horn. She munched contented on the dangling shrub. Barbadoros scratched her chin and kissed her cheek. "I call her Tafucha."

"Tafucha?"

Λ

"Yes. It means fluffy."

Dienekes dared to pet the creature. It snorted.

"And what will you do with us?" Asked a new voice.

"I hear you're polemarch now. Funny taking orders from a cocksprite," said another. "I almost don't believe the deeds 'Doros claims you've done."

For awe of the beast, Dienekes had not even seen the two Spartans following the rinokeros on a rope.

"Eurytos! Aristodemos!" Di recognized the two hippeians struck blind by water sickness.

"They nag me day and night to return them to the fight." Barbadoros complained. "But being blind, of course cannot wipe their own asses, let alone fight."

"We can still fight." Aristodemos snarled. "Just point the way."

Di waved a hand in front of their eyes.

"We're not that blind." Eurytos grumbled.

"Your orders were to return to Sparta." The Weeper reminded them. "You would disobey Leonidas?"

"Didn't you?"

Di could not deny the accusation. But he could pull rank.

"I am Polemarch."

"So order us to stay." Aristodemos half-demanded, half-begged.

"Our place is here. Just as it is yours." Eurytos seconded. "I don't want to die like Othryades. I would die with my brothers."

Di hesitated. It pained his honor to undermine his dead king, but they were right. He had disobeyed himself.

"We do both." He decided. There are two of you. One to stay, one to obey."

The Spartiates scowled, but accepted.

"Who then?"

"Dice for it." Barbadoros smiled, presenting his chance cubes. He put one in the hand of each Spartan. "Odd number, Eurytos stays. Even number, Aristodemos stays."

The Laconians nodded, and threw the dice to the dirt. Solemnly, they stared in the vague direction of their leader. They waited. And waited. And waited, until 'Doros whispered to Di.

"Read the cubes for them, you fool. They cannot see."

"Oh…" He stooped to read the dice and could have punched Barbadoros if he didn't think it would earn him another snake-fisted clout on the head. "You black-hearted bastard…'" Doros had switched the dice. The cubes on the ground were blank.

Λ

Dienekes appraised the last of the three hundred. Between the two of them, Eurytos was the more gaunt and sickly. Aristodemos, stouter, stronger, and with the greater reputation in battle, would count for more if he lived to fight in the battles to come.

"Odd. Aristodemos goes." The words stuck in Di's throat. The blessing of life was burdened with the curse of shame, the same shame that Weeper would rather die than face- rather die than see his son. With this grace, he damned his comrade. Though Aristodemos would journey home, he would never again be welcome. And he knew it. He accepted his fate.

Barbadoros clapped once.

"It is decided then. Leave us. Eurytos, help your brother back into his armor. The Weeper and I have things to discuss privately." 'Doros snapped his fingers and Tafucha, still munching acacia, led them back to wherever they had hid.

"You bastard." Di hissed when they had gone. "You bastard, bastard."

"Do not the being of anger with me, war kitten." Barbadoros said in his fake accent. "They deserved better than a fate decided by chance. Better to be chosen by their polemarch. Who knows them. Who loves them. Who understands their worth."

"So you made me kill one of my own. And damn the other to a worse fate than death. You would do that to me?"

"So your anger is not for them, but for yourself?"

"Why not, then? Why shouldn't I be angry?"

"Because you are already dead, Dienekes."

His own words used against him, The Weeper could not argue.

"What did we have to discuss, then?" He asked instead.

"When you were a boy, the King gave you a ring." Barbadoros inclined his head to Di's fist.

"How did you know that?" Di gave the iron band, awash in a trance of memory.

"And the other one?" Barbadoros ignored the question. Di had taken a ring from his dead mentor, larger but otherwise identical. The significance was lost on him till now.

"What do they mean?"

"And the other one?" Barbadoros skirted the question again, smiling devishly.

"I have no more."

"Don't lie to me, boy." He pointed at Thrasilaos's leather pouch still on Di's neck. The king's Thyrean sand. Di pinched his fingers inside and withdrew the lock of Lysimachos's hair.

"Deeper." Barbadoros urged.

Buried at the bottom was a third identical iron ring. Passing it over, Di finally noticed a fourth on Barbadoros's own finger.

∧

"What is this? What conspiracy did you weave me into."

"It was not me, you were a part since infancy. In death you will know the truth. Be patient, it will come soon enough."

"Tell me now. What do they mean."

"There was a vow attached to these rings." Barbadoros inspected them in the fading sunlight. "A vow you have kept, though you did not even know it. But these vows, like our duties, must be passed to those that follow us."

"What do they have to do with me?"

"Eight of us took an oath on the blood of the ninth who died to save us. We wear these rings to remind us, forged from the iron that slew him."

"Eight... saved by one..." Realization dawned. On a film behind his eyes, Di relived the story told to him by Thrasilaos on the steps of the hall of ephors. "These are from the axe head that killed my father."

"Not an axe. A plowshare. Beaten and bent into a weapon."

"Thrasilaos said it was an axe?"

"Perhaps he lied? To make the death seem more noble? Or perhaps he misremembered. My memory, however, does not fail."

"That means... You... You were there too?"

"Yes. Your father died to save me."

"You were the boy! The Skythian! Your name is Shukxa!"

"Ah! I have been discovered!" Shukxa clasped hands to his heart, as if shot.

"Then... you... your father died that same night." Though it was decades too late, he felt some solidarity in the shared loss.

"No. I mourned him, as he was dear to me. But he was my uncle. My mother's brother. Only pretending to be my father to keep me safe. My real father died only ten years ago. Skinned alive."

"No..." Dien only now recognized the resemblance. Remembering the diarch's face looming before his own and whispering...

Sometimes I cry too

Di thought he might faint.

"That's right, Spartan." Shukxa beamed. "Bow before your prince!"

Dienekes nearly did.

"I believe that concludes our business, unless you have more gifts for me?" Shukxa decided on behalf of the dumbstruck polemarch and whistled. Tafucha returned from the treeline, a single Spartiate in tow.

"I trust you will take my secret to the grave?" The son of Kleomenes straddled the back of the rinokeros. "It has been an honor, a privilege, and a pleasure to see you become a man, Dienekes, son of Hegisistratos. I hope you enjoyed the figs and fowl I left you as a boy. It warmed my heart to see you share with your brothers. Your

Λ

father in heaven saw as well, and he was -no- he is- at least as proud of you as I am. Farewell. I will see you again soon enough."

Silent Rivers streamed down Weeper's cheeks as his brother in blood spurred his strange mount to the south.

"Tell my son I died at Kolonos!" He cried, his voice shattering like glass. "Tell them I died with Leonidas."

Shukxa called over his shoulder, tears in his own eyes.

"Little brother, I will not tell them you died at all."

The stranger-bearing-gifts raised his voice to the sky, knowing that Persia might hear and come for him. Risking his life for a little bit of music, he left his comrades to their destiny.

The Weeper stood motionless long after the song had faded, letting the weight of fresh truths settle on him. Eurytos in his armor waited in patient silence until the sun had nearly set. In the amber light of dusk, he was the very visage of Lakonia, a vision Dienekes needed to see. The Weeper stared the blind man up and down, chest nearly bursting with forgotten pride. His own form, almost naked, mottled with mud and blood and black soot, had abandoned the shape he had been molded for. He could have kissed Eurytos for reminding him who he was. The hoplite's defiant red cloak billowed dauntless in the sea breeze. His bronze glowed gold in the failing daylight. He could have been anyone, face hidden, anonymous behind the Lakonian cowl. His eyes, though sightless, glowed with feverish dedication through hammered slits. This was why they wore no badges of office, no seals of rank. Under the helmet could have been a boy, a man, a common soldier, a king. In their armor, in the phalanx, they were all the same. They were all Sparta.

"Well?" Said the hoplite when he felt he'd waited long enough. "Are you ready to die, Weeper?"

"No." Said Dienekes. For the first time in his life he felt certainty. He turned north and Eurytos followed his silhouette. He walked with one foot already in Heaven, one foot still in Hell, but he knew the way. He had walked it long enough. "No, Spartan. I'm not ready to die." He smiled through tears that would never dry.

"I'm ready to live forever."

Λ

Λ

Afterward

Nearly five decades later, Herodotos traveled Lokris and Phokia to record the stories of Thermopylae. Though their deeds were remembered, the identities of the men responsible had been forgotten. For their exceptional valor in an already exceptional battle, the memory of only four names stood the test of time. Dithryambos of Thespia and the Spartans Alpheos, Maron and Dienekes.

Pantites, sent to bring the Thessalians over to the Hellenic side, arrived at the pass in the battle's aftermath, and overcome by survivor's guilt, took his own life. Aristodemos, the only other Lakonian survivor, was shunned by his peers on his return home. He fought and died the following spring at the Battle of Plataea where the Persian invasion was crushed by the unified forces of Hellas.

Only because the three hundred chose to stand at the Hot Gates and give their lives did the Hellenes rise up against the Persian and preserve their country. The defense at the pass provided proof that the invader did bleed like any other man and served as the rallying cry behind which all of Hellas stood up. Perhaps never has the world seen the like of what came to pass at Thermopylae and for their actions, they were eternalized by the poet Simonides in an epitaph on the hill where they gave their lives for the freedom of their nation and all of Hellas.

"Go tell the Spartans, stranger passing by,
That here, by Spartan law we lie"

9 780578 756592